About the Author

Mark Hayden is the nom de guerre of Adrian Attwood. He lives in Westmorland with his wife, Anne.

He has had a varied career working for a brewery, teaching English and being the Town Clerk in Carnforth, Lancs. He is now a part-time writer and part-time assistant in Anne's craft projects.

He is also proud to be the Mad Unky to his Great Nieces & Great Nephews.

Three Ring Circus

A Fairy Story

Twelfth Book of the King's Watch

MARK HAYDEN

PAW PRESS

www.pawpress.co.uk

First Published Worldwide in 2024 by Paw Press
Paperback Edition Published
April 2024
First Edition

Cover Design – Rachel Lawston
Design Copyright © 2023 Lawston Design
www.lawstondesign.com
Cover images © Shutterstock

Paw Press – Independent publishing in Westmorland, UK.
www.pawpress.co.uk

ISBN: 1-914145-05-4
ISBN-13: 978-1-914145-05-6

To Asen, Lore, Nina, Paula & Sheila.
The finest team of Moderators
Any author could wish for

THREE
RING
CIRCUS

A Note from #TeamConrad

Are you ready for this?

I don't think we are. When we set out to put this stuff together, we didn't think it would end up being *actually* published. I'd have done loads of things differently if I'd known.

Anyway, the publisher has helped us out by putting a list of new and recurring people from this story on their website. You can also find a full list of everyone from the previous books, and a glossary of magickal terms on the Paw Press website. Go to the "Extras" page and download the Dramatis Personae for *Three Ring Circus*:

www.pawpress.co.uk

And now on with the story.

Thanks,
Evie Mason.

Foreword

To Whom it May Concern

Before reading these testimonies, you should know how they came to be written down and collected here. This collection – *codex* if you like – comprises statements, reconstructions and what the Fae term 'stories'. They shed *some* light on proceedings, but as with all documents, they require careful weighing.

Just be careful there isn't a Spectral thumb on your scales.

Even a cursory reading will tell you that this Codex of Confusion raises more questions than it pretends to answer, though it does vindicate Dr Mowbray, and that was the main reason it was put together. As you'll see.

Along the way, you will also appreciate that Evie is primarily a writer of *fiction*, and, as we all know, Conrad can have a very selective memory when it comes to telling his tales; it now seems that this trait runs in the family, judging by Rachael's contributions.

After a lifetime of striving, straining and sweating (not to mention conniving, cheating and conspiring) to ensure that magickal writings are made available to all in the Queen's Esoteric Library, it feels very strange to be writing this foreword, knowing that the codex will be locked away in the Elvenham Grange safe. Very strange indeed.

In the end, I believe that these documents will be known as what the world believes them to be:

A Fairy Story.

Sealed under the Imprint of Dr Francesca Somerton ChD CBE, Keeper Emeritus of the Queen's Esoteric Library and Honorary Librarian of Mowbray College.

A Handwritten Note

Did Conrad make me the happiest woman in the world on our wedding day? Of course he did, but we shall pass over that because the very next morning he did his best to make me the grumpiest woman in the world, and for someone with my inherently placid and sunny disposition, that takes some doing.

In case you've forgotten, Conrad's negligence got us transported to Asgard. *Right in the middle of our wedding party.* I know!

He claimed – he still claims – total ignorance of the Allfather's intentions that day. Perhaps. It *is* possible. After all, the Elderkind *are* unpredictable, and Lord Ganesh *did* send a Nāgin to bless our union, so that might count in Conrad's favour, and if a wife cannot give her husband the benefit of the doubt occasionally, she may have a long marriage but she is unlikely to have a happy one.

No. It is what happened the day *after* our wedding for which he will be held accountable in the Court of Marital Grievances. Grr. Aiee!

The only problem is that whenever I try to focus on what he did, the wheel of time turns away from my righteous anger and suddenly Saffron is in surgery, Myfanwy is in labour and Alicia is missing in action, allegedly in Ireland.

It puts things into perspective, I tell myself (rather tritely, I know), and the word *perspective* makes me think of the pictures which Scarywoman is threatening to release into the wild, and *that* makes me think of the pictures of me and the stripper which not even Li Cheng could put back into the bottle, no matter what Thistle offered to do for him. And to him.

Kāla.

Time. Death.

A god and a concept.

The end is always in the beginning, and the beginning is always in the end.

No, I don't understand it either, and it does not tell you why Lucy's car ended up in the Manchester Ship Canal, which was one of the many questions to which Conrad was expecting an answer when I laced up the walking shoes he'd forced me to purchase on our first trip to Ambleside when I was still on weekend release from prison.

See? We have jumped straight to the end of his story – which is, of course, also the beginning of mine – and I can't tell him *this* story without going back to the beginning of Alicia's story, and that may never be told, unless the weird message I got from Francesca Somerton is true.

I mean, would the Fae *really* share all their secrets with a mortal, even one as widely respected as Dr Somerton, soon-to-be Keeper Emeritus of the Esoteric Library?

I shall tell Conrad what I know for certain, and I shall tell him what I am allowed to tell him, and I'm sure that he will tell me what he thinks he can get away with telling me. As usual.

As for the rest, it is in the hands of the gods. And of Kāla. We are all in the hands of Kāla.

Mrs Mina Clarke-Desai.
Or possibly Desai-Clarke.
No, definitely Clarke-Desai.

A Note on Translation, by Evie Mason

A lot of this stuff was a real eye-opener to me, I'm telling you. There's loads of things in here that I don't understand and for which I've had to take Corrib's word. And talking of words, there's a few places where I've left their words in the text instead of using the ones I was taught at school: *Hlæfdigan* is an obvious example. We use that word because we got it from the Gnomes, I think, and the Fae use it to talk to us mortals, but the manuscript landed with the word *Lady* instead, so I've left it in.

The same goes for *Sprite*. According to Francesca (who should know), the word came into use because we didn't know that Sprites were the same species as the Fae, and the Fae word is *Little One*. Makes sense.

The one word I had the guts to ask Corrib about was *profit*. I raided the thesaurus and suggested *benefit, gain* or *advantage* as alternatives, but no, Corrib insisted that only *profit* reflected 'The investment of life for a return.'

If it was up to me, I'd have gone with *benefit*, but there you go. So if it doesn't always make sense, don't blame me. Alright?

Evie Mason MA.

Part One — Hatching

Chapter One

The Story of Alicia-6th-Redqueen-Iris-Nymph Child, Handmaiden to Princess Faith

Translated from the Fae by Countess/Prince Corrib

Edited and revised by Evie Mason

One year before the Peace of Brothers Water,
fifteen months before the wedding.

The wooden needles clicked out a fast rhythm, like a troupe of clog-dancing mice, but Lady Agnes didn't notice. Her fingers didn't miss a beat, and her eyes never left the portal. They wouldn't be long. They were never long during the daytime.

At the end of the row of stitches, she had to glance down to feed the yarn correctly, and when she glanced up there he was, buttoning his shirt and thinking of other things. Horses, probably.

Agnes stood up and bowed. 'Her Grace is well, my lord?'

Prince Galleny looked up, and ran his tongue round his mouth before he replied, savouring the taste of Amrita. 'What? Oh yes. She asked for you when we were done. Something to do with a clutch starting to hatch. Damn these buttons, and where's my Gamekeeper?'

'She went in search of refreshment, my lord.'

Galleny left his shirt to flap open and strode off, taking his phone out of his pocket and muttering about having the wrong network. Agnes dropped her knitting and shook the Little One who'd fallen asleep on the grass; they all loved to nap, but this one was worse than most.

'Fetch a wet nurse,' she told it, reinforcing her message with a shove.

It ran, jumped and flew into a far corner of the bower. This one could be trusted, and Agnes left it to its work. She straightened her dress, tugging the loose shoulders to settle the high-necked collar, the style which she'd worn since the bosom underneath it had become purely ornamental. With her skirt straight and her hair patted down, Agnes stepped through the portal to the Queen's glade.

Her Grace had dimmed the light for the mating, and She was in no hurry to raise it. The May blossoms on the ever-blooming hawthorn trees which surrounded the glade glowed softly white, casting no shadows. Closer to the pool, the double ring of daffodils shone yellow and orange from their variegated trumpets and gave Her Grace's skin a blush of colour.

Lady Agnes approached and bowed. 'Your Grace, I am here, and help is on its way.'

The Queen had been lying on the grass, right next to the pool. She swung Herself upright and dangled Her feet in the warm water. She stared downwards and wiggled Her toes, the golden polish on Her nails winking like little fish just under the water. She looked up at Agnes and smiled the dreamy smile that showed that the mating had been successful. For that Agnes gave thanks, as she always did.

'No need,' said Her Grace. 'I'm keeping Galleny on short rations ahead of the Equinox, so I've got plenty of Amrita to spare. I haven't suckled a brood myself for quite a while, and who knows? There might be a new Prince in this clutch. Galleny could do with some competition. Let's look at the omens.'

Agnes went to stand behind the Queen, who withdrew Her legs from the pool and crossed them underneath Her. With slow, delicate moves, the Queen Inked the Web of the Future into the air. Fine strands of Lux glimmered brightly in the gloom, and then She cast them onto the water and spoke the words: 'From the Pool of Life they come, and to the Pool of Life they will return for re-birth. Water of Life, show me their future.'

The web of magick landed, and the water fizzed as the spell drew power and life from the pool. The surface cleared and the omens for the new brood were revealed.

Three Little Ones were walking towards the Water of Life in the pool, their wings huge and ready to overwhelm them. In the tracery of Ink through the veins of their wings, Agnes could see their essence: 1st at the front, walking proud and alone; 2nd guiding one whose name was hidden but who was clearly injured. It was as it should be and could be. Possibly. Like gold to the Diggers, the magick of the pool was a good servant but a terrible master.

Her Grace smiled and broke the charm. 'That would be a good return, would it not? Three from a clutch? Now, Agnes, sit beside me and take my hand.'

It didn't often happen, but when it did, Agnes cherished each and every moment next to her Queen. She smoothed her skirt under herself and sat down, offering her fingers to be held.

When they were joined, the Queen squeezed her hand and spoke. 'Your time is coming, Agnes. This will be your last brood, won't it?'

Lady Agnes felt it as the truth. She'd surprised herself by living through the winter, and now that spring was upon them, she knew she'd not see another Yuletide and would be lucky to make Samhain. She squeezed the Queen's fingers back and smiled sadly, reluctant to voice the future.

The Queen stroked the fingers of Her oldest Lady. 'It's time for Caroline to lead the household. Under your watchful eye, of course. I want you to do two last things for me, Agnes.'

'Your Grace?'

Their moment was broken by Lady Caroline herself rushing into the bower. The Queen released Agnes's fingers. 'Thank you, Caroline, for being so prompt. I have changed my mind, so fetch my vanity and wait outside.'

'Your Grace,' said Caroline with a bow, retreating backwards through the portal.

When she was gone, the Queen took Agnes's fingers again. 'Here is what I need,' said Her Grace. 'I want you to make this brood your swansong, give them everything you've given to me. And at Beltane, I want you to move to the stables.'

'Your Grace?'

'It's time that Faithful was let out of the sídhe. Persephone will soon be eighteen, and Faithful will supervise Persephone's treatment by Galleny. Not that I'm going to let the poor girl see Faithful's face, of course. Don't want to frighten the horses before we've ridden them.'

Princess Faithful was the ghost of Derwent: she'd haunted the lower levels of the sídhe all of Agnes's life, fetching and carrying and doing the most menial jobs. Only lately had she been allowed into court, and for the first month, Her Grace had made the Princess play the role of waitress. The whole court knew that this was to force Faithful to carry things. In both hands. That way, the drool ran down her face from the gap in her lips so that everyone could see her punishment, even if they never spoke of her crime.

'Your Grace is merciful and generous,' said Agnes.

'I know I am, and it'll be the death of me, but I can't base Faithful at Sprint Stables full-time, and I need someone there who thinks with their head and not with their dick. If I leave Galleny in sole charge of Persephone's bondage, he'll teach her to ride and try to seduce her. As well as raising the brood, I want you to watch out for the child.'

'Of course, Your Grace.'

'Good. Now let's see about this clutch. I laid them in the iris. Bring them to me.'

Agnes pulled off her dress and threw it up the bank. She padded around the pond until she reached the bright yellow blooms of the water iris. In the heat of the glade, they gave off pollen constantly. Agnes breathed in deeply as she stepped into the water and let the warmth tingle across her skin. For a moment, she felt young again and wanted again, and closer to her Queen than she'd ever been.

She dipped her hand into the pool and scooped up a mouthful, as only Ladies were permitted to do. It was rich in life, teeming with food and saturated with Lux. This would be the last time she tasted it, and that made it sweeter than ever.

She plucked a dragonfly nymph from under a leaf and sucked on it while she looked for the eggs. *There they are.* It was a big clutch, with good colour, fat and ready to burst. She counted them, looking for the omens. One, two, three … seven.

Oh. Seven was the mortals' number. That was not good. She moved the water lilies aside, searching for the completeness that eight would bring.

She was still searching when the first egg, a green one, burst open. The Little One emerged and swam up, reaching for air. Agnes caught it and brought it up to her shoulder. It smelled her teats and tried to slide down. *My, this is a determined one.* She cradled it in her left hand and stroked its lips, Inking some calm. The second egg burst open, and she plucked the Little One straight out of the water. The sooner Her Grace nurtured them, the quicker they would grow.

Agnes splashed out of the pool and skipped round the grass to give the first of the brood to their Queen. Her Grace took one in each hand and placed them to the teat with a smile.

The third, fourth and fifth eggs gave Agnes less trouble, and she was able to carry all three Little Ones in one trip. The first two were already flashing with Quicksilver as the magick worked in them. Agnes placed the three new arrivals in the Queen's lap and turned to go back.

'What shall we name them?' asked Her Grace.

Agnes stopped and blinked. She had *never* been asked about names before, and all she could think about was the flowers where she'd found them and her last meal from the pool. 'Iris-Nymph Child,' she blurted out. 'If it pleases Your Grace.'

'It does please me,' replied the Queen. She gently detached the first Little One and took Amrita on to her finger. With the speed and grace of a Queen, she Inked the name onto the infant: *1ˢᵗ-Redqueen-Iris-Nymph Child*, followed by the Locking Sigil, the hidden, personal name that bonded the Little One to Her Grace.

After the Name, Her Grace held open the Little One's jaw and Inked the People's tongue with quick strokes. It would be Agnes's job to try to teach them the mortal tongues in the months to come. If she lived that long. Would she even live to see their buds form into wings?

A cry from the pool made her jump. *The last two eggs!* She ran back as fast as her legs could carry her, arriving just in time to see one of the royal pets stalking the margin of the pool. By the look of it, the pet was a she-lynx crossed with a beaver. She cursed Galleny – how else could it have got in here without his negligence?

In the pool, both the sixth and seventh Little Ones were fighting for air, their big heads dropping underwater because their little bodies couldn't keep them afloat. Their panic was wasting all the life they'd brought from the egg, and if the pet didn't get them, they'd expire very quickly.

They saw the pet and cried for help, loudly and without words, desperate for some living thing to pluck them out of the water and save them. In their eyes, with none of the People nearby, the four-legged creature would have to do. The pet's tail twitched and its jaws opened wide, dripping saliva.

When the seventh Little One saw the teeth, it used the last of its strength to push its hatch-mate towards the bank, then dived underwater. The other Little One reached out its tiny hands and the pet came to its rescue, putting it out of its misery with a swift bite to the neck before dragging it towards the trees.

Didn't have the sense it was hatched with, thought Agnes. *We're better off without it.* She scooped up the surviving Little One from the water and felt the life within it, still burning strong. It would now become 6th not 7th because they don't get their names until they are presented to the Queen. Six was a much better number – a number sacred to the People rather than the mortals (it could be worse, like nine, sacred to the Great Goddess and to He who must not be Named).

1st-Redqueen-Iris-Nymph Child was standing by the Queen when Agnes presented the last of the hatchlings, and 1st took that moment to try out its newly Inked tongue. 'Too small,' it said, pointing to its sibling, about to become 6th. 'You're a too small, no-good *worm*.'

Agnes sighed. 1st was going to be trouble. She could tell.

'Open my vanity,' said the Queen. 'You can brush my hair while I finish Inking them.'

'Of course, Your Grace.'

Agnes's hand hesitated over the brushes nestling in the red velvet lining of the Queen's vanity. The everyday brush didn't seem right for such an auspicious moment, and she took a risk, picking up the special brush with the lacquered back made from ground lapis lazuli, the royalest of royal blues.

'May I, Your Grace?'

The Queen looked up from Her Inking. 'You may, and try putting a touch of auburn into the magick. And maybe a few soft curls.'

Agnes was no handmaiden. Her strengths had always been in the purity of her Amrita and the sharpness of her tongue, so when she made the Queen look closer to Christina Hendricks than to a young Julia Roberts (which is what Her Grace had been aiming for), the Queen took it in good part, laughing and showing off to the Little Ones who toddled around her.

'Keep it,' said the Queen to Agnes. 'You need to practise, and I expect it to be perfect next time.' She laid Her hand on Agnes's arm again. So special. 'I shall expect you to attend me whenever I ride at Sprint.'

It was a way of letting her down gently: *This is your last time in the glade, but you're still special.*

'My Lady is generous and kind. Thank you. Thank you for everything.'

Chapter Two

*Alicia's Story continues at Sprint Stables
four months before the Peace of Brothers Water,
seven months before the wedding.*

Lady Agnes *did* live to see Samhain, despite telling the brood many times that she wouldn't. She lasted until two days afterwards, as it happened, and then she went for a walk on a frosty morning before the brood was up and she never came back.

6th-Redqueen-Iris-Nymph Child missed Agnes as soon as it woke up, mostly because it couldn't smell anything cooking, and that meant something was *seriously* wrong. Lady Agnes existed to provide them with food, so where was she?

6th flew up to the perch and passed water while it looked round the nursery. Nothing. All was still, and the only sound to disturb the morning was the gentle *thump thump* of the mounts moving above the nursery nest. 6th used the perch to launch itself over the rest of the brood and landed next to Agnes's room.

The door was wide open, for a change, and the bed neatly made. 6th had sneaked a peek into the Lady's private space many times, trying to get its head around the mysterious things that the wingless surrounded themselves with. It took a quick scan and noted that her stout boots were missing. Agnes must be outside for some reason.

There were no herbs to gather now that autumn was upon them, so what was she doing? It looked back to the nest and heard grumbling. If it didn't move now, 1st or 3rd would wake up and lock it in the kitchen and not let it out until Agnes returned or until it had made food for them. That was not going to happen.

It scampered up the stairs to the ground floor of the roundhouse; the staircase down to their nursery nest was well hidden and Warded to stop their older cousins who perched in the rafters above from getting at them. To the left were the pens of the one-horned, the aon-adharcach, the mounts that only Little Ones could ride.

6th's first nursery nest had been at the Royal Sídhe in Borrowdale, where Lady Agnes had watched over their every step as their wings blossomed into life and they took their first hops, skips and jumps into the world of the People. 6th had little recollection of those early days, mostly because the Vortex for Inking Memories couldn't be realised until its wings were strong enough to bear the magick. Memory is the first of the Ways, and as their wings spread wider, Lady Agnes transferred more Vortices to help them master their powers and showed them how to mix the images of the Third Eye with their mundane vision.

She taught them much else besides the beginnings of the Ways: she chased them out of the nest to fetch and carry for the wingless, and she showed them how to mix the Fire of magick with the flames of combustion without burning themselves. As soon as they had mastered this, they were loaded into a horse transporter and brought to Sprint Stables.

Compared to the warmth, luxury and love which infused the Royal Sídhe, Sprint was a place made from cold stone, afflicted with cold winds and cold rain and ruled by the cold hard glare of the Count of Force Ghyll, master of the stables. That his second, the Gamekeeper, was fiery and fierce was no compensation.

On that first day in the stable yard, when the transporter had gone, Lady Agnes had shown them how to make Fire in their wings to keep themselves warm, and then she had led the brood towards their new home in the roundhouse.

She had held the lesson outside because 5th was quite likely to set the bedding on fire, and because 6th always needed two goes to get things right. 6th took *three* turns that day, and so the others had already gone in when 6th saw something which had been kept from the brood until now: mortals.

Two females led out a fearsome black stallion and began to groom him. 6th tried to see their magick, but either they had none or it needed more practice. It was about to turn away when one of the women wiped something from the other's face with a cloth. She also bared her teeth: the mortal smile. *So that's what it looks like! So strange to show your bite in a gesture of love.*

And there was more! The taller mortal had kissed the smaller one on the lips, both of them oblivious of 6th watching from the shadows. It could smell something in the air as they embraced, no wings to encumber them, and it stood entranced at the love flowing between them until something made them jump apart in shock.

5th had shouted in the People's tongue, and its message was for 6th. 'Hurry up, Littleworm! 4th says that you are a dead weight and will soon be dead!'

And from that day, Lady Agnes watched as they were introduced to the skills they would need to prosper: the Count taught them to ride the aon-adharcach, the Gamekeeper introduced them to the blade and all of the People present, including the Hidden Ladies, taught them more of the Ways.

They all had their strengths – 1st made the best Ink, 2nd was the best in the trial ring, already showing great promise with the blade, and 4th was the best rider in its brood.

6th hadn't found its strength yet but it wasn't failing at anything, and there were many little things it could do better than any of the others. It opened the gate to the pens and whistled, putting its favourite aon-adharcach's name into the sound. It gave a little jump for joy when the mount clopped over, rejoicing at its success. It could do *that* at least. 5th couldn't even whistle a mount, never mind sound the separate names with a whistle.

6th fed the one-horned horse a little treat, then grabbed its mane and jumped up, pointing its mount's nose at the pre-dawn light coming into the roundhouse. Beyond the doors, the frigid air tore at its throat. *In the Queen's name, it's cold!* it thought, and it turned its head to Ink some warmth into its wings – too long in this air and the fringes would turn brittle and the veins might even turn to ice.

It was about to urge its mount into a trot when it saw Lady Agnes standing at the entrance to the other roundhouse where the Queen's mounts, the High Unicorns, lived. 'My Lady?' said 6th. 'Has something happened?'

Agnes was holding her side, keeping her coat firmly in place over it. 'I had to,' she said, more to herself than in answer to 6th's question. Agnes turned to look at her brood-member. 'Let's walk to the pasture. The sun will crest the hills shortly. It's already lighting up the ghyll.'

'But what about food?' said 6th.

'In hand,' said Agnes. 'Come with me.'

The Lady was limping as if she were hurt, and leaning right over to the side. 6th had to pull back on its mount to stop him going ahead. For the first few yards, Agnes tried to make conversation. *Are the others awake? Did you light the fire? Why not?* Then she fell quiet and put all her strength into walking. 6th was becoming really alarmed now. It hated cooking.

Lady Agnes reached the wall and collapsed with her back to it. She held up one hand and commanded 6th to silence while still holding her coat in place with the other. 6th slipped off its mount and whispered calming words to the little beast, then squatted down, making sure its wings were away from the frost-white grass. Then it waited patiently for the sun to rise in the manner of its kind: it nodded off to sleep.

A groan from Lady Agnes woke it. The sun was now on her face. She screwed up her eyes and turned her head slightly. 'It was worth it,' she said.

'What was, my lady?'

For an answer, Agnes dropped her hand, allowing her coat to slip open. *Oh*, thought 6th. *That's bad. Very bad.*

Blood had soaked the Lady's dress and 6th could see her inside workings leaking out from her covering. Her *skin*, in the mortal tongue.

'I had to touch him once,' said Agnes, her breath coming in ragged gasps. 'Hipponax. So beautiful. So powerful. So sharp. So deadly.' With the lightning speed that had enforced discipline throughout the brood, she shot her hand out and grabbed 6th by the wrist. 'Listen, Little One,' she said in the mortal tongue. '*Unicorn.* Say it.'

Like all of the brood, 6th found it hard to sound the mortals' words in its wide mouth, but it tried. 'Unicorn.'

Agnes let go of its wrist and continued in the clickety-wet words of mortals. 'Good. What will become of you, eh? Who will take you to the pool and break the omen if you don't have something to offer?'

That was very scary. What omen? What was the Lady not telling it?

6th started to ask, but Agnes ignored it. 'Do you remember the first story I told you?'

'You told us of Gertha the Spider, and none of us slept that night.'

'No, fool, that was the first story I told you when we moved here. What about in the Royal Sídhe? By the pool?'

6th ran its stubby fingers over its thigh, where it kept most of its stories. 'Princess Livia and the King of Tribona?' it suggested.

'Yes.' Urgency gripped Agnes's voice. 'What does it mean?'

'You said it showed us why mortals hate us and love us and leave us.'

'And you couldn't see it, could you, my special darling? I've seen the way you hang around the grooms, pretending to learn their tongue. You need to learn that lesson quickly.'

'Yes, my Lady,' said 6th. It made one last attempt to bring comfort in the only way it knew. 'Shall I rouse the Count? He could carry you into the warm.'

Agnes shook her head with what little energy remained in her, then moistened her lips. 'Do you know what my last service to our Queen was?'

'We are your last service,' said 6th.

'Look in my pocket.'

Her eyes were turning dim, the sun no longer a bother to her. 6th reached into the pocket and found Agnes's greatest treasure, a hairbrush with a brilliant blue back. 6th knew that it was the Lady's greatest treasure because she put it under her pillow every night.

Agnes smiled. 'You are my last service to the People, not my last service to the Queen. You're wrong, *Sixth.*'

That word sounded *so* bad in the mortal tongue. 6th was not a number! The mortal word *sixth* only put it in a line between fifth and seventh, conveying nothing of the symmetry, harmony and love that came with its name in the People's tongue and which had been Inked by their Queen. It shifted uneasily, frightened that those would be the Lady's last words. That would not be a good omen.

Agnes managed one more breath. 'My last service to Her Grace was to brush Her hair while She nurtured you. Do the same for me, and I will name the brush to you.'

6th lifted Agnes away from the wall and began running the brush through the Lady's hair, gently sticking to the edges at first because it could see a matted tangle underneath and plunging the bristles into that would cause pain. As 6th worked, it felt the magick in the brush call to its essence.

It plunged the spikes deep and let the brush do the hard work, untangling the hair as it drew down. Lady Agnes gave a low moan of pleasure and relaxed her shoulders. After a few more strokes, her head slumped forwards and life finally left the brood's Lady behind.

6th immediately felt angry. How *could* she leave them! It wasn't *fair!* 6th was going to hit the remains of Lady Agnes for having the nerve to depart and raised its hand in frustration – but what would that serve? The Lady's voice came into its head. *Where's the profit in that, 6th?*

Nowhere. That's where. The profit would come from a hearty meal and currying favour with the Hidden Ladies in the sídhe below the roundhouse.

It dropped the brush and ripped open what was left of Agnes's dress, then sucked greedily on the open wound. It was in time: the Quicksilver was still running. It sucked the magick down to the wound and gathered the Quicksilver into a ball. *There.* Got it.

The pulsating ball of liquid metal dropped out of the wound and into 6th's hand. It paused to eat a little of the tasty remains before they got too squishy, then stood up and went to get its mount.

Something must be wrong because instead of *aon-adharcach*, the word *unicorn* came into its head. Strange. Whatever you called it, the beast had no interest in following 6th, so the Little One reached out to grab its mane with its free hand.

The sun had come higher, and the life-giver's rays made something glint in the grass. The hairbrush. It came from the Queen, and Agnes had gifted it. For the first time in its life, 6th knew what the wingless meant by *fork-pain*. It had three items and only two hands. Which was it going to leave behind?

It stood, flicking its eyes from the Quicksilver to the Unicorn to the hairbrush, torn by having to go down one fork and abandon the other. The Quicksilver *had* to be taken, so one of the other two had to be left…

To avoid the frozen ground, 6th flew as far as it could before it landed in the stable yard. As it did so, the two strange mortals emerged from the House of the Wingless, fastening coats around themselves and pulling on hats. 6th had been shocked when it discovered that mortals could grow up to be like these two. In fact, it had been told they were unique and nothing like lovely Flora and Verona, the two grooms who had introduced 6th to the mortal smile on its first day at the stables.

It called the taller of the special mortals the Headless One because she was using someone else's head instead of her own. The other was somehow like one of the People. 6th called her Eden because it couldn't pronounce the girl's mortal name, and it had heard the Faithful Princess talk a lot about 'the Eden line' when she came to visit.

6th knew that Eden was taking Amrita and that, with Faithful's help, she was binding it to her magick. The mortal was *very* valuable to the Queen, so 6th hopped up to her and offered the handful of animated Quicksilver from Lady Agnes. 'For you.'

Eden shivered. 'For me? That's kind, Little One, but I can only absorb it in Amrita.'

The Headless One recoiled and brought her hand to her nose. 'Eurgh, Perci. Where the chuffing hell has that come from?'

Eden glanced at her friend. 'Don't worry. 'Salright.' She turned back to 6th. 'Take it to the Hlæfdigan. We don't want to drop it, do we?'

'What the fuck are you doing?' came a shout. The Count of Force Ghyll.

6th was in trouble. Deep trouble. *Where's the profit?* Lady Agnes's words were never truer than now when she had left them. 6th bolted into the roundhouse where, below the floor, its broodmates were stirring. It threw the hairbrush down the steps to 5th, shouting 'Mine by right of gift!' and headed for the safety of the sídhe.

The steps to the nursery nest were off to the side – hidden and Warded, yes, but also very much of this world. Not so the path to the sídhe.

Not only was the path a shallow slope down which beasts of all sizes could walk, it also went up to the Fae Realm, away from the mortal world. Within the sídhe lived the Hidden Ladies who worked to breed, nurse and heal the Unicorns.

6th's favourite Hidden Lady made tears when it gave her the Last of Agnes. The other Ladies put their arms around her and led her away. 'Thank you,' she said over her shoulder, and she smiled the mortal smile at 6th. A clear profit.

When it left the sanctuary of the sídhe, 6th found 4th leading the aon-adharcach which 6th had abandoned near Agnes, and 4th had a smug look on its face. On the threshold the Count was waiting, and the Count's face was anything but smug. This was going to be bad.

The Count showed his teeth and said, 'Why in the name of the Morrigan did you leave a mount out there? Are you actually as useless as they tell me you are?' He folded his arms. 'Well? I'm waiting.'

6th threw itself on the frozen ground and covered its face. It knew one thing: any mention of putting the hairbrush ahead of its mount's welfare would mean certain death. 'Mercy. I beg mercy. Lady Agnes is dead, and I—'

'Shut up. You. Verona. Get me a hunting whip.'

The thin, waif-like mortal trembled and looked for her lover, Flora. When she realised she was alone, she ran and fetched the stout leather whip. The last thing 6th saw as the Count lifted his arm to strike was little Verona mouthing something silently and then turning away.

When the blows came, they were entirely without mercy. The most painful place on a Little One's body is the root of the wing where the veins mix with the carapace, and the Count beat at the roots until 6th screamed and its wings were broken and bleeding. Satisfied, the Count stopped and threw down the whip. 'Put that away and make yourself useful. If you can. If you can't, I could find you useful for archery practice.'

It took every last dram of 6th's strength to stand up. Its wings dragged on the floor with every step, shooting pain up its back. It took the whip and went down into the nursery.

Chapter Three

'Food,' said 1st. 'And quickly. We will be wanted for duties soon.'

6th limped into the kitchen. At least 2nd had already lit the fire and was putting the water on. The powerful broodmate stepped aside and let 6th soak a cloth.

'Let me, for favour,' said 2nd. It took the cloth and wiped 6th's wings gently, like Lady Agnes had once done when they fell over while learning to fly. 2nd also did its best to take the pain away with magick before tying up the wings with the cloth.

'The Hidden Ladies will help you,' said 2nd. 'For another favour, I'll cook tonight.'

'It is a bargain,' said 6th. 'Now go.'

When the pain had lessened a little, 6th measured out the oatmeal and dropped it into the water. It stood, watching the pan, and the stabbing pain in its wings was replaced by the slippery, dull ache of fork-pain. If it did nothing, it would be discarded or Matched with something so low that it would spend its short life among the wingless in the basement of Galleny's sídhe, cooking and cleaning until it threw itself on the fire to escape from life. *Where's the profit in that?*

Well, it knew where the day's second profit was coming from. 6th went to Lady Agnes's room, heaved the stool onto the bed, and carefully climbed up to reach the box mounted on the wall. With Agnes's life dispersed, her Ink was fading, and 6th breathed a sigh of relief: no one had beaten it to the cupboard. With a savage twist, it tore aside Agnes's Ink and punched a hole in the wood.

The force of the blow made it rock on the stool, and it had to grip the splintered wood to avoid falling back and dashing its brains out on the floor. More blood ran down its wrist from the splinters, but it was safe for now. It ignored the few treasures within and took the real prize: the key to the larder.

Getting down was much harder than getting up, and 6th had to risk tumbling onto the bed face-first. It was a good job it had eaten of Agnes, because without that, it would be fainting around now. It dragged itself back into the kitchen and reached up to the lock, barely accessible to the Little Ones. *Curse it and break it.* The Ink around the lock was keyed to Lady Agnes's hidden name.

The oldest of the brood would have it open in a blink, but 1st did not give favours. If it was going to get in, 6th would have to remember its lessons. It remembered the Last of Agnes, carried in its palm to the sídhe, and Agnes's full name came back to it in a swirl of Lux. The key turned, and 6th pulled open the door.

It wanted to hop for pleasure but didn't want the pain in its wing-roots, so instead it made a happy noise and made light inside. Perhaps it would get a stool, then it could work the wingless magic that made light from the roof *just by touching a dead knob.*

When it saw inside the larder, it *did* hop: there was plenty of meat. And other things, too. 6th had a bone to pick with its sibling. A very big bone, maybe even the size of a wingless horse, because there had been no sign of the hairbrush which it had left with its broodmate, and without Agnes's Heartstone, 6th could see very little profit in its future.

They all agreed who told the best stories in the brood: 5th. Their sibling could go to the Hidden Ladies and come back with the most amazing tales of Queens and Princes, mortals and Higher Ones. 5th would sit on the perch telling stories while Lady Agnes sat by the fire, knitting and asking them questions about what they'd heard. *Why did the Queen spare his life? Why should you never say your Name to a mortal?* And most of all, *Where's the profit in that?* It was how they learned of the world of the wingless.

6th loved the stories, and 5th was 6th's *favourite* broodmate. 6th had no idea whether what it felt for its sibling was the *love* spoken of in the stories and seen on display between Flora and Verona, but that was why it had given 5th the hairbrush to look after. After all, if you can't trust your favourite, who can you trust?

The porridge was nearly ready to bubble, and it would soon be time to add the meat. From beyond the kitchen, it heard the others return from their duties and descend the steps. 6th looked into the nest and called to 5th. 'Give me Lady Agnes's brush, and I will give you favour for hiding it.'

5th dug out the brush and looked at it greedily. 'Did this come from the Queen herself? It pleases me greatly. Fairly given and fairly taken. I will keep it, Littleworm.'

6th walked over, carrying a kitchen cloth. 'Lady Agnes named it to me with her last breath. It is mine forever.'

5th stared at its broodmate, taking in the broken wings and cuts to the chest. 'What will a kitchen maid do with a hairbrush, Littleworm?' it asked. 'For that is what you will become. It was told in the omens of the pool that only three of us would become Squires: 1st, 2nd and one other.'

'How do you know that? You lie!'

'Lady Agnes trusted me with the story for when she passed, and now she is gone and I have her gift. I will be the third who goes to the Matching, not you.'

Lady Agnes had told them many times that the pool did not tell the future: it told a *story* of the future, a story no more or less important than any other story, and 6th had a story of its own for today. Would its broodmate listen or not?

'Do you remember the story of Isabelle-9th-Nightwithstars-Moon-Wolf?' asked 6th.

5th giggled. 'You are broken and you smell of dead rats. You will not walk at the side of the Great Queen like Isabelle did.'

2nd had returned and flown up to the perch. It watched them with interest.

'How about the story of Her Grace and Trafalgar?' said 6th. 'Do you remember that one?'

Of course its broodmate remembered the story. The tale had been told to them by the Red Queen herself during nurturing, when they still lived in the Borrowdale Sídhe, and Lady Agnes had made them learn it, word for word, and had Inked it into their skin. 5th hopped from foot to foot, fluttering its wings. 'The Count has beaten out your brains as well as your wings,' it said. 'Your tongue is a worm with a life of its own and you have no power over it.'

'Challenge,' said 6th. 'Challenge here and challenge now.'

From up on the perch, 2nd spoke out. 'You're hurt. Withdraw!'

6th didn't look up. 'Challenge here and challenge now,' it repeated.

There was no need for a third challenge, with or without the magick to bind 5th to accept the challenge or submit to mercy. 5th jumped at the challenger, spreading its wings and lifting its hands to strike.

6th dropped the kitchen cloth and showed 5th the real reason why Lady Agnes kept the larder locked: to stop them grabbing the knives and stabbing each other. It plunged the blade into 5th's throat, twisted to cut, and pulled out.

'Your favour,' it said to 2nd, up on the perch. The broodmate licked its lips and hopped down to feast.

6th picked up the hairbrush and went back to the kitchen. It had a new favourite now.

Despite 6th producing a bowl of porridge with rat of which Agnes would have been proud, the Hidden Ladies of the sídhe decided that the brood were too young and too fractious to fend for themselves, and the Elder Lady, Morag, took it on herself to leave the sídhe and move into Agnes's room. She also changed the lock on the larder door as soon as she'd carefully counted the knives.

'It's a good job I came straight away,' she said to 6th after she'd taken one look at its injuries. 'Another few hours and your wings would never have flexed again or grown, and then where would you be, eh?'

'Making rat porridge for ever and ever,' it replied. 'Or hunting practice for the Pack. Ouch!'

'Finished. Well, I'm not like Agnes. She was as soft as the butter on the Queen's bread, she was. As lovely, too, but soft. There's no May blossom in the Sprint sídhe's glade, Little One, and we wear these garments all year. More in winter. You will cook for the brood until you can fly up to the perch.'

'As my lady wishes. My lady is kind and merciful.'

Morag straightened up and sat back on Agnes's bed – her bed, now. 'Before I dismiss you, tell me truly: what was your quarrel with 3rd?'

'It was with 5th, my lady. 3rd died at 1st's hand two moons ago.'

'Whatever. Tell me truly, and tell me in the mortals' tongue. Agnes was too soft about that as well. You'll soon need to talk to the grooms, and they don't take kindly to Little Ones who cannot be understood.'

6th's wings were unbound now, and it gingerly Inked the Sigil of Truth into the tracery. That was hard, but finding (and sounding) the words in the mortals' tongue was harder. 'Lady Agnes. Deading. Asked Favour, gave me her … Heartstone. Taken. *Stolen*. Mine.'

Lady Morag tilted her head to one side. 'Show me.'

The gift of Lady Agnes was fetched and shown, and Morag taught 6th the words in the mortal tongue. Later that day, Morag placed the stool next to her bed, gathered the brood around her, and gave lessons in the mortal tongue while 6th brushed her hair for the first time – and by the Morrigan, it was in need of care. 6th worked slowly and carefully, determined that Lady Morag would want it to repeat the service.

When 6th had finished, Lady Morag sent the brood early to bed because they would be riding at dawn tomorrow. Except 6th, of course, because you can't ride a one-horned horse without wings, and that was why 6th was able to watch what happened when the Lord of Death paid his first visit to Sprint Stables.

Of course, he wasn't the Lord of Death then, merely the Dragonslayer, and 6th didn't even learn *that* name until much later in the day. When the mortal first appeared at Sprint Stables, he was something which only Prince Galleny and Princess Faithful had ever seen before: a Witchfinder.

6th was making porridge and Lady Morag had gone back to the sídhe to make her toilet when a clatter of hooves upstairs announced the return of the little unicorns. 6th got the rat ready and went to look. Its older cousins were laughing at 1st, because 1st had been thrown by its mount. 6th wanted to laugh, too, but if it was seen enjoying its sibling's embarrassment, that would be a sure beating later.

And then everything changed.

Cries of alarm came from across the meadow. The Headless One was screaming, her voice carried by magick as she rode the great Keraunós over the grass at a gallop. When the mortal reined in the High Unicorn, the Count of Force Ghyll and the Gamekeeper rushed up to see what was wrong.

'Witchfinders on the Gallops!' shouted the Headless One. 'Two of them, and they're coming this way.'

'Witchfinders?' said the Count. 'Don't you mean Assessors?'

'No. They carry Nimue's Badge. One man and one woman.'

The Gamekeeper was not always at the stables, because she was also the personal driver and Huntsman for Prince Galleny, and at the stables she spoke with the Prince's voice. She had been gone for several days and had returned yesterday with the Prince's latest Knight – the Firefly, a rare talent who could mix Fire and Earth in ways that 6th had only heard of in stories.

The Firefly emerged from the House of the Wingless, and the Gamekeeper looked furious. She grabbed the Count's arms and made a Silence. When she let him go, the Count began barking orders, and the Gamekeeper ran towards the roundhouse where 6th was peering out. Scared at being caught gaping and not working, 6th put all the Lux it had into hopping onto a pile of straw and lying flat.

It needn't have bothered. The Gamekeeper ordered all of the Little Ones to mount up again and be ready to flee to the Gallops. Then she started collecting tools, the sharp ones that were kept locked away from the Little Ones' reach.

The mortal grooms were driven into the roundhouse where they were armed. 6th could see that they didn't look happy to be made warriors, especially the kind one, Verona. Of all the grooms, she was the only one who had ever let 6th come near the High Unicorns, holding Hipponax's halter to stop him spearing 6th like a *kebab* (a word Morag had taught them last night).

After the herd and their riders charged out of the roundhouse and the grooms had been pushed into the yard to join the combat, 6th had a good view of the battle. It used Ink in its wings catch their voices. This was going to be good sport.

And then 6th saw him. The male Witchfinder was the tallest wingless it had ever seen, and he carried a blade on his back. Sport indeed. They spoke many words in the mortals' tongue, and 6th didn't understand most of them. The Witchfinders offered peace, and 6th groaned. *No sport there.* The Count must have thought the same because he ordered the attack, and 6th gave a little jump for joy.

In its short life, 6th had seen fights and blood. It had seen Little Ones and the wingless practise with blades in the yard. It had seen the Pack released to go hunting on the Gallops. What it had never seen or smelled was n'Haeval, and that was what tinged the Witchfinder's blade. The waft carried over the yard, along with a ghostly howl of Wolf, and fear rose in 6th's throat, drowning the joy it had felt at the sport ahead.

It hunkered down, and missed the moment when the Count ripped off the Headless One's borrowed head. And when he shot nice Verona. In seconds, the stench of blood was everywhere, and 6th had to look up. The huge mortal and his partner were winning! How could this be?

With all power and no grace, the Witchfinder killed the Firefly and cornered the Count. When the Count's head tumbled off his shoulders, 6th gave the People's grin. There would be no more beatings from *him*.

What happened next troubled 6th for many days. The Witchfinder cradled the Headless One in his arms and they disappeared from sight, and when they came back, the Headless One had a new head. Their own head. How had he done *that*?

After the helicopter took the Witchfinder away, 6th learned that he was called Dragonslayer. No wonder he had triumphed. A few days later, when its wings were healed, 6th saw the Dragonslayer return and interrupt the hunt that Prince Galleny had set running, and suddenly the Prince was their Count and the Gamekeeper was gone.

On that night, the night of the Dragonslayer's second visit, Lady Morag told the brood that they all had to make a story out of the day's battle, and that the worst storyteller would be on cooking duty for a week. 6th surprised itself by winning the competition, and 4th was not happy that it lost.

Complaining only made things worse. 'You'll cook for a whole moon, 4th,' pronounced Morag. 'And you'll do it properly.'

The third time that 6th saw the Dragonslayer, he was no longer the Dragonslayer: he was the Lord of Death.

Part Two — Serendipity

A Note from Francesca

We will never know just how closely Evie's rendering of a Sprite comes to the reality of life in the sídhe, although I can tell you that it doesn't seriously conflict with what we know for certain about the Ways of the People.

However, when it comes to these papers on 'Chloë Greenwood', I'm afraid that what Evie wrote is pure speculation. Completely.

In my opinion, the only documents we should include in this codex relating to that unknown woman should be Mr Justice Morton's interviews with Juliet Bloxham and her husband. Alas, that suggestion has gone unheeded.

So long as you take what Evie wrote with a pinch of salt large enough to kill the mightiest slug, then enjoy them for what they are – another chapter in the fairy story.

Chapter Four

A Note from Evie Mason

When Francesca read what I'd written about 'Chloë Greenwood', first of all she rejected it, then she said it should be labelled 'based on a true story'.

I spoke to loads of people about what happened (except Chloë herself, for obvious reasons). This is as close to the truth as any of the other 'testimonies' in here, but if you prefer to think of it as *A dramatic reconstruction based on eye-witness accounts*, then that's up to you. Doesn't change what happened.

Clerkswell Village Green

Yuletide

The evidence was there if you looked hard enough for it. Questions on the village shop Facebook page. The Clerkswell Coven section on the cricket club website. Even the minutes of the parish council gave clues. And if you had spies in the world of magick, it wouldn't take you long to find out that, on one particular day around Yuletide, Myfanwy Lewis would be working in the shop while her fiancé enjoyed Sunday lunch with his parents.

A quick trip to the shop to make sure that Myfanwy was indeed behind the counter and showing no trace of morning sickness, and then back to the car for the short drive down Elven Lane to the gates of Elvenham Grange.

Was the Principal there? Almost certainly, along with the Sidekick and the Sidekick's partner. The partner was the one sent to ring the bell while the other two watched from a safe distance to see what happened with the Wards.

No one answered the doorbell, despite it being loud enough to be heard in the church, and the partner trudged back, blowing on her hands to warm them up.

'Good job we're not Fae,' said the Principal.

The Sidekick agreed. 'I know. I would not want to be a cockroach and get caught in *that* web. And when she gets back from playing shop, the Druid will know there's been a visitor.'

'And now there's been one visitor, let's have a closer look. If I'm not mistaken, that Trigger has to be reset to work again, and unless we cross the threshold, that's *all* the Druid will know: at least one visitor and no incursions.'

'Are you sure, Anita?'

'This isn't Merlyn's Tower. There are no Imprint scanners here. Chloë? Could you be a darling and watch the lane from behind that pillar? Keep out of sight and scream if someone comes. Unless it's a tractor. You can ignore that.'

The partner – Chloë – stood back and put her gloves on as the Principal and the Sidekick took cautious steps towards the house. When they were ten metres away, they stopped and stared at the carved stone which stood apart from the solid red walls of Victorian brick. 'Is that what I think it is?' said the Sidekick.

'Yes. It has to be. Let's go and look.'

The Sidekick hesitated. 'Look, we know for a fact that the Witchfinder General, the Keeper, the Earthmaster, the Royal Occulter, the bloody Mowbrays, Princess Cockroach and at least *two* gods have been here. Are you seriously telling me that *none* of them noticed?'

The Principal stared at the dragon. 'Have another look. What do you think was the biggest Charm bound in there?'

The Sidekick considered. 'Well, for centuries it was the one binding Spectre Thomas to the well.'

'Which was mostly about regulating the sex life of the Clarkes. Not something you'd stick your nose into if you considered them friends. And then what happened when Thomas departed?'

'There … there's another. Another Work connected to an Imprint.'

'Yes. And it's been trying to muddy the waters. With the house empty, it must be dormant.'

The Sidekick was still dubious. 'The inhumans would see that.'

'So? Pass me those plans.'

The Sidekick handed over a clear plastic map case which protected some yellowing documents. The Principal studied them for a moment then passed them back. 'Unusual not to have cellars in old houses. Are you sure these are accurate?'

The Sidekick *tsked*. 'I've told you: that well is here for a reason. The water table is just too high where the new house was built. Any cellars would be like an aquarium in no time.'

'Then where is it? The stone advertising the nest is here, so should the nest itself be, and where there's a nest…'

'Where would you expect it to be? Nearer the well and on a higher plane. Let's have a look at the gardens. We've another two hours yet.'

'Why not? I can't say this isn't giving me a thrill.'

'Whatever. I don't see why one of the Akademia Council couldn't just rock up and pay a visit. This is too personal. For you.'

'Then why don't you ask them to do it?' The Principal waited a moment, but no response was forthcoming. 'I thought not. Are you coming?'

The Sidekick turned and jogged back to her partner to give her some reassurance, and then ran to catch the Principal. They were quickly through the iron gate and into the remodelled gardens, heading towards the well.

'We need help,' said the Principal. 'We have time for a Summoning. A Spirit of Mother Nature would tell us.'

'You're mad. We might as well light a Beltane fire and tell the whole county.'

'If you have a better idea?'

The Sidekick pointed to the well. 'Why ignore the obvious? There's a gateway over there, so why don't we use it and see whether the Fae had a hand in this? One thing's for certain – there won't be any Wards on the well.'

'Won't hurt.'

With the time difference and the lack of mobile coverage in the Fae Realm, Chloë was beside herself with cold, panic and an urgent need to go to the toilet by the time the other two came back.

The Principal had a grim look on her face and went straight to stand by the passenger door of the car. She didn't speak until they were safely out of Clerkswell and had pulled up in the car park of a pub offering two for one at the carvery. She turned to the Sidekick and said, 'We *have* to have access, Beth. We *have* to. That sídhe must hold the answers, even if the nest itself is where you think it is.'

'And how the fuck are we going to get into the sídhe?'

The Principal turned to face the back seat. 'You're going undercover, Chloë. We need to know everything we can about the Clarkes and their weak points on home territory, and you're going to find out for us.'

Chloë returned the passion with a blank expression. 'Why in the mother's name should I do that? What the fuck is in it for me?'

The Sidekick took her partner's freezing fingers. 'You're doing it for us. This is what we've dreamed of.'

Chloë wasn't entirely sure about the *we* in that statement, but she squeezed back. 'And if I did, *how* would I do it? I've read those reports, you know. Clarke tracked the original codex all the way to Ireland and killed a Fae Queen. What do you think he'd do to me if he got a sniff of this? What would he do to *all* of us?'

'I've got an idea about that.'

Mark Hayden

The Inkwell Pub, Clerkswell

Just after New Year

Chloë made sure that she did all the dirty jobs when the pub closed for the night: it was the best way to ensure that Rosie, the Inkwell's senior barmaid (but don't let her hear you use the word *senior*), would keep talking. Not that it took much for that to happen – like the dodgy lager tap in the lounge bar, it was much easier to start Rosie going than to get her to stop.

'Shall I empty the glass bin into the recycling dumpster?' asked Chloë when she'd come back from putting the chairs on the bench seats ready for hoovering.

'Nah,' said Rosie. 'That's a job for the men, and it makes such a clatter that it might wake them. No point Reynold taking to his bed if we're gonna shock him to death. And the neighbours don't like it neither.'

'You reckon he's okay?' asked Chloë, with the appropriate amount of concern for someone she'd only met once.

'I told him that coleslaw was past its best. Self-inflicted is what I call it.'

It wasn't what Chloë called it. Chloë called it *Third Degree Tincture of Lobelia*. Rosie was right about the coleslaw, though, and the slight bitterness had been the perfect mask for the powerful, fast-acting emetic. Reynold would be fine in the morning.

Tonight was Chloë's first time at the pub, one of three probationary shifts she'd been assigned to before Reynold (and Rosie) would consider putting her on the roster.

As soon as Rosie had packed the owner off to his bed, it had taken her five minutes to get the measure of Chloë. As a barmaid, that is. 'You pulled that perfectly,' Rosie had observed as the head on a pint of Inkwell Bitter rose smoothly to the top of the glass, releasing the malty aroma. 'You better watch out or you'll be roped in to serve at the wedding.'

'Oh yeah?' said Chloë, trying not to sound interested. 'And what wedding would that be?'

'Take that pint and the G&T to that couple in Nookie Corner and have a look at the framed article on the wall when you come back.'

And Chloë had done just that, even though she'd examined the article online and already knew all about Conrad Clarke's first medal. When she returned to the bar, someone had ordered a pint of Guinness, and while they waited for it to settle, Rosie opened her mouth and started talking.

'Gonna be a huge wedding, it is. Church in the morning, then a big bash in the afternoon. Indian themed because the bride's from an Indian family...'

And on and on she had gone, with Chloë supplying the occasional 'Ooh!' or 'Wow!' to keep the tap running. Her one and only supplementary question had been this: 'Is the whole village going, or is it invitation only?'

'Open to all residents, apparently, though obviously the Bloxhams will have to think carefully before accepting.'

'Oh?'

'Hereditary enemies, they are.'

And that was music to Chloë's ears. *Hereditary enemies.* She asked plenty of questions about the Bloxhams, and with a bit of Googling during her break, she soon had her strategy in place.

At the end of the night, Rosie checked the kitchen doors, and then said, 'See you Tuesday, Chloë?'

Chloë fastened her winter coat around her and replied, 'You know what? I don't think so. I'd forgotten just how hard it is working behind the bar, especially one with hand pumps. I think I'll look for something where I can sit down.'

'Shame. I was enjoying getting to know you. Here. You've earned this more than I have, and I know how hard it is for you kids today.'

And with that, Rosie had handed over the bulk of the tips for the night, totally oblivious to the fact that she hadn't actually learned a single thing about her co-worker. She did remember Chloë's glasses, though, and that's how she would recognise her from the artist's impression DC Elaine Fraser would show her a few months later.

Chloë drove away from Clerkswell with aching feet from the cheap shoes she'd bought (and which Rosie had definitely noticed). She was glad that her revised plan meant going back to her *actual* wardrobe for her next disguise rather than to the clothing section of a major supermarket.

As well as learning about the Bloxhams, she had also picked up that the sad people of Clerkswell hated and distrusted everyone who came from or lived in the village of Allington, so that's where Chloë headed the next morning after making an appointment with Juliet Bloxham.

Chloë got to Allington in plenty of time. She parked at the pub (which didn't look nearly as inviting as the Inkwell) and went for a wander round the little village. The hood of her coat was pulled firmly up this morning, not for anonymity but to keep out the freezing rain. Anyone peering out of their curtains must have thought she was mad. Or lost. Or scoping out the place for a burglary. Which is exactly what she was doing, but not to burgle anywhere *here*. And when the neighbours (including Mrs Shaw) saw Chloë meet Juliet Bloxham outside No 4, Home Cottages, they had their answer: another potential new neighbour.

'Hi,' said Chloë as they shook hands. 'Good of you to come out in person. Horrible, isn't it?'

'Let's get inside,' said Juliet, trying to juggle her phone, her bag, her document case and a bunch of keys which any jailer would be proud of.

'Do you want me to hold that?' said Chloë.

Jules passed the heavy document case to her, and soon they were through the front door and into the little sitting room which had presumably once been home to an agricultural labourer, his wife and umpteen children.

'Bit cosy, isn't it?' said Chloë, putting the case on a battered IKEA coffee table and unzipping her jacket.

Jules did the same, hanging her coat on a hook behind the door before replying. 'If you mean that it's small, then yes, it is. Relatively speaking. If this was in the Lakes or Cornwall, or even up in the Cotswolds, we could turn it into a holiday let. Trouble is, down here on the plain there aren't enough magnets to make solos and couples give up the space. And then there are the holiday parks.'

'Have you thought of using this new Airbnb thing? I've heard it's growing massively.'

Jules stopped and took her first good look at Chloë, not that she could see much more than long dark hair and a pair of large glasses with photochromic lenses which made it hard to see her eyes. 'Are you after a short let? No 4 is only available on six-month terms.'

'That's what I want,' said Chloë. 'I was just wondering, that's all. It's an insane business model if Airbnb can keep getting away with classifying the properties as domestic and not businesses.'

Jules's eyebrows twitched. 'Obviously we'll need references, but there's no need for that unless you like it. Shall we?'

It didn't take long for Chloë to be shown round the single-bedroom cottage (the original second bedroom had become the bathroom). At least the kitchen was housed in a sturdy extension. During the tour, Jules asked her about her job – a polite way of finding out whether she had a regular income or whether she was going to try renting on benefits. In reply, Chloë told her that she was about to begin an MA at the Park Campus of Gloucestershire University and looked down as if she were blushing when she said that her parents were supporting her. 'I'll need part-time work as well, but I can't start looking until I know where I'm going to be living.'

'Do you drive?'

'Yeah. I parked at the pub. Does it get busy here?'

'You might jostle a bit with the neighbours but most of the time it's fine, and as you saw, there is the lane down the back. What do you think?'

Chloë made a show of looking around. It was perfect for her needs, and Jules had taken a shine to her when she had described the opportunities for media students in an increasingly digital world. Crucially, when Chloë had asked about the Park Campus, Jules had said that she knew nothing about it and had no connections there. Even more perfect.

Jules passed over a bundle of paperwork. 'If you're interested, all the details are in here, including the stuff we need from you. We can meet up again here to sign everything now that I can take pictures on my phone instead of having to photocopy everything.'

Chloë took the bundle. 'No need for you to come out. Your office is in Winchcombe, right?'

'Yes.'

'I could pop in if I decide to go ahead. And then I can take pictures of the gas meter and send them to you,' she added with a smile.

As they got ready to face the rain again, Chloë asked in an offhand way, 'Do you live near the office?'

'No. We live in Clerkswell. So long as you don't have to go through Cheltenham, getting around is quite easy.'

Outside, they shook hands again and went their separate ways. Once she got back to her car, Chloë sent a message to her partner in crime: *Looks great. And perfect for late night visits. XXX.*

Chapter Five

The offices of JB Lettings were on North Street in Winchcombe, squeezed between the sort of boutique fashion place Chloë's mother shopped in and a nail bar which Chloë thought might be worth trying. She had not been surprised to discover that Jules didn't work full-time, so Chloë had made sure her appointment was for a time when you might expect all the office staff to be in residence. All one of her, it turned out, so the four coffees which Chloë had bought were a little over the top. Not to worry.

'If those aren't for me, then whatever you want, the answer is no,' said the middle-aged woman behind the desk who absolutely *had* to be Jules's mother. Chloë smiled breezily to try to hide her surprise. It looked very much as if Mrs Smith was not just Jules's mother but a prototype of her daughter, a sort of Mark 1. The wardrobe was similar, they clearly went to the same hairdresser, and it was only age and a strong Birmingham accent which showed the improvements which had been made in the Mark 2 version. If the children in the photos on Mrs Smith's desk were Jules's, then Mark 3 was currently a difficult work in progress.

'Absolutely,' said Chloë. 'I'm here to see Juliet about No 4, Home Cottages in Allington. I've got a cappuccino, a latte and two Americanos, one with milk and one black.'

Mrs Smith ran a neat pink nail down yesterday's entry in an A4 desk diary. 'Chloë Greenwood? Excellent. You sort out the black coffee for me and the latte for Juliet and I'll give her a buzz.'

'Sugar?'

'No thanks, love. Sweet enough already, ain't I?'

That was a shame, because the Fourth Degree Tincture definitely needed something to hide the taste. Good job that Chloë had asked for an extra shot of espresso in all four cups. That should do the trick. She placed the cardboard cup holder on the window ledge and made sure that her back masked what she was doing.

Chloë took as long as possible to go through the documents, and took frequent sips from the rocket-fuel coffee to encourage Mrs Smith to do the same. By the time it came to her driving licence, Jules was starting to look at her watch.

'Oh no! After all that, I've forgotten it!' said Chloë. 'Can I bring it in tomorrow and collect the keys? I can organise a van and move in the same day.'

'Of course. Lovely to see you again, and I hope you enjoy Allington.' Jules paused. 'You're not into cricket, are you?'

'No?'

'Good. Don't want Allington recruiting you in the spring.'

Chloë had done her research: the women's cricket season didn't start until after the wedding, so she had plenty of time to decide if that needed to be part of her plan. On the other hand, sowing a seed might be useful. 'I did enjoy team sports at school, though. Hard to think about cricket in this weather.'

Jules stood up and Chloë knew she was dismissed.

She'd taken a good peek at the diary for the next day and seen that Jules had a couple of appointments, so when Chloë turned up at the offices half an hour ahead of one of them, a very harassed Juliet was on the phone and pacing up and down. Chloë sidled in and waited in the corner until Jules had promised to do what she could and then hung up.

'Chloë? Oh God, I'd forgotten you were coming in. Shit. In more ways than one.'

'Sorry?'

'My mother isn't well. Very bad dose of the runs, as in *seriously* bad. I might have to pop in and see her.' Jules massaged her forehead, trying to think.

'Is there just the two of you here?' asked Chloë.

'Yeah. There's a few admin staff at Stephen's place – he's a property developer, did I tell you? But he won't let the ones with a brain come over here in case I try to poach them.'

Chloë slid across the room towards the desk. 'Can I help? I need a part-time job, and I've got a car. Obviously I've got the computer skills and I used to work reception at the local hotel. It was in my references.'

'Would you? Oh no, you said you would have someone waiting with a van.'

Chloë made a face. 'And if it were a woman, she would be waiting, but I had to get a man, and he can't do it until tomorrow.'

'Have you got a couple of hours? We don't have much foot traffic, but if you could just take details and answer the phone, you'd be a lifesaver. Not literally, I hope, but Mum doesn't normally complain like this, and there's no point calling the doctor. Obviously I'll pay cash for today.'

'No problem at all, Juliet. Happy to help.'

Once she had started to work for her, it didn't Chloë long to discover that Jules was actually alright once you got past the cultured pearl necklace. On the other hand, Chloë was thinking of enrolling at the university for real, just so that she didn't have to watch her every step with Mrs Smith, who had both the time and the inclination to find out as much as she could about 'Chloë Greenwood'. It was a good job they didn't have to work together often.

It also became clear that Chloë was working for the wrong Bloxham: all the anger and well-rotted hatred of the Clarkes was stored up at the offices of Stephen's building and property company on the outskirts of Winchcombe.

Chloë had been sent there several times with messages or documents, and soon enough she met the man himself.

It made her flesh crawl when Stephen looked her up and down, and she understood immediately what Juliet's mother had meant when she'd said 'Dressed like that, you should be okay.'

Stephen pointed to a visitor's chair. This was his private working office, apparently, and bore no resemblance to the opulence of the executive room downstairs where he schmoozed investors and potential clients, and where Chloë had waited a few times. This room even had a cement-covered giant spirit level leaning against the wall, standing just above a pair of safety boots which the office cleaners must hate, judging by the amount of mud they were shedding.

'You're the new girl, aren't you?' said Stephen.

Chloë bit her tongue. She did not like being called a *girl* by middle-aged men. 'Chloë Greenwood. Yes.'

'Jules speaks very highly of you. Even says you've made an impression on her mother.' He smiled. 'You must tell me your secret: I've been trying to do that for years.'

Chloë's lips twitched reflexively. 'It helps pay the rent.'

'And I'm all in favour of that. What have you got for me today?'

She passed him the papers and waited nervously. The room smelled of expensive cologne, making her eyes water, and the one thing she'd had drummed into her about the glasses was *never take them off when you're in a room with someone else.*

Stephen grunted and scrawled a big *NO* on the front cover of one folder and a smaller *This One* on the other, then passed them back. Why on earth this couldn't have been done by email was beyond Chloë. She was halfway out of her seat when Stephen stunned her into dropping back into it.

'Jules tells me you bat for the other side,' he stated.

'Wh … what do you mean?' she said, the blood rising up her cheeks so quickly that it was visible well beyond the frame of her disguise.

Stephen looked unperturbed. 'That you might end up playing cricket for Allington. Can't have that.'

He was too old and too vile not to have meant it. *You're a dyke* was what he'd meant and Chloë had no idea what had given her away, because she'd been playing it straight with both Jules and her mother. A feminist, yes, but…

Still, she couldn't give up at the first hurdle. She swallowed and replied, 'Long way from that, Mister Bloxham.'

'Stephen. Please. Jules also tells me you're doing some techie course thing at college.'

'That's right. A Masters in digital media production.'

'I'm too old for that stuff. I don't mind technology. Love it. I hate computers, though. Do you know anything about websites?'

'That's a bit like asking if I know anything about farming, Stephen. Depends on whether you want to buy a cow or move into hydroponics.'

He grunted. 'Fair comment. I might have a job for you.'

It was what she'd wanted, and now the prize was in touching distance, could she swallow the bile and actually work in the same building as this man, and all the other men who were clearly in charge on the top floor?

'What is it?' she asked.

He sat back and folded his hands over an expanding waistline. 'The biggest challenge for any property developer is finding opportunities. I've got my spies locally, but sometimes you need an edge. There's this company who go through the planning decisions of every local authority. There are three hundred and thirty-five of them in England, and the company flag up indications and changes of use and all sorts of things. Trouble is, they charge an absolute fortune for it. Is there any way you could pull together the next batch with some fancy piece of software? I'm not interested in anything in the south east or beyond Yorkshire, so that should make it easier.'

There was no piece of software which could do that. Even Chloë knew that much. There would be a team of underpaid graduates in India somewhere who were doing it all by hand, authority by authority. Chloë had no clue how it was all pulled together, but she knew exactly how to replicate it.

She looked dubious. 'Sounds like a tall order. Can you send me the link?'

'I can do better than that.' He rooted in a pile of files on a side table and came over with a ring binder. The smell of cologne was almost too much for her. 'Here.'

She took the folder and glanced at the contents. Good. It had the company's name on every page. All she had to do was take out a subscription and re-format the output. It was only money. Providing she could hold her nose while she did it.

'I'll see what I can do.' She decided to play a card in her game. 'Would you sack me if I joined Allington Women? You're the President of Clerkswell, aren't you?'

It was a deliberate provocation: Conrad Clarke was the Life President of Clerkswell Cricket Club.

'Chairman. *Chair* now that we have women members. I still play, you know. Bit of spin.'

'I thought someone called Conrad Clarke was the spinner. I looked up the match reports to see if there was really that much of a rivalry. He won some sort of trophy, didn't he?'

'The team won the trophy, not any individual player. Not even the man of the match.' He looked at her steadily, and the flush which had started in her cheeks now went down her chest and round her back. 'That's rather dedicated. The research, I mean,' he added.

She grasped wildly for some excuse. She had enjoyed becoming *Chloë*, but today she'd overplayed her hand. In the end she opted for a version of the truth. 'I heard it in the pub. In Allington. They said you and this Clarke bloke didn't see eye to eye. I'm sorry, Stephen.' She offered the ring binder as a surrender.

He waved it away. 'No secret. If you go to the Inkwell they'll tell you all sorts of tall tales. It's all ancient history now that Jules and Clarke's fiancée are both on the women's team.'

Chloë could hear the gritted teeth. It would be a mistake to go in too hard now. She waved the ring binder at him. 'I'll take this away and give it some thought.'

He stood up and moved well back. 'You could discuss it with your girlfriend.'

She felt like she'd been slapped. Stephen picked up the two folders she'd come with and was supposed to take back to Jules. He held them out to her. 'Just banter, Chloë. Just banter. Allington has actually joined the twenty-first century. You can tell your girlfriend she needn't drive down the back lane to see you when there's a perfectly good front door.'

This time it was too much. 'And what business is it of yours?'

'She keeps waking the neighbours. They think they're being burgled. Jules has had a couple of complaints, but she's too polite to say anything to you about it.'

As she left the office building, Chloë remembered why she had never liked living in small communities – unlike her *girlfriend*, who loved them.

When she got back to JB Lettings, she gave a tight smile and said, 'Stephen told me about the complaints, yeah? You could have told me, Jules.'

Juliet Bloxham looked very uncomfortable. She also looked guilty and that meant she would probably overcompensate. Even better.

Chloë worked on Stephen through the end of January and into February. She forced herself to go into the pub at Allington and to endure the looks from some of the locals just so that she could go back to Bloxham Developments and say, 'Is it true about you and this Alfred Clarke guy? And the wedding anniversary?'

Stephen did not look happy. 'It was my father, and it was my mother who suffered most.'

'Oh. Right. What do the Clarkes do?'

'Alfred was a dodgy antiques dealer who retired to Spain when it got too hot over here.' Stephen thought this was funny. 'As for his son and heir, Conrad Clarke somehow got to be a hero.'

He hesitated. 'That's not fair. There's no denying he was badly wounded serving his country. I've seen the scars and they're not a pretty sight. Anyway, he's some sort of Secret Squirrel now – his mother used to work for GCHQ, so they're keeping it in the family.'

'Talking of family, why is the cricket ground called Mrs Clarke's Folly?'

Bingo. Eureka. Pay dirt. *Owzat!* Chloë could tell from Stephen's face that she'd suddenly asked the right question. If only she could work out why.

'We haven't always lived at Clerkswell Manor, you know. The family who had it before us were there for generations. Proper squires, they were. Jules and I are just looking after the Manor for the future.'

'Oh yes.'

'Yes,' said Stephen emphatically. 'It was during the 1800s. The then Mrs Clarke got religion, and so did the squire's wife. According to the stories, anyway. Mr Clarke bought the land right behind our house from the squire "so his wife could build a Methodist Chapel". That's what she said.'

Chloë had gone still, scared to disturb the flow of Stephen's story. When he didn't continue straight away, she dropped her voice and tried to make the conversation feel more intimate. 'There's no chapel there now.'

'Too fucking right there isn't, if you'll pardon my language. Her husband knocked her up and Mrs Clarke lost interest in Bible bashing. He donated the land to the village for use as a cricket pitch.'

Chloë almost whispered her next line. 'Isn't that a good thing?'

'No, it is not. The squire was furious and tried to reverse the sale, but the Clarkes had better lawyers. And possession is nine-tenths of the law. Anyway, it's all ancient history now and Jules gets to captain the Clerkswell Coven, so that's a win-win.'

Chloë knew when a subject had firmly been changed, and she left Stephen in peace. For the moment.

A few days after he'd opened up about the cricket ground, she presented a printout of the planning decisions. She'd had to get her girlfriend, Beth, to pay someone to re-format the consultancy's output into something she could pretend she'd done herself, and if Stephen noticed that there was no great insight in the new data, he didn't say anything: all he cared about was that he'd got it at half the usual price.

'What are you looking for?' she'd asked him. 'Maybe I can narrow the search criteria a little?'

He weighed the folder. 'Normally this is Scott's job, but he's gone skiing. Take a seat.'

Stephen shifted some reports off his desk and opened the folder. Either Chloë's nose was being destroyed from the inside out or he was wearing less cologne these days. She thought the former was more likely.

He chose a page at random and landed on Melton Borough Council in Leicestershire. He ran his finger down the listings (which already excluded single dwelling applications). 'See this here? Village envelope expansion. Twenty houses. That will already have a local developer tied up. And this one for converting a pub into flats? Too small for such a long distance. I'm looking for something which is too big for small developers but too small for the national boys. If you can narrow it down, you'll be saving Scott a lot of time. Tell you what, if you can find something, I'll give you a bonus.'

Chloë did not want any sort of bonus from Stephen and suppressed a shudder. Still, she was supposed to be at 'college' tomorrow, and Beth wasn't coming up from London until the weekend. Halfway through *Bargain Hunt*, she hit pay dirt for the second time and messaged her girlfriend.

On Friday she was back at JB Lettings (so Jules's mother could have a long weekend away). Stephen arrived to see Chloë and she saw him pause outside the office to examine the properties for rent, which were displayed behind Perspex covers and clipped to vertical wires.

That had been the first job Mrs Smith had delegated: getting the printouts between the Perspex layers was a swine, and Chloë had been forced to make an emergency visit to the nail bar next door.

Satisfied with what he saw, Stephen walked into the office and spread himself around, peering and poking and using up the oxygen. 'I wish Jules would put this place in the window.'

'Sorry?'

'She only uses this building as an office because it's too small for most businesses. He put on a smile. 'I think her mother likes the location. Handy. Still, it's not my decision: her business pays rent on this place, so we're not losing out overall. You said you had something for me?'

'Thanks so much for coming in. I can't abandon my post.'

He inclined his head graciously. 'No problem.' He sat down. 'What you got?'

She passed him a printout. 'This.'

She was going to reel him in, but it had to be slowly. He took out his reading glasses and studied the document. 'This would be a challenge if it was just round the corner, never mind at the arse end of England. Be a real coup if we could get it, though. But we stand no chance of that.' He put the document down and smiled. 'Good call, though, Chloë. That's exactly the sort of thing I'm after.'

She smiled sweetly. 'What if I said that I know someone who knows someone?'

'Then I'd say you've already mastered the first rule of property development. Tell me more.'

Chapter Six

S ooo … How do we do this?

Right. Okay. Rachael Clarke here. You may know me as the Gloucester Under-14 girls tennis champion; you may know me as the youngest woman to matriculate at Harwood College Oxford (still got that one btw); you may know me as the cover girl from last year's March edition of *City Beat* 'Top Ten Women to Watch in the Square Mile'; you may know me as the co-author of *Anomalies in Bond Yield Distribution*; you may know me as the founder and CEO of Occult Estate Management, and you may even know me as the beautiful assistant to La Gitana.

Shall I cut the crap? Thought so. Let's face it: I'm the Dragonslayer's sister. No, the mundane one.

Yes, Conrad Clarke is my older brother. Get used to it: I've had to. What's he like? Well, how long have you got? I'll just say this for now: he's not as clever as he likes to think he is. Evidence? Well, when our half-sister burst into the gardens at Elvenham, Dad's infidelities were news to Conrad. They weren't to me. I've known that he's been unfaithful since I was old enough to know what *infidelity* meant, and that was at my first under-12 tennis competition.

Dad took me to the competition, because it started at four o'clock in the afternoon and Mum didn't finish at GCHQ until the evening. Mum didn't care about my tennis aspirations much. She saw it as a way of keeping my brain oxygenated so that I could play chess better, and therefore not worthy of her attention. Dad was more indulgent.

I won my first tennis match, and I saw that Dad was talking to the other girl's mother and giving her his business card. 'She has a Georgian table she wants me to value,' he told me. 'Shame about her daughter's forehand.'

When she (the mother, not the daughter) turned up at the next competition, I knew what was going on. Not that I ever said anything. Didn't need to, did I? After all, Dad had agreed to lay a tennis court in the gardens and hire a coach, so why did I need to say anything? Conrad thinks that the key to managing our parents is to keep Mum onside. Why bother? She's sooo stiff. Much easier to work on Dad.

I know Conrad's told you about the night I discovered magick, and looking back, I have no idea how he planned to keep me *out* of the world of magick much longer, but that's Conrad all over for you: ignore problems until they get so big they can slap you in the face. Maybe it was a Freudian slip on Sofía's part that Entangled me, or maybe it was just statistically inevitable, what with half a dozen Mages hanging around most of the time, not to mention Conrad's relationships with the non-humans.

All of this gossip brings me neatly to the subject of the Grange Invasion and my part in it. Well, it started a long while before the wedding. In January, in fact, not that I knew about it until afterwards, and it happened in several places at once. That's the power of video-conferencing for you.

You know all about the Mowbray-Ahearns, right? That's my BFF Eseld, her siblings and their relations from Ireland. Yeah? No, I know that *strictly* speaking the Ahearns aren't related directly to Ez, but the Mowbrays stick together, and that's what gave me the headache.

You remember that Eseld's dad married an Irish Witch called Aisling? She was Aisling Ahearn, and there's a whole bus load of carrot-topped relations who came with the package, but they're not my clients, unlike Aisling's children: Kenver (who took after his dad) and Morwenna (definitely ginger).

Aisling was killed by her own octopuses in circumstances that no one really understands, and Morwenna disappeared for years. When Morwenna showed up again for the final time, she was terribly wounded and pregnant with twins. You know, I'm so glad I'm not a Mage because I don't think I could bear the thought of twins.

My brother being my brother, he couldn't let a tragedy pass by without turning it into a three-act opera (preferably by Wagner), and so he promptly turned the dial up to the max and tracked down that book he was so obsessed about, the Codex Thingy, and went to Ireland. Naturally he needed someone who knew what they were doing, so he took me and Eseld as well, and that's how I got to meet the rest of the Ahearn crew, apart from the one in London.

The London one actually works alongside Eseld, and Mages are usually very polite to mundane people like me. They are usually good value at a party, too. What they *don't* do is take your number or return your calls. Too busy making magick. And that's why I didn't get to meet Oighrig Ahearn until she wanted something.

The first thing I knew about it was when Eseld asked if I fancied hitting the gym then going round to Mowbray House for supper – Chris was away doing something to the Ley lines of Wales. You know, Ez actually has a full-time cook at Mowbray House. A *cook*. And a good one, too. While we were getting changed for spinning class, she said, 'Going to be three for supper tonight.' She also gave me an evil grin which told me there was no way I'd find out who the extra person was until they showed up.

To prove what a good friend she is, Ez added, 'And before you get your hopes up, it's not a potential client.'

'Then it's either a blind date or they want something from my brother. Or both.'

Eseld gave it some serious thought. 'I don't think you're her type. In fact, I'm not sure she dates much. Apart from Tinder. Shall we say she's got *niche appeal.* Come on, class is about to start.'

Eseld's thighs could enter the Tour de France all on their own, as you'd expect from someone who could ride before they could walk. She doesn't do much cardio, though, and I beat her on the sprint finish (after losing the hill climb). That meant I got to choose the wine, and they have the sort of wine cellar that matches having your own cook.

On the short walk from the gym to Mowbray House (which is in Mayfair and worth more than most embassies), I suggested a few possible dating niches that our mystery supper companion might fill.

'Does she like a threesome?'

Ez actually stopped to think about that one. And to light a rollup. 'I have no idea. You should ask her.'

'Plays video games and always loses to boys?'

'No chance.'

'Is an undying supporter of Queens Park Rangers?'

'Not even sure she knows what they are.'

Before I could get on to some seriously kinky options, we'd arrived, and the housekeeper gave it away by saying, 'I've shown the Oracle into the drawing room.'

'Aah. She's ginger,' I said. 'Now that *is* niche.'

'Shh! She's also a member of the Inner Council and can hear a mouse fart in Cornwall.'

Oighrig Ahearn is the senior Sorcerer at Salomon's House and gets the job title Oracle to go with it. I've heard a lot about her, one way and another, from Ez (colleague), from Sofía (one of her students) and even from Conrad. She is also Morwenna's second cousin or something.

Ez started walking away. 'I'm going to sort the food. I'm starving. Go and introduce yourself.'

'Coward.'

Mowbray House is an early Georgian property. Not the biggest or grandest Mage mansion in London, but one of the nicest, and not because Eseld has good taste (she doesn't). I went into the panelled room complete with a real fire, and said a breezy, 'Hi! You must be Oighrig.'

She sprang up from one of the incredibly comfy sofas and gave me a radiant smile. 'Rachael! I'm thrilled to meet you at last.'

We air-kissed, and I got a good look at her. Mina (and others) have told me that she rarely wears anything which exposes her skin, even in winter. Not only is she incredibly pale, *her whole body is covered in freckles*. Every centimetre, or so I'm told. During the day she uses magick or foundation to cover it up, but they were all on show tonight.

'I love that dress,' I told her. 'So does Eseld. So much so that she bought a copy of it.'

She gave me an uncertain look. 'Right. Did you enjoy the gym?'

'Yes. I beat her. Have you got a drink?'

'I didn't want to start until you got back. Where's Eseld?'

'Gone to gee up the cook. I thought you could hear everything?'

She flashed a half-smile. 'I heard the front door. To do more would mean magick, and that's rude. As Eseld well knows. Why, what did she say?'

She looked completely transparent. In all sorts of ways. Oighrig Ahearn seems one of the most open, honest Mages I've ever met, and if that's her using magick to make me believe her, then she's so damned good it doesn't matter. It almost made me confess to being gingerist.

'She was wondering if you liked threesomes.'

'I … That was a joke, right? Of course it was. You have your brother's sense of humour, that's for certain, and you must get it from your ma, coz Sofía's is quite different.'

'Do you blame her? It's not easy being dumped into a shark tank like Salomon's House. Or our family. Talking of family, how's Fiadh?'

Fiadh Ahearn had been imprisoned under house arrest for fifteen years. Yeah, her house was a pub, but still. She's been making up for lost time ever since Conrad sealed the deal which released her. She's as honest as Oighrig, I think, but more guarded. As you'd expect.

Oighrig blinked rapidly. Even her eyelashes are ginger. 'Did Ez tell you what I've come about?'

'She wouldn't. I just wondered if Fiadh had worked her way round *every* nightclub in Ireland. North and south.'

'Did she not send you the pictures from Ibiza? She went there for new year, and…' She thought for a moment. 'Perhaps not, with you being so respectable and all. On the surface anyway. Some of those pictures need a lot of explaining.'

'I'm respectable all the way through, thank you.'

'Not what Ez told me.'

'What did I tell you?' said Eseld from the doorway. 'Supper's ready, and we're having champagne, even if it is a school night.'

Oighrig kept forgetting herself. One minute she was trying to be a senior academic at England's third oldest seat of higher learning (I went to the oldest. Just saying.), and the next minute she was having a laugh with the girls.

As I said, she wasn't rich enough to be a client, and I didn't want to get Eseld in (too much) trouble at Salomon's House, so I just went with the flow. The second bottle of champagne was nearly gone when Oighrig finally got round to why I was there.

'It's about Conrad and Mina's wedding.'

Of course it's about the bloody wedding. Couldn't possibly be about the Salomon's House investment portfolio, could it?

'What about it? I know you're on the invite list for the main event,' I replied.

Oighrig glanced at Eseld, and Ez said, 'Raitch went through the main guest list and made a note of everyone she might tap up for business.'

See? I told you Ez was a good friend.

Eseld rushed on before Oighrig could get embarrassed (the scientist in me did wonder what that would look like, but hey, some other time). 'She also helped Mina sort out the seating plan by filling in some of the gaps. Go on, Oighrig.'

'We've been thinking – that's me and the others. Fiadh's going to come, and we've been thinking that if Cathal could get an invite, then we could all get to meet Morwenna.'

Eseld sat back and frowned. She'd known this was coming. 'You've all been invited to Pellacombe.'

'I know, and that's grand and all, but we can't all just drop everything and fly around the country. Not like some people. Fiadh owes Conrad, you know that, and she'd come regardless. Me too, come to that, and if Cathal could make it, then we could, you know, make it a proper visit. Have a bit of time to get to know her. And to see more of Kenver, of course.'

Eseld nodded slowly. It wasn't her call. 'We're going to the Beltane feast on the Saturday, so we're heading up on Thursday to give Morwenna a chance to settle in. We could go up a day earlier…?'

'That would be grand, apart from one thing.'

Eseld could see what was coming. So could I, and Oighrig confirmed it: 'Accommodation. Is there nowhere we could all fit in? Take over a hotel or something?'

The Mowbrays were booked into the Old Rectory in Allington, a little village about ten minutes away, and their chauffeuse was going to be a busy woman. Eseld grimaced and looked at me. 'There's a bit of a shortage of accommodation that weekend, isn't there, Raitch?'

'There is. How important is this?'

'Very,' said Oighrig. 'To us, anyway.'

'And to Morwenna,' added Eseld. 'She's dreading it for all sorts of reasons, but she still wants it to happen. Is there nothing you can do?'

'There's only one property even vaguely big enough, and that's going to be a *big* ask. It's Clerkswell Manor.'

'Shut up!' said Eseld. 'You're joking! From what you've told me, there's more chance of Heidi Marston being on *Strictly* than there is of Stephen Bloxham renting the Manor to Conrad.'

'But Jules might rent it to me and Mina. Tell Heidi she might need her dancing shoes.'

'You haven't met her, I take it,' said Oighrig.

'I have. Twice. At the Fire Games. If there were a professional dancer who could take her on, that would be something *I'd* pay to watch.'

Eseld snorted, and Oighrig would have gone pale if she weren't already white. 'Do you know what she did the other day?' she asked rhetorically.

'You mean when she arm-wrestled the postgrad?'

'That's the one.'

'What's wrong with that?' I asked.

'They were doing it over an open fire,' said Oighrig.

Eseld shook her head. 'Don't. Look, Raitch, do you really think there's a chance we could get the Manor?'

'Leave it with me. I don't get down to Clerkswell much, but for this I'll make an exception.'

Chapter Seven

The night of the Peace of Brothers Water,
three months before the wedding.

The brood was broken up at the moon before Yuletide.
4th had stayed at Sprint to continue horse-magick, and (much to 6th's disappointment), 2nd had also stayed at the stables, to practise the blade with the new Count, formerly Prince Galleny. 6th and 1st were taken away to Borrowdale.

The Queen's own sídhe was luxurious, of course, and being in Her presence was an honour every day of 6th's life. Even so, as the veins grew in its wings, 6th started to really worry about what it would become when it shed its wings. And *where* it would shed them.

The omen from the Queen's Pool that only three of the brood would return to Borrowdale for Matching weighed heavily on 6th, and for that reason, it clung closely to the Queen's Ladies, who were more than happy to have a loyal servant. 6th was in the bower when Countess Bassenthwaite rushed in one night to bring the news.

'Have you heard about Galway? The Fair Queen is dead and the Dragonslayer is become the Lord of Death!'

The sídhe was abuzz with rumour for days, with much debate about whether the Digger who had struck the fatal blow and killed the Fair Queen was the *real* Lord of Death. The consensus seemed to be that the rock-born could *never* have that title, a view reinforced when Princess Lussa of Mull attacked Birk Fell. Somehow, in some way they couldn't divine, the Dragonslayer/Lord of Death turned Princess Lussa's own People against her and walked away with not even a scratch on him. And shortly after that came the Day of Revolution.

The Red Queen had planned her attack carefully. For days she had been closeted with Countess Bassenthwaite and her Princes, then towards the end, she summoned Princess Faithful to her inner council. On the day of the attack, the Royal Household split up and travelled separately before gathering again at Broadwater, where they were to wait for the horses and the Wolves to join them. But when the first arrival came, it wasn't a Pack of Wolves or a troop of the finest mounts. It was Hipponax, and he was carrying Faithful and a small mortal on his back.

6th was on watch duty at the bridge when Hipponax galloped across the snow. The mighty Unicorn pulled up before them, frightened of the spear wielded by Saerdam Adam of the Queen's Guard. 6th couldn't see the little mortal's face for the hood, but it could smell some form of magick radiating from under the thick coat, and anyway, what had happened to Princess Faithful? Her bright blue snowsuit was torn and covered in blood splashes. The People's blood.

'Hold,' said Adam. 'Why are you here?'

'The Queen is betrayed. Force Ghyll has wrought a Change on the Gamekeeper and Proclaimed her Queen. Appleby is besieging the Pack.'

The woods around Broadwater came alive with light and sound as the People repeated and digested Faithful's words. Could this possibly be true? Surely not. Surely tonight the Queen would triumph over the mortals and get justice for their sacrilege.

Saerdam Adam raised his spear. 'What are you doing here? Your orders were to remain on the Gallops with the Lord of Death. And who is that mortal?'

In a shocking breach of behaviour, Faithful ignored Adam, switched to the mortal tongue and spoke to the woman behind her. 'Mina, lower your hood.'

6th had expected a child Witch, but the pillion was a grown woman *with brown skin*! It could only be her: the Consort of the Lord of Death.

Faithful waited until the Guard had seen who it was, then raised her voice to the woods. It was a measure of Lady Morag's skill as a teacher that 6th understood every word, even though she spoke in the English language.

'People of Derwent, hear me! On this day, I submitted to the Dragonslayer. I am a Princess no longer, and have become Rani Desai's handmaiden. You are betrayed, outnumbered and about to be attacked. Rani Desai is sent as the Lord Guardian's emissary, to offer a path to peace.'

This time the woods were stunned into silence. For a moment. The People are rarely quiet for long. Unless they are ordered to be quiet, as 6th had been ordered to be. Because it couldn't join in, it had time and thought to look more closely at this … apostate? Was that the word?

Quicksilver flickered around Faithful's fingers, *and also around her wound of shame*. 6th was the first to see what others only learned later: that if she lived tonight, this servant of the mortal princess would one day become a Queen.

'I will fly to the Queen and bear witness,' said 6th, then turned and opened its wings before Saerdam Adam could argue. Because of this, 6th was in the sídhe, not the woods, when Faithful and Rani Desai were brought inside. No

Ladies had been brought on campaign, and the wingless were in such a flap that no one objected when 6th fetched and carried for the Chamberlain, and no one saw what happened when 6th waited outside the earth closet for Faithful to emerge.

6th was taking a huge risk doing this. It could easily be struck down for daring to address a future Queen, but it knew that it would have no better chance to defy the prophecy. It offered Princess Faithful a ewer and towels, and as she washed her hands, it said, 'Your Grace, may I be the first in your household? I have much to offer as *your* handmaiden.'

Faithful laughed, spittle flying everywhere. 'Who are you, Little One? Haven't I seen you at Sprint Stables?'

'6th-Redqueen-Iris-Nymph Child, of Lady Agnes's last brood.'

'The one with the Queen's hairbrush?'

'Yes, Your Grace.'

'I'm no one's *Grace* right now. Fetch fresh water for Rani. She won't be long.'

6th did what Little Ones rarely do: it bowed. Of course, it also overbalanced (which is why they don't bow much), and landed face-first in the dirty water.

It thought that was the end, that it had lost so much favour that its future was over, but no: Faithful roared with laughter.

'Nice timing, Little One. Maybe I'll revive the old traditions and have a court jester. You'd be perfect.'

6th froze face down in the water. A *jester*! UnMatched and doomed to be a Little One forever? No. It was not possible. Her Grace would not allow it. But if Faithful became a Queen, who would stop her?

'Get up,' said the Princess. 'I'm joking. Clean yourself up and be quick with Rani's water. And don't, whatever you do, smile at her. Or speak.'

6th rushed to fulfil the Princess's command, and returned to the closet as Gustav escorted the Dragonslayer's consort down the tunnel. The mortal did not look happy, and was saying, 'I still don't see why I have to go back outside. You do know that it's freezing out there?'

'Indeed, my lady,' replied the Chamberlain, 'but someone has to mind the High Unicorn, and there is no one else suitable.'

'Yes, there is! The Red Queen and Faith can have their tea party in the snow, and I'll wait by the fire. How about that?'

'There is indeed a fire, my lady, and we've used it to heat this water for you. For after you've finished.'

Gustav pointed to the closet, and Rani folded her arms. 'In *there*? Why is there no proper bathroom?'

'Alas, Broadwater Sídhe is more of a hunting lodge than a palace. I shall give you some privacy, and this Little One – Sprite – will summon me when you are finished.'

Rani had been standing with her back to 6th while she spoke, and now she turned and the Little One got its first close-up look at the female chosen by the Dragonslayer to be his mate. The Dragonslayer had apparently killed a Queen Proclaimed tonight. Did that make him Lord of Death twice over?

Rani's face was flushed and scraped raw from her High Unicorn ride through the freezing air, and her skin was almost pale. And then you saw her nose. It was long, sharp on the bridge and pointed. She lifted it and strode into the closet.

Her face had relaxed a little when she emerged, and 6th held up the ewer, having used some Lux to bring it back to a nice temperature. It had learned its lesson and did not bow.

Rani approached cautiously, as if 6th might bite. Faithful had told 6th not to smile, but did the Princess mean only the People's smile or the mortal one, too? 6th was about to bare its front teeth in a mortal smile when Rani spoke.

'Is that water as hot as it looks?'

The other order had been equally clear: don't speak. 6th shook its head, and Rani cautiously placed a finger in the water, then plunged in both hands.

'You have no idea how good that feels.'

She closed her eyes for a moment and wiggled her fingers in the water. When she opened her eyes she gave the mortal smile, but her face didn't move properly: there was something about the left side of it... 'Do you have any idea how cold it is out there? Conrad tells me that Sprites can regulate their body temperature.'

6th shook its head. There was no profit in speaking now.

'Thank you,' said Rani. 'Do you have a name?'

6th had many names, but not one it could share with a mortal. Not until Matching. For the third time, it shook its head.

'Oh. Right. Can you fetch the Chamberlain, please?'

6th carefully placed the ewer on the ground and hopped off in search of Gustav, who was hurriedly organising refreshments. It seemed that Faithful was right: there would be no vengeance against the mortals tonight. It told the Chamberlain that Rani was finished, and returned to find her doing something with her hair, which was half in and half out of her hood.

6th longed to speak up and offer to get Lady Agnes's gift, but while it hopped from foot to foot in fork-pain, Rani abandoned the struggle and pulled up her hood regardless. 'You look so weird trying to fly,' she said. 'Yet your wings are beautiful in this light, especially with the golden tint.'

Gold? *Gold?* There was no *gold* in 6th's wings! What was this madness? Did Rani have ice-fever? 6th opened its mouth to ask after her health, and she flinched back.

'You! Get to the kitchens,' shouted Gustav in the People's tongue from down the corridor. The Chamberlain bowed to Rani and switched to mortal words. 'My lady, I have hot refreshments which you can enjoy outside, and

Saerdam Adam will escort you.'

Behind Gustav, Adam stood with a hunting bag and a mortal smile on his face. Rani saw the Guard and said, 'Oh. Is he coming with me? Then yes please.'

A huge risk had been taken tonight. By laying itself down and offering itself to Princess Faithful on a plate (or on a ewer), 6th had run the risk of dying alongside the Queen-to-be. There was a fairly high death rate for aspiring royalty – just ask tonight's would-be monarch. Or worse, Faithful could have rejected it, and who would take the leavings of a disfigured servant Princess?

6th watched the tiny form of Rani Mina disappear up the corridor, and it wondered if there *might* be an alternative path. It knew that there was so much that it could offer to mortals, if it were only given the chance. Mortals were frail, delicate and easily broken, it's true, but they also had the power of Water.

6th summoned the story of Prince Morignac and the Enchantress, the one where the Prince had been Fire which the Enchantress quenched, Earth which she dissolved into mud, Air which she turned to the densest fog, and then Void which she had filled with rain and life. It was only when the Prince became the sixth element that the Enchantress had been vanquished.

Hadn't Lady Agnes always said that being with mortals gave a view of the world which you could never get in the sídhe? At least, that's what 6th thought she had said.

Rani turned into the main corridor and disappeared like rain into dry ground: another power of Water. 6th was at the bottom of the pile when it came to the People, but mortals…

It remembered luckless Verona's kindness, Flora's sadness, and now Rani's charity. They were all there. All out in the open, ripe for the plucking.

Chapter Eight

The Derwent People had been summoned to the Royal Court, an order they could not ignore even if they wanted to, although no one with a choice was going to miss it.

Every noble seemed to be there. Two had flown in from afar, and the platform looked almost full once the lesser nobles had taken the seats vacated by the traitors, all of whom were now dead.

The nobles had brought their Knights and what Squires could be spared from duties, and with the Royal Household also assembled, the Derwent People filled the Grand Chamber to the rafters – which was where the Little Ones perched.

6th was late. It usually was – there was always some little job which needed doing. It hopped towards the packed bodies of its People, ready to launch itself towards the perches.

'You! 6th-Redqueen-Iris-Nymph Child! Come with me.'

What was Lady Morag doing here? And why had the Lady brought 6th's broodmates with her?

It scuttled to join them, and 4th shoved it to the back of the group. 'You smell of the privies,' it said to 6th.

'And you have horseshit under your talons. You suck at it and think it's honey,' countered 6th, ready to scratch at 4th's wings.

'Oi! Quiet!' ordered their Lady. 'All four of you will join me at Her Grace's left hand, and if any of you so much as hop once before you're called, I'll turn you all into frogs.'

They fell into line and took a place at the bottom of the dais just before Countess Bassenthwaite emerged from the wings.

The hum of anticipation reached fever pitch when they saw that Bassenthwaite was wearing all white. What could this mean? And the room almost burst with the pressure of gossip when, instead of taking her chair at the right hand of the Queen's throne, she stood two paces in front of it.

'Silence!' boomed Gustav, and his Ink called to the sídhe. The People's tongues froze in their mouths and their eyes bulged. 'Megan will now speak in the Queen's name.'

What was this? And where was Princess Faithful? Could Her Grace have gone back on Her bond so quickly?

'People of Derwent,' began the Countess, whom no one called *Megan* unless Her Grace was present. 'The revolution is over. The traitors have paid the price. Our Queen was as triumphant in the negotiation as She has always been in battle. The stories of Her genius are only now being begun. She will hear the first of them at the coming Equinox and has new favours for the best.'

Gustav had slowly relaxed his command, and the room began to buzz again at the news. Before the noise could build, Bassenthwaite continued, 'Within ourselves, the despicable treachery of Force Ghyll will always be known as the Outcasts' Revolt.'

Will it? thought 6th. *Why is that?*

'However, Her Grace has let it be known that whenever and wherever we speak of the revolt in mortal tongues, it must be known as the Peace of Brothers Water. In the same way, the Guardian of the North shall be the Dragonslayer. You should mind these things carefully.' She waited for the message to sink in, then she stepped aside, taking her normal place.

'Kneel for the Red Queen,' declared the Chamberlain. As one, the People of Derwent took the knee. Except for the Little Ones – whether on the perch or down by the dais, they bent at the waist and opened their wings for balance, crossing each others' and making a rainbow carpet, a moving tapestry of Ink and honour to their Queen.

6th stole a glance, and was shocked to see two People emerge before Her Grace. One was the Duke of Bowness, in white like Bassenthwaite, his mortal-aged face familiar from the stage and screen posters which lined one of the sídhe corridors. The other new arrival was Princess Faithful, and she wore two-tone blue: a dark blue surcoat over a long-sleeved light blue gown. Neither fitted her well.

Finally the Red Queen of the Derwent People emerged, and she scanned the room of lowered heads. She sported Her colour today, glowing brightly from the fire-red armour She had worn in the Wild Hunt of Trafalgar, at Gretna Green and in every victory of Her life. Her ears were raised to delicate points, and when She spoke, Her second jaw showed teeth capped with silver.

'Arise, my People, and join me in celebration.'

The Great Chamber echoed as their Queen led them in victory song, and Her Grace glowed as the music reached its climactic conclusion. 'We have much to do,' She announced at the end. 'And I give you new royalty to join our lands, just as we prepare to lose the greatest jewel in my crown. This is your moment.'

Bassenthwaite and Bowness got down in front of their Queen, knees to the floor. Her Grace offered them Her ring and they kissed it, and then she drew them to their feet and pronounced them Princess- and Prince-to-be. Because they had not yet even *begun* to Change, there would be no Inking of new names today, and that also explained the white garb; colours would come later.

Faithful, of course, already had her colours, and it was now her turn to kneel and kiss the ring. When the Queen spoke, it was low and personal, and the assembled People had to strain their senses to hear.

'One day soon, my most loyal girl, you will be Inking out my name. Until then, let me restore what Galwyddel took away. Would you resume your

Matching name, Mielle?'

'If Your Grace pleases, I won my freedom as Faith, and as Faith I would begin my journey. Mielle died at the hands of the Heather Queen.'

Her Grace's face was unreadable to 6th because it bore a thoroughly mortal expression; Her words were clear enough, though. 'Neither of us are exactly free at the moment, are we? It pleases me, however. Give me your arm.'

The loose sleeve of the sky-blue gown slid down the Princess's arm when she raised it, and the Queen Inked a new name into the skin, sounding it aloud as She did so.

'From this day, I Name you Faith-Princess Staveley in Cartmel-Mistress of Hipponax-Redqueen-7th-Bee in Lavender-Springtime.'

7th! She was 7th! *How has she lived so long with such an inauspicious name?* wondered 6th.

'And now it is time to work,' announced the Queen.

The People bowed again, and She left the stage, followed by Her royal nobles. As soon as She was gone, a thousand conversations broke out.

Not much of a victory … no heads on pikes … Lord of Death … mortals in disarray … Dragonslayer … Pale Horsemen are saddling up while we wait here … Dragonslayer … Dragonslayer …

'You heard our Queen!' declared Gustav. 'It's time to work. To build on *Her* victory.' His Silence pressed down on their heads until those nearest the doors bolted and the rest soon followed, but not 6th, for Lady Morag barred the way.

'We're wanted in the cabinet chamber,' she said, then turned and led 6th's brood through the curtains.

Lady Caroline, head of the Royal Household, was removing Her Grace's armour; Princess Staveley – Princess Faith – was standing in a puddle of dress fabric, hitching up a pair of royal blue jodhpurs, and Bassenthwaite was dressing in what 6th had learned to call a 'business suit'. There was no sign of the other nobles, and it was only then that 6th realised who had been missing from the podium: Prince Harprigg. His head groom had been there, but not the Derwent People's only Prince. He must have had permission.

6th saw a profit in misbehaving and barged into 4th, who barged back; an exasperated Lady Morag pushed them apart, which is what 6th had wanted, and it was able to hop away from its broodmates and catch the words exchanged by Her Grace and the others. For some reason they were sticking to the mortal tongue.

'…about as well as can be expected,' said Countess Bassenthwaite.

'Only just,' replied Her Grace. 'Faith? Have you heard from Conrad Bloody Clarke?'

Ooh! Another of the Dragonslayer's titles. This one definitely suited him.

'That's why I was late. Apparently Alexandra Greening has been to see

Nimue and got the true story about James. So have the Sisters of the Water, and they have let it be known in no uncertain terms that they stand with the Assessors in cementing the Peace of Brothers Water. The Greenings have stood down their militia and put Blenheim up for sale. Word is spreading, My Lady.'

'Good. That should buy us some time. And the Clan?'

'Running round telling anyone who'll listen that they would have stood with the Commissioner if only they hadn't all been locked away in the First Mine.'

The Queen spat on the floor and held Her arms up so that Lady Caroline could drop a court gown over Her head. 'How fucking convenient. That's what gets me the most, you know. The Clan risk no one in the field and somehow end up as the victors. Makes me sick. These have been *our* lands since well before any Gnome figured out which end of an axe to hold.'

She paused while the laces were tightened and the bodice adjusted. When the Lady stepped aside, the Queen looked at the royal nobles and said, 'The wheel of time turns. The mortals banded together, and when they find that the Clan have bought and sold them, they'll come crawling to us for help. The Peace of Brothers Water is between us and the humans. It says nothing of the Clan.' She pointed to Faith. 'And I'll expect you to be at my side when we ride out.'

The Princess bowed her head and spoke in the People's tongue. 'We all serve the Great Queen. Though I may be bound to a mortal, his days are numbered.'

'Good. Are you off to see the lawyers, Megan?'

The newly promoted Countess squeezed her feet into a pair of gleaming black heels. 'I am. There is much to discuss.' She hesitated. 'Should I try contacting Harprigg again?'

Red fury glittered in the Queen's eyes. 'No. He can stew in his juices a while longer.'

Bassenthwaite picked up a handbag and prepared to leave, but Princess Faith looked at the Queen. 'Is that wise? He is your only Prince at the moment.'

'Then he should start behaving like one. He's Master of Wolves, not kennelmaid to corgis. If he'd attacked Appleby, we might have stood a chance in the field.'

Princess Faith raised her eyebrows but said nothing, and it was Countess Bassenthwaite who turned and faced their Queen. 'You keep telling yourself that, Charley, if it makes you feel better, but you'll be the only one who believes it. The mortals had us cornered like rats in a cornfield. If it wasn't for the Dragonslayer, these Little Ones and their Hlæfdige would be pledging obedience to the Queen of Grace, and you, me and Faith would only be alive in stories.'

The Queen stood and held out Her hand. When the Countess went to kiss it, the Queen grabbed her head and dragged it up to Her face. 6th felt a thrill, anticipating a de-nosing at least, but no. The Queen kissed Her noble on the lips.

'I knew there was a reason I loved you,' said Her Grace. 'Sorry about your lipstick. Good luck with the lawyers.'

The Countess nodded and retreated, her heels echoing down the corridor.

6th tried every trick it knew to remain silent and still and overlooked as the Queen turned to Her Princess.

'That was brave of you, taking the name "Faith". Why did you do it?'

'Conrad Bloody Clarke. He knew I'd been punished with the name "Faithful", yet he ignored the slur and called me "Faith" as if it were my chosen name, just like any other. I'll change it when I Change.'

'If you live that long.'

What was this? Was Her Grace planning to punish Her Princess's failures to hide Her own sins?

The Queen continued, 'Word has already got round. The High Queen's obnoxious child will not be happy, and Princess Birkdale is not someone I'd want as an enemy unless I had no choice in the matter.'

'It's worse than that, Your Grace. Princess Birkdale has her claws firmly in the Dragonslayer's associates.'

'What are you going to do?'

Faithful bowed. 'I shall be as Gertha the Spider. I shall watch and wait.'

'Good.' The Queen turned to Lady Caroline. 'Hose and shoes.'

The Little Ones waited until Her Grace had finished dressing and had taken Her seat on the Chair of State, then Lady Morag led them forwards to show their respect.

Faith and Lady Caroline stood to the side, and the Red Queen addressed her Princess. 'You can keep Saerdams Jessica and Karl until the Matching. This brood are closest, and you can have three from this clutch for now and two from the next when they're ready.'

'Kneel,' said Lady Morag, and the Little Ones nearly toppled over as their wings pushed them forwards.

Faith smiled a mortal smile. 'Right, Morag, who have we got here?'

'This is the Iris-Nymph Child clutch – Lady Agnes's last, and a fine bunch they are, if you don't mind the aggravation. They can be fierce, I'm telling you.'

'An auspicious brood,' added Her Grace. 'I was even moved to take an omen for them. Six were named, and the pool told me that 1st, 2nd and one other would Match together. What happened to 3rd and 5th, Morag?'

'3rd died in a duel with 1st, Your Grace, and 5th tried to steal from 6th. There was a fair challenge.'

'Tell me their colours,' said Faith. 'I see red in 2nd, and much Ink in 1st, but what of the other two?'

'4th is reigning Northern Champion at the Unicorn Gallops, my lady. I believe you were there for some of the races.'

'So I was. It has superb camouflage skills. And now I recognise the other one. You're the one with the hairbrush, aren't you, 6th?'

'It is,' said Morag, speaking for it. 'It was Your Grace's final gift to Lady Agnes.'

'And I expected to get it back when Agnes left this life,' said the Queen. 'I had it so long I've forgotten where it came from and can't be bothered to read the story. It was fairly given and fairly gifted to this Little One, so Agnes must have known best. She usually did.'

'What else is 6th good for?' asked Faith.

'The court love it,' said Lady Caroline. 'Quickest to serve, and always handy if you have a message. And it can do hair without the brush, too. And it's making progress with skin-Ink.'

The Little Ones had stayed mute, as they must in the presence of the Queen, and only their wings and their shifting eyes gave away their nerves. 6th was bursting with pride when Lady Caroline told of its worth. All those cups of tea, trips to the laundry and hours spent making the Mirror were clear profit.

Faith was speaking with a Glamour to assist her. She no longer dribbled from her mark of shame, but she found it hard to enunciate the People's tongue with the scar which still froze much of her face, and she had raised her handkerchief to the wound several times, even though there was no saliva to wipe away. After staring at their wings for an age, she spoke.

'I need a Guard who has been with me from Matching. Perhaps that can be you, 2nd. Step forwards.'

6th's favourite broodmate was allowed to kiss the Princess's ring, and Lady Morag ushered it to the side.

'Your Ink is mysterious,' the Princess told 1st. 'I'd be foolish not to find out where it takes you. If you're ready, of course.'

6th knew that 1st was proud. So proud, in fact, that it thought the broodmate might reject the offer – but no, it kissed the ring and joined 2nd next to Lady Caroline.

Faith turned to 6th, and its blood rose, heating its wings. *It was going to be chosen!*

'Sorry, 6th,' said the royal blue Princess. 'My head groom is mundane, and I need someone who can work with beasts more than I need a handmaiden. If the last forty-seven years have taught me anything, it's how expensive vanity can be. Good luck to you, Little One.'

The prophecy! 6th would not be going to the Pool with the others! It was *not* going to be rejected like that. Not while it had strength in its claws…

It jumped on 4th, striking at the root of its wings and breaking several veins. Blood and Quicksilver spurted out and 4th howled in pain, raising its hands to protect its face. 6th Inked iron and swung it at 4th's feet, chopping into the ankle. It was going for the killing blow when it found itself rising into the air with a fierce grip round its throat.

'Enough!' said Lady Morag. 'Agnes did not raise you to do this!'

Actually, that was exactly what Lady Agnes *had* done, because 6th had been focused entirely on the profit to be had from putting 4th out of the Matching. 6th twisted in the grip, feet in the air and wings pinioned. The Red Queen was grinning, as was 1st, and then 6th realised that 2nd was the one who had stopped the attack and was now holding it up in the air.

'You have betrayed me!' squeaked 6th.

'Have not. Have saved you,' said its favourite.

'Put it down,' said the Queen, rising from Her throne. 2nd dropped 6th to the floor, and the Queen spoke to Her Princess. 'Matching here on the first of March.'

The room bowed, and Her Grace left them alone.

Faith examined 4th closely. 'Looks like your wings will heal by then. Morag, take my three Squires-to-be back to Sprint Stables, and I don't think I've got Karl's number…'

6th didn't hear the rest, because Lady Caroline grabbed its hand and dragged it all the way to the laundry, then threw it into a tub of cold water. 'You do not leave here until I say so. Is that clear?'

6th didn't reply, partly because its mouth was full of suds, and partly because Lady Caroline hadn't waited for an answer. She had spoken in power, and there was nothing more to be said.

Cleaning the privies was the dirtiest job in the Royal Sídhe, but the worst job was undoubtedly in the laundry, and the reason for that loomed over the vat with a leer.

Saerdam Ajax had arms the size of tree trunks and no hair. His scalp glowed in the gloom and steam of the laundry, and he plucked 6th out of the water as if it were a piece of wet silk.

'I'm going to enjoy this,' he said. 'You're not, but I am.'

Chapter Nine

Lady Agnes had called it the dance – the People and the mortals have danced together since the first egg hatched, and still they dance today, sometimes one leading, sometimes the other. She had paused then and added, 'It's been the mortals leading for a good while now, though things have changed a little in my lifetime.'

She had told the brood this when she was explaining the mortal calendar: when mortals had given themselves respite from their labours on Saturdays as well as on Sundays, the People had followed their lead. All of which was one way of saying that on Saturday night, the laundry was quiet. Even when tonight's revels were ended, instead of rushing down the corridors with trolleys, the chambermaids and parlourmaids would leave the soiled linen where it lay and enjoy their rest. The Queen, it had been voiced, was entertaining a group of climbers from Japan who were visiting the Lakes, and Her Grace would no doubt let one of them stand in for Prince Harprigg (who still hadn't been seen in the Royal Sídhe). Now that would make for an interesting clutch…

Two groups worked in the laundry: those assigned to it and those sent there for punishment. Saerdam Ajax had a very simple way of running things. He called his methods an 'HR Policy' – a joke which sailed as far over 6th's head as the perch above the gently steaming vats. Ajax made those being punished wash the linen, the towels and the uniforms without Ink, leaving the others to handle the finery.

Following the Outcasts' Revolt, a dozen Squires and two Knights had been sent to the laundry for showing insufficient enthusiasm in defending the Queen ('You are still here! You should have laid down your lives! Well, you can reflect on that for a year.'), and Saerdam Ajax had worked one of them to death already. The survivors were huddled in a corner, exhausted and resting, and 6th had watched Ajax lead his team out of the laundry at sunset for revels of their own.

6th was the only Little One in here, and at first it had thought it would join the groom whose arms had dropped off into the water. Ajax had set 6th to keeping the linen tub at exactly the temperature which would clean the cloth – which was also the temperature which would boil the blood in its wings.

'And if the water gets too cold, I'll push you in and heat it up myself until it's perfect.'

Squatting on the platform next to the tub, 6th had passed out twice from the steam, and only another prisoner taking pity on it had saved it from Ajax's wrath. Now, of course, 6th also owed the prisoner favour.

Once 6th had got the hang of Inking the Fire through the copper rivets in the tub instead of working directly with the water, things had settled down, and Ajax had taken notice. From that moment on, it was put to minding the sinks where the silks were laundered, which was boring but less likely to result in 6th becoming the prisoners' evening meal.

And so here it was, on a Saturday night, well fed and rested and perched over the vats, keeping two of them ready for emergencies and letting the rest cool down. It had fed well on porridge with rat in the royal kitchens, and it reflected that there were worse jobs in the sídhe, but no worse fate. From here, it could see only one future: a late Matching and being assigned to what Ajax called his Grey Scrubbers. An assignment for life.

There was the only conceivable route out of the steam. 6th needed to become Ajax's favourite, and then one day replace him. It had heard Ajax rutting several times, and he seemed to have a preferred partner, so…

Footsteps coming down the tunnel. Urgent footsteps. An emergency.

6th flew down from the perch, ready to rouse one of the prisoners. It would deal with the emergency itself if it could, but Little Ones were not allowed to wash the laundry for obvious reasons: their talons played havoc with fabric.

Lady Caroline, skirts lifted off the ground, ran into the laundry room and stopped when she saw 6th. 'You. Come with me. And bring your Heartstone.' As soon as she'd spoken, she turned and ran back up the tunnel.

What was this? 6th grabbed the Queen's hairbrush and flew to catch the Queen's Lady. Instead of turning towards the heart of the sídhe, Lady Caroline veered left, towards the public spaces. She passed through the Great Chamber and took the royal path towards the entrance, as only the Ladies could. When they arrived at the reception hall, she pointed to the doors. 'Wait outside. You will be collected, and I shall be here when you return. And remember: say nothing and keep your jaws inside you.'

Lady Caroline made Ink for the doors to open and left 6th alone to discover what the fates held in store for it.

The approach to the Derwent Sídhe was big and grand and watched by the Guard, who all ignored the Little One. 6th was starting to shiver – the night air in Borrowdale was a chilling contrast to the steamy cavern where the laundry lay. And then the silence of the lake was broken by the roar of an engine. It was a noble's car, loud and fast and large, and it stopped away from the doors. The Guard watched it, but their spears remained down.

'Get over here, 6th,' said Faith from inside the vehicle. 'And you'd better have your brush.'

6th hopped over, nodding its head. The Squire, Jessica, came round from the driver's side and opened the front door. 'In you get. I'll mind your wings.'

Little Ones rarely travelled in ordinary vehicles, and 6th had to fold its wings as tightly as it could. Jessica eased the door closed, and 6th looked eagerly into the back of the car.

The first thing it had noticed when it clambered up the running board was the smell: smoke and Wolf, and not the toxic stench of the Dragonslayer's tobacco. Woodsmoke, pungent and harsh, was mixed with the smell of SheWolf and blood. What in the name of the Great Queen had Princess Faith been doing?

6th gasped when it saw the other passenger. *What has Rani done and why is she here?*

The Dragonslayer's consort smiled at 6th, and said, 'Hello again. Remember me?'

6th nodded, scared to do anything else. Jessica got back in the front and drove the vehicle away from the Royal Sídhe.

'My lord has what's known as a sense of humour,' said the Princess.

'Do the Fae not have this "sense of humour"?' asked Rani Mina, her eyebrows going upwards in a gesture which 6th had practised but never tried in public (because it didn't have any eyebrows and because it had been warned that mortals found it very scary).

'No,' said Faith. 'We are inherently funny, so we don't need a separate sense of humour.'

'The jury is still out on that. I have found that laughter is not something I enjoy when with the Fae. Utter terror, yes, and trembling knees on one occasion, but laughter not so much. This is why I prefer Conrad to Lord Ashford.'

Why would the mortal's knees tremble? And who was Lord Ashford?

'Whatever,' said Faith, then the Princess looked at 6th with a stare that could not be ignored. 'Whether he thinks it funny or not, my lord has given me not one job but two as part of his judgement on me. First, I am to become Madreb to the Birkfell Pack and live in a cottage by the Wolf's Lake.' Before 6th could object that this was simply not possible, not with a Royal Sídhe to build, the Princess held up a stern finger. For once, 6th bit its tongue (which was not as tasty as you might think).

'Second, I am appointed handmaiden to Mina. I am to dress her at the wedding and before, at what we call the Virgin Feast and what mortals call the "hen party". And you are to assist me.'

6th moaned with delight. *All my dreams have come true. The prophecy is toilet water! I will be Matched!*

Mina's voice broke through 6th's dream. 'Is he okay? She? What are they?'

'It. Little Ones are sexless. Well, technically they're infertile immature females.' The Princess waved away the topic. 'And it's fine. It's happy, aren't you?'

6th nodded.

'Does it have a name?'

'Not one you can hear, I'm afraid. When it's Matched, it will have a nice name, I'm sure.'

'And you say … it … has what we need?'

'Call it *serendipity*, Mina. I wasn't looking for a handmaiden until Conrad put me in my place, but now the gods have sent one in my direction, I'm not about to say no, even if it will need more work on it than I'm going to have time for. Oh, would you prefer it to have a male or female skin?'

'I have no idea what you mean, but if you mean *do I want a man to come on the hen party*, then no thank you.'

'As you wish.'

Jessica brought them to a stop, somewhere dark and without lights. Princess Faith was a noble on a mission. She held out a rather grubby hand and said, 'Give me your brush.'

6th struggled, beset with fork-pain. It wanted to serve the Queen-to-be more than anything, and the Queen-to-be was asking it to give up its only true possession.

The grubby hand snapped its fingers. 'You'll get it back in a second. I need it, and I'm not doing this anywhere near the sídhe.'

That was alright, then. 6th handed over the brush. The soon-to-be-royal hand disappeared and darkness rose between the front and back of the interior, blocking out both magickal and mundane sight.

The Queen-to-be was as good as her word. In less than half a turn, the Ink dispersed and 6th heard the second half of Rani Desai's sentence: '…better not forget your strength again, Faith. That hurt.'

'Here,' said Faith to 6th. 'Don't touch the brush again. Not until the Matching. Clear?'

'Yes … Yes, Your Grace,' it whispered in the People's tongue.

The brush was now in a cream cotton bag adorned with a label which 6th recognised: *Gucci*. It was one of the Red Queen's favourite marques, and it was radiating magick. 6th took it carefully from the Queen-to-be and settled back. The noble's car drove off and pitched into a tight turn.

'I will attend Mina myself,' said the Princess to 6th. 'You will assist and do the hair and make-up for the bridal party. And don't get too excited, because most of them are Mages and the Matron of Honour is the Anointed Guardian.'

Egg and wings! Is this true? Would 6th really be doing the hair of— It tried to raise its eyebrows and made a mewling sound.

'Well remembered,' said the Princess. 'And no, Hannah Rothman does not have her own hair. That's going to be interesting.'

'And dangerous,' added Rani. 'The first time she met Conrad, she nearly blew him in half.'

6th shrank as far as it could into the seat. One of Saerdam Ajax's sayings bubbled up in its Ink: *Out of the boiling tub and into the furnace.*

Faith rattled off a list of things which 6th should ask for as Matching favours, and then they were back at the Royal Sídhe. 6th hopped down from the vehicle, which sped off towards the mortal town of Keswick.

6th took a moment to dance inside (dancing outside, in front of the Guard, was not a good idea). Its dreams had come true: it was going to live in the Staveley Sídhe and prepare to work on mortals. It would be at its lady's side for the Dragonslayer's wedding. It would almost certainly be Knighted in double quick time. And it would be part of the household with 2nd, whom it had completely forgiven for grabbing hold of it and stopping it from attacking its broodmate. 2nd was only looking out for its favourite, and when they had formed a team, they would be unstoppable. It was in all the stories. It had to be true.

Back inside the sídhe, Lady Caroline was waiting, her knitting needles flying through a ball of the finest thread. She stood up and announced, 'You are relieved of the laundry and will return with me to the royal quarters.'

6th felt a crushing around its heart. Part of it wanted to skip behind the Lady, but… 'I must return to the steam. I owe favour there.'

'Who?'

6th named the one who had saved its life twice, and Lady Caroline grunted. 'I will discharge the favour for you.' She grimaced. 'Ajax can do things my way for a change. Follow me.'

When they returned to the royal quarters 6th kept its word about not touching the brush, but there was no harm in looking, was there? It opened the bag and saw that the Ink in the brush had been heavily modified and was now bound to many long strands of shiny black hair, some natural and some dyed, which could only have come from Rani herself. What was that all about? It couldn't be for the Matching, could it?

It could.

Fran,

There is a whole chapter which has not been translated and which almost certainly deals with the shedding of wings and the Matching, the only parts of the Sprite life cycle which have never been documented. You could send it back to Corrib if you want. I wouldn't.

Evie

I did not send it back for translation; I may be old, Evie, but I'd like to get older, thank you very much. If you're not familiar with the speculation about Matching, Evie, could I humbly suggest Chapter 4 of my own work, Sídhe Dreams: De Quincy and the Fae?

Francesca

Chapter Ten

And so it came to pass that the prophecy was fulfilled. 1st, 2nd and 4th made their way to the Royal Pool in the Derwent Sídhe, and 2nd had to help 4th when it was savaged by a Unicorn because it had been slow to heal after 6th's assault in the cabinet chamber, and 6th did not go to the Royal Pool with its broodmates.

Instead of the Queen's bower, 6th got the dark and hidden waters of the pool at Sprint Stables during a flying visit from Her Grace. Its new name and new lady were Inked rapidly into its skin while the Red Queen drank hot punch after an early morning gallop.

And thus it was, two days later, that Alicia-Staveley-6th-Redqueen-Iris-Nymph Child stood facing the doors out of the Sprint Sídhe, with all her worldly goods packed into one large wheely case and one large sparkly pink rolling beautician's case. She had fire burning in the nubs of her wings as the Ink unravelled itself and took hold of her new skin.

And clothes. For the first time in her life (Its life? Their life? Whatever) there was fabric wrapped around her, tugging her new boobs up and gripping her bum – and other places – in a way that made her keep looking down to see if there was someone there playing a joke on her. And then there was the hair! So much hair, so far down her back, and so *heavy*.

The Ladies of Sprint had admired it and told her how beautiful it looked, but Alicia had a sneaking suspicion that it was their handiwork in creating the black waterfall which they were admiring, rather than its impact on the wearer's appearance. Lady Morag rubbed her hand up and down Alicia's bare arm which was currently afflicted with little molehills of flesh.

'Why are they called goosebumps, my Lady?' Alicia asked as a way of postponing the inevitable.

'For the last time, I'm not your Lady any more, and I have no idea why they are called goosebumps. Your lady is Princess Faith now. And Rani Desai. Are you ready?'

'No.'

'Which is what Robbie said when I asked him the same thing last week. And look at him now, eh? Imogen said she was ready, and so did Nadya, and I didn't believe them. Come on, girl, Robbie's waiting for you.'

Alicia did not feel in the least ready to join the world of the wingless, but she was excited to see 2nd again. No, not 2nd; it was now *Robbie*, just as 1st was *Imogen* and 4th was *Nadya*.

'Go with my blessing, Alicia,' said Lady Morag. 'You are the last of a fine clutch and the future is yours now.'

When the doors opened, Lady Morag gave her former charge a shove in the back and propelled her up the ramp into the half-light of the roundhouse, just above where she'd lived as a Little One. She was about to glance over at the staircase down to the nursery when she noticed Robbie and forgot all about her past for the moment.

He was immense. A real tribute to the Matching. From his tousled blond hair to the muscles on his thighs (and several places in between), Robbie was a perfect blend of strength, grace and beauty. Something released and unwound from Alicia's wing nubs, and she shivered all the way down her spine. *Now I know why Rani's knees trembled when she met the Duke of Ashford. And it wasn't her knees that trembled, was it?*

'Come here,' said Robbie, his voice a delicate baritone counterpoint to his bass of a body. *And where did that image come from!*

Alicia took a few steps away from the door, dropped her cases and flung herself into his arms. *Up* into his arms – she was going to have to get used to men towering over her. Being in Robbie's arms was every bit as exciting as she had imagined. He lifted her bodily into the air and swung her around. She pressed her now smooth skin into the roughness of his face, and another shiver went through her. 'My favourite. Always my favourite,' she whispered into his ear. *And why do I want to nibble his ear? What is wrong with me?*

'And you were mine,' said Robbie, gently lowering her on to the floor and standing back. 'You look … perfect, Leesha. Perfect.'

A tiny frown fluttered across her forehead like a butterfly on a flower. 'It's *Alicia*,' she replied. 'And I'm not perfect. Unlike you.'

Robbie gave a little grin and shook his head. The mortal smile seemed to come naturally to him, and Alicia gave him a big beam in return (at least she hoped it had been a beam – the mirrors in the sídhe didn't come with a built-in tutorial on smiling). 'I never thought I'd get here, Robbie, but I did, and here I am, and there you are, and *that* is what's perfect.'

A voice from outside broke the moment. 'You done in there?' It was female, young and mortal. One of the grooms, probably, though she must be new since Christmas. It definitely wasn't Flora, so the most likely candidate was her lady's first mortal servant, Sophie.

'Let me,' said Robbie. He picked up Alicia's cases as if they were shopping bags and headed for daylight. Alicia followed him and saw who had been speaking.

'Leesha, this is Sophie. Sophie Guest. Still getting used to mortal names.'

'And I'm still getting used to being defined by the fact that I'm gonna die one day,' said the mortal. 'Robbie says you're called Alicia, right? And he wasn't joking about the hair, neither. That's … that's just amazing.'

'Yes. It's a real triumph. Pleased to meet you. I look forward to serving our lady together.'

'I'm still getting used to that as well. The *serving* part. This is a *job* for me, okay? If I serve anyone it's the horses. And Hipponax.'

Sophie looked like all the other grooms in most ways – shorter than Alicia's new skin, dressed for dirty work, and with brown hair held firmly out of the way. In other ways she was different. For one thing she was rounder in the face and had a bigger nose – not sharp and pointed like Rani's, just *bigger*. And Sophie talked back. That was *very* different.

'I'm your lift,' said Sophie. 'On account of there being a distinct shortage of drivers among the *Staveley People*.' She said the last part with a mortal hollowness in her voice, as if she were not part of their lady's household. Then again, perhaps she wasn't. And she spoke the truth about driving: it was a skill with which you did not emerge after the Matching.

'Why? Where am I going?'

'To Staveley for a few days, then on to Birk Fell.' Sophie looked at Robbie and raised her eyebrows (a skill which Alicia had been practising furiously). 'Robbie says it's for the best.'

'We'll break bread first,' said Robbie, with colour coming to his face. 'Could you come back in half an hour, Sophie?'

'Sure. No skin off my nose. See you round the front at one o'clock, yeah?'

'Thanks.'

Sophie turned and headed for the row of loose boxes where the mundane mounts were stabled, and where Flora had been watching from a distance. Alicia felt uneasy, as if there were a predator around somewhere, and she had no idea why. She was Matched. She had left the nest. She was with her favourite and she was in the household of a future Queen.

So why didn't she trust the way that Sophie had looked at Robbie? And why was she being sent to Staveley, where as far as she knew there was nothing but an empty field? And then on to Birk Fell? What was *there*? Wolves, she supposed, with their unique magick and their burning hearts consuming their lives so quickly. Where was the profit in *them*?

To reassure herself, she grabbed Robbie's hand. 'It's so good to see you. *So* good!'

'I know. And you look really … amazing. So healthy, Leesha. I am so glad to have you around. You've no idea what it's like out here.' He followed up the reassurance with another hug, then released her and grabbed the cases again. 'Is this your first time in the cottage? Remember when we used to call it the House of the Wingless? Well, that's you and me now.'

Alicia could see the muscles rippling under Robbie's tight jacket, and there were no prominences where his wings had once been. Surely the nubs couldn't have withered already? Could they?

She followed him into the little garden which separated the cottage from the stable yard. Standing by the door was someone whose smell she could not mistake, even if the form was totally unexpected: Nadya, formerly and still 4th of the Iris-Nymph Child brood.

It was like looking at their lady's younger sister. Nadya was slightly shorter and leaner than Princess Faith, but she had the same prominent cheekbones and triangular bone structure. *She wants to be the first Princess*, thought Alicia.

When Lady Agnes had taught them the rudiments of Construction, she had also taught them a mortal saying: *Imitation is the sincerest form of flattery*. There is a corresponding saying among the People, which begins *Look like, sound like, smell like, feel like, think like, become and then die*. It was a warning of sorts, and if Nadya did want to become the first Princess of the Staveley People, she had chosen to play a dangerous game.

'Look what the cat dragged in,' said Nadya.

Alicia was about to respond when a Memory Inked deep inside her tickled and then swam away. Something to do with someone being dragged *away*, not *in*.

While Alicia hesitated, Robbie spoke out, mistaking her silence for submission. 'Lay off, Nadya. We're all in the same boat. Don't rock it.'

'She's not worth the bother,' said Nadya. She sauntered away from the door, and as she came closer, she shifted to barge into Alicia's shoulder. Alicia saw it coming and raised a tip of Fire close to her skin, so that when Nadya made contact, she bounced off and staggered through the gateway, shooting venomous looks over her shoulder. 'I won't forget that, Littleworm.'

'See?' said Robbie. 'You don't need the aggravation. You'll be much happier at Staveley.'

He led her through the boot room and into the kitchen, which took up all of the ground floor of the old cottage and was where the wingless took their meals, mortals and the People alike. Even the Queen ate in here when she visited.

'But you won't be at Staveley!' said Alicia desperately. 'In fact, who *is* at Staveley?'

He looked away and busied himself, first with moving her cases, and then with a pot on the stove. 'I made your favourite. A last meal before we get split up.'

Alicia pulled her top away from her chest and looked down at her boobs.

The Ink was still just visible, but soon it would become part of her. It was one of the stories which Lady Agnes had told them: 'You'll not just lose your wings and grow taller. You'll have things inside you that you don't have now and that I can't explain.'

Tears dripped from her eyes and splashed onto the soft skin. Lady Morag had shown her the Ink and said that it was part of being wingless. That Alicia would feel things she hadn't felt before and that she would feel them in different ways. 'It's connected to producing more hormones, Alicia, like the beasts, but that's only part of the story. You can't control it, either. You just have to let it become part of you. You've got a bigger heart and a bigger head than you did yesterday. Don't be afraid of them.'

Through her heart was a spear, and on the spear was Inked *Robbie doesn't want me.* Her hand was trembling, her lips were pressed together. Her face was on fire with the shame of mortals, blood burning her cheeks. Was this what the wingless lived with every day?

'Hey, hey. Dry your eyes, Leesha. You know I'll always have your back. You'll always be my favourite.'

She didn't want him to have her back. She wanted him in front of her. On top of her. Lost in her, as she'd seen many times at the Revels. But instead of grabbing her and lifting her to his face, he took her hand and kissed her fingers.

'Saving our lady, I will always be your Champion, Leesha.'

That was nice, but she wanted all of him, not just his sword arm.

He lowered her hand gently and stepped away to serve two bowls of steaming porridge with rat. They weren't normally allowed to cook it outside the sídhe or the nursery, but he'd made sure there was no one around to notice – Alicia could see primitive Wards around the kitchen. No wonder Nadya was waiting outside. It would piss off the mortal grooms no end.

She ate as much as her stomach would let her and pushed the rest aside. 'You never could cook, Robbie. The oats are like paste and the rat is as stringy as Nadya's hair. At least you didn't ferment the Amrita.'

He blushed. 'I know. Sorry. I was so nervous I started cooking it ages ago.'

She took his hand. 'And I'm grateful. Truly I am. Now, tell me who's at Staveley.'

'Imogen is starting work on the sídhe, as best she can. And the Diggers are doing something. You'll be going to Birk Fell as soon as our lady can come to collect you.'

Great. 1st had never liked her; becoming Imogen wouldn't have changed things. And *Diggers.* She shuddered. That the People's oldest enemy should be helping to make Princess Faith's Royal Sídhe was just *wrong.* 'Great. I suppose I'm on kitchen duty.'

'Probably. It's only for a short while. A chance to clear your head. We'd better go.'

It was Sophie who thought about the practicalities when Alicia emerged from the House of the Wingless. 'Have you got anything a bit less salon-ready?' she asked.

'What do you mean?'

'The trainers. White doesn't go well with a muddy field, and if those are your best leggings, I'd save them.'

There was more fussing around, and Alicia ended up with a pair of Sophie's old jeans, some wellingtons and a pair of fluffy pink socks. Apart from the socks nothing quite fitted, but Sophie had been correct: Alicia had not been dressed for a muddy field near Windermere.

'I owe you favour,' said Alicia to Sophie, then she turned to kiss Robbie goodbye. Neither of them went for the lips.

She got in the car, and Sophie said, 'I'll buy new clothes and put in a claim for expenses. Win-win, eh? And there's no point relying on Robbie to think of these things. Not exactly his strong point, thinking. He's got other strengths, though.'

'In what way?'

'Seat belt. You've got no wings now, so you have to wear a seat belt.'

Sophie never answered the question about Robbie's strengths, but she did say that Nadya was a complete pain in the arse, and that if she didn't adjust her attitude, she'd find herself on the wrong end of Hipponax's horn one day. That was music to Alicia's ears, and she contented herself with that learning as they made the slow and winding journey from Longsleddale to Staveley in Cartmel. She also learned that Princess Faith was finding it hard to get away from Birk Fell on a regular basis.

'Those Wolves can be a bit of a handful. Apparently,' observed the young mortal. She turned her head and grinned. 'I'm fairly sure that *brañahoona* is a swear word in Fae. The Boss uses it a lot.'

Alicia was impressed. 'It's actually *braña_hoo*nah*, but you can't hear or make the _ or the * sounds with mortal ears and lips, Sophie. It means "go fuck yourself in a quagmire".'

'Impressive. And talking of sounds, I don't want to cause offence given that we've just met, but is your name pronounced *Aleesha* or *Alees-ya?*'

'It's *Alisiya*, with a tiny little *i* in the middle. It was that or call myself Serendipity, but Lady Morag said that no one would call their child by that name, so I wanted to become Alice after the human story. It was one of the few mortal tales we were told, but Alice is a reserved name.'

'Reserved for who?'

Alicia shook her head. She'd already said too much. 'Doesn't our lord have a brood-sister with the same name as yours?'

'Erm, if you mean *Does Conrad have a little sister called Sofía*, then yes he does. But she's like exotic and fierce and a wizard at magick.' Sophie laughed at her own joke. If it was a joke.

Sophie the non-Mage took what she described as a "shortcut" which nearly killed them when a lorry cut across a junction. When they were on a bigger road, Sophie relaxed again and said, 'What does it feel like?'

'Sorry?'

'I nearly got on a horse and galloped away the first time I saw Sprites. Scared me shitless, I'm telling you. You lot look proper creepy when you've got wings, but then I saw one fall flat on its arse. Right comical. Got easier after that. Anyway, you were like *one of them* a few days ago, and now you're well fit. Wouldn't look out of place running your own salon and getting some award or other. Apart from the hair, obviously. How does it feel to be so different so quickly?'

Alicia went quiet. She sifted through some of the stories, looking for an answer but no answer came. 'I dunno, Sophie. It's just how I am. There's loads and loads I'm trying to get used to, and there's so much to learn, and … I just don't know.'

'Well, you've got several lifetimes to learn. We have to get it right first time.'

'Is your mother still alive?'

'Yeah. Alive and kicking and living in Grange-over-Sands. I'm gonna nip down and see her when I've dropped you off. She said she had something she wanted to talk to me about, and she sounded funny. I asked her if it was bad news, thinking the worst, you know.'

'No, I don't know. What would be bad news?'

Sophie looked at her again with a strange expression, then shook her head. 'Like she was leaving Dad? Like Dad was having an affair? Like she'd got cancer? That sort of bad news.'

'Oh. I'm sorry. Please tell me she doesn't have cancer. I've never met your father, so I don't know about him.'

'Mum laughed and said it was a weird surprise and not bad news. Anyway, why do you want to know about whether my mum is still alive? Do you miss having one?'

There was a story about that. *The pool and the nest are your mother…* It meant that Alicia had several mothers, in reality – Her Grace, of course, Lady Agnes, Lady Morag, Princess Faithful… 'No – I have a mother, Sophie. If you fell on your arse like that Little One but did it in a wingless way, what would your mother do?'

'You might need to unpack that a little, Alicia.'

'I don't know. If you killed Flora in a quarrel and Hipponax escaped. That sort of thing. What would your mother do?'

'Shit, Alicia. Don't say things like that. I have enough trouble writing up the horse passports properly, never mind coming over all *Fatal Attraction*. I dunno. Mum would cry a lot and age ten years overnight, then come and visit me in prison every month until I got released.'

'Well, if it happened to me, I'd either be executed on the spot or chained in the privies until I killed myself or the Queen died. Whichever came first.'

Sophie didn't laugh. 'You're not joking, are you?'

'No. We don't have several lifetimes to learn, either.'

'Fair enough. Let's change the subject, shall we? What do you think I should do with my hair?'

Alicia gave it some serious thought. 'Get a job in an office, and if you can't do that, start using masking conditioner every week. And don't put it into a ponytail until you've given it a good brush first.'

Chapter Eleven

There were still a couple of hours of daylight left when Sophie drove up the track to the Staveley Sídhe. In theory.

In practice, thick rain clouds had blown in from the west, and if there had been street lights within five miles, they would have responded to the gloom by bursting into life. Alicia was not a street light and bursting into life was off the agenda. She shuffled around until she could zip up her coat, then turned to Sophie.

'Thank you so much for the lift. And for the learning.'

'Pleasure. Nice to have someone bonkers on the team. As opposed to weird or psycho. Bonkers I can cope with. Look, can you get the cases on your own? No point in both of us getting soaked and covered in mud. I'd take you closer to the Portakabins, but there's a stuffing great lorry in the way.'

Alicia read the name on the lorry. *Skelwith Construction*. The Diggers. The Gnomes. She shuddered inside and forced herself to be cheerful for Sophie.

'Now I have your wellingtons, I'll be fine. Better than armour. Enjoy your mother time.'

'Right. See you around, Alicia.'

No one came to greet her or help her with her cases. At least the Portakabin with the lights on wasn't locked. And it had a heater. Alicia took her coat off and wandered around looking at the papers and drawings. Most of the papers were meaningless and seemed to have been produced by Clan Skelwith. The drawings did mean something – they were Layer Sketches in Void, describing the new sídhe. She knew that much. The ability to travel between realms is born in the egg, and all the People can do it. *Making* is different. The Void is the hardest of the Lenses to master, and constructing new realms is one of the most difficult Ways.

Alicia was about to put the kettle on when the door banged open. A mortal stood there, staring at her.

'Who are you?' he asked with a look of sheer bafflement. 'Are you supposed to be here?'

'I don't know. That's in the lap of the gods. I'm Alicia, and I've just come from Sprint Stables to live with Imogen.'

He was not young, and his face told of hard work in the sunshine and the rain. He did not look angry or afraid, either. 'You one of the Fae?' he asked.

'I am of the People, yes. I am in the household of Princess Faith.'

'Right. I'm Andy, the site manager. Put the kettle on and I'll give Simmo a shout. I think Imogen is off travelling.'

'Travelling?'

'Or whatever it is you call it. Higher plane stuff. Won't be a sec.'

Alicia put the kettle on and lined up some mugs. She had kept her nails short after the Matching, and it was nice not to have great talons getting in the way while making the drinks.

She sensed and smelled the Digger before she heard the door bang open, and her nostrils filled with the hot iron of Mother Earth. She had seen Gnomes from a distance, but never before had she come face to face with one. Her hands wanted to reach for something sharp, so she stuffed them in the pockets of her tunic.

'Well met, sire,' she said with a bow.

'Well met, Squire,' he returned, Ink rippling over his body. 'I am Simpson of Clan Skelwith.'

'Alicia of the Borrowdale People in the service of…'

'Yes, I know. Sorry. It's pouring with rain out there. Is that tea on the go?'

Alicia made tea for Simpson, Andy and three other mortal men. Simpson sat well away from her, talking to Andy, and the men kept looking at her out of the corner of their eyes. In their faces, she caught a mixture of fear, uncertainty and a glimmer of the sort of look which she'd hoped to see in Robbie's eyes: *bodylonging*. In mortal words, *lust*.

'Alicia?' said the Digger. 'Thanks for the tea. If you're looking for Imogen, she said she was working on the Primary Anchor.'

'No, I…' It suddenly hit her that the Gnome wanted her out of the room. 'I'm not sure I can find her, sire.'

A look of pity came into the Digger's eyes. 'Are those your cases? If they are, you should put them in the other cabin. That's the bunkhouse. Do you need a hand?'

'Thank you, sire. You are generous.'

One of the men, the middle one in years, picked up her beautician's case and opened the door for her. She put on her coat and trudged round to the other Portakabin. This one *was* locked. And Warded.

Alicia was wet and starting to get cold. She smashed the Wards with Fire and used a simple Work of the mortals to unlock the door.

Inside, there were three rooms: two with bunk beds, and a bathroom/shower room. Imogen's belongings were strewn around one room, so Alicia carefully folded them into piles. As Imogen had been sleeping on the bottom bunk, Alicia put her few belongings on the top one. Then she sat down on a chair and waited, Inking memories and wondering what on earth was going to happen to her.

Instead of spending time getting to know Robbie at Sprint Stables, she had been sent here to dwell in darkness, and then she would be going to live with Wolves at Birk Fell, and Sophie would be the first to find out just how *complete* Robbie's package was.

They had been taught some mortal beliefs – fate, luck and fairness among them. Alicia reflected that to mortals, her *fate* would not be considered in the least *fair*, and she would be seen as having some shitty *luck*, just as Sophie had feared bad luck had befallen her mother.

The People do not suffer *bad luck* or expect Fate to deal fairly with them. They do not get cancer and their husbands do not have affairs because they do not marry each other. What would be the point?

Lady Agnes had followed the lesson on mortal luck with an observation and a story.

'Everyone is subject to *chance*, Little Ones,' she had begun, then paused to make sure they understood the difference between chance and luck. 'You can't escape chance, but you can escape being eaten by Gertha the Spider, because Gertha doesn't eat the tastiest or the fattest. Oh no. Gertha eats the ones who wander blindly into her lair, and she eats the ones who mistake her honey-coated silken web for Amrita. Don't let that be *you*. Now, whose turn is it?'

Alicia let the Memory return to her skin and rolled her shoulders with a grimace. Had Lady Morag really given her the correct bra size?

It was completely dark when Imogen returned to the cabin. The engines of the Digger vehicles had long since roared into life and disappeared down the track, and Alicia would have slept except that the churning inside her meant she couldn't just lie down and close her eyes like she used to be able to.

The door to the Portakabin banged open and closed. 'What the fuck are you doing sitting here in the dark, Littleworm?' said Imogen in a husky voice. She flicked the switch and the bunk room was flooded with cold, white light. 'And don't think you're sleeping in here.'

Alicia's broodmate looked exhausted. The edges of her aura were blurred and fractured, colours spinning away and dripping into the ether. Underneath, the new form was striking – angular and tall, pale and intense. Some of the Witches from beyond Albion looked like that, and so did some of the mundane mortals. *Gothic* was the word. The pale skin was framed by long black hair, currently pressed down by a woolly hat, and the angular body was softened by several layers of warm clothing. When Imogen saw Alicia's own hair, she blinked and screwed up her face.

'Are you copying me, Littleworm? And why have you got so much hair? Looks ridiculous with that face.'

Alicia stood up. She was as tall as Nadya, but a couple of inches shorter than Imogen. Heavier, though. 'It is made from Rani Mina's hair, and I am to be handmaiden for the wedding. It is an honour.'

'Get you. I'm starving. Have you made any food yet?'

'I didn't know where the kitchen was.'

'It's in the other cabin. Well, it's bolted to the back of it, and you have to use a separate door. I'm going for a shower. I'll see you in the office when I've finished, and you can move your stuff into the other bedroom. Don't take the bunk on the left because the roof leaks.'

Not only did the roof leak, there was also mould on the walls. Alicia laid out her belongings again and went to make food. Or to heat food, because there was no fresh produce, only ready meals. There weren't even any oats for porridge.

Imogen was a little calmer after her shower. No one had told her that Alicia was going to train as handmaiden, or that Alicia would be living with their lady in Birk Fell, but the real reason Imogen was weighed down was this: she couldn't cope. She had gifts in making spaces from the Void, yes, and was trying her best, but this was bare earth. Even a Queen would be taxed doing this.

'Shall I tell our lady?' asked Alicia.

'You will keep your mouth closed, Littleworm! You will not discuss what you don't understand, is that clear? It's none of your business. I just need to go back to Derwent and get some guidance, that's all. And you're going to Birk Fell tomorrow – I've just been on the phone to sort it out.'

Alicia made soothing noises, and when they retired to bed shortly afterwards, she offered to brush Imogen's hair. 'And give you a special scalp massage. It will help.'

Imogen saw the gesture as submission, and allowed Alicia to work on her. Alicia used the gentlest strokes to ease out the knots in her hair, then used a little Ink into the scalp and soothing fingers to ease away the knots in Imogen's shoulders. Alicia brushed again, and Imogen purred.

'I'll plait it for you,' said Alicia. 'Easier to keep together.'

'Thanks, but not for sleeping. You can do it in the morning.'

'Oh, I need to do it now. See?'

Alicia stepped in front of her broodmate and showed her the hair, now removed from her scalp and cradled gently in Alicia's fingers. With a quick twist, she made a plait and offered it to Imogen, who couldn't believe what she was looking at until she touched her head and felt scalp, not hair.

'Whaaat!'

'I used the little Healer to stop you feeling anything, and I've killed all the roots. You will be bald until you can return to the pool. And, by the way, my name is Alicia. Call me anything else again and I will give you monkey fur on your face.'

With that, she dropped the skein into Imogen's lap and stepped backwards. When Imogen sprang up to attack her, Alicia pulled her knife out. 'We are forbidden blood among the brood until after the first clutch is laid. Goodnight.'

They might be forbidden blood, but Alicia slept with her sharpest scissors under her pillow and her knife planted in the floor next to the bed with a Trigger wrapped around it.

The next morning, Imogen announced that her transport had been confirmed for the afternoon.

'Shall I cook breakfast?' asked Alicia. 'I would break bread with you before I leave. Before I leave to dwell with our lady. You know the first question she will ask.'

Imogen already had her woolly hat firmly planted on her newly bald head. She stared at Alicia for nearly half a turn before she sat down. 'We are both young and have much to learn. Tell our lady that I crave to visit her and ask favour. I will share your bread before I go.'

After food and a little more discussion about what could be said to their lady, Imogen asked, 'Do you have a phone?'

'No.'

'And are *all* your possessions in those cases?'

'Everything.'

'Then I'd put your personal seal on them. They'll be going to Birk Fell separately, and you don't want anyone tampering with them.'

'A good thought. Thank you.'

Imogen stood up. 'Your ride will be here at four. The mortals will not expect refreshments, but they will be grateful for any.'

Imogen left, and Alicia cleaned up as best she could. The mortals arrived soon after, and by mid-morning the air had cleared and Alicia could see Windermere from the front of the sídhe. Princess Faithful (as she then was) had chosen well when she claimed her ground. It was far from mortals but near a big road. It had a small reservoir on the ground above, and best of all, it was a long way from the Royal Sídhe in Derwent.

When Alicia (still 6th at that time) had been dumped in the laundry, she had not lost interest in what was happening to her People, including the Queen-to-be. Alicia had asked the prisoners about Princess Birkdale, and she had discovered that although the town from which she took her name and lived with her mortal husband was many hours away by horse, the Princess kept a Pack of Wolves very close to the Westmorland border. One of the oldest Knights had said, 'Why do you think Faithful was allowed to claim ground to the south when she rose from Countess Mielle to Princess Mielle? Her Grace expected someone to move north towards the Particular at some point, and she expected Mielle to be the buffer.'

Alicia turned and looked to the south, wondering if Robbie would one day lead their lady's army into battle against Princess Birkdale, and if he did, would Alicia be by his side or stuck here, running the laundry?

After walking the grounds, she made more tea and took it to where the mortals were digging a hole in the ground with a big machine. Simpson had joined them, and Alicia forced herself to hand over the steaming mug in person, adding a slight curtsy. 'Does all go well, sire?'

'It does.' Simpson blew steam off his tea and raised his eyebrows a little. 'Help you with anything, Saerdam?'

'I am not a Knight. Alicia is my name.'

'Better safe than sorry. Are you as new as Imogen?'

'Newer. I know nothing. Why are you digging this hole, sire?'

'For a septic tank. Do you know what one of those is?'

'Oh yes. It is the ultimate prison.' She practised the mortal smile. 'And I know its other uses! I was taught.'

'Then you might know that they don't last forever. The existing one disintegrated after the old sídhe was dismantled. We're putting in an upgrade. A Royal Sídhe will have a much bigger outflow.'

'Would the new tank cope with automatic washing machines if they were installed?'

Simpson peered at her. 'They actually use less water than open laundries. I think. I can double check.'

'It would be a favour if you did, sire.'

'Pleasure. Keep supplying us with tea and I'll even have the fibre optic cable installed by Friday.' He paused. 'That's for the internet.'

'I have heard much of the internet but seen little. I look forward to learning. I will bring more tea at noon.'

By noon Simpson had gone, so she practised on Andy instead. 'Have you got any holidays planned, Mister Andy?'

'I have, as it happens. We have an apartment in Tenerife, and we're going there for the last week of March.'

'Is that far from here?'

Andy pointed to the youngest of the workmen, who was studying his phone. 'Ask Callum to show you the map, if you really don't know.'

When she sat next to Callum, he went red. Good. Alicia was glad to see she could have that effect. Callum coughed and brought up a map on his phone. 'There. That's Tenerife.'

'Nice.' She put her hand on his thigh to lean closer. 'Where are we on this map?'

Callum shot up as if he'd been burned. 'I'll get that heap of spoil moved, shall I?'

She took the mugs back to the cabin, and the oldest of the three workmen grabbed her arm. She'd seen him coming, so she didn't lash out. Yet.

'Callum's my lad, okay, and he's just got engaged. Lay off him, understand?'

Alicia was tempted to accept the challenge, but she would be leaving in a few hours, and upsetting the workers would be bad news. 'Forgive me. I meant nothing, and I will do nothing to upset the apple cart.'

He backed off, muttering 'All the bloody same' to himself. Alicia gave them a wide berth from then on and left a tray for them at two. At four, she put her smart clothes on and waited for her lift. The Diggers' lorry was leaving when a motorcycle roared up the track, swerving round the lorry and bouncing over the grass. She was supposed to ride on *that?*

Chapter Twelve

The rider was a Squire from the Royal Sídhe, one of the chauffeurs who occasionally rode with the hunt. 'Where's Imogen?' he asked.

'At work beyond.'

'Never mind. I'll catch her when I've dropped you off. Put this on. It's easier than making a Glamour.'

Alicia didn't need a helmet, but the Squire was right that the real thing was easier. And it would do something to hold her hair in place. While she squeezed it on, the Squire turned round.

There was something odd in the visor, and she tried to lift it but the fastening was stuck.

'Get on,' said the Squire. 'Put your hands round my waist and imagine you're on a horse.'

As they waited at the gate, he turned and touched the helmet, and something happened to the visor. Suddenly, it was a little blurred.

'What are you doing?'

'Sorry? Can't hear!'

He roared off down the road, and Alicia felt sick. She spent the rest of the long ride to Birk Fell trying not to vomit. When they arrived, she almost threw off the helmet and it took her a moment to realise that they were not where she expected. 'Where are we?'

'It's an hour round to Birk Fell by road but ten minutes across Ullswater by boat. The King of the Wolves will be over to pick you up at six. The jetty is just down there.'

He took the helmet from her and was gone before she could ask further questions, so she shrugged and walked down the tiny track towards the lake, the light behind her already fading. She passed some mortals' cottages and a big hall, now partly derelict and partly some sort of meeting place. She read the name and thought it very odd that Coniston Sailing Club should be based at Ullswater, but that was mortals for you.

She found the jetty easily enough and settled down to wait. She wasn't worried when the boat did not appear on time, taking the chance to review some of the Memories she would need at Birk Fell and trying to decide whether Robbie was just waiting until later or whether he really wasn't interested in her. After meeting the mortal workmen and the Digger, Robbie's form and face were even more appealing. She was still thinking about this when she heard a mortal approaching behind her.

She turned round to smile and saw a man in middle years, wearing several layers to keep out the cold. Alicia, too, was feeling the chill and was gearing up to use Fire, but not in front of any mortals.

'Are you alright, love?' asked the man. 'You've been here ages.'

'I'm fine, thank you. I'm just waiting for a boat. It's a bit late, but I'm sure it will come.'

'Oh. Right. Where are you headed?'

'Across the water. To the right of the big house, I think. Is that Sharrow Bay?'

He started to look worried. 'That's Brantwood, not Sharrow Bay. Sharrow Bay is on Ullswater. Is that where you're going?'

'Nearby, I believe. Is Ullswater further up? Further down?'

'What do you mean, "further up"?'

'If this water is not called Ullswater, then is Ullswater this way or that way?'

'Are you being serious?'

'Why would I not be?'

'Well, if you're not trying to wind me up – and I wouldn't blame you if you were, me being a middle-aged man and you being a young girl – but if you're not winding me up, then someone's winding *you* up. This is Coniston Water. Ullswater is a completely different lake about twenty miles away.'

There was no guile, lies or hesitation in the mortal's words. He spoke truth, and Alicia was sitting on a jetty with no phone, no transport and no mortal money. Imogen had had her revenge in the sweetest way.

She sprang up and came closer to the man. 'Oh dear. How would I get there from here?'

'There's no buses until tomorrow. You could call a taxi from Coniston, but they'd charge a fortune.'

'Which I don't have. Nor do I have a phone. Is it hard to find?'

He hesitated, flicking his eyes to the (appropriately named) hall owned by Coniston Sailing Club. 'What did you say your name was?'

'I didn't, but it's Alicia…' She cast her eyes around. 'Alicia Lake. If you give me directions, I'll get there.'

'Would you like me to call someone for you?'

'No need. Just point the way.'

'It's dark. You can't be walking around at night.'

The mortal seemed to care about her situation, but he wasn't helping at all. Time to change that. Surely he must have a car, and he clearly found her attractive, so…

She thrust out a hip and used the excuse of pulling back her hair to push her new boobs forwards. If this didn't produce bodylonging, nothing would.

The man stepped back, his eyes showing alarm rather than arousal. What had she done wrong?

'Are you sure there's no one we can call?' he asked. 'We have a computer of sorts in the club house. I could look up their number.'

She let her hair drop, and for the first time in her new body, she let out a sigh. It came naturally and seemed the right response. She looked around again, her sight easily piercing the gathering darkness. If she couldn't bend this mortal to her will by using her body, perhaps she should stick to what she *did* know and just walk to her new home. After all, she was still in the Lakes. Surely it couldn't be *that* far?

She knew that there was a town called Coniston on the lake, so she said, 'Just tell me the way to Coniston and I'll sort myself out.'

'That's okay. You look young and fit. Back to the main road and turn right. It's only a mile from here.'

'Then thank you. You have saved me a long wait for nothing.'

'Are you local?'

'Born and bred.' It was a safe thing to say because it was true.

'Fine. Take care, Alicia.'

She felt him watching her all the way out of sight, then she forgot about him and put some Fire into her legs. In no time she had to slow down again, because she was in the town and looking for help. A petrol station with a shop was still open, so she went in there.

The mortal behind the counter didn't look up from her phone, so Alicia took her time wandering around, tempted by the smells (and put off by some of them). A wire rack of maps gave her an idea. The mortals were sometimes friendly and sometimes hostile, so what had she got to lose by asking? No risk of loss, but much promise of profit.

The maps were all different sorts, and they had mini-maps on the covers showing what was contained inside. It took her a few minutes to find one which actually had both Coniston *and* Ullswater on it, and then she was in a quandary, because the mortal maid was staring at her with a strange expression on her face.

The mortal held a landline handset to her head and spoke into it. Alicia listened in and heard, 'Looks like her, yeah. She's eyeing up the maps. What shall I do? ... I'm not going over there if she might be a nutter ... whatever. Hang on.'

The maid lowered the handset and said, 'Are you alright? Need any help?'

Alicia walked towards the counter. 'I really need to look at this map, but I have no money. Would you let me have a look? Just for a minute?'

'If you fold it carefully, yeah.'

As Alicia started to unfold the map, the mortal moved away from the counter and lowered her voice, presumably thinking that she would have privacy. 'She's looking at the map ... Yeah. Bye.'

Alicia quickly found Coniston, then ranged her gaze around until she lit on Ullswater. There were two or three ways of getting there from here, and if she could understand the difference between the brown parts and the green parts...

'Are you alright there?'

She recognised the mortal behind her as being a police officer straight away, and immediately called up the Lesson: *If you have committed no crime in mortal law, tell the truth and go in peace, saving only our secrets.* There was a second lesson on what to do if you *had* committed a crime in their eyes, but she didn't need that.

'I'm fine, thanks. Is this green area forest, do you know?'

'Would you be Alicia Lake?'

'That's me! How did you know?'

'We received a report that you might be a bit lost.'

'I was! I'm not now, though. Are you sure you don't know what these symbols mean?'

'It's coming on to rain. No night for being about. Let's see if there's someone we can call to help you out. Where do you live? And who's best to get in touch with?'

That was a difficult question. Where *did* she live? And how would the mortal police contact anyone? Everywhere she could think of was Hidden. 'I don't know. Well, I do, but I don't think there's any way of getting in touch, and no one would care anyway.'

'We're concerned about your welfare, Ms Lake. Why don't we talk it over round the corner?'

Alicia racked her brains trying to think of who they might call, and the only name she could think of was Skelwith Construction. 'Call Simpson of the Clan. He is with Skelwith Construction.'

The mortal looked slightly alarmed and took a step back just as another name came into her head. Why hadn't she thought of it before? 'Or the Commissioner! You must know Conrad Bloody Clarke.'

The officer took another two steps back. 'In that case, I'll leave you be, Ms Lake.' His mouth twitched, halfway towards a smile. Only mortals did that for some reason. 'If you really want to know, the green is forest and the brown is mostly mountains. Goodnight.' He looked at the maid behind the counter. 'Cheers, Chelsea. Thanks for that.'

Alicia started re-folding the map, its ways and obstacles dancing before her eyes. She returned it to the rack and bowed to the maid. 'You have my thanks and favour. I wish you well, whatever team you support.'

And then it was out into the night. She hoped to be at Birk Fell by morning. After all, what could possibly go wrong?

Starvation and lack of Lux were the first things to go wrong, but those shouldn't be problems, should they? Alicia was going to hop on top of a house until she remembered that she didn't have wings any more. A smaller building with open sides looked more promising, and she quickly scrambled onto the roof. Her hand flew to her mouth when she looked to the north west, for there was a glow of deepest red pulsing from beneath a mountain. 'The Old Man,' she whispered, and she gave thanks that her route didn't involve trespassing on the Dwarf's territory, and then turned in a slow widdershins circle.

Nothing to the south except the great Ley line heading to the old Radiant Sídhe, and nothing to the south east. Due east was a different matter. There, in the forests above the upper portion of the lake, glowed the barriers and protections for something which looked *very* interesting. If only she'd heard the household use the mortal words for these places, she might be able to match them up to names she was familiar with. She glanced north, her preferred route to Waterhead, but there was nothing. East it was, and the road to … Hawkshead. That's the one.

She hopped down, then nearly jumped with fright.

'You lot! You're a bloody menace,' said an elderly mortal man. Where had *he* come from, and why hadn't she sensed him?

She bowed quickly. 'The People serve and support.'

'You don't serve or support me. Bloody anarchist free runners, jumping onto things with no respect. That bus shelter wasn't designed to have people sitting on top of it, and the next thing is you'll be suing the council when it collapses under you.'

Alicia understood almost nothing of this. All of the words made sense, but as for *meaning*…

'I meant no ill or harm. Please forgive me and let me go in peace.'

'You'll go whether I forgive you or not, but if I see you round here again, I'm going to call the police.'

'I understand that. Thank you.'

She jogged off into the night, intending to put Fire into her legs until she realised that she simply didn't have enough Lux, so she walked. Ten minutes later, she discovered that the police officer was a true oracle: it had started to rain. It didn't take her long to get round the lake and find a concealed and Warded entrance to some mortal property. There was a sense of much being hidden here, and the Ink around the entrance was opaque. Far too risky.

It wasn't *unreasonable* of Stephen Bloxham to ask Chloë to the offices at seven o'clock in the evening. After all, it was in the Bloxhams' shared calendar that Wednesday was Chloë's long day at university, and Stephen often returned late from site visits or meetings. There was no reason for Chloë to say no until she got to the building and found it locked, and by then it was too late, because she'd already told him that she was on her way.

She took out her phone, desperately thinking of a reason to postpone, and a message arrived from Stephen. *Just seen you pull up and remembered that you don't know the code to get in. The lights are on a motion sensor. The code is 8275.*

Of course he would have seen her arrive – the sun had set behind thick clouds half an hour ago, and the building was in a quiet corner of the business park, so her car lights would have been obvious. She went back to her car and got the pepper spray out of the glovebox, then went to enter the security code.

The hidden lights which came on when she entered the lobby were just enough for her to see the staircase and to move safely, but no more. They certainly didn't penetrate the shadowy corners, and when she got upstairs, only the lamp on Stephen's desk gave any illumination.

'Come in, Chloë,' he called.

She stopped, braced her shoulders, and with a smile painted on her face, she strode into his office with all the false confidence she could muster.

The chaos of his desk was gone. This happened sometimes, but rarely at the end of the day. All the files, catalogues and drawings had been put in their proper places and his desk was naked but for three pieces of paper. She didn't know whether to be worried or relieved that there was no sign of champagne and two glasses, or any other seductive cliché. 'Hi, Stephen.'

He gave her a thin smile that lasted only for a brief moment. Then he sat back and stared at her, his eyes now lost in shadows. 'What's your game, Chloë – or whatever your name is?'

Chloë was so used to being *Chloë* that her denial was instinctive. 'What are you on about?'

He rocked forwards, putting his elbows on the desk. Now his eyes were back in the light, they were as hard as the diamond-tipped drill she'd once had to move off the visitor's chair.

'You must think I don't talk to my wife if you expected to get away with this.' He held up one piece of paper, with the Mowbray boar visible at the top.

'You appear out of nowhere, and five minutes later you're telling me to bid for a development owned by Ethan Mowbray.' He swapped papers. 'And then the entire bloody Mowbray family, including two people who don't seem to exist, book themselves into Allington Rectory *as guests at the Clarke wedding.*'

The mood Stephen was in, even if it *had* been a coincidence he wouldn't have believed it. Chloë had expected a moment like this and she had a lie ready, but she never got to tell it because Stephen had picked up the third piece of paper.

'You can get a private detective to do an online report for a hundred quid these days. And this report tells me that almost nothing you've told Juliet is true. Not your name, not your college course, nothing.' He leaned forwards. 'I'd say that my wife is too trusting, but as she trusts me, that would be dangerous ground. Exactly like the dangerous ground you're standing on.'

Shit. Double shit. Beth had *promised* a cover story would be put in place for her.. She stepped backwards and put her hand in her bag, gripping the can of pepper spray.

'Are you working for them? Are you working for the Clarkes?' His fist slammed on the desk. 'I will *not* have Juliet dragged into this.'

It was a lifeline, thrown by Stephen's anger. Did she have the guts to grab it and turn it from a lifeline into a fishing line, with Stephen re-cast as the fish? She rotated the can of spray until her finger was on the button and said, 'Okay, okay. I'm sorry. I am *not* working for the Clarkes. I'm on *your* side, Stephen. Beth and me. Both of us. By accident, yeah, but it's true. We can work together.'

He didn't believe her. 'To do what?' he said with a frown.

'It's simple. We both want something from Elvenham Grange, and we can help each other get it.'

The irritation in his eyes disappeared in a blink and was replaced by … fear? Yes. And the way he suddenly took his phone out told Chloë that Stephen Bloxham did actually have an imagination inside the poured concrete of his skull, and that that imagination was painting Chloë as an assassin sent to rub out Conrad Clarke. Her fish was hooked…

'Yours isn't the only family the Clarkes have stolen from,' she said.

'Why am I not surprised? Does that explain how Conrad can afford this wedding?'

She hesitated, then realised that if she painted Conrad Bloody Clarke as the enemy, she could end up in all sorts of trouble. 'I have no idea, Stephen. Seriously. It wasn't him, it was one of his ancestors. As with the owners of Clerkswell Manor, there's something of ours we want back.'

'What?'

'You think there's evidence somewhere in the house, don't you?'

'I know there is. Clarke's grandfather taunted my father about it. I even know that it's in the safe. Do you think there's something in there for you, too?'

She shook her head. 'Did you know there used to be an old farmhouse there, before the Gothic place was built?'

'I did know that.'

'Did you know it had a cellar, and that the cellar was never filled in?'

'How the fuck could I know that? And more to the point, how do *you* know that?'

She was on a roll now, and went with it. 'We've always suspected, and when they remodelled the gardens we got some aerial photos. Hi-res, infra-red, the lot. There's something *ancient* there, Stephen. I can show you. You know a lot about groundworks and stuff.'

She crossed the fingers of her hand not holding the spray. Their Principal could afford to buy a drone and send it up one morning, and Beth could fake the rest of the pictures, no problem. It was time to reel him in.

'We can do it together. Both of us can get what we want out of this.'

He opened his mouth, then closed it. The fear in his eyes had switched to apprehension. 'I've been in that house three times and we couldn't even *find* the safe, never mind open it. Jules was there a dozen times last summer with the cricket team and there was nothing. I'm not sure it even exists, and now that Myfanwy lives there, the place is never empty.'

'It will be empty soon enough. On the day of the wedding, *everyone* will be in church, and then hanging around for the photos afterwards. We can be in and out, and don't worry, we'll find the safe.'

He raised his eyebrows. 'True enough. About the wedding, I mean. Hadn't thought of that. But there's a huge difference between a bit of safe-cracking and digging up old foundations. Even my best lads couldn't get the equipment onto the site before they've said *I do*.'

'Aah, but there's a tunnel from the well. We just need someone with a bit of muscle who's handy with a crowbar.'

Flattery. It gets to men every time, and she could see him wriggling on the hook. And then he gave a jerk that nearly pulled the rod out of Chloë's hands, picking up the boar-headed printout and saying, 'If this contract comes off, I won't need the old deeds – which might not exist, by the way – but I would owe you. I don't need to know who you really are, Chloë, but I do need to know about this. What's the truth about you and the Mowbrays?'

'Never met them, but I really do know someone who has. Someone who can tell you things about the way they work. The sort of inside knowledge you won't get from anywhere else, no matter how much you pay a private detective.'

His eyes went involuntarily to the printout that had exposed 'Chloë Greenwood'.

'Does Jules know?' she asked.

He picked it up and folded it in half. 'She does not. It can be our secret for now. We'll continue this discussion closer to the wedding, shall we? When you've got something useful to say. If you haven't disappeared back where you came from.'

'I'm going nowhere, Stephen.'

'We'll see. Goodnight.'

She turned and walked out of the office, stiff-backed. The motion sensor lights came on and she somehow made it down the stairs without breaking into a run. She only dropped the keys twice as she tried to unlock her car, eyes from the upper floor burning into her back. She knew he was looking, even without turning round to see it.

The strangest thing was that once she arrived at her rented house in Allington, she actually felt relieved. The Bloxhams might own it, but the house was her sanctuary. She poured a *very* large glass of wine and called Beth. 'We need to talk. Things have changed, and I'm scared.'

It took Alicia another two days to find her way to Birk Fell. To survive, she lowered her sights – literally lowered them and found a rabbit warren halfway up the hill, beyond the mortals' domain. There, she coaxed some food out with a little song and fed herself on it, and then rested overnight. That was enough to get her over the hill and down to Hawkshead, where the mortals played at justice in their courtroom.

The house of justice was secure enough, its entry Wards much tighter even than at the private property on Coniston Water, but the protections were sloppy in execution and Alicia fed herself deeply on the Lux flowing around the buildings. All she had to do now was get to Ullswater without encountering any mortals, Wolves, Diggers or (perhaps worst) the People.

On the next stage of her journey, from Hawkshead to Waterhead, she saw a signpost to Tarn Hows which stirred a Memory from just before her Matching. She had heard Her Grace saying something about it as a joke, and Alicia hadn't been able to understand what was funny. She moved on past the signpost and saw the homes of mortals which few of the People ever get to see – mostly because they have way more sense and much more forewarning.

As the road dropped towards the River Brathay, she saw the high walls of the Diggers' Halls, thick and foreboding and filled with an ancient hatred of the People. Except when it came to septic tanks, it seemed. How had that come about, she wondered? Was it a sign of change?

At dusk she followed the river to Windermere, and there she came to the grounds of Waterhead, the school for Mages. The girl she had called 'Eden' was studying here, and Alicia had learned to pronounce *Persephone* properly while she was in the Sprint Sídhe waiting to emerge. Persephone was a mortal with Fae blood; the world was much more complex than the stories had told her it would be. Or perhaps she just hadn't listened hard enough.

At dusk on the third day, she took a track out of the little village of Patterdale and struck off on a path which followed the eastern shore of Ullswater. Not long now, and then it would be time to face the music.

When Lady Agnes had told them of the dance with mortals, she had said that some sayings were so old that it was not known whether the mortals had learned them from the People's tongue or the other way around. Either way, *facing the music* summed up what was waiting for Alicia when she finally got to Birk Fell. She went to zip up her coat against the night, then remembered that it was broken. She sighed and set off down the path.

The low growl was delivered as a friendly warning, and it came from up the slope, away from the water. Alicia scanned around again, and still she found nothing. That was good and also disturbing: first the mortal in Coniston and now the Wolf had approached with no warning.

She took a few steps off the path and away from even the keenest eyes or telescopes. When she got closer she smelled the Wolf, and as she must, she bent the knee to the animal. It approached cautiously, a young male with a glossy coat and bright eyes. It circled her until satisfied, then spoke in Wolf to the air and lay down in guard. Alicia stood up and waited.

A crashing through the trees told of haste, and a SheWolf ran up. The People take the knee to the Wolf, but the HeWolf and the SheWolf know their lords and masters. Or should do!

The offering of the neck was little more than a token lowering of the head and sweeping away of the hair. Things must be very different here at Birk Fell.

'Are you Alicia, my lady?' asked the SheWolf.

'I am.'

'Welcome to Birk Fell. I am Maria, Chantress to the Pack and chosen of Rani Mina. I am to escort you.'

'Thank you.'

Maria looked at Alicia properly, and her eyes showed surprise. 'Your journey must have been a dangerous one, Leesha. Madreb Faith says you have been busy working your way through the students in Ambleside, but it looks like you've fought a stag and lost.'

Since when did Wolves use the People's names in this way? Well, if that was the rule, at least they could follow it properly. 'It's Alicia, not Leesha. Please, lead the way.'

The Wolf on guard slipped away through the trees, and Maria led her to a hidden path running parallel to the mortal trail which hugged the water. 'Madreb Faith says it's a good job, actually, because our Guardian is gone away, and it will be easier to get you settled in without her knowing. And we have a special visitor, too.'

Alicia was suddenly very conscious of the dirt on her face, the rips in her leggings and the stuffing leaking out of her torn coat. Surely the Dragonslayer…

'We're special,' Maria was saying. 'We have a Guardian as well as a Madreb and a Protector, and our first Guardian was Erin Slater, Enscriber of Sprint Hall. She is come to visit while Guardian Karina is abroad.'

They passed another hidden track, leading even further up the fell. 'The landing zone for the helicopter is up there,' said Maria. 'It's how we got to Brothers Water. That was a night and a half.'

The SheWolf's grin was feral. *Lupine* even, and Alicia felt a tiny shiver of something.

'Here we are.'

And there they were, and this would be Alicia's home until Princess Faith could find a new Madreb and move into the Staveley Sídhe. They were at the top of a down-sloping yard which had wonderful views of the lake. To the right was a metal shed with big doors, and to the left was a small cottage, and in between, scratching around the floor, were several chickens.

It was not quiet here: there was woodworking going on in another building and children were playing a game somewhere, but it was peaceful. 'I like it, Maria. I hope I get to stay.'

'I am to take you to Guardian Erin in the Pack Hall. Madreb Faith will join us later.'

Inside the Pack Hall was a communal living space with beds, tables, a kitchen, and clean and neat storage cupboards, even if some of them were a little battered. Adult SheWolves and Elders moved around preparing the evening meal, all of them turning to stare when Maria introduced Alicia to the Pack, then turning back to their work. The exception was a mortal Mage who sprang up and bustled over.

'Well met,' she said with a bow. 'I'm Erin Slater, and you must be Alicia. Welcome to the Pack Hall.'

'Well met, and thank you.'

The woman and the Squire contemplated each other for a moment. When Alicia looked at Erin, she saw a mortal with an honest and open face, a sense of humour, and blonde hair which had most definitely come out of a bottle. Erin was wearing old clothes on top of new clothes, and had clearly eaten several meals while wearing the old clothes, judging by the stains down them.

'You so need a shower and change of clothes,' said Erin. 'Good job you didn't damage your hair on your little walkabout or you might be in *serious* trouble. Unless you're into something *very* kinky – you've not been shacked up at Charlotte Mason college with the PE students, have you?'

Alicia shook her head, unwilling to say more to a mortal, no matter how closely linked to their lord.

Erin gave the mortal half-smile. 'We need to have a little chat away from the Pack. Come with me.'

What was this? A mortal doing the People's business? Alicia shook her head and followed the Enscriber down the slope and into an open space where banked log seating faced a long fire pit. In the bottom of the pit were half-burnt logs, signs of general trash and what appeared to be a *lot* of fabric.

Erin sat on one of the logs and pointed for Alicia to join her. 'Take the weight off. You are one very lucky Squire, Leesha, and you've got me to thank for that.'

'I pay all my debts. What do I owe you for?'

'Strictly speaking, it's my partner, Barney Rubble, also known as Detective Constable Smith. That means he's a policeman.'

'Oh.'

'That's right. Look, it wasn't your fault that Imogen stitched you up like that and had you dumped in the arse end of nowhere. And respect for getting here alive and without *too* much trouble, but you need to know a bit more about how we mortals see you. The ones who aren't Entangled, anyway.'

'What do you mean? I tried my best to keep out of their way.'

'And you almost succeeded. Look, mundane mortals see you as a very young, attractive woman on her own. A tiny weeny number of men would actually look on you as prey, as the wolf does the deer.'

Alicia felt uncomfortable about that. There was nothing of that in the stories.

'And there's some places in the big cities where you would be attacked for being alone and a stranger, but out here in the country people are *interested* in you. And they want to help.'

'They did. They were kind, and I found it hard to get away.'

'That's because you came over to them as a vulnerable adult. It means they thought you had mental health issues and might have come from a secure unit. In old terms, the police thought you were a loony on the loose.'

Alicia didn't know whether to be amazed or insulted. 'You mean they thought I was Eclipsed?'

'If Eclipsed means you're wrong in the head, then yes. Exactly. Good word, that. *Eclipsed*. I'll have to use that at work next time Pihla tries to mix the Ink with olive oil.'

Alicia sat back. She had no idea at all how that could have happened. What had she done wrong? What had she said? If this were true, she had indeed been fortunate. Her voice was almost a whisper when she said, 'They wanted to bind me?'

'No. The nice policeman would have Sectioned you under the Mental Health Act for your own safety. You can look it up later. That was until you mentioned Conrad, then the penny dropped. The responding officer's an old mate of Barney's from Barrow nick, and he called Barney as soon as you left the petrol station. Barney called me, and I called Faith. She was not amused, but she was grateful. So yeah, someone must have been watching over you, Leesha.'

'And the other mortals?'

'The cashier? The bloke by the lake who called it in? You're just a story to them.'

Erin stood up. 'You'd better go and get yourself cleaned up. Faith's having a lie-down so be quiet, but Cathy's in the cottage. When you've sorted yourself out, I'll show you my surprise. I can't wait. This is going to be epic, Leesha.'

A Becoming-Queen needs Amrita. Lots of it, and Cathy, their lady's Lady, had expressed some earlier. When she saw Alicia, she took pity on her and passed her a golden flask of the elixir.

'You're sharing with me in the little room. The Wolves have built us a bunk bed, but watch out for splinters. Shower's at the end of the landing. Welcome to Birk Fell and to our lady's household.'

With the Amrita and a venison sandwich inside her, followed by a hot shower, Alicia felt almost normal again, and the good news kept coming when she examined her cases. They had been delivered yesterday by courier (and boat across the lake) and were waiting in a corner of the tiny bedroom. Imogen had tricked her and sent her to Coniston, yes, but her brood-sister had left the seals on Alicia's belongings intact: the motorcycle to nowhere had been the end of her revenge. That was good. They could move on. Alicia dressed in clean clothes and returned to the Hall.

With a flourish and a 'Ta-da!', Erin collapsed a Glamour to reveal something like a hairdressing station. Something like one, if an old dining chair and a mirror on a low chest made a station. That was another favour and Alicia was grateful, but it was the wall behind the station which Erin the Enscriber was most proud of. She had created an Enchanted display board and put a banner across the top. *Operation Barnet*, it said.

'Rhyming slang,' said the Enscriber. '*Barnet* means *hair* in London. These are your subjects, Leesha, so you can see what you're up against. Do you know them all?'

Underneath the banner, the board had been divided in two. One third was blank, except for a living picture of Rani Mina in her native costume. The larger portion of the board was filled with similarly Enchanted pictures of women arranged in three rows, the top row having only two pictures and the others four each.

'I don't know many at all. I recognise ... you. And that's it.'

'Ah well, I suppose Faith had a lot on her mind. And I don't think she had any pictures anyway. The top two are the ones you don't mess with, okay, 'cos that's the Matron of Honour and the Chief Bridesmaid. When they're not plotting the most hardcore hen party this side of Marbs, they're known as Hannah Rothman and Vicky Robson.'

Alicia felt her mouth go dry, an entirely new sensation. She swallowed hard and said, '*That* is the Anointed Guardian? Do you know why she has no hair?'

'You say Anointed Guardian, I say Peculier Constable. Either way, she's the Boss, and she's got no hair 'cos she had her head caved in by a Revenant. Have you not heard that one?'

'If the People were not involved, then no, why should I have?' She considered the Chief Bridesmaid. 'Has no one told Vicky that her hair has less life than a bowl of cold rat porridge?'

'Ew. That's proper gross. Hmm. Vicky got loved up not so long ago, so she *might* have changed it. Dunno. She's lovely really, though. Proper friend. Right, next row down there's yours truly, then Lucy Berardi. She's mundane but Entangled. Runs a chain of coffee shops and lives with Tom Morton. You know him, right?'

'I do. Lucy has a lovely face. Very curly hair, though, if a little too short to take away from the round face.'

'That's the Italian in her. And the next one is Saffron. Have you not met her before?'

'The Hawk! I have heard much of her and her family. Please tell me that hair is real.'

'The jury's out on that one, but it does run in the family. Good luck. Anything familiar about the next face?'

'Ooh! Is that a young Duchess of Cambridge?'

Mortals rarely hit the People (unless they're trying to kill them, of course), and the dig in the ribs knocked Alicia off balance, which was a good job because she lashed out with her inner talons and missed.

'Did you just try to slice my face open?' said the Enscriber, her face rigid with shock.

Alicia righted herself and bowed. 'Of course not, my lady. It was a reflex Glamour. I beg your pardon for shocking you.'

Erin squinted at her, then shrugged. 'Fair enough. No, that is not Princess Catherine,. That is Rachael Clarke.'

'Aah. The mundane one.'

'You could say that, and I could hit you harder next time. Rachael is a tricky customer and most definitely not friends with *her*, the first one on the third row.'

'She is little more than a child.'

'She's in her forties, but she cheated and stole a teenager's body. That's Tamsin Kelly that was. Now calls herself Tammy Pike.'

'A bodysnatcher! Really?'

'Yeah, but she sees herself as more of a working mother and wronged woman, and the woman who did the wronging to her is most definitely not up on *this* board.'

Erin had been honest with Alicia, so it was time to be honest back. 'I'm sorry, but you've lost me completely.'

'Keep up. I thought you were all supposed to be geniuses before they let you consort with *mortals*. That's what I've always found anyway. Geniuses, or well-endowed in other departments. Talking of which, is it true what I've heard about that Squire Robbie?'

'I do not know. What is it you've heard?'

'That he works at the stables? And that he fits right in with the stallions in terms of equipment?'

A deep sigh came from the entrance to the Hall. 'I think that's a question you'd better not answer, Leesha,' said Princess Faith.

Alicia whirled around and dropped to her knees. Her lady, her future Queen, had begun the Change, and Alicia's throat closed up with pride, wonder and awe as she beheld the full glory.

Princess Faith's Skin was fractured, tiny fissures emitting the glow of Quicksilver, and her eyes were blank silver orbs. Truly the People are beautiful.

'Approach,' whispered her lady in the People's tongue. Alicia crawled up to the gleaming beacon and kissed the offered hand.

'Welcome to my household, Squire. May you live to the last square.'

'My lady is gracious and merciful.'

Alicia felt the level of Ink swirling around them drop, and Princess Faith's skin became human-coloured again. Around them, the Enscriber was rubbing her eyes and all the Wolves but two had looked away. Behind Faith, Maria and a cub were also on their knees. What did that mean?

Alicia stood up and shook herself. Now that her lady was returned to normal form, she looked tired and drawn with no splendour about her. Princess Faith took a deep breath and pointed to a tray on the table. 'Maria will serve us, and you will say nothing about Squire Robbie's endowments. What else have I missed?'

Alicia was eager to please. 'The Enscriber was just about to explain Tammy Pike's geometry.'

'That's one way of putting it,' said Erin. 'Tamsin was married to a powerful Mage called Chris Kelly. He's the Earthmaster of Salomon's House. You must have heard of *him*.'

'I have heard of the Earthmaster.'

'Good. Right, well, Chris was having an affair with Eseld Mowbray, and that's where it gets complicated, because—'

'We'll skip that, thanks,' said Faith. 'I'll tell her later.' She turned to Alicia. 'In fact, you'll get to see Tammy in a week or so, I believe. According to Conrad.'

The Enscriber looked a little hurt at having been deprived of a good story, but she moved on. 'This is Evie Mason, housekeeper at Middlebarrow Haven. That's where the hen party will begin.'

Alicia nodded her understanding and ran her fingers over the fringe descending *way* too far down the mortal's forehead. 'I look forward to meeting her. I do like a challenge.'

'No comment.' Erin tapped the picture of a woman holding a newborn baby. 'This is an old picture of Kelly Kirkham. Never met her, but Mina says she's a proper old friend. She's the only one here not Entangled. Make sure it stays that way. She's only on day one of the hen party.' She tapped the final picture, a smiling woman with cornflower blue eyes and naturally blonde hair. 'And Myfanwy here won't be at the hen party at all, but she's third in line at the wedding, after Vicky and the Boss.'

'And you shall meet her when we visit Clerkswell,' added Faith. 'That is another trip I can't wait to enjoy.'

What was that tone in her lady's voice? Surely not *sarcasm*. Why would a trip to their lord's mansion be unpleasant?

'Suck it up, Faith,' said Erin with a little sharpness.

Princess Faith pointed to the picture of Lucy. 'Has Erin told you about Ms Berardi's friend?'

'Which one?' said Erin.

'Leesha, you should know that Lucy is in the favour of Princess Birkdale, also known as Tara Doyle, and Princess Birkdale will be a principal guest at both the hen party and the wedding.'

Oh. Had someone done this deliberately? Forcing Faith to be around her future enemy so soon after beginning the Change was a risky gambit if it was intentional. Would the Dragonslayer have done this? Surely not – where was the profit in that? And ditto for the Red Queen. Perhaps it was merely chance and nothing to do with Gertha the Spider.

Alicia nodded to show that she understood, and Erin continued. 'That just leaves these two.' She pointed away from the board towards Maria and the cub. 'Maria you know, and this is her daughter, Lottie. Maria's not on the hen for obvious reasons. Lottie here will be leading the flower girls up the aisle in the church, won't you, love?'

The cub nodded enthusiastically and spoke up in a high voice: 'And I am on a special diet to stop me growing too tall to fit in the special dress.'

'No, you're not,' said her mother. 'That was Rani's joke. You will grow as tall as Great Fang wants you to grow.'

'And the dress is also Mina's little joke,' said Princess Faith, with some suppressed emotion. 'When our lord returned from Ireland, he brought some silk. To be precise, it was the shift worn by the Fair Queen just before she was hacked in two by the Dwarf. Rani thinks it's symbolic that a Wolf cub wears a dress made from that silk at the wedding. You may have another opinion.'

Alicia did not know what to make of that. Erin broke the awkward silence by plonking herself in the chair. 'You can make a start on me, 'cos I have to get home and get ready to go out. Not often Barney and I get a Friday night together.'

Maria handed around mugs of tea, and Alicia took a slurp then went to examine Erin's hair, taking the chance to thank the Witch for the living renders. 'Being able to try styles on their images will be a boon indeed.'

'Glad you like them. They were fun to make.' She pointed to the mirror and said, 'I thought about getting an Enchanted one, but they're expensive.'

'This is enough,' said Alicia, parting the sections and examining the roots.

'I am skilled in the Ink of Reflection. See!'

Alicia didn't need the battered semi-antique to make a Mirror of Possibility, but it *did* make life easier. She cast the Ink upon the glass and there was Erin the Enscriber, with her natural muddy brown colour restored and glossed into a smart bob which gave sophistication to her face.

'Good work,' said Faith. Praise indeed.

'Is it hell,' said Erin. 'I am blonde on the inside and it's your job to make the outside reflect that. Got it?'

'Of course, my lady. You'll be coming here again, will you not?'

'Off and on. Mostly off now that Karina is Guardian. She does get a bit jealous.'

'How could she? Just promise me that you won't go to any salon other than this one from now on. At least until after the wedding.'

'That's what I was hoping. Do you know how much they charge in Kendal, of all places? Oh, and talking of Alicia's salon – you need a name, don't you?'

'Do we?' said Princess Faith.

'You do,' said the Enscriber emphatically. 'And I've got one for you. *Shear Magic*. Without the *k* in *Magic*. Perfect.'

'Shear Magic it is,' said Faith.

'Can I have an embroidered tunic?' said Alicia eagerly.

'When it comes to the salon, you can have pretty much what you want,' said Faith. 'Mina's given me a blank cheque for that, and believe me, a blank cheque from Rani Desai is about as common as a Unicorn mare.'

The next day had much learning, and Cathy took pity on Alicia by preparing a glowing bowl of fresh porridge with rat, laced with the fragrant Amrita.

'Don't get used to it,' said Cathy. 'I'm saving almost all of my Amrita for our lady, but I thought you needed something to build you up. You can take hers upstairs when you've finished eating. She wants to see you.'

Alicia savoured the treat and gladly took the loaded tray upstairs when she was done. She knocked and entered, and found her lady sitting up in bed, pinched lines around her nose and sweat on her brow.

'Move that bedding off the chair. Sit down and wait on me,' said the Becoming-Queen, and Alicia did as she was bid. The sheets she removed were soiled with sweat and a little blood in the middle, but still fresh at the edges.

Her lady saw her looking and grimaced. 'Do you know the one piece of advice that Her Grace gave me about the Change? She said, "Get on to LinenWarehouse and order lots of extra bedding." We've had a lot of bonfires so as not to overload the washing machines. The Wolves don't like the smell.'

As Princess Faith came to the end of her breakfast, she lay back and signed for Alicia to remove the tray. 'I'm glad you're here, Leesha. I don't know how I thought I could manage without a handmaiden. You've a lot to learn, though.'

Alicia bowed. 'My lady is wise. I look forward to discovering the Ways at your hand.'

The Princess waved that away. 'Later. You've got a lot to learn about being wingless first. You shouldn't wind Imogen up like that. She's got a vicious streak.'

Alicia lowered her head. 'It was fair return for what she called me, my lady.'

'Not the hair, you cracked egg. It wasn't the hair that wound her up. Think about the timings.'

Alicia ran through the Memory, and then it struck her. 'Did she order the motorcycle *before* I scalped her?'

'Of course she did, and she ordered it to stop you coming here and telling me that she has less chance of making our sídhe than Robbie has of winning Miss World this year. She sent you packing so that she could come to me and tell her side of the story before you landed her in it.'

Alicia trembled inside. *How did I not see this?* And the worst thing was that she could see no useful learning from it.

'At least you got your revenge in first,' said Faith. 'Serves her right. Thank you, Leesha. Cathy will show you some of the things that need doing around the place.'

Alicia put the tray together. 'But what of the sídhe?'

'In hand. You'll see. Sometimes there are benefits to kissing a mortal's blade.'

Downstairs, Alicia put the dishes in the sink and then realised that it would be an insult to Cathy not to wash them. She ran hot water and thought of how far she'd come since the night when Princess Faithful and Rani Mina had ridden Hipponax over the snow to Broadwater to declare that there were rebels abroad. She'd come a long way, yes, but not in the direction she'd dreamed of.

The clutch which hatched *before* Alicia's were still in the Borrowdale Sídhe – those which had survived the rebellion, anyway. They were being coached in the Ways while learning the skills of the wingless and beginning their interactions with mortals, and here was Alicia, washing the dishes, not because she was destined for the kitchens but because there was no one else to do it.

She was still thinking about what this meant when Cathy returned with some fresh eggs for lunch. The young Hlæfdige was grateful for the clean kitchen, and took the unexpected extra time to tell Alicia what the Madreb's role might be.

After making a Memory of her duties, and with Maria's help, Alicia went forth and answered the Wolves' questions, nodded wisely and generally tried to let the Pack get on with things. They clearly knew what they were doing and it seemed like Faith had inherited a well-oiled machine from Guardian Karina. In fact, Alicia spent most of the morning walking the grounds with Lottie, and Lottie, being both a child and a cub, had a lot to say. Alicia nodded sagely and played games with the little girl and then filed the information away for the future.

When Lottie skipped off to join her mother, Alicia found herself smiling at the cub's special mixture of insight and assumption. It was like nothing she'd ever come across before, and it brought a joy which seemed to outweigh the simple learning of routines. Unlike lunch, which managed to turn the fresh eggs into something less than they should have been.

Alicia was at the dishes again when Faith emerged and said that she was taking the car and King Alex and was going shopping, and did Alicia want for anything?

'Err…'

'Good. See you later.'

What Alicia would have *liked* to ask for was a phone. She was going to need one. Perhaps next time. Back in the yard once their lady had gone, Maria begged for her and Lottie to sit in the chair, and Alicia started with the cub.

They had great fun with the Mirror of Possibilities, and Lottie screamed when Alicia turned the reflection green. Lottie had strong, straight hair and styling it would be easy, if only she could get the cub to sit still for more than five minutes. It was when Maria got in the chair that the learning began.

Wolves obviously keep their hair down to avoid complications when Exchanging, although they'll sometimes risk tying it up loosely with a simple headscarf or (now that we are in the twenty-first century) a scrunchie. HeWolves and SheWolves alike have mutual grooming as part of their daily bonding, and many a gobshite Squire has mistaken their simple hand-me-down clothing and rough toilet for filth and ignorance. Alicia had known better from the day she'd first seen the Harprigg Wolves brought to Sprint Stables, when she'd noticed that the back of the minibus was as clean and neat as the creases in their kilts.

'Are you going to cut my hair today?' asked the SheWolf.

'Probably. A little.'

Without another word Maria whipped off her top, exposing not just her breasts but also her scars, including the livid red weal around her neck which could only have been caused by the enforced wearing of a collar.

Maria saw her staring and said, 'Rani will buy me a high-necked blouse to wear for the wedding. She says it will be too warm for a turtleneck jumper.'

Alicia moved on without comment, and by the time she'd finished, Maria looked less like a feral child and more like a student at a mundane university. The rest of the SheWolves had been casting glances, and Alicia had been listening carefully as Maria told her more about the history of the two Packs who had merged to become Birkfell. When Maria got out of the chair, the other Wolves looked away.

Alicia swept up the fallen hair and took the broom to Lowri the Elder, who spent most of her time sitting on a high chair because her Mage's Curse was so bad that anything else was painful. 'Would you like to be next?' asked Alicia.

'Not me,' said Lowri. 'Choose someone with more life ahead of them.'

'It should absolutely be you. The Elder should show that she is the power here.'

'Owww! Curse it! And how am I going to do that?'

'Come. Let me show you. Satisfaction guaranteed or I shall scrub the Hall tonight on my knees.'

'Did you hear that, girls?' said the Elder. 'What do you reckon?'

'I reckon we'll have a clean floor tonight if making you look good is the challenge,' said one of the Wolves from the shadows.

'Less of that, you,' said Lowri. 'Come on then.'

Alicia offered her arm, and the Elder took it, leaning heavily on her. The People make great supports. Once she was in the chair, she stared at the reflection of her almost waist-length hair. Barely a tenth part still had its natural colour. 'What you gonna do? Anything that puts me in the skin of the lamb and I'll set Guardian Karina on to you.'

What was that? *Skin of the lamb*? Aah. Wolf in sheep's … no! *Mutton dressed as lamb*. That's what the Elder meant. And good advice, too.

Alicia bent forwards, nearly resting her chin on Lowri's head and staring at their reflection, ignoring the rest of the Pack watching eagerly from where they were gathered behind them. 'How about this? Why be *grey* when you can be *silver*? Let me show you.'

Becoming accepted by the Pack was only the first step of Alicia's journey, though it did make life much easier. Her wing nubs were hurting, trying to unwind the rest of the Ink from Matching, and Alicia needed learning in the Ways, learning which her lady had scant time to offer and which life at Birk Fell did not make easy.

The Wednesday following, Alicia was taking time out from these thoughts and having some fun with Maria and Lottie when the world of Birk Fell shifted in a totally unexpected direction. The more she got to know Maria, the more Alicia was tempted to think of her as Eclipsed, and it was Faith who'd told her of the crimes committed by Sura in the past. Maria loved to dress up, and as a treat, Alicia had said that she would give them proper Elsa hair to go with their *Frozen* costumes. The white-haired Witch from the film was Maria's heroine, and Lottie was very much her mother's daughter.

The SheWolves did not want their face shapes changed but they did want the extravagantly blushed cheekbones of the cartoon character, and the light inside the Pack Hall was just too *yellow* for that. The low light suited Lowri's new look but make-up needs daylight, and why use Ink to make it when the sun gives light for free?

The three stepped out of the Hall, and Alicia was poised with the brush over Lottie's face when the cub screamed 'Auntie Kay!' and lifted her skirts to run up the yard. Alicia jerked her head up and beheld a strange sight indeed.

Three figures, two mortal and one of the People, stood by the gate. Both mortals were young, female and wore Goddess braids, but there the similarities ended. One stood braced for combat in sturdy outdoor wear, her Ancile glittering, and the other wore robes of the Sisters and was moving to stand behind the Warrior. No, not the Warrior. This must be Guardian Karina, the Archer.

As for the little Squire, Alicia could barely see her – there was so much Ink around her tiny frame that her mouth was obscured and her arms invisible.

Lottie ran up to the Archer, and then pointed to the unknown Squire. 'Who's she, and why does she smell of Quicksilver and death?'

'Lottie! Shh!' said Maria, who'd followed her daughter and dragged Alicia with her. 'Don't talk to the Guardian like that. She's probably captured an enemy, that's all.' Maria moved Lottie to one side and bowed to the Archer. 'Guardian, may I present…' She lifted her nose and tried to remember what to say. 'May I present Alicia, Squire of the Borrowdale People in the service of Princess Faith of Staveley in Cartmel.'

Alicia bowed to the Pack's true heroine – if the stories were true. 'Guardian, it is a great honour to be here. I am exalted beyond my time and I thank you for the hospitality.'

'What is she doing here?' asked the Archer.

'I can guess,' said the Sister of the Water, who seemed to find the situation amusing. 'She's doing the girls' hair is what she's doing. Why she's doing it is another matter.'

'It's Operation Barnet!' said Lottie, as if that explained everything. 'You have to come and see.'

Before the Archer could object, Lottie grabbed her hand and started dragging her towards the Pack Hall. 'Lottie, has someone been straightening your hair?' asked the Guardian.

'Yes, Auntie Kay. Well, Leesha tried to but she blew the floozy, so Madreb Faith had to get a Digger to fix it.'

'I...' The Archer stood lost for words, staring at the display board and the now slightly upgraded salon station.

Alicia felt very uneasy. The Pack held their Guardian in the highest esteem, and the look on the Archer's face did not bode well for Alicia. Princess Faith had made it very clear that in their lord's hierarchy, the People came well below the mortals of all description – human, Digger or Wolf. 'We're about level-pegging with his bloody dog,' her lady had concluded. 'On a good day.'

She was still staring and calculating, and the Sister of the Water still had a strange grin on her face when the mood was changed by Princess Faith's arrival. The Archer had not noticed that Faith was here, and Alicia started edging away towards the entrance.

'Guardian! You're back! I wasn't expecting you,' said Faith, then added in the People's tongue, 'Leesha, stop looking like the world has just ended and try to look like a handmaiden, not a spare part. Cathy, serve the tea.'

Cathy approached the mortals and said, 'Guardian? Miss Lewis? Refreshment after your journey?'

The Archer looked surprised for some reason. She took the mug (which Alicia had been warned against *ever* using) and sipped her tea. Then she placed the mug on a table and said, 'What's going on, Faith? Why is Alicia here and what's ... this? What's Operation Barnet?'

Faith walked to the wall and gestured at the picture of Mina. 'My lord has made me handmaiden to Rani for her wedding. I will attend her myself, and I have brought Alicia to work on the rest of the bridal party. And for practice, of course.'

'Of course what?'

Faith took Alicia's shoulder and lifted some of her glossy hair. 'Alicia was late shedding her wings because I wanted her to grow Rani's hair. It's an exact copy so that I can practise on it.' She let the hair fall and smiled.

The Guardian mulled this over for a second. 'What's this about the fuse box?'

'Aah. That. The power supply to the Pack Hall was not designed to cope with two Dyson hairdryers and professional grade GHDs. I got Clan Skelwith in, and they said I needed a new consumer unit, whatever that is, so they fitted one.' Faith gave the Archer a fun smile. 'At my own expense, of course.'

While the Guardian drank deeply from her mug, Princess Faith glanced at the shadows where the little Squire was lurking. 'Where on earth did you get her, and what's she doing here?'

The answer came from the Sister of the Water. Well, not the answer perhaps, but certainly a flood of words. 'We've been on an adventure, which goes to show that you should be careful what you wish for. Does Mina really have hair like that? Are you going to put it up for the wedding? What sort of wedding is it, anyway? Indian or English? Karina doesn't know, or she wouldn't tell me.' She dropped her voice to a whisper. 'What are you going to do with the Constable's hair?'

The Guardian interrupted, addressing Princess Faith. 'I'd like you to look at … Thistle. She has the runes which will free Corin, the ancient Guardian of the woods, but she also has what I'm told is a Hyde's Knot. I would have Corin freed, but not with Thistle's life as the price. She had no part in the evil.'

Princess Faith immediately took the Ink in her hands and examined it. 'Yes. It's complicated, and it's not without risk, but I can do it.' Then she stood back and grinned at the Archer.

'What do you want, Faith?'

The Princess pointed to Thistle. 'This one is mine to keep, and you will owe me a favour, Guardian.'

'What's the favour?'

Their lady did not reply, save with a smile.

'Done,' said the Guardian. 'Let's go straight away. Alex! Get the launch.'

Alicia was a little disappointed not to be going with them. She quite liked the lake and the boat, but that was work for those appointed above her. She went to help Cathy prepare refreshments, and while she was there Cathy told her about the Witch, who, it seemed, was around a lot and normally known as 'Becca'.

'What do you think of the Squire? Thistle, I mean,' she asked.

'I think that she'll be trouble. That's what I thought about you, too, and I was right. Let's hope she can cook something other than porridge.' Cathy sighed and lifted her top away from her overworked nipples. 'I've enough to do without having to learn the kitchen.'

Chapter Fifteen

Princess Faith and the others returned within the hour and brought the new Squire straight into the cottage, where Alicia and Cathy emerged from the kitchen to greet them. All of the Ink which had bound Thistle had gone, and Alicia got a good look at her. *She is barely an adult*, she thought. It was very, very rare for a Squire to emerge from the Matching in so young a form. For one thing, she would find it hard to move among mortals without causing trouble or attracting the wrong attention. The Great Queen alone knew what the nice policeman from Coniston would have done if he'd come across a *child* acting as if she were Eclipsed in the petrol station.

'This is Thistle, formerly in the household of the Duke of Tiree and fifteen years a Squire,' announced Princess Faith. Displeasure streaked across her face. 'Tiree has been heavily into the skin game for some time. It's why he's been banished, and Thistle here was one of his stars, weren't you?'

'No so much a star, my lady. 'S why I was banished tae the kitchens.'

'What did she say?' asked Alicia. 'What was that language?'

'Scots,' said Cathy. 'I think.'

'Well, I'm not going to play the skin game,' said Faith. 'Thistle, if you join my household, you will be cook, cleaner and maid while we live here. It will be hard, and you'll have to make your bed by the fire as there's no room upstairs. Or I can send you to the Derwent Sídhe to join Her Grace. She is merciful and she will welcome you. Your future there would be safe and guaranteed.'

Thistle fell to her knees. 'You saved me. I was made death and you saved me.'

Faith extended a hand for Thistle to kiss. 'I will Ink your new Name when the mortals have left. Welcome. Cathy and Alicia will look after you.'

Faith left to see to the Guardian, and Cathy took the new member of the household into the kitchen. Alicia was left to wander outside and check on the Wolves, where she saw a strange thing up by the gate, hidden from general view. The Witch with flame hair took the Guardian's face in her hands and gently kissed her lips.

Mortals. They never ceased to amaze.

Alicia had heard of the 'skin game', of course – providing sexual pleasures for mortals was as much a part of the People's world as hunting, racing and warfare were. Indeed, Alicia had fetched and carried behind the scenes at several parties in the Borrowdale Sídhe when she still had wings. However, there was a *big* difference between inviting mortals into your bed for sport and charging them for it, and Her Grace the Red Queen would have nothing to do with it. Neither, it seemed, would Princess Faith.

That night, the Pack were celebrating the release of Corin of the Woods, and for the first time since Alicia's arrival they made a hunt, with all the adults

Exchanging at once. When it happened, Alicia was filled with awe and respect for their grace and their power. Not so Thistle. The little Squire had been almost clinging to Cathy all day, and as the Pack slipped easily into their new forms, Cathy had to grab Thistle's arm to stop her running away. And that was not all.

Alicia had asked for tea to be brought to the Pack Hall, and when it had been delivered with no biscuits, Thistle had cringed and nearly dropped the tray, bracing herself for a beating and jabbering an apology which Alicia barely understood.

The next day, Princess Faith announced a surprise: she would be going to the Equinox celebration at Waterhead, and Alicia was to accompany her. 'If I collapse, you won't be able to drive me home, but at least you could call for help. We're going to meet someone special. Someone you need to see, Leesha.

'Right now, we're going shopping. The Wolves need some stuff and we need to get Thistle something else to wear.' She gave the new kitchen maid a dark look. 'Thieving from the Pack will always be noticed. Five minutes and we're off to Penrith.'

Four minutes later, Alicia and Thistle met outside and both reached for the front door to get in with their lady. They were both Squires, and Squires do not have a hierarchy – as such. Every Knight and noble has a place in their lord or lady's household, and they all have a place within their People, as recorded in a book kept by the Chamberlain in the Royal Sídhe. Not so the Squires. They have to fight it out for precedence, and that's exactly what Alicia and Thistle did.

Alicia was Princess Faith's Bonded Squire of the same People, but Thistle was much older. Alicia was bigger and stronger, but Thistle was faster and had been in a lot more fights. If there had been another of the People there – a neutral one, of course – they would have watched and licked their lips at the prospect of an evenly matched contest.

Faith had still been in the cottage when Thistle and Alicia both approached the car. Their eyes locked in challenge. Thistle whipped out a kitchen knife from the belt of her kilt and made a stab at Alicia's leg; Alicia knew it wasn't a blood blow, just a threat to force her back. She still had to avoid it though: the People do not pull their punches with each other.

Alicia jumped back, and that left Thistle in pole position by the front seat. Thistle pulled the handle and cried in frustration: locked. Alicia took the long scissors out of her beautician's tool belt and stepped forwards. Thistle had her back to the car, and nowhere to go. It was fight to blood or surrender the door. She surrendered by dodging to the side.

That left neither of them by the door, and with both of them armed, there was no choice but to carry on in blood or wait for their lady's judgement. Alicia looked at Thistle's knife hand, and it shimmered a fraction, moving slightly away from the mortal realm. Alicia grinned. Blood it was.

'Pack it in, you two,' shouted Faith. She strode towards them, fishing in her bag for the car keys. 'You're worse than bloody children, the pair of you.' She found the keys and unlocked the doors. 'Today, you will both sit in the back. Next time, you'll toss a coin then take it in turns.' She fastened her bag. 'And, Thistle, I'm warning you. Scullery maids are ten a penny and you're easily replaced. However, even though handmaids are just as common, I cannot get another qualified hairdresser at this short notice. Understood?'

Thistle had bowed her head. 'My lady is wise. Rani's needs must always come first. I understand.'

'Good.'

That night, when their lady and Cathy had retired for healing, Thistle invited Alicia to join her by the hearth and said, 'It will be a year before our lady becomes a Queen. If we work together, you can become her handmaiden for life and I can become housekeeper. At least. Maybe even Counsellor for you and Chamberlain for me! What do you say?'

Before Alicia could react, Thistle clutched her arm and said, 'I've never known anything but pots and pans and baring my body for a mortal's beating or worse. You can teach me, and I can teach you.' The clutching fingers became an iron grip, and Thistle hissed, 'Sisters in the Sídhe.'

Alicia's mouth became dry, and she whispered back, 'What could I teach *you*? You are fifteen years a Squire.'

'To read, for one thing. And how to use a phone.'

That was true. It would also make Thistle much more useful to their lady. 'What can you teach me?'

'The Ways. The nubbins of your wings have scarred and will soon be gone from your back. I saw them this morning. I worship our Lady and owe her my life, but you can't deny that she has little time for your teaching, does she?'

Thistle bared her teeth and showed her People's smile, and Alicia knew it for the truth. She forced her mortal jaw back and brought out her inner teeth, then locked them with Thistle's. They were now Sisters in the Sídhe, bound to each other and second only to their bond with the Princess.

Alicia liked looking at maps, she had discovered. The People mostly use them as part of treaties – to agree boundaries and to show ownership. When it comes to roaming the world, they rely on their senses. All of them.

But when you are bound to a diminutive holding like Birk Fell, escaping by map can be fun. And there is much learning to it.

When they needed a break, Thistle and Alicia liked to go in opposite directions: Thistle went down to the small jetty because she loved the lake and the water; Alicia went to the helicopter landing zone.

It wasn't that she didn't love Ullswater – she did. It's just that the LZ had artificial grass, was well drained and showed her the fells to the east and south. Up there, Alicia made Memories, tried (and usually failed) to practise the Ways, and when exhausted, she would look at a map.

Alicia had found herself trying to copy Maria the Mannwolf's magick the other day, and it was a good job they'd been outside at the time. Even so, Alicia had lost several nails rebuilding the dry stone wall after the *accident*. Oops. To show that she could learn, Alicia had Inked all of that, too, including her failures.

And then there were the mortals, humans and Diggers both. Their lord and lady were their sun and moon, of course, but Rani was a princess, not a Priestess, so she could teach Alicia nothing of magick. As for their lord … How in the name of the Great Queen was Faith going to…? Alicia shuddered at the thought. The Lord Protector had come out one day to work on the – what was the name? *Ley line*. That's it. The Ley line from the Pack Hall to the Smurf's landing zone. Not only did his blade smell of n'Haeval, *his magick did too*. And if his magick did, then…? She forced herself not to think about *that*.

Their lord and lady were with them much, but the most frequent mortal visitors were Guardian Karina (with or without Becca the Witch) and Enscriber Erin. The Guardian didn't like the People. At all. A fact she made plain every time she set foot on Pack ground. If it wasn't so ridiculous, Alicia would have said that Princess Faith and Guardian Karina were engaged in some sort of battle.

In one of her grumpy moments, when the Change was upon her, Faith had called the Guardian 'The Pale Footman'. It was not wise to joke about such things, in Alicia's opinion. Lady Agnes had never joked about Pale Horsemen, and thinking of Lady Agnes brought Alicia back to the subject of her new Sister.

Thistle was doing her *best*, Alicia supposed, but the problem was that Thistle had never had to teach anyone anything and she was not someone with natural patience.

When Alicia failed yet again, Thistle would say, 'Can you no see it? It's as plain as the nose on Sophie's face. Emphasis on the *plain*, you ken? And why do you think Robbie's wasting his time with *her* when he could have *me*, eh?'

The first encounter between Alicia's Sister and Alicia's broodmate had been like a strike of lightning. Princess Faith had taken them on an expedition beyond Birk Fell, with a trip to Kendal so that Alicia could visit the beauty wholesalers and to Longsleddale for Thistle to see Sprint Stables. When they walked into the stable yard, Thistle ignored everything but Robbie, whom they encountered with his shirt off and the hoof of the great stallion Scipio braced between his legs while he examined his shoe.

'Tell me tha's no Robbie,' Thistle said. ''Cos if it is, then all the gods have smiled on me this year.'

'Yes,' said Alicia. 'He is 2nd in our brood.'

Thistle turned to her Sister and said, 'He's yours if you want him, then. Do you?'

And at that moment, Alicia realised that she *didn't* want to compete for Robbie. Not now. Not yet. One day, perhaps, when Sophie had been put aside, and hopefully after Alicia had found her own Sophie (male or female), they would be together. Until then…

'Robbie is my noble Champion. There is no traffic between a noble Champion and his lady.'

'Then game on, eh … What? Who's that skanky mortal feeling his arse?'

'Sophie, our lady's head groom. Nadya will be trainer if she lives, and Sophie is head groom.' Alicia nudged Thistle to get her undivided attention (not easy when there were Robbie's rippling abs to focus on). 'Sophie has the personal favour and protection of our Lord Protector. The Dragonslayer. Him. Remember him?'

'Oh. Aye. Good to know.'

And so the competition had begun. Or it had begun in Thistle's head, because since that day, neither Squire had gone beyond Birk Fell. Until today – and it was Alicia who was getting the day out.

She hadn't believed just how far away from mortals her home at Birk Fell was until she had traced the road on a map with her finger, and now she knew why Princess Faith kept a vehicle on the western shore and usually ventured there by boat. That was how they began their trip to Waterhead on the night before the Equinox.

They had to be at Waterhead before dawn, and Faith was taking no chances. A lot of VIPs would be there, including their lord and lady, and they would get to meet someone whom Faith saw as a potential Void Engineer and who was a member of the bridal party (which is what bothered Alicia). The fact that Tammy Pike was also a bodysnatcher fascinated both the Princess and her Squire.

King Alex turned the boat around and headed back to Birk Fell while Faith dismantled the Glamour on her car and got in. At this hour on a Sunday morning, the lake was utterly quiet and still except for the receding sound of the Pack launch.

Faith pulled onto the road and sped off towards Patterdale. 'I don't want to do this, Leesha, but I'm going to have to. There are going to be way too many people with way too much power at Waterhead today. I simply can't risk you running amok and, I don't know … calling out Tammy Pike as a murderer, or telling the Clan Chief that he stinks like a night in a skin house, or taking a bite out of Alex Greening's thigh.'

Alicia lowered her head and blinked. The heating was going full-force into her face and making her eyes water. 'I would do none of those things, my lady.'

'Better safe than sorry. I'm going to bind your mouth before we enter the grounds. Don't worry, I'll hide it completely so that no one will know.'

Alicia had seen many Memories of the grounds in front of the old School House at Waterhead Academy – including the fateful night of the Waterhead Chase, when the horrible crimes of the Greenings and Ripleys had been revealed. When they emerged from the trees which concealed the park, she tipped her hat to the mortals: they had made the most of an imposing space and turned it into something filled with power and menace. *Respect.*

They were here for the mortal celebration of the Equinox. Not a festival celebrated by the People, but one they acknowledged and were happy to join in with from the sidelines. Today the mortals would be sacrificing their pride to the sun by burning their Yuletide decorations. It was fitting.

As Alicia and Faith closed the gap to where the ceremony would take place, right by the water, Alicia dropped two paces behind her lady. Faith was heading for a group in which the Dragonslayer stood out, head and shoulders above three women – one young, one old and one both old and young. Oh, and there was his dog, too.

Faith approached and bowed to Conrad and Mina. As she stood up, the Dragonslayer said, 'Morning, Faith. May I introduce the Keeper of the Queen's Esoteric Library, Doctor Francesca Somerton? And this is Tamsin Pike.'

'Well met,' said Faith.

'Well met indeed,' said the Keeper. Now there was a mortal with hidden depths: Alicia could read almost nothing of her, so carefully guarded was her magick. There was certainly a lot of it, though.

'How d'you do?' said the Bodysnatcher, offering a handshake after bowing.

Princess Faith shook both the women's hands, and when she saw them staring at Alicia (in particular at Alicia's hair), she pointed behind her and said, 'This is my handmaiden, Alicia Lake.'

'Excuse us,' said the Dragonslayer. 'Tammy? Would you mind holding Scout during the ceremony? Thanks.'

He passed over the lead of a very bored (but very handsome) sheepdog, and then he and Rani Mina went to stand closer to the ceremony, as befitted the Commissioner. Alicia sneaked a glance at the Bodysnatcher, but the mortal was too far away for her to assess either her magick or her hair and features. She had a trim and toned body, and would almost certainly show up some of the other bridesmaids unless Shear Magic were very careful.

As the young mortal made the sacrifice, Alicia said the words in her head and looked down, and when the voices stopped, she could hear the waves lap on the shore. She was still looking down when screams and shouts shattered the silence. The young Mages were running around throwing powder and magick everywhere, and the congregation was descending into chaos all around. Now this *was* unexpected. Alicia jumped and clapped her hands with excitement as colour exploded and Scout the dog ran riot. She was a little disappointed that the students avoided their group (for some reason), so she followed them to School House unadorned by powder. At least she wouldn't have to wash it out later.

It was good to get out of the cold and Inside the cosy warmth of the old building, and even better to have her lips released so that she could eat breakfast. Princess Faith did not do bindings by half.

'You'd better leave that seat,' said the Bodysnatcher, when Alicia went to hide in the corner. 'That seat's next to the radiator, and if I know Mina, she'll want it for herself.' Alicia was going to back away, but Tammy had more to say. 'Can I look at that hair? It's … amazing.'

Alicia smiled and stood for inspection, then retreated and asked what she could get them from the canteen servery for breakfast. The others were talking about people Alicia had never heard of as she served them, and then Rani joined them and all the talk was of the wedding, and the Bodysnatcher became quite animated. Alicia could see something wrong with the woman's aura but couldn't put her finger on it, or couldn't put it into words. No denying her power, though.

And then their lord's business was finished, and so was Alicia's breakfast. As previously ordered, she left them to it and retreated to the hallway. A pair of mortal women with a well-swaddled child in a pram emerged from the depths of the building, and Alicia jumped to hold the great doors open for them. Alicia thought that the woman who hadn't given birth might be … yes. A Daughter of the Earth.

'You can have a look if you want,' said the other one, the mother. A Witch, in fact. 'So long as you're not planning to swap him for one of yours.'

'Gloria!' said the Daughter of the Earth. 'You can't say that. Are you one of Faith's new Squires?'

'I am,' said Alicia. 'Well met.'

'In peace, well met. I'm Grazia Brathay-Whitfield, this is my wife, Gloria, and that's our son, little Grant.'

The baby was not Grazia's at all, but that's mortals for you. 'You are the Chief's daughter. I am honoured. I have heard my lord speak with fondness of his time at your hotel.'

'That's good to hear. Thank you.'

Alicia peered down at the swaddled infant. 'He is beautiful and healthy.'

The women smiled with pride, and Alicia remembered something she'd been thinking about for days now. 'A question, if I may, my lady. How do you clean the sheets at your hotel?'

Gloria snorted with laughter. Her hair was newly dyed and cut short (and not by an expert). Grazia, though, answered the question without hesitation. 'Lakes Laundry. They take it away and bring it back.' A sly grin came over the

Daughter's face. 'Unlike the Derwent Sídhe, or so I've heard.'

Alicia nodded an acknowledgement and, as the women hadn't yet moved away, added, 'And how do Lakes Laundry clean the sheets?'

'With a conveyor washing machine and a rolling-press steam iron. According to the website. I don't have first-hand experience of it.'

'You are kind and gracious, my lady. Thank you.'

The women finished wrapping themselves up and headed into the cold. To get away from the dark hall, Alicia followed them outside and found Jocasta Greening trying to walk Scout. Jocasta was their enemy's child, but Scout was their lord's hound and Alicia had nothing else to do, so she ran up and offered to help – Jocasta's arm was still in a sling, and it had been Her Grace who had broken it.

'Do you want a hand with the dog?'

Jocasta looked at her. 'Why would you help me? What are you after?'

'You are my enemy, but this is my lord's hound. If he pulls you over and breaks your arm again, he will be in trouble, and so will my lord. I would avoid that.'

Jocasta shook her head and said, 'Totally weird. Every time. Here you go. Mind if I find some shelter? It's freezing out here when you don't have a thermostat like you lot. And you can have these, too. I think the Commissioner got a bit confused when he handed over the treats. Not sure I'd risk *these* on a dog. Not one I was gonna put in the car, and I wouldn't wish that on my worst enemy.'

Alicia took the lead, and now that her good arm was free, Jocasta dug in her pocket and offered Alicia a small bag of treats and a larger bag of … *curried worms*!

'Thank you,' said Alicia. 'The Dragonslayer says that these have been vital in saving his life. You're right, though – I don't think they'd agree with Scout's digestive system.'

'Good luck, and, erm, well met and all that,' said the mortal, before scuttling off and pulling a phone out of her other pocket.

Scout looked at Alicia and spoke to her, rather indignantly. 'Arff!'

'And the same to you, workhound. Would you like to smell something nice?' She made the scent of venison in her hand and offered it to the dog (easily done – she'd eaten little else for days). He sniffed, then licked, then barked with joy.

Alicia was filled pleasure at the day. She had kept her obligation to the immortals, she had seen the mortals at play, she had been complimented by Rani at breakfast ('You should think of going fully Indian, Alicia, you totally rock that hair already!') and she had not disgraced the Princess, who now, it seemed, would have a mortal working on the Royal Sídhe. It was the perfect preparation for the coming week, when in just four days her lady would be taking her to Elvenham Grange.

'Come on, workhound. Let's go for a run.'
'Arff!'

Chapter Sixteen

Alicia was more excited than on any day since the day she'd dropped her wings, submitted to the Matching and turned from *it* to *she*. What a day that had been, and what a day today was already becoming.

She was more excited than when Faith had accepted her pledge of service, more excited than when she'd been presented to Rani Mina, more excited than when she'd seen just how *fit* Robbie had become, more excited than when she'd met the Pack (and their weird Guardian), more excited than when the Enscriber presented Operation Barnet, more—

'Shut up! Shut up, shut up, shut UP!' said Princess Faith through gritted teeth. 'If you start drivelling like that at the Grange, I will cut out your overworked tongue, slice it up and make you serve it to Conrad and Mina on cocktail sticks.'

'Do mortals eat ... oh. Sorry, my lady. Was I speaking aloud again?'

'Yes, you effing well were. We're not at Birk Fell now, you know, and you don't need to speak *all* your thoughts to practise your English. In fact, the fewer thoughts you speak from now on, the better. Clear?'

'Mmm!'

'May the Great Queen give me strength! I'd forgotten just how hard it is to work with Squires, especially when someone else hasn't broken them in, and I've got five of you. *Five!*' She laughed. 'Knowing my luck, I'll end up having to get you to break them in for me in the future, and then where will the household be?'

Alicia shrank back from the swirl of Ink leaking from her lady's hands. She did not want to arrive at the Dragonslayer's house with no voice. Even so, she'd been asked a question: *and then where will we be?* Unless...

'Was that rhetorical, my lady?'

'In one hundred yards, turn right into Elven Lane. Your destination is on the right,' said the Dwarf. No, not the Dwarf – the *satnav*. Why they made satnav voices sound like Dwarves was a question that had worried Alicia since they left Birk Fell, a question which she was now too afraid to ask.

The car turned, and in unison they turned their faces away from the House of the Crucified God on the corner, where they were no doubt gearing up for their big festival this weekend.

'Arriving at your destination.'

They couldn't miss it. Not with a gleaming plaque proclaiming *Elvenham Grange*, and then the gravel drive and the Wards that were going to ping an announcement of their arrival any second ... *now*.

'They're strong,' said Alicia.

'And according to Conrad, stronger still on the house. He reckons we'll get nowhere near it.'

'But that was before you came! You'll get through, my lady.'

The house came into view. Seconds later, Faith slammed on the brakes, scattering gravel and slewing the rear wheels. 'I don't think we will, you know.'

'Hmm,' whimpered Alicia. All she wanted to do was get out and run away: every swirl of Ink on her body was throbbing painfully. Faith glanced right, then grabbed the gearstick and looked over her shoulder. With more gravel spraying around, she reversed away from the front door and towards a gate in a brick wall to the side.

The pain subsided, and Alicia felt *sticky* in places she didn't want to feel sticky. Not if she was going to meet Rani. 'Those Wards, my lady! A mortal made them?'

'Yes. Mortals can slay Dragons and raise the dead these days. Or so I've heard. And that was irony.'

The front doors of the house opened, and Rani Mina was standing on the steps, beckoning them over.

Faith got out first and leaned on the car. 'Sorry about the gravel. Leesha will rake it later,' she shouted, clearly reluctant to get any closer.

Rani Mina jumped down the steps and came towards them. 'Are the Wards that bad? And how is your leg? Thank you for getting in the way and saving Conrad's life.'

'Leg's fine, thanks. Unlike the Wards. They *are* bad. Doctor Mowbray will have to do something radical to them if you want us inside the house at any point.'

'Then that is what she will have to do. I shall arrange it, and don't worry about the gravel; that is what we have men for.' She paused. 'Unfortunately, we are a man down: Conrad had a late start because of that business with the Warden, and now he's stuck in traffic.'

Rani gave Faith a long look that Alicia couldn't understand, then said, 'Was there anything I should know about what our twice-deceased late Warden said?'

Faith shook her head. 'Conrad was more bothered about the isolation unit in Furness than anything else. Even for me, it was pretty distracting.'

When Faith had come back from the Radiant Sídhe, she had been more troubled than at any time since the Outcasts' Revolt (or the Peace of Brothers Water, as she was supposed to call it). Alicia had been going to ask what was wrong, but Thistle had taken her arm and whispered, in a weird voice, 'Only a fool goes looking for more trouble.'

Mina nodded thoughtfully. 'Thank you, Faith. I am under orders from Conrad to say that even if you're not going inside the house, you still have to greet the dragon. After that, if you follow the path through that gate, you'll find the stables. They're unlocked and ready.' She glanced uncomfortably towards the gardens. 'I'm really sorry, Faith, but I have to go out. The Tesco delivery today had so many bizarre substitutions that I shall have to go and do the job myself or we'll be eating toothpaste-flavoured chicken paneer with dried pasta. Ugh.'

'No problem,' said Faith. 'Is anyone else here?'

'Only Myfanwy, and she's having a lie-down. I shall give her a nudge and tell her you're here. She'll be out shortly. I have no idea when everyone else will arrive. This is *not* how I planned things.'

'It will all come off perfectly, Rani,' said Alicia reassuringly. 'Bound to.'

'If only I had your faith, Leesha.' She glanced at Faith and gave a crooked smile. 'I suppose I do have your Faith. See you later.'

Rani Mina went back inside with a wave, and Alicia studied the house properly. She had a very small sample to compare it against, even from the outside. Their cottage at Birk Fell was tiny compared to this, of course, and Elvenham Grange was tiny next to the Derwent Sídhe. It was much bigger than the farmhouse at Sprint Stables, but not as grand as School House at Waterhead, though it did have some of its features. And that exhausted Alicia's range of comparisons.

'Can you see the dragon?' said Faith.

This question didn't *sound* rhetorical, so Alicia looked again. The Grange was built from red bricks, apart from the white patch over the door … Ah. Why couldn't she see what it was? 'Do we have to go closer, my lady?'

'I very much think we do. Give me your hand, Little One.'

Faith had spoken in the People's tongue. Alicia had heard other nobles use 'Little One' as an insult to the newly wingless but her lady sounded serious, as if she needed to give Alicia comfort, so Alicia said nothing and took the Princess's hand.

Their Ink merged, and Alicia took strength as they walked a few steps. 'By the Lords of Neverwhere, that is *deep*,' said Faith, still in the People's tongue.

'What is it?'

'It *was* the sign for a Dragon's Nest. Still might be, somewhere, but not here in the house. And it's been re-used and re-formed an awful lot.' Faith switched to English. 'Let's get it over with before I bite another hole in my lip. I'm going to let go, so try not to scream.'

Their hands – and their Ink – slipped apart, and Alicia felt the acid burn of copper magick crawling across her skin once more. Oh, this was baaad.

'Great Wyrm, we come in peace,' said Faith.

'What she said,' echoed Alicia, her feet moving backwards of their own accord.

When they'd both retreated and caught their breath, Alicia risked a question. 'Are you going to tell the Dragonslayer about it? About something living here?'

'If he didn't already know, I'm sure he was told all about it by the great and mighty Eseld Mowbray, shagger of other women's husbands. And don't repeat that.' Faith shuddered and looked again. 'The way La Mowbray draped her Wards over the *m'Ghenz* is arrogant, to say the least.'

Alicia didn't like this. 'If our lord knew, why did he not tell us?'

'Because our lord has more secrets than Gertha the Spider, that's why. Get the cases, and I'll see just how deep my humiliation is. Working in a fucking stables indeed.'

The Princess grabbed her bag and limped off, banging the iron gate open as if it were made of chicken wire. Alicia spent a long time dragging the cases over the back seat, then remembered there was a button to open the lid on the car. By the time she'd carried the first load through the gate, her Princess had calmed down.

'What are you staring at?' said Faith. 'Anyone would think you hadn't seen a Herbal garden before.'

'I haven't! The Herbal at Derwent is nothing like mortals' work. This one is so … mysterious. In a good way. I can't furlong it.'

Faith laughed. 'Fathom. You can't *fathom* it. Conrad told me that there's a huge marijuana bush hidden somewhere. You'll have to try it later, but watch out: unlike opium and opioids, cannabis works a treat on the People. Let me give you a hand – the stables are actually quite nice.'

Alicia had spotted the marijuana straight away: the Ink hiding it was surface deep. No, it was something else that was strange. Something she couldn't put her toe on. She giggled: *put her toe on.* She'd have to remember that one.

The stables were indeed *quite nice*. The one where the Enscriber used to work was perfect, and it even had a Hawker's Board outside. When Alicia had finished bringing the cases in, Faith had said, 'I need to walk the grounds. There's a lot going on, magickally, even without Mowbray's Wards. You unpack, and why don't you have some fun with the sign?'

Shortly later, Alicia stood in front of the Hawker's Board. It was sleeping at the moment, and having it function would be a joy to the day. If only she could manipulate the stupid thing.

A Memory uncurled from her shoulder, and she was back in the Derwent Sídhe, her wings still wet from the Pool, her tongue barely loose in her mouth. *Begin with what you know.* It had been Lady Agnes's first lesson in Inking, so Alicia brought the Board to life and read its dormant message. *Erin's Ink. Calligraphy, Illustration and Enscribing by Erin.* Ugh. Why did she have to debase the word *Ink* like that?

Lady Agnes was right. From here, it was actually easy to reformulate the script to something new. A quick twist and it was done. *Shear Magic. Hair and Beauty you can only dream of.* Alicia stepped back with a smile, and then she discovered what mortals mean by *jumping out of your skin.*

'Hello, Mina! What … Oh. I'm sorry. I thought you were Mina, from the back.'

Egg and wings! It was Lord Alfred, father to the Lord Protector. Alicia bowed low. 'Forgive me, my lord. I did not hear you approach. I am Alicia Lake, handmaiden to Faith.'

You could see that Conrad was his father's son from the twinkle in the older man's eye. 'Are you now?' he said. 'Are you a friend of Rachael's or Victoria's? Outdoor theatre? Something to do with the wedding, perhaps?'

Hadn't their lord told his father who they were? Strange. Alicia was at a loss, so she waved her hand at the Hawker's Board and smiled the mortal smile. It had worked a treat on the man at the motorway service station.

'*Shear Magic*. I like that. Sorry, Ms Lake, I really did think you were Mina. That's not a wig, is it?'

'Oh no, my lord. See?' She tugged hard at a fistful. 'It is Rani's hair from the root to the tip. It will become a wig in time. Would you like to feel it?'

She stepped forwards and offered it to Lord Alfred to stroke. He couldn't examine it with magick, of course, but the texture was rich and silky, a pleasure to the fingers.

Lord Alfred touched two fingers to his lips and lifted his eyebrows. 'Well, that's not an offer I get every day, but I'd better say no. Thank you all the same.'

Another mortal appeared, and again, you could see the Lord Protector in her height and her bearing. It must be Lady Mary. 'You most certainly better had say *no*, Alfred!'

Her lord looked hurt for some reason, and said, 'I did, didn't I? And that was before I knew you were creeping up on me.'

'Hmmph,' said Lady Mary, then her eyes narrowed and bore right through Alicia. Even Her Grace couldn't match *that* stare. Not without Ink. 'You're one of those Fae creatures, aren't you? What are you doing here?'

Lord Alfred leapt to Alicia's defence. 'I'm sure it's part of her professional persona, Mary.'

'Go and take the luggage inside, Alfred, and see if Mina's left a note or something.'

Alicia bounced up on her toes. She could help with that one. 'Rani Mina has gone to market, my lady, and the Druid is asleep. And Lord Conrad is—'

A cough from behind. Faith was back. Alicia felt very comforted.

'What Leesha is trying to say is that we got here earlier than expected, so Mina asked us to wait outside while she shopped for food.'

'I'll deal with this, Alfred. Cases. Please. It's to do with … the hen party. Women's things.'

Lord Alfred looked from his lady to Faith to Alicia. He clearly didn't believe a word. 'If that's the case, then I'll go. Pleased to meet you both.'

Lady Mary pursed her lips while her lord extended his hand and shook with Faith, then offered it to Alicia. *Don't kiss it. Don't kiss it. Don't kiss it.* She returned his firm but gentle grip and bobbed a slight curtsy.

He smiled and walked slowly away. The three of them stood still until Lady Mary was satisfied that he couldn't hear. '*Are* you Fae creatures? Both of you? And did Conrad not tell you that Alfred is blind to magick? Completely blind?'

Faith went still for a fraction of a second before bowing. 'I am Faith of Staveley, Princess of the Borrowdale People and bonded servant of your son, Mrs Clarke. This is my handmaid, Alicia. Mina invited us and welcomed us in peace. As you may know, we are unable to cross your threshold. I am sorry for Alicia's behaviour.'

Lady Mary was clearly *not* blind to magick, because Alicia saw her nose dilate when Faith introduced herself using Power-in-Name. Lady Mary blinked. 'Oh. I see. Looks like Conrad needs a lesson on *need to know*. Not your fault. And what is it exactly you do for him?' She waved a hand. 'I assume that this is just a sideline?'

'I do what my lord bids me. So far he has bid me supervise his Wolves and become Mina's hairdresser and beautician. One is far more interesting than the other.'

'*Wolves*, did you say? Never mind. I'll get the story from him later.' She turned to Alicia. 'Just one thing, dear. Don't call Alfred *lord*, and I don't mind people calling my daughter-in-law *Rani* as an occasional joke, but it doesn't do in public and I can't believe she made you do it.'

Alicia trembled. *What have I done wrong?*

'Forgive her,' said Faith. 'Her English is still growing, and she tends to translate literally from the People's tongue. It's Conrad and Mina, and Mr and Mrs Clarke from now on.'

Mrs Clarke smiled. 'Conrad has a lot of explaining to do. And it's Alfred and Mary.'

She hadn't finished with Alicia, though. 'What was that nonsense about your hair?'

When Faith offered no explanation, Alicia did the only thing she could. She told the truth. 'It was given to me when I shed my wings so that my lady can practise styles for Mina. When it is done, I will shed it and weave it into a wig for Mina so that she will always have it, no matter what. A wedding gift.'

'It does look creepy, you know. To us *mortals*.'

Faith had the answer to that. 'Only to those without magick. Leesha's hair will be gone before the actual wedding weekend, don't worry. She's still deciding whether or not to become a redhead. For a change.'

Mary sighed and shook her head. 'I was thrilled when Conrad brought Mina home, criminal record notwithstanding. I couldn't wish for a better daughter-in-law. I just never thought that their wedding would turn into such a three ring circus. Have you been offered refreshment? No? I'll sort it out and then have strong words with my son.'

Alicia didn't wait for her to go, nor did she attempt a Silence. She just reverted to the People's tongue. 'Have I done you great wrong, my lady?'

Faith *did* put up a Silence. And stuck to English. 'No, Leesha, you have not. I think that *Conrad* and *Mina* are going to be very uneasy tonight, and it will be all their own fault.' She cancelled the Silence. 'I also think I'd better stick around.'

'What did you find in the gardens, my lady?'

'Later. Looks like we have some refugees on the way.'

'Refugees?'

'Displaced people escaping conflict. In this case, the conflict between Mary and her son. See?'

As it happened, none of the wolves had been with cub since Alicia had arrived at Birk Fell, so the Druid was her first experience of a pregnant mortal. Very pregnant in this case, judging by the size of her belly. And next to her was their lord's brood-sister, the one called Rachael. They looked to be laughing at something. Rachael was carrying a tray with four steaming mugs on it.

'Try to act more human,' said Faith.

'I'm trying!' Alicia responded. 'It's not easy when you've only met a few of them and they're all so *different.*'

'Then channel someone and act like them.'

Their clients stopped laughing, and the Druid said, 'Well met, ladies,' and bowed.

Chapter Seventeen

If you want to know all about the Elvenham Incursion and what happened at the hen party, then you really have to know about Easter, and about Maundy Thursday in particular. I'll try not to tell you about it with *too* much hindsight but, you know, some of the things that didn't make sense at the time make a lot more sense now.

I hate driving in London. Not only is it an utter pain in the arse, but I can rent out the designated parking space allocated to my flat in Mayfair and receive enough income from Faisal on the ground floor to pay for as many Ubers as I want, so when I leave London, I usually take a train to the nearest decent city and hire a car. Much simpler. And when I have to pick up the parents, it's even better because Birmingham airport is only an hour and a quarter from Euston and there are loads of options for car hire from there. Sometimes I can even charge it to the business. Only sometimes, and I'm not just saying that because Detective Chief Inspector Economic Crimes is going to read this.

Eseld had invited me to Pellacombe for Easter, and I was sorely tempted. I *do* love that house, and I really wanted to meet Morwenna and see what all the fuss was about, but I couldn't be in two places at once. Conrad says that Dwarves can, but I wasn't going to grow a beard for anyone. As ever with me, duty won out over a hedonistic weekend of luxury, and I picked up M&D from Arrivals like the good girl I am.

Obviously I didn't mention Elvenham's non-human visitor in the car: it's really awkward having to remember that Dad has rejected the world of magick, and I'd almost forgotten about her myself until we got home. Seeing the glossy 4x4 reversed up to the garden gate was a bit of a giveaway, though. Mina had WhatsApped me to say that she'd nipped out to Tesco, so I assumed she'd left Conrad behind. Big mistake.

'Who's that?' said Mum, pointing to the Fairy chariot.

'The wedding hairdresser,' I replied. 'She's doing the hen party too, so she's come down to cast her eye over me and Myfanwy and try a few styles on Mina. She'll be in the stables.'

'Come on, Alfred,' said Mum. 'Let's go and see what they're up to. You can sort the cases, Rachael, because Conrad's leg will be playing him up after the journey.'

See what I have to put up with? Conrad gets himself in trouble and it's a free pass for life. I grumbled but said hello to the dragon before dragging the cases up the steps. I'll say one thing for Mina coming into our lives: her insistence on getting the front door fixed has made arriving home a lot simpler.

Except that when I say *home*, I'm talking poetically, of course. I pushed open the great Gothic door and was immediately swept away by the Celtic tsunami of Myfanwy.

She was standing at the bottom of the stairs, her tunic scrunched up over her boobs and fighting a losing battle with her leggings. 'Hiya, Rachael. I could have sworn these were over-the-bump leggings but I can't get them up, and I can't find the special red ones I was gonna wear for Mary 'n' Alfred coming.' She gave the top seam another fruitless tug. 'I can't have grown in my sleep, can I? Or did I just pick up the wrong pair? Shall I change them? Nah, can't be bothered. Had a good journey? Oh, I love that top, is it silk? Of course it's silk, silly me. Where's Mary and Alfred? Come to that, where's Conrad and Mina?'

'Mina's nipped out to Tesco. Have you only just got up?'

'Prepping for the weekend didn't half take it out of me, so I had forty winks. I expected Conrad to be here by now, and I only woke up when Faith tried to get through the Wards. Like a fire alarm in a match factory it was! Proper gave me a fright.'

'You mean Conrad *isn't* here?'

'No.'

She paused to lower her tunic, and I dumped the cases and headed for the kitchen before she could start again. 'I think we should put the kettle on. There may be a need for hot sweet tea shortly.'

She followed me down the corridor and asked, 'Whatever for? I have my cravings, but I still can't stand sugar in tea. And I'm feeling fine.'

I filled the kettle and put it on the Aga as my phone pinged with another message from Mina: *Forgot to tell you. Conrad stuck in traffic.* Coward. If I'd known, I'd have taken the long way round.

'The sweet tea's not for you,' I told Myfanwy. 'It's for Mum and Dad.' I glanced out of the window. 'Here they come. Brace yourself.'

'Why? Oh, that doesn't look good. It's not often we see Alfred *stomping* down the path. Not a great stomper, is he? And what's got into Mary?'

Dad came into the house and *stomped* straight past the kitchen towards the hall. I grabbed a tray and put three mugs on it: a fast exit was going to be called for.

Mum did stop at the kitchen. In fact, she stopped in the doorway and stared at me. 'Where's your brother, and why has he brought two of those *creatures* here? Alfred should *not* be exposed to magick. Did you know about this, Rachael?'

The trick with mother is always to answer the least important question first. 'Conrad's stuck in traffic. Apparently.'

'Did you say *two* Fae?' asked Myfanwy.

'Yes. Faith something-or-other and another one who's trying to take Mina's place. What's going on?'

I added an extra mug and poured water in it, then grabbed the milk. What I needed now was a human shield, and luckily there was an extra-large Welsh model standing right next to me. I picked up the tray and nudged Myfanwy in the back. 'After you.'

Mother had no choice: it would have been rude to carry on standing there, so she stepped aside and let us pass.

'You're shameless, you are,' said Myfanwy when we reached the safety of the gardens. 'No wonder you never go out to Spain on your own. With no one to run interference, you'd actually have to deal with Mary.'

'That's not fair! I've always used Dad as a shield. But you're right – it's the reason I've never taken up bridge. That, and the fact that I'd rather die.'

'Mind you, I'll get her upset more often if it means you making tea and carrying the tray… By the dragon, would you look at that?'

I stopped and stared, and our guests stared back. I'd seen pictures of Faith, and in the flesh she was just as polished as her image. If you want to know what she looks like, just Google *women's equestrian clothing* and point at the blonde model. She looks like that. But the other one…

Myvvy touched my arm, and I got the faintest tingle of something that had to be magick – a Silence, because she said, 'I cannot believe it, Raitch. Imagine walking around looking like *that*.'

'Wow,' was all I could muster.

I knew it must be Alicia, because I'd heard about her. Mina said that Faith had recruited (bought? hatched?) a junior Fae to assist her, and that she'd been given a copy of Mina's hair so that Faith could practise. Nice idea in theory, but the reality…

Mina's hair is long, rich and a lustrous black. It suits her. It's part of who she is. But on Alicia… Wow. Alicia is slightly shorter than average, and her legs are sturdy: made for standing all day, not for riding like Faith's. And Alicia has the hips to support them, too. She was wearing a black salon tunic with *Shear Magic* embroidered on the chest, to match the signboard outside the stables. And then she had the hair.

A great curtain of the glossiest, blackest, straightest hair you've ever seen hung down her back. Wow again.

Myfanwy coughed and stepped forwards. Faith and Alicia stood up to face us.

'Well met, ladies,' said Myfanwy, and she bowed (as much as she could without falling over).

'Well met,' responded Faith. 'You do me a kindness by sticking to the rules. As Conrad's servant, it should be me who defers to you.'

'Sod that,' said Myvvy. 'Check this out, will you? Rachael Clarke with a tea tray. Haven't seen that for a while.'

I wasn't going to bow, for obvious reasons, so I looked sideways at the other human (sounds weird). 'It was either make tea and meet the Fae, or watch Mother in a strop.' I put the tray down on a corner of the table inside the stable. It's very well appointed for a stable: Erin used to rent it to use as a … *scriptorium*. That's the one. 'Normally I enjoy watching Conrad get the GCHQ treatment from Mother, but when he's not here, she goes for the nearest substitute. Me. So here I am.'

Myfanwy had shuffled closer to the junior Fae, and broke into a grin. 'Come here, you, I wanna see that hair. I didn't believe Mina when she told me about it.'

Faith used her eyes to urge Alicia forwards, and Alicia beamed at Myfanwy. 'Hello, lovely.' She tossed some of the gleaming black locks. 'Good, innit? Right pain to look after, though. Dunno how Rani does it.'

It was a bloody good job I'd put the tray down. Out of Alicia's mouth had come the *exact* voice of Erin Slater. Myfanwy let out a little squeal of shock. 'Duw duw! Where did that voice come from! You sound just like her, cy, don't she, Raitch?' She paused. 'Did I just scream?'

'My fault,' said Faith. 'I told Alicia to channel someone, and she chose to channel Erin. She still takes me literally. I give up, Leesha. Just be the quietest version of yourself. If such a thing exists. Get chairs — and don't, whatever you do, don't call our clients the *Druid* or the *brood-sister*. It's Myfanwy and Rachael.'

So that's what they call me behind my back: *brood-sister*. I'm back to being Conrad Bloody Clarke's effing sister. I bet they don't call Sofía that. Oh no. I bet they call her *La Gitana* or something.

Alicia looked confused at the order she'd been given, and I swear she stapled her lips closed from the inside. She grabbed two chairs, putting one close to the door and the light, and the other in the corner next to the tray. She offered that one to me, and ushered Myfanwy into the first one. At a signal from Faith, Alicia began to assess her task, and Myfanwy began talking: 'I never have a lot of luck with my hair for some reason. Dunno why. Can you do something *proper dramatic*, so at the wedding everyone will focus on my hair and not on the fact that I'll be the size of Elvenham Grange by then? I'll have a bump bigger than all of Mina and Sofía put together at this rate. Do you know what I call the twins? Burger and Chips, they are…'

And on she went. This could take some time.

Chapter Eighteen

While Myfanwy rattled on to Alicia, I passed a mug of tea to Faith and took one for myself, and we both sat down to size each other up. Given that we've never met each other, you'd be surprised how much we have in common, and for once I'm not talking about my brother. I'm talking about the Bodysnatcher.

Another lie I've told Conrad is that I didn't know Eseld was shagging Chris Kelly on the sly. I suppose it wasn't a lie, technically, but unless there are two six-foot-six Geomancers with bald heads, I was pretty certain I knew what was going on. So far, so none of Faith's business. That was until she employed Chris's soon-to-be ex-wife. And of course, Faith has this weird bond with Mina (according to Erin), and the divine Tamsin has Mina firmly in her corner.

Why do I care? Because although Tammy and I aren't at daggers drawn, she is going to be a bridesmaid, and she was third on the list for the hen party. I know I was last, because Vicky let it slip. The one thing I do not want is for Team Tamsin to decide that my loyalty to Eseld makes me a target. Always best to be certain, so Faith and I were looking each other over weighing each other up. She didn't like it one bit.

When Alicia stepped aside from Myfanwy, she announced. 'No problem at all. It will be a pleasure to work with someone who has their natural colour.'

Unlike Erin Slater, who — despite being able to afford a house in the Lake District — always goes to the cheapest hairdresser she can find. Talk about a bottle-blonde.

Alicia wasn't ready for the assault. Quick as a flash, Myfanwy's elbow shot out and hit Alicia's thigh. Hard. It was a good job the Fae didn't have scissors in her hands. 'Hey, you,' exclaimed Myfanwy. 'That's my friend you're talking about. Wait till you meet Saffron Hawkins. I'm still sure she uses magick to get it that colour.'

'I know,' replied Alicia. 'My lady is going to take me to somewhere called Garstang soon to see the Hawk and Lucy Berardi. I can't wait.'

'I thought you were going to Middlebarrow,' I said.

'Maybe,' said Faith with a frown. 'I need to negotiate access with Nimue, and she may need a sacrifice. It's not top of my to-do list, but I need to sort it before the hen.'

'Oof,' said Myfanwy. 'That tea's gone straight to my bladder, that has. Excuse me.'

She held out a hand, and Alicia jumped to help. When Myfanwy had muttered off to the toilets round the back of the stable block, I took my place in the hot seat. Instead of whipping out her comb, Alicia stopped and stared at Faith, unable to move, and Faith was staring at me with a look that said she wanted to do magick on me. Believe me, it was not comfortable, and I got the feeling she was waiting for me to say something, so I went on the attack.

I crossed my legs and leaned back, then said, 'So, Princess Faith, has she tried to bribe you? Told you she'll put in a free minstrel's gallery if you arrange for Alicia to have an *accident* with the peroxide on my hair?'

Faith pointed to Alicia. 'If Leesha had an accident with your hair, she would answer to me, and I would answer to Mina, and Mina would answer to my lord the Dragonslayer. I'll let you decide if Tammy Pike could overcome those hurdles. And FYI, Miss Clarke, I can afford to pay for my own minstrel's gallery.'

That was some comfort, I suppose. It didn't make Faith a neutral party, though.

I shrugged. 'Point taken. About the money, that is. And I'll give Mina the benefit of the doubt, but what about you? You're not going to ambush me out of sisterly solidarity with Tammy?'

Faith bristled, and at that moment, I got it. Vicky has said I have *some* latent gift for magick. Just enough to be aware of when it's being used in great quantities or, in this case, being held back. Faith still looked like she'd wandered in from a country house party, but underneath I could sense that she would be just as at home in a cage full of starving lions or leading a charge of Valkyries or whatever. *This* is what Conrad meant when he said she's a Queen-to-be.

Faith's lips barely parted as she said, 'Again, for your information, the closest I have to a sister is Leesha here. The affairs of mortals are of no interest to me.'

'Nice pun. I was just testing. Confidentiality of the salon and all that.'

Myfanwy reappeared, and Faith stood up from her perch. 'Would you be so good as to show me your garden? I've heard it has hidden surprises.'

'Really? Well, come on then.' They left, and I could hear Myfanwy carrying on to Faith. 'When I was a little Druid, I dunno which I thought was less likely: seeing a dragon with my own eyes, or having not one but two Fae princesses admire my garden...'

I breathed a sigh of relief, and so did Alicia. Interesting. She took out the most elaborate antique hairbrush I've ever seen and clutched it like a surgeon about to perform a heart transplant.

'Wow, Alicia. What a brush,' I said, a little nervously.

She beamed. 'It is my Heartstone.'

'Eh?'

'Oh. It is my most treasured possession. It was bequeathed to me, and it was *made for a Queen!* It can do amazing things with anyone's hair, but on the People it can totally transform the skin. It's how I got this!'

She flicked the totally inappropriate mane of Indian hair and grinned. 'And when I offer my hair to Rani Mina, I will be able to grow any style I like in the swoop of a dragonfly.'

'Wow.' I looked up at her happy face and couldn't resist it. 'Could you cure Conrad's bald patch?'

She wrinkled her nose. 'That would be a favour indeed, but no.'

She bent to study my hair. It didn't take long. 'You have beautiful, glossy hair, my lady. Sorry. I meant Rachael. You really look after it.'

If you're wondering why I didn't let them get on with it while Faith was still here, fear of a peroxide-related accident is only a cover story. What I really wanted was to find out more about how they interact with us mortals in an everyday way. You know that Conrad roped me in for his Irish adventure, right? Well, I met the Queen of Galway and some of her People over there, and I gave the Queen my card in case she fancied some help with wealth management. Let's face it, when it comes to *wealth*, they have a lot of it, and they're so busy getting one up on each other that surely they could do with some expert help, right?

Wrong. Conrad saw me handing over the card, and he got Eseld to actually *sit me down and give me a lecture*. That's right, a fraternally mandated lecture on dealing with the Fae. I could have saved him the trouble: 'Don't start by drawing your sword.' That just about sums it up.

I did listen, though, and Ez told me way more about these creatures than I'd guessed in my wildest dreams. And she'd never had much to do with them, unlike some of his crowd.

I looked up, and I saw what I'd glimpsed in Alicia before: youth, vulnerability and a desperation to please her lady. And having felt the pent-up power of Faith's anger, I actually felt sorry for Alicia. I've had some bad bosses in my time, but never one who could rub me out like a mosquito between her fingers and had no scruples about doing so. I locked eyes with Alicia and said, 'You're a Squire, right?'

She nodded.

'So how old *are* you? Do you even measure age like we do?'

She shook her head. 'Oh no. We measure age by status and add sixteen years for when I was what you call a "Sprite". In your terms, I was hatched last year and Matched a few weeks ago – and don't ask what *Matched* means because I'm not allowed to tell you, but that's when I dropped my wings – so we would say, "Alicia is a Squire of six weeks." If the hen party goes well, I am to be Knighted. A mere Squire could not attend the wedding as handmaiden.'

She pronounced her name differently to the way that Faith had done, and I added a mental note to use her preferred pronunciation. 'How's it all going then, Alicia? Are you on track for a promotion?'

She was speechless, and did the fish out of water thing with her mouth. When I raised my eyebrows, she stammered a reply. 'I don't know, my lady. It is in the hands of the Princess.'

I took one of her hands in mine. It felt perfectly normal – warm and soft but strong underneath. 'There's a mortal saying, you know. *Change what you can, live with what you can't.* I know you're ... different, Alicia, but still. I'm sure you'll be fine. And yes, my hair is good. Given what I pay that salon in London, it bloody well better be. Keep it simple for the hen party, yes? Then do whatever you think for the wedding. We're still in the dark over what the bridesmaids' dresses will be like.'

It worked. She sort of bent herself into a knot on the spot and I knew I'd got through to her. She slipped her hand out of mine and started to lift and twist my hair. I nearly jumped backwards when she pointed at the wall and turned part of it into a Mirror. Bloody hell, and as if it were totally natural to do this stuff (something I can't get used to), she carried on talking. 'You know the real reason Faith doesn't like Doctor Mowbray?'

This sounded good. Alicia was willing to talk now that Faith was out of the room, and I might never get the chance again to *really* test what Ez had told me about the way the Fae work. 'I didn't know Faith and Eseld had met. You know Ez is my friend, right?'

'I'm sure she's a good friend too, and no, my lady and Eseld have not met. The Princess knows all about her, though. When my lady comes back from Staveley, she says that she's been brainwashed and that if she has to hear about E-Slag Mowbray one more time, she might kill her first to stop it happening. But she doesn't mean it. Two minutes of Reflection and it's like rain in summer. Gone.'

Oh. Right. I suppose I asked for that. What on earth is *Reflection*, I wonder? Even so, it's rather worrying that Tammy is still blaming Eseld for Chris's cheating. 'That's rather ... extreme.'

'I know. Have you ever worn a Goddess Braid?'

The Mirror shifted to show what my hair might look like if it were twisted into one of those freaky things the Witches use.

'Perhaps not,' said Alicia.

'Definitely not.'

'But that's not the real reason Faith doesn't like Eseld. The real reason is that Doctor Mowbray has beaten her. Even together, we couldn't get through the Wards on our lord's house. I don't think a whole nest of the People could do it. None of us like being bested by a mortal.'

Something I couldn't see, couldn't understand and couldn't control. Like all magick; even the illusions that Sofía does in her act are utterly invisible to me. Forces that Conrad can see and Mina can sense, but to me they just look like ... magic. I know, I know: just because it's invisible, doesn't mean it doesn't exist. Like radiation. Yet magick had kept Faith away from 'her lord's home'.

'Who likes being bested? I certainly don't. Listen, Alicia, if I ask you a question, will you give me an honest answer?' She smoothed down the sides of my hair and added a fringe in the Mirror.

'Ew. No, Alicia. Stop it, now!'

She banished the fringe and asked, 'You can't see the Ink of truth, can you?'

'I have no idea what you mean, but no, I can't.'

'I swear by your hair that if I answer, it will be true.'

I laughed. 'Fair enough. Okay, Squire, tell me this: if I said to you that Eseld Mowbray is a good person, would it mean *anything* to you?'

'That's an easy one to answer. No.' She let go of my hair completely. 'I could tell you one of our stories about it, if you want.'

'I'd like that, but not now. Your boss is coming back, bearing gifts. Remember, Alicia, confidentiality of the salon.'

'Of course.'

So, I had my answer: Alicia really doesn't believe in goodness and badness. Exactly as Eseld had told me. Even the idea of good and evil has no place in Alicia's world view at all. I wonder, does that make life easier for them? Does it take away some of the spice? I looked at Myfanwy, still chattering away and pointing at flowers. She is *totally* a good person. Apart from the dragon-hatching thing.

How can you live your life without knowing about that? I have no idea what Conrad has been telling you about me behind my back. No need: what he says to my face is bad enough. I know he loves me and all that, but I think his vision of me froze a long time ago, and he's constantly surprised when I think about anything other than maths, tennis or money.

Now, I don't want to go all biblical on you or anything, but doesn't Alicia remind you just a little bit of Eve in the Garden of Eden? From the time *before* she ate the fruit of the Tree of Knowledge of Good and Evil? Am I on to something here, or are they basically just another species who consider us in much the same way that we consider the cows in the field? Maybe I'll ask Francesca about it when we put all this stuff together. She seems very nice. For a librarian.

Chapter Nineteen

I'd been resting my phone on my lap while Alicia offered me nightmare visions of alternative hairstyles in the Mirror. Or should that be the Mirror of Trichological Doom? These Mages do love an inappropriate capital letter. Myfanwy and Faith were just walking back into the salon when my phone burst into life. I flipped it over and saw that Jules Bloxham was calling, so I answered and said hello.

She did not sound happy. 'Hi, Raitch. Something's come up in Tenerife. We're off to the airport in an hour, so if we're going to sort this out it needs to be now.'

'Now! Shit, Jules. I was going to soften the boys up over Easter and tell them on Sunday.'

'Sorry, Raitch. The Trabajadores are threatening to walk out on the whole development. Stephen's got to go, and I need to be with him.'

'The *who's* gone on strike?'

'The Trabajadores. Ask your sister about them. Can I come over or not?'

Just when I thought I could sit back and relax with my family. I massaged my forehead. 'Yeah. Course. Mina should be back soon. Park in the meadow and come to the stables.'

'See you shortly.'

I ended the call, then swore (in case Alicia needed help with mortal curses) and dialled Mina. It wasn't just the boys who I'd left out of the loop on this one, and if Mina didn't find out now, I would be in serious trouble. 'Hi, Mina. Where are you?'

'On my way back. Everything okay?'

The Mirror thing was still working, and Alicia's eyes lit up when she heard Mina's voice. She looked more excited than Scout when she knew there was food in the offing, and that was just wrong. Not even Conrad looks that excited when Mina's coming.

I put the Squire out of my mind and focused on the emergency. 'Mmm. Bit of a situation, Mina. Can you park in the meadow and come round?'

'I have ice cream in the back!'

'I'll get Alicia to take it … no, I won't, will I? Sod the ice cream. This is important, Mina. Important to me.'

'Then I will see you in five minutes.'

'What's up?' said Myfanwy. 'You've got a face like a slapped arse, Raitch.'

I hated that expression, especially when the Mirror was telling me that Myvvy was actually correct. Not that I've seen many slapped arses.

'Jules Bloxham is coming,' I told her. 'She's coming here, and so's Mina.'

'You what? Let us have that chair, Raitch, it's got a cushion.'

I got up and saw Faith looking at Alicia with fun in her eyes. 'Would you like us to leave? Not that there's anywhere we can go, as we're barred from the house. We could go to the pub.'

'Nah,' said Myfanwy. 'So long as the boys stay indoors, it'll be fine.'

'Who is it?' said Faith. 'I've never heard of this person, but she's clearly important.'

I didn't want to wash the Clarke dirty linen in public, but Myfanwy got in first. 'Did Conrad never talk about the Bloxhams? Too mundane, I suppose. You know that the Grange isn't the big house in Clerkswell, right?'

She'd started, so I sighed and sat down in the uncushioned chair.

'No,' said Faith. 'Who on earth lives there, and where is it?'

'On the Winchcombe road, just past the cricket ground – which is important, by the way. Clerkswell Manor is proper old, it is. Older than Elvenham Grange by centuries.' She paused. 'Older than the Derwent Sídhe, as it happens.'

Alicia couldn't help herself. 'I thought the Clarkes were the oldest family in the village. Our lor … Conrad told me, and he spoke truth.'

'For once,' I said. 'Doesn't happen very often. The old, erm, *squires* – the human ones. They died out a hundred years ago, and the Bloxhams bought the Manor in the seventies.'

Myfanwy wasn't to be put off so easily. 'But Miss Parkes – that's the old schoolteacher – she told me that the Bloxhams were sniffing around before the seventies. Whatever the reason, the Clarkes and the Bloxhams have hated each other since Alfred's dad's time.'

'Sounds good,' said Faith. 'Nothing like a multi-generational feud to make life interesting.'

I gave up at that point and let Myvvy get on with it.

She shuffled her bum and said, 'Yes, well, we know that the People's definition of *interesting* is a bit different to ours, don't we? Apparently the feud was quite bad until Alfred and Mary moved to Spain. Conrad's not so bothered. Not really. And us girls have been getting on fine since the Clerkswell Coven was founded.'

Faith frowned. 'It's not what you think,' I told her. 'Though I have my doubts sometimes, Clerkswell Coven is the name of the women's cricket team. Jules is captain, Myvvy here is vice-captain and Mina is wicket keeper. Erin Slater was their star fielder until she ran off to Westmorland.'

'Cricket!' said Alicia, earning a dark look from Faith. 'Erin and Karina had an argument about it. Karina said that it went on for days and nothing happened, and Erin said that not everyone was an adrenaline junkie, or any kind of junkie.'

'I've never met her, but I'm with Karina,' I told her. 'On the other hand, it's nice not to have the boys bouncing their heads together like rutting stags. Dad once bribed the landlord of the Inkwell to cancel the Bloxhams' wedding anniversary party – Stephen's parents' anniversary. You don't want to know what the Bloxhams did for revenge, Myfanwy, because you'll mention it in front of Mother, and I'll be in serious trouble.'

'We *do* want to know,' said Faith. 'I'll get it out of you one day. Where do these Bloxhams get their power?'

'Property. Stephen develops it, and some of it he keeps for Jules's lettings business. They've come close to bankruptcy as often as Conrad has come close to death, I reckon, yet like him they always end up smelling of roses.'

'He doesn't smell of roses! He smells of …. Shh!' said Alicia, whose ears were clearly magickal. 'I've just heard a car.'

Myfanwy's voice dropped to a whisper. 'So what's goin' on, Raitch?'

'Hello?' said the musical voice of Jules Bloxham. She was big in the St Thomas's choir until she took over the cricket team. 'Where are you?'

'In here, where it's warm,' I shouted back.

Jules was dressed in her everyday lady of the manor outfit, complete with green gilet, woolly hat and golden Labrador. You wouldn't think she grew up in Bromsgrove, just outside Birmingham. She looked outside the salon and found a ring which she tied the dog lead to. 'Sit, Floss. Good girl.' Then she rubbed her hands on her jeans and came to stand in the entrance.

'Hi, Jules,' I said. 'Mina will be here in a sec. This is Faith and Alicia. They're going to be doing the hair and make-up at the wedding. Girls, this is Juliet Bloxham.'

Juliet looked at the sign, which now looked like a rather permanent advertisement for Shear Magic. '*Shear Magic*? Are you opening a branch here?'

'We're mobile,' said Faith. 'We're based in the Lakes, and you could say that Conrad helped get the business started as an investor, so we're returning a favour.'

Juliet accepted that without question, and smiled fondly at Myfanwy. 'You're blooming, I see. How are you?'

'I'm blooming enormous, I am. Not so bad, though.'

Jules looked around the room. 'Erin would never let me in here. Did Conrad get planning permission for it?'

'I'm sure he did,' I replied as smoothly as possible. 'Is that Mina I hear?'

It was. She scuttled into the stable and made straight for the heater before she lowered her hood. 'If they must have Easter as a movable feast, why can they not move it to June or something? Having two big festivals in March is two too many.'

'What's the other festival?' asked Jules, and three voices spoke three words.

'Holi,' said Mina.

'Ostara,' said Faith.

'Alban Eilr,' said Myfanwy.

'Right,' said Jules. 'That's me told.' When Alicia stayed quiet, Juliet raised an eyebrow at her, then noticed the hair. She opened her mouth to say something, then shook her head. 'Whatever. The sooner we get this sorted, the sooner I can take over the packing.'

'Sort what?' said Mina.

'When you told me to block out the weekend of your wedding for *all* of my casual lettings, I didn't think you were serious, Mina. I've actually had people trying to pay double to gazump each other. One offered to buy one of the houses outright. Then I got a call from Rachael here.'

'Oh?' said Mina.

'Yeah, because Oighrig got a call from Fiadh Ahearn,' I said. 'Sorry, Mina, I was going to tell you all about it over a drink at the Inkwell. It's basically good news. Complicated, but good.'

Alicia had retreated towards her rather glitzy rolling salon trolley, and I thought she was lost in her own little world until she suddenly started reciting poetry.

Lonely sat the maid of the Inn,
Lonely in her fortress pure,
The cries of drunkards made her heart-sore.
Vengeful shadows of the Dark Queen's wrath
Were prison bars around her hearth.

'Fiadh Ahearn! The Market Tavern in Galway!'

'Yes,' drawled Faith. 'That Fiadh Ahearn. Sorry, Rachael. Carry on ignoring Leesha.'

'And I'm sorry, Jules,' I said. 'These people have a complicated family. There's a cousin from Ireland and a cousin from London who both want to meet their long-lost cousin from Cornwall, and they want to do it on neutral ground. Here. At the wedding.' I turned to Mina. 'So that's why I called Jules and asked, and please, pretty please, can the Mowbrays and the Ahearns rent Clerkswell Manor?'

'What!' said Myfanwy.

'You have to be kidding me,' said Mina.

'This is interesting,' said Faith, flashing a weird look at Alicia.

Mina shook herself. 'Why are we even discussing this? Surely Stephen would never agree to it. I'm not sure I would in his shoes.'

'Rachael can be very persuasive,' said Juliet. 'I came to check with you, Mina, rather than just take it from Raitch. This family really seems to have a lot of money to throw around, so why haven't you said before that you know them?'

Mina was unfazed. 'Because they hate publicity, because they have connections to national security and because they have people like Rachael here to hide their money where the newspapers can't find it. In fact, they now have the actual Rachael here doing it. Oh, and they're Cornish, so who cares about them?'

'Stephen does,' said Juliet with a grim smile. 'He cares a lot about the

Kellysporth Marina Development Scheme, and so do I.'

There was a tense silence in the salon. I will swear any oath you want that I had no idea the Bloxhams had *any* interest in the marina until Jules told me there and then in the salon. The relationships between the Mowbrays and Mina were complicated enough without this being thrown into the mix. Mina looked like she was thinking it over and may have been about to speak, but Alicia had another priceless contribution to make first.

'The Headless One! She lives and she's coming here!'

'Great Queen protect me,' muttered Faith.

'Just ignore Alicia,' said Mina serenely. 'She can't help it, and it doesn't hurt anyone.'

'How do you know about Kellysporth Marina?' I said to Jules, trying to sound curious rather than anxious.

'Conrad doesn't have a monopoly on finding things out,' she replied. 'Here's the deal: the Mowbrays and their family, with or without heads, can stay at the Manor from the Thursday before the wedding for a full week at two-and-a-half thousand a night, subject to Stephen getting a meeting with whichever of them is in charge of the development.'

When she finished speaking, Juliet folded her arms over her Barbour gilet and leaned against the door. I looked at Mina, Myfanwy looked at Faith, and Faith stared at Alicia with her finger on her lips. Alicia got the message.

As for Mina, no one knew where she was looking, because her hair had fallen in front of her face. When she straightened up and swept it back, she had made her decision. 'And here's *our* deal, Juliet. The Mowbrays are more Conrad's friends than mine. Most of them. I will get Lena to speak to Ethan — he's your man — and they can come up a day earlier and stay at the Inkwell. They still have rooms for Wednesday night. You can see the Cornish Mowbrays and offer them dinner to save me the trouble. How about that?'

Juliet nodded while she considered the offer. 'That's fair. Very fair, Mina. Thank you. And if you could put in a good word in advance, Raitch?'

'They are my biggest clients, Jules. I promise not to mention all the crap that our menfolk got up to in the past, but when Ethan sets me on due diligence, I've got no choice but to give him the facts about your and Stephen's businesses.'

Juliet unfolded her arms and sighed. 'Coming from a Clarke, that's more than fair enough. Happy Easter, everyone. Enjoy your eggs.'

'And safe journey, Jules,' I replied. 'Hope it works out in Tenerife.'

'Incoming hound,' announced Faith with some urgency. 'Conrad must be back.'

'Right. Bye,' said Juliet, disappearing into the dusk.

She'd barely untied her dog and got round the corner when the bright eyes of Scout bounded up the path from the house. He made straight for where Floss the Labrador had been tied up and sniffed around with interest, then gave up and headed for Mina. He stopped in front of her and barked happily. She bent to scratch him and said to the group, 'We'll keep this to ourselves for a while, shall we? I'll break it gently to Conrad after Easter.'

'Evening, ladies,' said the man himself. 'Are you going to be much longer?'

'Not me,' said Myfanwy. 'That casserole will be nearly done.'

'And I'd better go and make my peace with Mary,' added Mina.

'In that case, I'll wait a bit,' I said. 'I don't fancy being collateral damage. Did I see you with a stash of Sofia's finest, Faith?'

'Come on, boy,' said Conrad. 'We know when we're not wanted. Let's go herd some sheep.'

The group broke up, and Faith got out a bag with something vibrantly green inside it. Alicia, having been standing awkwardly for a couple of minutes, glanced at the door. ' 'Scuse me. Back in two shakes of a lamb's tail.'

'Fine, but don't say that again,' said Faith.

'She's right,' I added. 'You sound like Dad, Alicia, and that's not a good look for an aspiring handmaiden.'

With Alicia gone, Faith slumped back into her chair and closed her eyes. It was like seeing an actor backstage after their exit, vulnerable and … human. Only way I can describe it.

'You okay, Faith?'

She let out a low 'Mmm' but didn't answer my question. She snapped out of it when Alicia returned from the loo, and started to roll two monster joints. With a smile, she passed one to Alicia and one to me. 'Enjoy.'

'You not joining us?' I asked.

'One of us has to drive home tonight, and as Leesha can't ride a bike, never mind drive a car, that would be me. I can purge alcohol, but not this stuff.'

'Oh. Right. Is that really true?'

'It is. Leesha, could you use a little Fire and light Rachael's spliff?'

The last thing Alicia truly remembered about her visit to Clerkswell was her trip to the toilet behind the stables.

When the beautiful, graceful and wonderfully clever Rachael Clarke had said 'You sound like Dad, Alicia, and that's not a good look for an aspiring handmaiden,' she had spoken with warmth and love as if she really did care about what happened.

Alicia had dashed outside, where it was getting very cold, and went to the (unheated but clean) toilet. When she'd rolled down her leggings and relieved herself, she looked at the Ink on her thigh from earlier in the day. On an impulse, she made a Reflection of the whole time she'd just spent as Assistant Stylist at Shear Magic. It had been wonderful. Scary, but wonderful. She added an extra jump of joy when she pulled up her leggings.

And then she had gone back inside and lit the joints. Alicia couldn't believe how it made her feel. The closest comparison was Amrita, and that was no comparison at all. When she went outside for air, she had tried to unfurl her lost wings again, and it was a good job they weren't standing on top of the tower above the Dragonstone or she'd have jumped right off and splattered herself on the ground.

What with one thing and another, she forgot to ask Faith for a tour of the grounds. In fact, when they got back to Birk Fell at midnight, the feeling of flying was the only thing she *did* remember from those last moments in Clerkswell: everything else was a happy blur. Or a blur of happiness, which is much better.

Part Four — Luckless Saviour

During the two weeks after her visit to Clerkswell, Alicia perfected her plan for Operation Barnet Phase One: the hen party. Not that she had as much time as she would have liked.

For one thing, she had somehow ended up doing more work with the Pack than she had expected. Princess Faith was often away at the new sídhe, and Thistle was having a hard time bonding with the Wolves. For another thing, Alicia only got brief chances to work with the hens (except for Erin, though to be fair, Erin did need a *lot* of work). Still, it was a wonderful day when Princess Faith said, 'You're good, Leesha. You'll crack this and do a better job than me.'

Alicia got to meet two more hens on her second trip away from the Lakes. It began auspiciously as dawn crept over Birk Fell and lit up the mist rising from the lake on a rare still day. Thistle gave her arm a squeeze and said, 'What a beautiful day. You've got this, hen.' Alicia hefted her smaller case onto the launch, and Thistle cast off the rope.

A very junior driver from the Royal Household was waiting for her at the western jetty, and she relished in the chance to catch up on some gossip from the Derwent Sídhe. It seemed that Her Grace had held a secret trial for some of her Guard and that there would be a new Prince to go with the new Princess Bassenthwaite. Alicia had been prepared to say *nothing at all* about Princess Faith's business and was slightly disappointed that her driver showed no interest anyway.

Ninety minutes later, he dropped her off at a coffee shop down an alley in the small town of Garstang. Alicia was excited again, and not just because she had a chance to do her job. This would be her first time on her own in a mortal place of pleasure (the toilets in the motorway service station did not count). She admired the bold red and black colour scheme outside and the intricate logo for Caffè Milano. The People like coffee almost as much as mortals do, so Alicia swung her case from her arm and went inside with a smile on her face.

It was early by mortal standards, and the barista was lining up several takeout cups for the queue to have their pre-work fix in. The aroma was rich and wrapped itself around her like a comfort blanket. Alicia liked this place already, and thanks to Erin's briefings, she recognised the hens straight away. They were sitting in a corner and talking animatedly: Lucy Berardi and Kelly Kirkham, a farmer's wife from nearby. This was, of course, Lucy's coffee shop (or one of them), and Lucy sprang up to welcome Alicia and to introduce Kelly.

'Only Mina could do this,' said Kelly with a shake of her head and a smile.

'Do what?' asked Alicia.

'Hire not one but two beauticians, and send one of them round the country trying out hairstyles.'

Her lady's parting words rang in Alicia's ears. *Think mortal, act mortal and talk mortal. If you Entangle this Kirkham woman, I'll have you back in the Derwent laundry so fast your shoes will still be in Birk Fell.*

The only problem was that Alicia had no real idea what mortals thought and frequently misconstrued what they said, so she channelled Rachael Clarke. 'Mina is a good person. She only wants the best for her friends, and when it comes to hair, I'm the best. Are we doing it here?'

'Erm, no,' said Lucy. 'I've bagged the staff room for half an hour. This way. Would you like a coffee, Alicia?'

'Ooh, yes please.' She had been thinking about this ever since Faith had told her where she was going. Coffee was always on the go in the People's homes, but this was the first time she'd had to order it for herself from a mortal vendor, and she so wanted to fit in with the role she was playing for Kelly. Last night she had wrestled the shared phone from Thistle and tried Googling *what sort of coffee do hairdressers drink?* Sadly all the answers were about buying a machine for the salon (which was a good idea, but...), so Alicia ordered what Faith had ordered at the motorway. 'A triple shot espresso with equal water. That should get me fired up.'

Lucy raised her eyebrows and shouted the order to the barista, then almost hustled Alicia through the door at the back, past the toilets and into a small room with lockers, a table and four chairs. At least it had a mundane mirror on the wall. Lucy pointed to the chairs and went to get Alicia's drink.

'So how do you know Mina?' asked Alicia while she unpacked her case. Kelly looked uncertain, as if she didn't want to talk to a stranger. 'Don't worry, Kelly. The salon is sacrosanct and anything you tell me will go no further.'

'We met Conrad first, before they were even dating properly, never mind engaged.'

Alicia got out her Heartstone and prepared to attack Kelly's hair, which had the remnants of at least three barely adequate dye jobs mixed together. 'You mean when Mina was still in prison?'

'Oh, you know about that, do you?'

'I do. They've moved away from the Lakes now, but I did see a lot of them.'

'How's Scout? You know he came from our farm?'

'Did he! He is an amazing dog. You could almost think he's a Wolf some days.'

Lucy reappeared with a tray of coffees, and Alicia asked questions to discover more about Kelly's home life. She learned that Kely lived on a farm called Ribblegate along with her husband David, ('Everyone calls him Joe 'cos he looks like his dad'), her father-in-law, her daughter from a disastrous relationship, and her son with Joe. She also discovered that Kelly found it very difficult to get away from the farm on her own: 'I've only got childcare today because I promised Joe that I'd go to the cash and carry after I'd seen you.'

Alicia stood back, drank her coffee and considered Kelly's hair. She also considered her age (early thirties), and the relative ages of the other hens: only the Anointed Guardian was older than Kelly, and she was a special case. 'I think you should go dark brown. Glossy, with auburn highlights.'

'Really? I was thinking blonde again.'

'Lucy, can I borrow your phone? And sit this way, Kelly, so I can get the light right.'

It wasn't a question of light, it was a question of stopping Kelly from seeing the Mirror; Lucy looked uncomfortable but handed over her phone. Alicia got to work with her brush, adding volume, colour and shape to Kelly's hair while Lucy stared and her jaw dropped open. Alicia took a quick picture and then cancelled the Glamour.

'It's a new app,' said Alicia. 'Allows you to see what your hair *could* look like. See?'

'Wow. You've convinced me. I look proper classy. Might even compete with Tara Doyle. Did you know that Mina *and* Lucy know her, *and* that she came to the farm once?'

'I did, and I can't wait to meet her,' Alicia lied. 'Let me write the colours down, so you can give them to your hairdresser. I can re-style it at the racecourse if necessary.'

Kelly got her things together and said that she had to go or Joe would rush off to the cows and forget that he was supposed to be looking after their child. 'God only knows when I'll fit in a visit to the hairdressers. And I think I'd better go to Preston if I want it done like you've shown me. Nice to meet you both.'

When Lucy got back from showing Kelly out, Alicia had moved the chair and cast a Mirror onto some boxes of takeout coffee cups. Lucy sat down and said, 'I still can't get over how magick comes so easily to the Fae. The way you made Kelly's hair change like that… Wow. I so wish I could do that.' She gave one of the uniquely mortal smiles. 'It must be nice to have so much power at your fingertips.'

Alicia was at a loss. 'If only. I'm barely keeping my head above the effluent, and the septic tank is getting fuller by the day. Enough about me – did you meet Princess Birkdale at Clerkswell?'

'No. It's a long story.'

'We have time. I want to try a few things, if you don't mind, so tell me.'

Alicia was shocked as Lucy unfolded the tale of the Count of Canal Street, and how Tom Morton and Mina had been kidnapped by Diggers *who were working with the People*. Why had Princess Faith not mentioned this?

Alicia could see that the kidnap of her beloved and her new friend was the main thing to Lucy, as was the involvement of Wolves (also strange), but why had another People wanted the Count dead? 'Did your clever boyfriend ever discover a motive?'

Lucy looked up. 'You might want to dial back the flattery, Leesha. It's okay to tell me I look beautiful and that I'm a successful businesswoman, but hairdressers shouldn't praise the boyfriend. You can agree with me if I say he's the handsomest detective in Lancashire, though. That's allowed.'

'Is he? I've only met Barney, so it's hard to judge.'

Lucy laughed. 'Barney's in Westmorland, so I don't have to choose.'

'And did the handsomest detective in Lancashire find a motive?'

'Apparently the Count was running a high-class brothel and there was blackmail involved. And he didn't play fair with the Gnomes who kidnapped Tom and Mina.'

That was a lot to digest: the Count was clearly well into the skin game, and some of it had been with his Princess's approval.

'And when it was all over, Tara was really interested in my business. So much so that she's invested in it.'

And that investment would no doubt make sure that the full truth never came out: a wise move from Princess Birkdale, not that the mortal seemed likely to be playing the great game.

'You are blessed, Lucy,' said Alicia. 'The sun shines on you.'

'I don't know about that. So what are you going to do with me?'

Alicia stood behind Lucy and smoothed out her curly brown hair. 'This doesn't like being straightened, does it?'

'It does not.'

'Then how about this?'

Alicia drew extensions down from Lucy's scalp to form a soft background, lightening the colour a little and making a dramatic statement. 'It will only take me an hour.'

Lucy stared at her reflection. 'How long will it last?'

'If you avoid violence, it should last indefinitely.'

'You know this is Conrad's wedding we're talking about? What are the chances of avoiding violence there?'

'Don't worry about that. Leave the security to the People and focus on looking your best.'

'And you can do this in a morning?'

'I can.'

'Done. Go for it, Alicia.'

Alicia made a Memory of the image and cancelled the Ink. It was a wonderful morning and a joy to experience. The same could not be said of the day she met the other hen.

Chapter Twenty-One

'Look on it as a family outing,' Princess Faith had said. 'It's about time the whole household got to see our new home, and the stables will be moving soon – Her Grace is going to start charging me a fortune for livery.'

Alicia was unsure about this because she had yet to hear a good word about *family outings*. If the evidence from television was reliable, then she could expect illness, trauma, destruction, huge expense and police involvement. At a minimum.

Princess Faith piled Alicia, Thistle and Cathy into her 4x4, and for some reason Maria went, too. When they got to Windermere, Imogen and Tammy were waiting at the entrance. The others were due soon.

Robbie and Nadya were still learning to drive, so Sophie was bringing them from Sprint Stables in the horse transporter, along with Hipponax (who was most definitely part of the family). When Alicia locked eyes with Imogen, she felt cold water running down her back. Her brood-sister was still wearing a thick woolly hat, despite the weather.

'I see you've not grown an inch,' said Imogen, peering at Alicia's Ink.

'Knock it off,' said Faith. 'At least Leesha doesn't need a mortal to do her work for her.'

Oh dear. That was not a good thing to hear. Imogen would hold Alicia responsible for that remark at some point, and Alicia also knew that her brood-sister had spoken the truth: her skills with the Ways had barely changed since she had been sent chasing wild geese on Coniston Water.

'We're going to look at the Primary Anchor,' said their lady, signalling for Imogen and Tammy to follow her. 'You four wait for the others and put the kettle on.'

Alicia led Thistle and Cathy to a newer, larger Portakabin which had a separate office for Tammy as well as a bigger crew room and kitchen. Maria had taken one look at the building and then said 'May I Exchange and explore?' before stripping off and turning into the Wolf. There was definitely something going on there.

'This is a bit cleaner than you said,' observed Thistle when she'd put the kettle on.

'Because it's new. I believe that our lady ordered it when the Bodysnatcher joined us. She wouldn't spend this much on Imogen.'

'She really doesn't like you, does she? There's more to it than a scalping, I reckon.'

'From the egg,' said Alicia with a shrug. It was the People's way of saying that the future had cast them as enemies. It was also said of lovers, and that's how Alicia had thought it would have been with Robbie. It wasn't *fate*, but when a clutch is laid, the web of life is spun, and you have to work very hard to avoid being wrapped up in it, just as she had done with the prophecy. She sighed, then brightened up as the horsebox's rattly engine strained up from the road which skirted Windermere below them.

They piled out of the cabin and Alicia had a lovely moment when she was able to be of use – helping Sophie find the road leading to where the stables were being erected by the mortals of Skelwith Construction. They followed the transporter and watched Sophie park neatly, with the back of the horse transporter close to the Warded field gate to Hipponax's new pasture.

'Will you look at that!' exclaimed Thistle. 'He's totally too good for that horsey lassie. I am gonna get me a piece of our Robbie.'

'Join the queue,' said Cathy. 'Our lady said I could rut at liberty until her first clutch.'

Alicia said nothing. She was too busy wiping moisture away from her eyes, which was strange because today was quite warm.

Nadya had hopped down from the cab without giving them a glance, then she had gone to the back to unfasten the ramp. Robbie grinned at them and waved in a friendly way; Thistle growled, and Cathy whispered 'Mmm.'

Sophie got down, too, and shouted, 'Come on, Robbie. I need your muscles.'

Thistle, Cathy and Alicia looked at each other and shared a meaningful glance as Robbie trotted round the back of the lorry like an obedient version of Scout the dog. Thistle shook her head and said, 'He's wasted on a mortal. Did you see the way his mouth dimpled when he smiled at us? I think I'm in love.'

'Sod the dimples,' said Cathy. 'Those thighs look like tree trunks, and as for the package…'

Thistle put her hand on Alicia's arm. 'Did he really knock you back, hen?'

Alicia couldn't bring herself to answer.

'Then I'm going to break his heart.' She squeezed Alicia's arm. 'It's what Sisters do for each other.'

They moved forwards and watched Sophie coax Hipponax down the ramp and into the field. Alicia was in awe of the Unicorn's power and grace (who wouldn't be?), but she wasn't jealous of the Sophie's access to Hipponax; it was her access to Robbie that clutched at her insides. Unlike Nadya. Her brood-sister found riding, chasing and hunting much more precious than their well fit brother, and Nadya was being eaten up from the inside as she stood well clear of the mighty beast; unless Nadya could become a Princess, Hipponax would remain as deadly to her as he'd been to Lady Agnes.

Suddenly, there was a cry from round the hill. 'Our lady!' said Alicia. 'Quickly!'

The People ran towards the shout and found Imogen supporting Princess Faith as Tammy stood to the side wringing her hands. Robbie ran fastest,

Cathy on his heels, and he scooped the Princess up in his arms to carry her into the accommodation cabin. Cathy followed them inside and the others gathered on the steps.

'What happened?' asked Tammy. 'We were testing the main transition and she went white and fell over.'

The People glanced at each other, and Alicia decided that if Tammy was part of the household, then she had a right to know. 'It is the Change. It comes upon her often. Cathy will minister to her. We should make refreshments.'

'You mean *I* should make refreshments,' said Thistle. 'You're right, though. Why don't you two go and play salons while I get some food for our lady? I'll bring tea in a minute.' Nadya, exiled for the moment, looked longingly at the bunkhouse, then followed Thistle next door.

Alicia put Fire in her legs and was back with her beauty case in two shakes of … no. She was back *like lightning*. The accommodation unit was also new, and this one didn't have a leaky roof or mould on the walls. As soon as their lady was safely ensconced in Nadya's room, Tammy led Alicia to a spartan bedroom. 'This is where I sleep after a late shift or when I'm drained. Good job I've got Siona.'

'Who's that?'

'My nanny. I've rented a place in Bowness for now. It was hard to find somewhere that would take three toddlers and a single mother with no job references.' She laughed. 'Erin had to forge me a reference and then she pretended to be a HR manager from BAE Systems when the lettings agency called to check.'

Alicia was at sea again. 'I understood *toddlers*, but the rest…'

Tammy pulled a chair out from under a small table. 'Never mind.' Her face changed and a darkness came over it. 'Have you heard the latest?'

Alicia turned her back on her and opened her case. 'No. About what?'

'Mina called me yesterday. You are *not* going to believe this, but E-Slag Mowbray is going on the stag do! The fucking *nerve* of the woman.'

'Which one? Rani or Eseld?'

'Mowbray. And Myfanwy, a bit. I can't blame Mina because she was blindsided. Myvvy suggested to Vicky and Hannah that the stags needed a chaperone who they could trust not to get drunk and who could stop them getting in trouble, and for some reason they thought the Mowbray woman was the person to trust.'

'Oh yes?'

'It's a shame she can't be trusted not to shag other women's husbands. I hope Chris gets legless and she sets her sights on Ben or Conrad. Then Mina might see what a total slag she is.'

A response bubbled up Alicia's throat until she bit its head off. It would not do to reveal that the radiant Rachael Clarke had told her that Eseld was a good person. 'Your hair is young and strong,' she said instead.

'Yeah, yeah, I'll calm down,' said Tammy. 'At least the bitch won't get to walk down the aisle behind Mina. Right, what do you reckon?'

Alicia bent to draw her brush through Tammy's hair, giving life and easing the tangles. Then she stopped and frowned. 'Your hair is lustrous. When did you stop parting it on the right? It's fighting the brush.'

'I have *never* had a side parting. What are you on about?'

'Nothing, my lady. Forgive me. What is your dream for the hen party?'

'Make me a sexy ass bitch. I'm the only single lady, so I'm going to be putting myself right out there.'

Alicia felt warm inside. 'My pleasure, but don't blame me if Mina complains that you're hogging the limelight. Oh, and Rachael is single.'

'Sod her. In fact, there's a bonus in it for you if you make me sexier than Rachael. A double bonus if you have an accident with the peroxide bottle.'

Alicia's brush stopped mid-stroke. *Did Tammy have Second Sight?* She thought of her lady's words and tried not to tremble. 'If I have an accident, then I will answer to Faith, and she will answer to Mina, and Mina will answer to Conrad, and Conrad loves his sister.'

Tammy sighed. 'I suppose someone has to love her.'

Alicia realised at that moment that it wasn't just Conrad who loved Rachael: she loved her, too. It was a shame she didn't have bodylonging as well. Perhaps in the future. Right now, she just wanted to spread the love around. 'I have heard Mina say that Rachael is a good person, and she should know.'

'I'll take that under advisement and get back to you,' said Tamsin, in a voice which distinctly said the subject was closed.

'I think we keep it simple,' Alicia told her. 'You have the best skin of all of the hens, and the more we work on showing off your face the better.'

Tammy, for some reason, made cat noises. 'I like you a lot better, Leesha. Keep talking.'

When the plan for Tammy's hair and make-up had been agreed, they joined Thistle, Cathy, Nadya and Imogen outside the Portakabin.

'Where's Robbie?' asked Alicia.

'Running a *hosepipe* for dough-face,' Thistle replied with a spit.

Cathy told them that Princess Faith was getting better but needed some rest, and that where they were bound for was not a place for mundane mortals like Sophie (or Wolves, although no one had seen since Maria since she Exchanged). Tammy stood at the back of the group. Imogen led them over the threshold and into the foundations of the new sídhe.

They emerged at the top of a deep, deep bowl which cupped the base of where the hill was rooted in the mortal world. Above them, the higher slopes were covered with healthy trees, gathering Mother Nature's bounty and sending it down through their roots to shape and support the future royal bower.

'Why have you gone for a sphere?' asked Nadya. 'I've never seen a sídhe made like this.'

'This is the twenty-first century,' said Tammy. 'Spheres are much stronger, and the Primary Anchor isn't like a great piece of iron, you know. It doesn't need to sit at the bottom to hold the structure in place, and having it in the centre gives the maximum protection.'

'So where is it?' said Cathy. 'I can't see a thing.'

'Even higher,' said Imogen with a small voice. 'Tammy has attached it to the base of Godshome.'

There was silence for a moment. Alicia couldn't work out whether the Bodysnatcher was a genius, a sacrilegious firebrand or simply filled with false pride, the sort mortals called *hubris* and which the People referred to as *being like the Queen of Paris*.

'And before you ask, Faith has signed off on all the details,' said Tammy. 'It's hard to visualise where everything's going to go, but the Great Hall will be quite high and have transparency: when your future Queen holds court, she wishes to gaze on Windermere in all her glory. Seen enough?'

Nadya grunted and turned to leave. When they got outside, Princess Faith had recovered and was talking to Sophie and Robbie. Their lady looked up and said, 'Leesha, Thistle, Cathy, you come with me. Nadya, you and Sophie need to have a look at the plans for the stables. Robbie, I want you to walk the perimeter and give some thought to security. Let's go.'

Princess Faith led them around the hill on the opposite side to the road. It was a steep climb up a bank still sodden with spring rain, and Alicia had to help her lady reach the summit. When they did, the whole of the claim was laid out before them: the mound where the sídhe was being built, the levelled area for the stables, the great scar left by the Diggers and three small concrete structures well hidden by Glamour and containing by turns a transformer, a pump and a propane tank.

'It's beautiful,' said Thistle. 'Such a spot is a blessing.'

'It's a start,' said Faith. 'I wouldn't be anywhere else to lay my first clutch. Whether I'll lay my last here is another matter. Any suggestions about the sídhe?'

There was silence for a second, until Alicia put up her hand. 'My lady, may I make a plea for when you craft the laundry? Could we do what Lady Tamsin has said and join the twenty-first century by having machines instead of sinks and coppers?'

Princess Faith raised her eyebrows and locked eyes with Alicia for a second, then turned to her right. 'What do you reckon, Thistle? Should we do the same in the kitchens?'

'I will craft you kitchens fit for a Queen,' said Thistle. 'As for yer laundry, my lady, ye don't want none of that machine nonsense. Where are you going to send folk for punishment if you've only the septic tank as an option?'

'A good question. Come on. Tammy has brought a hamper full of afternoon tea goodies – and, by the way, stop calling her Lady Tamsin. Neither word is correct.'

On the way down the hill, Thistle asked, 'Have you given Robbie leave to rut with mortals, my lady?'

'You can all do what you want for now. I've enough to think about without trying to direct your liaisons. There'll be time for that later. But *try* not to get into trouble.'

'There's little chance o' trouble locked up at Birk Fell,' muttered Thistle. 'I've even found maself dreaming of the guy who delivers the oil, and he's no oil painting, tha's for sure.'

Chapter Twenty-Two

'Leesha, could you go and fetch Sophie?' asked Faith. Alicia nodded and took a shortcut, running over the hill, the day putting a spring in her step she hadn't expected. Perhaps there was something to be said for family outings, after all.

She paused at the far end of the pasture and whistled for Sophie. The young mortal jumped and looked around, then reluctantly gave Hipponax a final stroke before coming up to the fence. 'What's up, Alicia?'

'Time for food.'

Sophie gave her an eye-roll (another mortal gesture often practised in the nursery, especially by Little Ones planning to take a female form). 'You could have said. I'm not climbing over this fence in my best jodhpurs.'

'No problem.'

Alicia wasn't a great tumbler – the People's unique cross between gymnastics, acrobatics and dance. None of her brood were, but she could do the easy stuff so she swivel-vaulted over the fence, then crouched and offered her cupped hands to Sophie who, for some reason, was staring at her.

'Fuck me, Alicia. Where did you learn to do *that*? Shit! Hipponax!'

The Unicorn did not look happy, presumably seeing Alicia's entrance as a threat to his favourite female.

'Quick, Sophie! Stand on my hands.'

Sophie hesitated, clearly thinking about trying to calm the Unicorn, then put her foot in Alicia's hands. Alicia dug her shoulder into Sophie's behind and thrust the mortal up, up and over the fence, then followed her with Fire as Hipponax broke into a gallop towards them.

'Whoa … aaah! Oof!' said Sophie as she sailed through the air and landed on the grass beyond the pasture.

Alicia stooped to offer a hand, and then her blood ran cold: just beyond Sophie's head was a rock, lodged in the turf. Another six inches…

'Please don't do that again without warning me,' said Sophie, examining her jodhpurs for grass stains. 'Oh, shit, will you look at that?'

'Allow me. I can use Ink to clean it. It's only a small mark.'

'Yeah … what you doing? Gerroff!'

'Hold still and let me get my tongue on it.'

'You are *not* licking my thigh, Alicia…'

'But—'

Sophie started to laugh, and put her arm around Alicia's waist. 'You're mental, you are. *Eclipsed*, innit?'

'Woo woo woo,' said Alicia. She'd seen it on a film, and it worked just as well in real life. Profit! 'This way. A shortcut.'

'Only if you have superhero skills. I might ask the Gnomes to put a gate in that corner for the future.'

They walked slowly towards the Portakabin, and Alicia remembered their last conversation. 'What secret did your mother have that made you so anxious?'

'What? Oh yeah.' Sophie looked towards the south, to her family home. 'She was adopted and she's trying to locate her birth family. Conrad's looking into it. Probably too late now.'

'Is there anything our lord cannot do?'

'Well, he'd struggle with that fence for one thing. And he's proper going deaf, you know. Mind you, he's nearly as old as my mum, so only to be expected. You know what, he's gonna be *forty* next year. Hey, I saw Imogen take her hat off before, and it was all I could do to not shout *slaphead*. Did you really do that to her? And is it true she dumped you at Coniston Water with *no phone*?'

Alicia's eyes darted around, guilt and fear mixing together. It would not improve things for Alicia if Imogen's humiliation was widely known. 'How did you find out it was me?'

'Saerdam Felix. The new custodian at Sprint? You know him?'

Alicia nodded. He was one of the lesser Squires, suddenly promoted for picking the winning side in the rebellion.

'Well, he heard it from the helicopter pilot.'

Alicia stumbled. *It's all around the Royal Sídhe. Egg and wings, I'm in trouble.*

Sophie thought Alicia had tripped. 'Watch out, yeah? How come you can do a vertical flip then fall over a rock? Mind you, maybe Imogen will re-think the Goth look. It's *so* old. I had a friend at Cartmel Priory who was proper Goth, but she wasn't a moody cow like Imogen. I think she should go for space alien with a head like that.'

'I didn't know you'd been a nun. Aren't you too young for that? And aren't nuns supposed to be celibate?'

'What you on about now? Oh, right. Cartmel Priory hasn't been a nunnery since forever. It's the name of the *school* in Cartmel, and no, since you ask, I have never been celibate. Very hard to be celibate when Robbie's around. He even got Flora worked up, and she is *totally* into girls. You know, I caught her pining after Nadya the other day, until I told her that Nadya only has eyes for Hipponax. If you see what I mean.'

This was too much for Alicia, and she stopped to sit on a grass tussock.

Sophie touched her shoulder. 'Hey, you okay? You didn't pull a muscle or nothing doing the flip?'

'Only my heart!'

Sophie's eyes widened in alarm. 'Do you need me to get Cathy? Is it serious?'

Alicia's hand flew to her mouth. 'NO! Do not say anything, I beg you ... It is an expression: *the heart is only a muscle*. It's what we say when thwarted in love.'

Sophie sat down, nudging Alicia's bum further along the tussock. '*Thwarted in love.* You don't half talk nonsense, you know. Look, I'm really sorry about Robbie. After I brought you here he told me you fancied him, but he said you were totally okay about him and me.'

Alicia had to pause and sort out the pronouns. And calm her nerves. It was the Unicorn's fault. If Hipponax hadn't charged at her, she wouldn't have got upset. Yes, that was it: the Unicorn did it. A stupid man-beast.

'Hey, hey. No need to cry. I didn't know your lot *could* cry.'

'Ignore me. Everyone else seems to.'

'No, they don't. Erin said you were awesome, and not just with a hairbrush. She said you've got the Pack proper eating out of your hand. Not that I'd want a Wolf doing that. See? Fearless, you are, Alicia.'

The mortal's words were a real comfort, until Alicia realised where they'd come from. 'How do you know the Enscriber?'

'Who?'

'Erin Slater.'

'Is that what she does? Whatever.' Sophie took a deep breath. 'When you'd left Sprint, just after you did the Matchy-thing, Robbie came on to me so hard I thought I'd better ask someone neutral. Conrad, again – not that I actually wanted advice from *him*, gross – but he sent Erin to see me.'

'Why her?'

'Because she's been in a few Fae beds in her time, but don't you *ever* say that to anyone, 'specially not Barney. She said to me that so long as neither of us was … what was the word? *Forsworn.* That's it. She said it was the old word for *exclusive.* So long as neither me nor Robbie was promised to someone else, like engaged or married, or exclusively dating, then it didn't matter. It was just fun. And Robbie swore blind he wasn't foresworn. If you see what I mean. He wasn't lying, was he?'

Alicia shook her head. What Erin had said was all true, and she must have had it from the People. Whether or not Erin knew the second part of the saying was another matter. *The People will always wait.* But Alicia didn't *want* to wait! Not for Robbie to finish with Sophie, not to be Knighted, not to learn the Ways. None of it.

Sophie dropped her voice to a whisper. 'Erin also told me about the glands. Sorry, but I must say I didn't believe Robbie when he said those big boys were just for producing testosterone, not sperm, and I had to make sure.'

Alicia couldn't help herself. 'Are they really that big?'

'Yup. And he has the complete package, and now I'm beginning to think that I'm the one who's Eclipsed for sitting on wet grass with a Fairy, talking about the size of another Fairy's balls.'

'Don't do that, Sophie. I love you, but there are many who would cut your face for using the *other* F word. Starting with Imogen and Nadya, probably.'

Sophie nudged her hip again. 'Well, you're not them, are you?'

Alicia sighed, and wondered why they didn't practise sighing in the nursery. 'I am not them. I am not secure in my lady's household. I am a half-formed Eclipsed Squire who has an Enchanted Hairbrush and no future. You know why I scalped Imogen? Because she called me "Littleworm". It was my nickname. To them. Not to Robbie, though.'

'No wonder you liked him if the others bullied you like that.'

'He was my favourite.' Alicia was about to tell Sophie why her *first* favourite wasn't her favourite any longer when she suddenly realised that a story about slicing open your broodmate's neck with a kitchen knife might not come over in the right way.

'Quite right, too,' said Sophie. 'And you've got a great future ahead of you, Alicia. It's me who needs to consider her life choices.'

'You are amazing, Sophie.' Alicia's heart swelled, despite the bruises. 'If our lord's brood-sister were here, she would say that you were a good person.'

Sophie blinked, lost for words.

Alicia desperately wanted her love to come over, so she doubled down. 'I mean it. Rachael would *totally* say that you are a good person.'

'Rachael! I wondered who the flip you were on about there.' She paused. 'And why can't *you* say that I'm a good person?'

'Because we have no gods, that's why.'

Sophie looked like Alicia had spoken in the People's tongue, and Alicia was about to repeat herself when Sophie held up a hand. 'Are you serious? What do you mean that you have *no gods*? You lot have gods coming out of the blinking woodwork, and what have the gods got to do with goodness?'

'Isn't it obvious?'

'Look,' said Sophie, a tinge of hurt on her face. 'I know I didn't pass all my GCSEs, but I'm not thick. I got a B in biology, actually, but what you said's so far over my head I can't see it, never mind understand it. Why do you need gods to be good?'

'It was told in the story of the first egg, but that's a *very* long story.'

Sophie looked towards the Portakabin. 'We'd better get going or we'll both be in trouble. Is there, like, a short version?'

Alicia stood up and offered Sophie both her hands, desperate to feel a warm touch. 'I—'

'What are you two up to, eh?' barked Thistle. 'There's tea in the pot going cold and you're oot here making hay.'

It was Sophie who jerked her hands away (yes, they were warm, but they were calloused, too). 'Sorry, Thistle. I was in the field. My fault. Is there a toilet in there?'

Why had Sophie taken the blame? Before Alicia could ask, Thistle said, 'Aye. You can use the one round the back, but be sharpish. Our lady's not for lingering.'

Sophie strode off, and Thistle switched to the People's tongue. 'And what are you doin', being pally with her like that? I hope you were trying to prise her away from Robbie.'

Alicia rubbed her face. That had not gone as she planned it. Nothing ever did, except hair. You could rely on hair. 'Why did you send Sophie to the Portaloo? That's the one the men use, and … ew.'

'Why do you think? Sod that, what *were* you talking to her about?'

Alicia opened her mouth to say *the first egg*, but that made her think of other egg-shaped things, and then she was blushing, so she lied to her Sister. 'She asked if Robbie were forsworn to me, and I was about to tell her that she should leave him and then you interrupted.'

Thistle looked suspicious. 'If that's what it was, then good, but it's no' the girl you need to speak to, it's Robbie. He's newly wingless and he doesn't want to get in too deep with a mortal or the next thing you know is he'll be petitioning to roam. Now, get your arse in gear, Sister, and make friends with one of us, not one of them. Robbie trusts you, and I'm relying on you to show him what a fool he is.'

They put Fire in their legs and arrived in time to avoid a tongue-lashing from their lady. Nadya looked ready to call them out but Tammy was being hostess, assisted by Maria (now thankfully dressed) and, with Princess Faith looking fully recovered, the atmosphere turned as sunny as the April weather.

The afternoon finished with the whole company cracking open a bottle of champagne and drinking a toast to the Staveley Sídhe. 'Excuse us a moment,' said Princess Faith to the three mortals. 'This needs saying in the People's tongue.' Their lady lifted her glass and intoned the traditional blessing. 'May the walls of our home see the walls of Merlyn's Tower crumble into dust.'

Alicia felt a little traitorous joining in the toast. Just a little. It wasn't as though this would happen in the Dragonslayer's lifetime, was it?

They split up, and Alicia saw Thistle intercept Robbie on his way back to the stables. She put her hand on his arm, moved closer and tilted her head right back to look up at him. Alicia expected Robbie to move off, but he laughed at something Thistle said, then cast his eyes towards Sophie before laughing again.

When she returned to Faith's car, Thistle had a glint in her eye. Alicia was pleased for her Sister, of course, but she was a little worried about Sophie. Someone like Thistle should not happen to a good person like Sophie. If that's what she was.

Chapter Twenty-Three

Two days after the family outing, Alicia began the day as she had become accustomed: gathering the cubs from the Pack and leading them into the woods while the adult Wolves sorted out breakfast. Lottie enjoyed this sport hugely, and the little SheWolf found it a release – later she would have to spend time with Thistle, learning to suppress her instinct to bite things and generally preparing to fit in with the human children at the wedding. As much as Rani Mina loved Maria and wanted Lottie leading the flower girls, the bride was not going to risk an *incident* with so many mundane guests there.

A cold wind had blown in from the north, bringing rain, but the cubs were enjoying themselves so much that Alicia carried on regardless, not caring that she would have to spend an hour drying her great mane, unlike the cubs who would dry themselves with a quick shake. Still, not long now: Thursday was the maiden feast and she could shed the hair *and she might be Knighted!* Everything was in place: Operation Barnet had been settled, the hens had sent pictures of their outfits and Vicky had finally let Alicia in on the secret of the second night. Now *that* was going to be fun! Still no news on the second or third daytime activities, though.

The cubs scampered down the yard, naked bodies glistening in the rain, and the bigger boys took their chance to jump in puddles to splash each other. Alicia smiled to herself and was about to head to her salon when she saw Thistle waiting under the overhang, arms folded and a sour look on her face.

'Come on, Lottie,' said Alicia. 'Thistle's waiting.'

'She's early! Can't I eat my breakfast? It's *sooo* hard to concentrate when you're thinking about eating your teacher.'

'It's no' the wean I'm after, it's you.' She managed a smile for the cub. 'Off you go, hen, and get your breakfast. No school today.'

When Lottie had scampered off, Thistle examined her Sister. 'Look at the state of you. Soaked to the skin and enough water in that hair to drown a whole pack of rats.'

'Easily sorted. Mind if I start work on it?'

Thistle pushed herself upright. 'You shouldn't *need* to be drying your hair.'

'It'll soon be gone.'

'Yet again you're missing the point, Alicia. You're not a Wolf. You dinnae have oiled fur. You are of the People, and we do not get wet. It's not what we do: we have Ink for that.'

'I know, and I'm sure I'll learn.'

'Get your top off and stand by the mirror.'

When Thistle put her foot down, there was no arguing, and Alicia was getting changed anyway. Her top removed, Thistle's deft hands swept the soaking hair off her back, then she grabbed the hand mirror and held it up.

Thistle was little practised at this, but Alicia had spent days working the Ink so that the hand mirror acted like a Skyway capture, projecting what it saw onto the big mirror in front of the client. Much easier that way.

'See?' said Thistle. 'Your nubs are still there, and they're starting to look angry. You need to finish absorbing them, or they'll burst and you'll be in serious trouble.'

Alicia had avoided looking at her back, for this precise reason. If she didn't look, maybe her wing nubs would merge into her skin of their own accord. Alas, it didn't work like that.

Thistle put down the hand mirror and handed Alicia the Dyson hairdryer. 'It's breaking me up, this is, on top of everything else.'

'Oh? What's happened?'

'Our lady is feeling a lot better this morning, and she had me in for an update. She's decided that we no longer need to take Robbie as Guard to the hen party. I had it all worked out, you know. All worked out.'

Alicia was genuinely sorry. She had reflected on the family outing and decided that she'd rather fall out with Robbie than either Sophie or her Sister. She was beginning to agree with Flora the groom about men: they caused all the trouble in the world and did nothing to make it better. On that basis, Alicia had decided to stay neutral and comfort the loser in the battle for Robbie's affections. 'That's not fair,' she told Thistle. She was about to switch on the hairdryer when the look on Thistle's face turned down even more. 'What's up?'

'It got worse. Our lady has had the Dragonslayer on the line, and this time it's a direct order: I've tae grow up and look twenty-one minimum before the wedding. How am I gonna snare Robbie if I look older than pudding-face?'

Alicia didn't think about it when they were on their own, of course. To her, Thistle was every inch nineteen years a Squire, and it was only when in mortal company that Thistle's skin stood out for what it was and what it had deliberately been made to do. *Ma sweet sixteen sex kitten* was apparently what the Duke of Tiree had ordered, and because the Borrowdale People were not invested in the skin game, the reasons why some mortal men found flowering children so attractive was lost on Alicia – the look certainly did nothing for her.

'It will be for the best,' she told Thistle. 'If we perform well this weekend, we will be Knighted, and then you can put that skin behind you. Don't forget, Sophie has command over the great horses and over Hipponax. Perhaps that power is what draws him in.'

Thistle shook her head. 'Some days I can't decide if you're half-breed or half-witted. Hurry up with your hair and I'll make *my* favourite breakfast for us. The one that doesn't involve dead rodents.' She turned and walked off, muttering about ruining perfectly good porridge.

Alicia turned on the hairdryer and watched Thistle pause theatrically on the threshold before raising a shield over her head and crossing the yard without a single drop of water hitting her curly locks.

'What have you got for us, then?' asked Stephen.

'Give her a minute,' said Juliet. 'She's barely got her coat off, and she hasn't got a drink in front of her.'

They were meeting in an old pub down a side street in Winchcombe. When Chloë had asked 'why there?' Stephen had told her, 'I've got my eye on it for development. I like to pop in and make sure it's still losing money. And it's quiet.'

Juliet had stood up and taken a step towards the bar, which was round the corner and out of both sight and hearing. 'What would you like, Chloë?' she asked.

'Diet Coke, please.'

'Coming up.'

Chloë smoothed out her hair and looked at Stephen as defiantly as she could. He just smiled and looked right back at her.

Juliet came back with the drink and placed it in front of Chloë, then sat down. 'How was college?'

'Great, thanks. Did that guy take up the lease on Bishop's Cleeve terrace?'

Juliet frowned. 'No. It's getting to be a bit of a white elephant, that one. Too far from the station to walk and with no parking … Might have to re-think the way we market it.' She smiled. 'Might even have to stoop to students.'

'On your head be it,' said Stephen. 'You know what they're like.'

'If only more of them were like you, Chloë,' said Jules.

'Indeed,' said Stephen. 'Now, let's get serious. There's a lot at stake here, especially as Juliet now has to cook for multi-millionaires.'

Chloë hadn't believed it at first when Stephen told her, and she'd got straight on to Jules to double check, but yes: the Mowbrays were renting Clerkswell Manor for the wedding, and Juliet was even having them over for a meal to discuss the marina project.

When Jules didn't rise to the bait, Stephen continued. 'With what they're paying to stay at the Manor, we could easily get that chef to come in and cook.'

Juliet shook her head. 'There's only six of them. And Rachael. I can do twice that without breaking a sweat.'

'I know you can, and you'll be amazing. Like always.' He stared at Chloë again. 'Are you sure you can't join us?'

Beth had been quite clear on this: *under no circumstances can you be in a room with five Mages.* 'If it was any night but that Wednesday. It's my parents' silver wedding anniversary.'

Stephen gave a quiet snort of disbelief; Juliet was full of support. 'I only hope our kids feel the same when it's our turn.'

'So, what *have* you got for us, then?' said Stephen.

While her girlfriend had been firm about Chloë not attending the dinner, Chloë had been just as adamant that every word she spoke about the Mowbrays must be both true and helpful. If Stephen suspected for one second that he'd been set up to fail, there was no way that Chloë would get them onside for the wedding day raid.

'Above all, they're very private,' Chloë began. 'And rich. Don't be surprised if they say almost nothing about themselves, especially Ethan. He has the social skills of Cornish granite, but don't let that fool you. Don't let any of them fool you. It will be Ethan's decision, but he listens to all of them, especially his fiancée, Lena. With the others, it's like this. Cador is their legal brain, but it's all a game to him. Don't let him wind you up.'

'Posh lawyer. Right.'

'I have no idea whether Morwenna will be there. She's pregnant and had a terrible accident, so she might duck out. If she turns up, spoil her rotten and then you'll have Kenver on your side. He dotes on his sister.'

'Gotcha.'

'As for Eseld, she's a bit of a loose cannon. Just give her a bottle of wine and don't say anything negative about the Clarkes to her. She's a friend of both Rachael *and* Conrad.'

Stephen made air quotes. 'A "Friend of Conrad"? Does Mina know?'

'Of course. Eseld has a boyfriend, but when it's family business, he's kept at arm's length.'

'How does that work?'

'No idea. She does love horses, though.'

'Oh, that's good,' said Juliet. 'Plenty to talk about there.'

'And that brings me to the most important thing,' concluded Chloë. 'Don't be surprised if they don't say Cornwall and call it "Kernow" all night.'

'Why would they do that?'

'Because they actually believe it should be a separate kingdom to England.' She raised her hands. 'I know, I know. Trust me on this. If you don't have Cornish contractors lined up for most of the work, you've got no chance.'

'Seriously? This is one of the biggest projects west of Exeter in decades.'

Chloë raised her Diet Coke. 'Which is why they need a developer with outside experience to help the locals fulfil their potential.'

Stephen sat back, his face showing that his brain was overheating. 'And it's three weeks tonight. Shit.'

Juliet gripped his forearm. 'You can do it, Stephen. You got the NEC Annexe, didn't you? With my beef Wellington under their belts, they'll be a pushover.' She turned to Chloë. 'Thank you for this. We wouldn't have got this far without you. And if we don't get it, they're paying so much rent that we'll be off to the Maldives in the autumn.'

'I'll drink to that,' said Chloë, first raising her glass to Jules and then looking at Stephen. 'Something good will come of this, one way or the other.'

Two nights later, Alicia found herself standing naked in the rain outside the Pack Hall on the night they were due to leave for Middlebarrow Haven and the start of the hen party – without Robbie.

Alicia's cases were packed and stashed in the back of the minibus, and she would have gone to rest if Thistle had not told her that a Squire who could not keep off the rain was no Squire at all. 'If it doesnae rain on Ladies Day in Liverpool, then it will be a miracle. You don't want to see all your hard work on the lassies' hair go down the drain, do you?' Alicia did not want that, so she had followed a very determined Thistle out of the cottage and into the downpour.

It was the perfect time to practise the Ways because the Pack were asleep and the Archer was in residence in case of sudden emergency while they were away. Thistle led Alicia to the amphitheatre and said, 'If you cannae get this right soon, you'll be no use tae anya'an, and that's a fact.'

At least, that's what Alicia *thought* her Sister had said – to make sure, she asked Thistle to repeat herself in the People's tongue.

Thistle's best feature was her nose. It was small, cute and dusted with freckles. When she'd tried to seduce the Pack King, she had almost made it twitch with mischief, and a glint had lit up the hazel eyes above it. Thistle was still very wary of the Wolves, and that attempted seduction had done little to endear the Squire to Queen Cara.

Alicia wondered if the cute nose and hazel eyes would survive Thistle's enforced skin change. Right now Thistle was staring at Alicia with an entirely less inviting light in her eyes and wrinkling her nose with frustration or distaste; it was hard to tell which. She did, however, switch to a less incomprehensible language.

'You will be worthless to our lady without magick of your own: anyone, including a mortal, could use that Enhanced hairbrush you're so attached to.'

Alicia thought that was unfair. With or without Lady Agnes's dying gift, Alicia already knew that she was a *good* hairdresser and beautician, as good as any mortal, and she also knew that she had it in her to one day become a *great* one. She had Inked Sophie's words extolling her skills into her Memories, and they were as true as a Dwarf's framing square: Alicia *was* good at her job. For what that was worth. Unfortunately, she couldn't argue with Thistle's assessment of her future among the soon-to-be People of Westmorland: a Squire with no magick to speak of was destined for a short, hard life and a painful, lingering death.

Every day it was up and down: when Alicia groomed Lowri, she basked in the love from the Pack, and then Thistle would show her a post from Sophie's new, anonymous Instagram feed with a shirtless Robbie brushing down Evenstar (much to Thistle's annoyance). And then Alicia would take all the cubs at full moon and let them hunt her through the forest, and she would be their heroine, and then the next morning she would have to call the Archer and have her reset the Wards because the Ink was beyond her.

A shiver which had nothing to do with the cold Lakeland air ran down Alicia's spine. 'What am I doing wrong?' she asked.

The rain was bouncing off the metal roof of the Hall behind them, but they were dry – thanks to Thistle's magick. Alicia could see it swirling gently on her Sister's skin, making the water pass above and beyond them. 'Bring up Fire,' said Thistle.

Mastering the Six Lenses had been the first of the Ways taught to them by Lady Agnes. They had been shown how to draw Lux and use a Lens to focus it into Ink. It was a different approach to mortals, who called the Lenses 'elements' and could only see five of them. Using Lenses was the first Way, and most of the People's magick was built on that, though mastery of them was but a first step, as Alicia had been reminded many times.

It was, however, one of the few things which Alicia could do without using her fingers to scribe the shapes on her body. She raised her left arm to her waist and rotated her wrist. *Fire* appeared on her skin, summoned from within and ready to burn.

'Tha's pish,' said Thistle, reverting to English (or Scots) as she often did when swearing. She breathed in and calmed down. 'It needs to be a lot bigger, and you need to push the Latitude out. Our lady shouldn't have settled for this.' She peered closer. 'I like your Knot, though. How come?'

'It's how I dry and straighten hair when I'm not using mortal implements.'

'Might have known. Push the Latitude out.'

Alicia focused on the swirl of Ink and dug the nails of her right fingers into her palm to stop herself doing it by hand. She drew Lux from the wet ground and, slowly, the Latitude became a bulge, and then a spiral. She would need much more Lux for a Vortex than she was used to using on her Heartstone.

'Good. That's very good. Can you go further? Make it brighter?'

Alicia wasn't cold any more. Sweat was leaking from her armpits, and Thistle wanted her to *make it brighter*. 'Great Queen, give me strength,' she muttered, and then she pushed it further. She hadn't known she had it in her.

'Excellent! Keep it there and look at my hand. I'm going to show you the Vortex, and you're going to make it out of that spiral in the Latitude. Okay?'

It was very much *not* okay. Alicia was getting wet all over now, from sweat, from bodily discharge and possibly from leaking blood. She desperately wanted to collapse the Ink and collapse her body onto the ground. She summoned the image of Robbie, shirtless and bending over the water trough at Sprint Stables to wash his face. That would keep her going. No Vortex, no Robbie.

Thistle held up her palm, and the neat, efficient lines of the Vortex throbbed in her Ink. Alicia tried to see it, and then the great curtain of black hair slipped its moorings and flowed in front of her eyes, and she didn't have the strength to push it back. On her arm, Fire burned, and the only thing she could think of was to unpeel the bleeding fingers of her right hand and touch her forefinger to Thistle's palm.

'Eurgh,' said Thistle, but she didn't snatch her hand away.

Alicia's blood ran over her Sister's hand, and the lines of the Vortex became clear inside her. *I can do this.* She merged the lines into the Latitude, and the Vortex became part of her. Her knees shook and she was ready to drop.

'Lift it!' said Thistle. 'Lift it into the sky and push that water away. You can do it.'

And she did. Alicia floated the Ink off her arm and let the magick rise into the air until it met the Lakeland rain. She expected a drenching, but the Vortex did its work and every drop bounced off the magick and rolled down the slope to fall beyond the amphitheatre. She *had* done it.

Now that the Vortex had become part of her, the drain of Lux slowed to an efficient trickle and she was able to drag her hair back and give her Sister a silly grin.

'Well done, hen,' said Thistle. 'Okay, it's something most Squires can manage before they're allowed out of the sídhe, but hey, it's a win, no?'

Alicia looked at her right hand. Oh dear. She wiped the blood onto her stomach and peered more closely. No real damage. Good job she kept her nails quite short (the Princess was much better at nail art, anyway). She drew some skin over the wounds, and then jumped with fright.

'LEESHA! THISTLE! Where are you?'

Their lady's voice boomed over Birk Fell and the Vortex collapsed. Water flooded out of the sky and drenched the girls as they ran round to the yard to see what was going on.

Chapter Twenty-Four

Princess Faith was standing, furious yet regal and dry, in the centre of the yard. The same could not be said of the Archer to her right. The Pack's Guardian was armed with her bow and wearing sodden flannel pyjamas in a red tartan. Behind them in the doorway, Cathy shivered, clutching her dressing gown tight around her.

The two Squires stopped at a respectful distance from the Princess and bowed. Thistle brushed her fingers against Alicia's thigh and established the connection which allowed Sisters to Share without words aloud – the mortals called it *telepathy*, but it was really just silent speech.

'Becca,' said Thistle.

'Where?' said Alicia in alarm. For the Guardian's woman to turn up here like this would be … unprecedented, to say the least. They were all expecting the flame-haired Witch to rock up after they'd left for the hen party, but not yet. Not with the People as witnesses.

'The pyjamas! Must be a present from Becca. She'd no' buy them herself.'

Alicia broke the Sharing with a hissed, *'Time and place.'* Thistle could be *such* a gossip. 'My lady?' she said out loud.

Faith had her phone in her hand and lifted it. With a gesture of Ink to Memory which summoned the recent conversation, the voice of the Seer spoke into the rain.

'Sorry, pet, but Nimue's put her watery foot down. There's nae chance of her letting you into Middlebarrow without a sacrifice. I tried me best, but no dice, I'm afraid.'

'What are we going to do?' asked Alicia.

Faith grimaced with real pain, and her outline shimmered for a fraction of a second. 'You two, get dressed and get ready. We're leaving now and going to Rydal Water. I'll have to deal with the Nymph myself.' She turned and bowed to the Guardian. 'Please forgive the interruption. I'm sorry to have disturbed your rest for no reason.'

Guardian Karina gave the Princess a foul look and retreated into the cottage without a word. Alicia had heard about the instability in Lakeland's instantiation of Nimue, and was not looking forward to seeing it for herself. It was a good job she'd done all her packing earlier.

'Let's just grab our clothes and get dressed in the back of the bus,' said Alicia. 'Our lady is not in a good humour tonight.'

'Aye, and for once it's not our fault. Good thinking, Sister.' They flew into the cottage, scooped up armfuls of things and ran back outside. The Guardian watched them go from the sitting room, the flannel pyjamas discarded and a fluffy dressing gown tied securely around her. 'Here,' she said. 'Conrad left these for you. Said I had to hand them over before the hen party.' She pointed to a padded envelope on the table and Alicia darted forward to grab it, not wishing to get within striking distance of a very unhappy Guardian. She dodged back and looked inside.

'My lady? These are curried mealworms.'

The Guardian had what mortals call a 'poker face'. No way of telling what she was thinking. What she said was this: 'Conrad said that, knowing those girls, you should be prepared for any eventuality.'

'Erm. Thank you.'

Faith already had the engine running and nodded her approval at their swift return. In seconds, they were on the tiny lane that led along the shore of the Wolf's Lake, travelling at speeds no mortal would dare, especially in weather like this. When Faith took a bend which threw Alicia on top of Thistle, she began to wonder whether the Princess would be the best teacher if she ever decided to learn to drive.

Even with the Princess's magick and no regard for safety, it took forty-five long minutes to travel what the raven could cover in eight. At the end, they bounced down a rough track off the main road and Faith jerked on the lever. 'Come on.'

They were twenty yards from the lake and a dozen feet higher than the water. Alicia's Third Eye had never come to life so strongly or with such colour as it did when she turned to her right. Hovering over the mortal world was the great twisting join of Ley lines which made the Four Roads Cross. The beauty was in the Lux, and the giant iron cross was no more than the cork in a wine bottle. And it had all been the work of her Foremothers.

'Hurry up,' hissed Thistle. 'This is no time for gawping.'

'Right.'

Faith was already on the Fae bridge which led to the upper island, using Fire to move like the wind. Alicia put on a spurt and caught up with the others in a wind of her own. Now that was one of the Ways she *had* mastered: life would definitely be very short if she couldn't escape from mortal perils.

Their Princess slowed down and came to a stop by the edge of the lake, and made the Ink keeping off the rain into a static structure. Thistle and Alicia stopped two paces behind Faith and stilled themselves. So strong was the light from the cross behind them that Alicia could see the surface of the lake start to move and then glisten with magick as Nimue formed herself from the water. As one, the three People bent the knee, as all Creatures of Light must do before the Higher Ones.

Alicia's breath caught in her throat when the Nymph spoke. Her words were in the People's tongue, and she formed them with beauty. A song like that would silence even the Great Queen.

'Well met, Princess of the People. I think I can guess what brings you to my shore.'

Faith stayed on her knee, but for some reason she was holding her side as if to stay upright, and there was a big pause before she spoke. 'We crave permission to cross the Wards of the Middlebarrow Manse,' she finally said.

Before answering, Nimue looked around at the mountains. She seemed to be looking *through* them. 'These are strange lands, Princess. The rocks are ancient and have seen much history. It is a quiet land, and yet not so quiet.'

The Nymph drifted off somewhere, and Alicia thought they had blown their chance. Faith emitted a quiet groan and gripped her side more tightly. The faintest smell of blood came through the night air. 'My lady is wise,' said their Princess. 'I could learn much from her.'

'Could you? Could you really? Or perhaps I could learn from you. Perhaps you could tell me why the children of Albion have decided to store their heaviest poisons where the sun sets.'

'What's she on aboot?' hissed Thistle.

'Not a Scooby,' replied Alicia. It was her new favourite saying. She used it a lot, because there truly was so much about which she had no clue at all. Then again, it didn't look like Faith had much more of an idea, though she did seem to understand the question and opted for silence as an answer.

Nimue made a watery hand and let it drip. 'Plutonium is well named for the lord of the Underworld. It is nothing but death to the unwary, though it can serve you if you are careful. Like Quicksilver.'

This put Faith on firmer ground, and she said, 'Plutonium is deadly to all but the Dwarves, and even they cannot stomach it for long. Quicksilver is life to us.'

'But deadly to me. I do not blame your Queen and her Foremothers for doping the Eden line, but she is accountable for what Madeleine did here.'

'Who?' said Thistle.

'Maddie, from the Lord Protector's story.'

'Oh. Right. Her.'

Their lord, Conrad Clarke, had become associated with a Spirit who, in mortal life, had purged Quicksilver – mercury – into Nimue's Vortex of Memory, with disastrous consequences for the Nymph.

The water dripping from Nimue's fingers became brighter and metallic, and the air reeked of the tang of Quicksilver. 'If you would earn my favour, you will take back more of it,' she pronounced. 'And you will do it now.'

Faith's shoulders stiffened. That was a high price indeed, and Alicia guessed that it was about more than just a security pass to Middlebarrow Haven: this was the price Faith would have to pay to ease her path to royal status in more than just her form.

The Princess bowed her head, then stood up and opened her arms. 'It will be as my lady requests. I will ... Aargh!'

She gripped her abdomen and collapsed in agony. Without thinking, the girls rushed to her side. Pain wracked Faith's face and she bit her lip until blood ran. And then she screamed and arched her back in a spasm, and blood stained the crotch of her jeans.

'The Change is upon her,' said Thistle in awe.

Faith collapsed onto her back and breathed deeply.

'What can we do?' said Alicia. This should be happening in the sídhe, and it should not be happening yet.

'Not the Change,' said Faith through gritted teeth. 'Just losing a bit of mortal. That's all. I'll be fine.'

'In the days to come, I hope you will be,' said Nimue. 'But you are not fine tonight. Return when you can open yourself to me.'

'Got. To. Get. To. Middlebarrow,' said Faith with short, hissing breaths. She put all her energy into a lungful of air. 'One of you two do it. Make the sacrifice. Now!'

Their Princess blacked out and went limp. The girls looked at each other, fear and panic freezing their faces. They both knew that if neither of them attempted the sacrifice, Faith would kill them both as soon as she awoke. They also knew that for a Squire to take on extra Quicksilver without the help of the Hlæfdigan would be to court death with roses.

Thistle reached for the knife at her belt.

Light and Lux glittered on Thistle's blade, and Alicia knew why her Sister had kept putting off any teaching of the Ways of the Blade. They had both known that this moment might come, when blood called for blood and the bond of Sisterhood was dissolved in death. One of them would fall here, mortally wounded, and the other would throw the loser into the lake to make the sacrifice. After tying on a line so that their corpse could be pulled out, of course.

Alicia retreated and uncurled one of her oldest Memories, written high on her back. The Memory rolled into her mind like hot wine in winter, and Lady Agnes's voice was there to comfort her.

And the Sisters came again to the wood. Neither girl could get a clear lead, for Ygraine ran faster on the paths, while Iseult could slip around the trees and follow the scent better than the Great Queen's hounds. They were in danger of finishing the race together, and then neither would win, because the Morrigan had been clear in her words. 'Only the winner will serve as my Messenger. No winner, no place in my house.'

They plunged into the woods, thick with the oldest oaks and full of hidden pools. Ygraine leapt over the home of a Nymph and Iseult made a tunnel through a Dryad's tree, yet still they could not be separated. They converged on a path, and there before them was Ysgithyrwn, the wildest wild boar in the land. The mortals say that one of their heroes plucked the comb and scissors from his bristles, but that is not so. It was Ygraine...

She absorbed the whole story in one draught, and it became part of her without having to listen to every word. When it was absorbed, Alicia knew what she had to do. If she fought Thistle, she would lose and be pitched into the water minus a kidney. Or her liver, if Thistle got angry. But if she chose to do it herself…

She whipped out the Queen's hairbrush and brandished it at Thistle. 'Goodbye, Sister.'

'You're mad,' said Thistle, circling to her right. 'Madder than those Wolves, you are.'

Alicia made light pour from the hairbrush, and Thistle flinched back. The way was clear, and Alicia brought the Fire from her arm to move her like the wind. She flew over the shore, and with a leap like Ygraine's, she plunged into Nimue's water. Time slowed as her feet left the ground and the last line of Lady Agnes's story echoed in her head.

And so the profit went to Ygraine, Little Ones, even though she died. What do you think of that, eh?

Chapter Twenty-Five

Water, water everywhere, and drink as much as you like!

Alicia giggled at the Memories which floated towards her little boat, because that's what she had become: a little boat on a sea of thoughts. A juicy fish jumped from the water, and she grabbed it like she used to grab the dragonflies in the Queen's bower when she was a Sprite. She stuffed the fish in her mouth and savoured its flesh.

The lake around her was still, still enough for the little paper boats to bob gently in her direction, each one bearing a naked flame. She thought of a video she'd seen of Diwali, with lights floating on a river in India. Little tea lights, she supposed. One of the fragile vessels came within reach, and there was nothing so mundane as a tea light. Instead of wax and wick, the flame burned from a little delicacy, a cake of some sort – cooking it, yes, but at the same time consuming it. Alicia lowered her hand into the lake and let the boat float onto her palm.

She lifted it and couldn't stop herself. She rammed the boat, the flame and the tasty morsel into her mouth, using her People's smile to force her jaws open. That was *very* tasty, if surprisingly sweet – a caramel smoothness with notes of … pepper? Yum.

Two more were nearby, and she snaffled them, one light and floral, and then one which nearly took the roof off her mouth with spices.

She wanted more. More of those little boats. She pointed herself at the flotilla of flames, but they had parted, and in the middle a fin showed above the water. *Shark!* Now what would *that* taste like? She had to know, and she got ready to intercept it.

The shape glided towards her, and she leaned out of her self-boat to harpoon the beast, but she was too late. The shark leapt from the water and crashed into her, its jaws as wide open to eat her as hers had been for the fish, with rows and rows of teeth glinting silver.

She twisted at the last moment, and the shark crashed into her, crushing her legs and smashing the boat. She tried again to stab it, and caught the beast with a glancing blow as it sank back under the waves. She was alive, but her boat was gone, and she was floating on the lake. She looked frantically around, spinning as she trod water.

The shark was circling round on one side, and on the other, probably drawn by the taste of blood, something bigger and even scarier was coming for her.

Whatever it was, the shark sensed it too, and the fin shot away. If the shark was scared of it, what chance did she stand?

Three Ring Circus

Note from Evie Mason:
Just to be clear, I asked Corrib whether the above section was a dream, a vision or a metaphor.
She said, 'It's a story,' and I didn't want to push her on it. You can make up your own minds on this one.

'Wake up! Wake up, Alicia! Come on, Sister.'

Alicia coughed and vomited bitter water onto the grass. Grass? How? And why was she shivering?

'Urgh,' was all she managed by way of response.

'You're alive! Oh, you beauty.'

It was Thistle, and she was holding Alicia from behind, around her waist, and shaking her. Alicia retched, but nothing came up, and she collapsed when Thistle released her. 'Ooh, oh, my head. Where am I?'

She felt Thistle's hands pulling her hair away from her face and trying to disentangle it. She was lying on her side, and she was completely sodden. Cold, yes, but not freezing like she should be. Maybe it was the warm, sunbaked ground, because the light was strong.

Daylight! Had she missed the hen party? She opened her eyes in panic, but no sun shone here: the light came from the river of Lux that flowed into Four Roads Cross, and that was what warmed her. Beyond the glow of Lux, the clouds were starting to part, revealing stars. It was still night. Hopefully the same night that she'd … Had she really jumped into the lake? Had she really taken on more Quicksilver?

Thistle looked strange, glowing cyan with the Ink which protected her from the river of Lux. Alicia tried to lever herself up, but collapsed back onto her side. 'Our lady?'

'Over there. Behind you.'

Alicia managed to roll over, fighting a wave of nausea. Princess Faith was also lying on her side, her lower half covered with towels from their stash in the bus. Nearby was a pile of blood-soiled denim and discarded shoes. 'Is she…?'

'Still out of it. The blood has stopped, but she's awf'y pale.'

'The Nymph?'

'Satisfied. For now. She's going to let us into Middlebarrow, but she demanded that our lady come back. If she lives. Here, take my hand and try to sit up.'

The Lux was helping. Alicia's world was beginning to stabilise, and she risked coming up to sitting, with Thistle's help. 'What happened to me?'

'I dinnae ken.' Thistle squatted down to Alicia's eye level. 'You landed in the lake, and then it lit up like Hogmanay fireworks, and the water *boiled*. I covered my eyes, Leesha. I didn't want you to lose life. I wanted you back, and I begged the Great Queen not to desert us.'

So Thistle had begged the Great Queen to save them, had she? And in the moments before Alicia leapt into the arms of Nimue, had Thistle also begged the Great Queen, saying *take her not me…?*

Alicia flinched. There were new Memories all over her body, in strange places and in shapes she didn't recognise, almost as if they weren't of the People at all. That would be *so* wrong. She looked at the lake, and a stray image of something vast and scary floated over her eyes. 'Perhaps it was her. I don't know, Sister.'

'Well, anyways, Nimue bore you from the water and placed you on the shore. She pronounced her word and disappeared. I thought it best to get you both up here. You must be *freezing.*'

'I will be when I walk out of the river of Lux.'

'I'll go and see to our lady,' said Thistle. She stood up and strode across to their Princess, then bent down and stroked her brow tenderly.

Alicia looked away and looked at herself. She was feeling composed enough now to do something, and decided to start with the great clump of dripping, matted hair pressing against her back. How in Mother Nature did Rani live with it?

She made Fire on her arm, and then jumped back, trying to get away from her own flesh. *What was that?*

In the midst of the Fire Ink, a new stroke was winking at her. It was part of her, but not from her. It could only have come from the lake. From the Nymph. From the Vortex of Memory under the water. Alicia felt alien in her own skin, a very uncomfortable feeling.

She moved her finger towards the Fire Ink and traced the new stroke. It was powerful and strong and … what was *that?* Away from Fire, something was sketched into the thinly populated Lens of the Void, the magick which mortals call 'Plane Shifting' and which the People call 'moving between worlds'. When her finger moved, Alicia got a whiff of caramel from the Void Ink, and something like one of Rani's curries from the Fire stroke. She didn't dare attempt the stroke now, not like this. Instead, she scooped the gluey mass of hair over her head and in front of her face, then made the Knot which would bring warm air to dry it.

'AARGH!'

'Oh my God! You're on fire!'

Somehow Alicia had set fire to her own hair, and only a quick squirl of cold air saved it from all going up in smoke.

Thistle ran across and made bug eyes. 'What in the name of the Morrigan have you done to yourself?'

Alicia held the damaged strands and dialled back the life in the Knot. Gentle winds started to blow, driving the water away from her thick locks.

'I've no idea,' she said. 'Call me Gertha the Spider.'

'Who? What is it with your brood and this *Gertha* that I've never heard of? Whatever. Our lady is awake. Up you get.'

Alicia took her Sister's hand and groaned. No dizziness. Good. She carried on discreetly drying herself and went to see how their lady fared.

She was weak. Weaker than Alicia had ever seen a noble before. And so *pale*. Not good. At least she was alive and aware.

'It's over,' said the Princess. 'For now. But I'm spent. I can't ... well, I can't drive, that's for certain, so we can't leave here.' She looked at Thistle with true love. 'You have done well for the sídhe. Your name is already written. I need one last thing of you: feed me.'

Thistle's knife was out in a flash, liquid fire from the river of Lux washing up and down the blade, and the tip pointed at Alicia's heart.

Alicia didn't bother reaching for her scissors. Instead, she turned the Fire back into Thistle's palm, and her Sister dropped the knife. Before she could look up, Alicia had dived again, this time knocking Thistle to the ground and placing her in a chokehold, just like Nadya used to do. Thistle was restrained, yes, but this was bad. Very bad.

One of the new, alien Memories unfolded from the small of her back. *Ask not what you would do. Ask what the Hound of Gloucester would do.*

The Lord Guardian? Conrad Clarke himself? What could he bring to *this* party? Alicia bought herself some time by pushing Thistle's arm up her back and rolling until she could drag Thistle to her knees and present her to their lady. Her Sister's body went slack in Alicia's arms, and Thistle whispered. 'I am done. I will give myself, Sister.'

Alicia released her hold and stepped back. As they took turns sitting in the front of the car, so they would take turns with offering the ultimate sacrifice. It made Alicia's own heart swell with love that her Sister was renewing their bond. With precise, nimble fingers, Thistle unbuttoned her shirt and shook her hair back. 'I am ready, my lady.'

And when Faith had fed, Alicia would be alone at Birk Fell. And Faith...

'No!' said Alicia suddenly. 'Don't let my sacrifice to Nimue be in vain.'

The Princess frowned, eager to feed. 'What are you wittering about, child?'

'If you take her life, her remains will pool here and run down to the lake, and there is no guarantee that you can drive us to Middlebarrow. You would be out of the cauldron and into the fire.'

Faith looked uncertain. 'What would you have me do?'

'Ask for help,' said Alicia simply. 'It is what the Hound of Gloucester would do.'

Faith flopped back on the grass. 'The Queen will demand a heavy price. Very heavy.'

'She's too far away. Ask a mortal ... there are plenty who would help.

You have the Diggers and Tamsin building your sídhe, so why not let them save your life?'

'Have you been smoking weed again?'

Thistle scanned their faces, hope bursting into life. 'She's right. We work tonight for Rani, not ourselves. Choose one of the mortals who would put themselves out for Mina.'

The Princess looked at the lake, now almost still. 'Carry me out of here and call … call Sapphire Gibson and swear her to secrecy. And tell her to bring all the raw meat in the house. Including the frozen stuff.'

Faith smiled at Alicia, her lips twisting when she saw the singed ends of her hair. 'Looks like you've discovered microwaves, Leesha. Defrosting a few shoulders of pork should be a doddle for you. Good work tonight. You have served me well, Leesha, and your lady is grateful. Pissed off, but grateful.'

The girls bowed and muttered their thanks, but Alicia only had one thought in her head: *Microwaves? Really?*

Chapter Twenty-Six

Sapphire Gibson, a photographer and wife to George Gibson of Clan Skelwith, emerged from her vehicle into the dark lane by Rydal Water like a creature from Netflix, not a Daughter of the Earth. The moon had set, the stars were dim, and the creature's sapphire blue eyes shone brightly into the darkness like living torches, giving out light instead of taking it in like eyes should do.

The girls were forced to support Faith, because their lady could not stand on her own and it would be wrong to greet the mortal from a prone position. Besides, their lady was barefoot, and only towels covered her lower half: she needed to stand to have any chance at matching her Name as Princess (or 'having any dignity' as she had put it in English).

The creature's eyes dimmed, and the Daughter of the Earth (if that's what she truly was) bowed low to their lady.

'Well met,' said Faith. 'You find me at a disadvantage tonight. There is one who would be most grateful for your help in conveying me to Middlebarrow.'

'Aah yes,' said Sapphire, drawing out the words. 'The hen party. It's a good job Mina didn't invite me, or I wouldn't be here to give you a lift.'

Sapphire spoke in a friendly tone, but her words had many ways of telling. Was she jealous? Was she glad? Or could those eyes see something that the People were missing?

Alicia's own vision had stabilised after the dazzling blue light, and she could see the Daughter quite clearly now. Sapphire tilted her head to one side. 'You're in a bad way, aren't you, Faith?'

'There's no point denying it,' said their lady. 'I wouldn't say my life is in your hands, but hers certainly is. You wouldn't want me to feed off Thistle here, would you?'

'No skin off my nose.' Gibson opened the back of her car and fetched out a large cool box and a smaller bag. She swung the bag onto her shoulder and hefted the cool box. 'But sacrificing Thistle would benefit no one, would it? I give you this food as a gift, freely given. And I will drive you to Middlebarrow Haven.'

She stepped forwards and placed the large box down, then stepped back so that the food was closer to them than to her.

'Name your boon,' said Faith. 'I don't write blank cheques to the mothers of Diggers.'

'Tsk. Get with the programme, Faith. I'm not defined by my eighth child.'

Faith showed the People's smile, and the Daughter flinched back. 'Yes, you are, Sapphire. Get used to it. And when you have, name your boon.'

The mortal paused, then raised herself slightly on her toes before saying,

'I was going to ask for a portrait but, as you've reminded me, I am part of the Clan. My boon is *eight* portraits. Time and subject of my choosing.'

Faith had rallied when they were in the flow of Lux, but Alicia could feel the weight on her shoulders increase. Their lady was flagging.

'That is not so far from a blank cheque as I would like, but you leave me no choice, mortal. I grant you your boon, but you should remember the words of Methingolias.'

Sapphire bowed. 'You are generous, and don't worry, I will be very careful what I wish for.'

When her head came up again, her eyes were once more living sapphires in her head. 'Say *gammon*.'

The flash blinded Alicia, and she blinked twice to clear her vision. When she could see again, Sapphire was zipping a large camera into the shoulder bag. 'I'll just move my car a bit so we can get the bus out. You can tell me what you were doing here when you've got your strength back.'

'I'd rather put a tongue beetle in my mouth,' muttered Faith in their mutual Silence. She eased her arm off Thistle and fumbled for the keys. She passed them over and said, 'Open her up and get the food. Leesha, you'll need to use that new strength of yours to lift me inside. Try not to set me on fire. And if either of you can find a way to delete that image off her camera, I'll make you a Count on the spot and put the other one in her service.'

On the journey to Middlebarrow Manse – *Middlebarrow Haven* in the mortal tongue – Alicia managed to suppress her questions about her sacrifice at the lake and what it meant for her future. She made that suppression to preserve her integrity and stop the new Memories crawling over her skin like the giant ticks which occasionally infested the sídhe, and she achieved that suppression by focusing on three questions about the mortal who had their lives in her hands:

One: Who is the more dangerous driver? Our lady or the Daughter of the Earth?

Two: Are those eyes a Work of mortal magick, are they Artefacts, or are they part of her nature?

Three: Will our lady kill her before or after we arrive, and if before and if we crash, would that count as suicide?

Other than driving like she was Eclipsed, Sapphire Gibson was as good as her word, and left the People to recover in peace while she threw the minibus down the roads towards the motorway. However, after they'd stopped for coffee and for Faith to get dressed at the service station, the Daughter of the Earth became as relentless as a digging Dwarf: asking questions about the People, the Peace of Brothers Water, the Staveley Sídhe, the other Queens of Albion and even about their lord's adventure in the Emerald Isle. Alicia had been amazed: she had no idea there were quite so many ways her lady could say *no comment, none of your business,* and *fuck off* without being rude. Alicia filed some of them away for use during the hen party, especially when talking to Rachael Clarke.

After the comfort break, Sapphire had dumped her camera bag in the back of the bus, along with all the hot pies that had been in the shop and a giant Toblerone (why Toblerone? Was it a Gnomish thing because of the mountains on the box? Whatever. They were thankful for it. And for the pies.).

When Sapphire had asked Faith, for the sixth time, to give the real reason why she had been wounded and sent to the kitchens, Thistle got up and broke off some more Toblerone. She leaned her arm over the front seat and said, 'Would like you some, my lady? Keep your energy levels up?'

'Ooh. Thanks. I am getting peckish. Drop it there.'

On the way back to her seat, Thistle stumbled and fell over. Alicia thought that this was because Sapphire had just executed a near-death experience overtaking a lorry-load of *Bargains*, and maybe it was, but it was also Thistle's chance to swipe the camera bag and put a Glamour in its place.

This was clever but way too dangerous in Alicia's eyes, because Sapphire kept turning to look over her shoulder (swerving into the other lanes when she did so). Alicia was convinced those eyes would see through a Glamour in a heartbeat, but Thistle had been clever: she had struck while the Daughter was eating Toblerone. Their driver had her mouth full, and she focused on the road ahead. Until Thistle screamed.

The brakes slammed on, Alicia fell off the seat and Faith landed on top of her. The sound of horns blared around them.

Thistle knelt in the gangway, wide eyed and quivering with pain and fear. Her right hand gripped her left wrist, and the jaws of a mousetrap gripped two of her fingers on her left hand. Alicia gagged, unable to process the sight, and unable to move with the weight of their lady on top of her.

Sapphire broke the silence. 'Ooh! It worked. Do you want me to take it off, or do you want to self-amputate?'

Alicia felt Faith go rigid with rage for a fraction of a second: to ask Sapphire to remove it would mean being in her debt.

The Princess forced herself to relax. 'Forgive me, noble Daughter,' she said. 'I apologise for my bondmaid's actions, and if you could remove your clever device, I will make sure it never happens again. Once you've driven onto the hard shoulder, that is. Please. I do not want my obituary to be a traffic statistic.'

Sapphire drove the bus off the carriageway and onto the embankment. Faith scrambled off Alicia and grabbed Thistle by the shirt, dragging her to the front and flopping her over the seat.

'Hold her arm still,' said Sapphire.

Faith gripped Thistle's left arm, and the Daughter quickly prised off the mousetrap. The Princess and the Daughter of the Earth locked eyes for a second. The People's special eyes and the hard stones of Mother Earth saw something in each other, and Faith extended a hand. 'Peace. I shall teach Thistle the story of the Chequered Queen and the rabbit hole. It will be good learning for her.'

Sapphire shook hands. 'Nice try, Faith. Look, I don't want you as an enemy, so I promise: no more surprise pictures, and you get a veto on the final selection.'

'Understood.' Faith let go of Sapphire's hand and gently picked Thistle up. She placed her on the double seat and took her hand to begin the Healing. If possible. 'You need a new name,' she said in the People's tongue. 'It shall be *Thistle Lightfinger*. Let me tell you a story…'

They arrived at the hamlet of Little Barrow without further incident, and if it hadn't been for the occasional jolt and swerve, Alicia would have fallen asleep. As they wound slowly through the lanes approaching the Manse, Faith got her phone out. 'Our timing is shit. Mortals do not like the Angel's Hour.'

'What's that, my lady?'

'Four o'clock in the morning. It's when the Angel of Death stalks them.'

'Really?'

'How should I know? Shut up a minute, will you.'

Faith dialled a number and put the phone to her ear. It rang for a few seconds, then a sleepy voice said, 'Gnrrgh?'

Faith lightened her voice a touch. 'Hi, Vicky. So sorry we're late. We'll be there in five.'

'Righty-ho. I'll tell Saskia the good news, eh?'

'Who?'

'Saskia Mason. Guardian of the Spring. Evie's mother.'

'Oh. Her. See you in a minute.' Princess Faith disconnected and leaned forwards to talk to Sapphire. 'I think it's along here on the right. I take it you won't have a problem seeing through the Glamours.'

'What makes you say that? Oh, here's the turning.'

The bus pulled off the lane, past a sleeping cottage and through imposing stone gates, then up a short track. The headlights briefly picked out the blue shape of the Smurf off to the left, sleeping quietly. If helicopters sleep.

To the right of the Smurf, Alicia could see more magick than even the Derwent Sídhe possessed, even though the Manse was a fraction of the size. Wards upon Wards, nested Glamours and some vicious traps marked out the boundary of Middlebarrow Haven, and Alicia felt one of her new Memories stirring. She suppressed it and focused on the welcome committee.

The two women waiting for them had chosen radically different approaches to the long wait. The older one had stayed up and was layered in country clothes. She didn't look happy, either. The younger one had gone to bed.

The chief organiser of the hen party, Victoria Robson the Seer, was wearing a fluffy dressing gown with a big logo on the chest. Alicia tried to get a look at her hair, but it was tucked into a big knitted hat. If Sapphire took a picture of the Seer looking like this, the caption would read *asleep standing up*.

Alicia sensed more life beyond the humans. Was that Scout lurking in the background? Yes, it was.

The People wearily exited the minibus, and the only one of the assembly with any energy at all dashed up and barked loudly at the People. Then he ran round in a circle and hid behind the Seer.

'Welcome in peace,' said Saskia. Her eyes flicked along the line, resting on Sapphire. 'I don't believe I've had the pleasure.'

The Daughter offered her hand. 'Sapphire Gibson. Relief driver.'

'Oh. Pleased to meet you.' Saskia took two Artefacts from her pocket, handing them to the Daughter as she was nearest. 'You'll have to share these. Ms Gibson will need one to herself, and you three can hold hands. I am now going to the lodge and going to bed. I may see you before you go, and I may not.'

The Princess bowed. 'In peace, thank you.'

The Guardian of the Spring marched off with a stiff back, taking a shortcut through the grounds to her cottage; Scout thought about following her, but stuck to the Seer. The visitors stood quietly for a second, then Sapphire offered the second token to Faith. 'You sort yourselves out, and I'll get ready to drive us down.'

Alicia and Thistle helped their lady onto the bus. Alicia went to close the door, but the Seer was standing there, suddenly looking wide awake.

'By the gods, this bus *stinks* of blood and Quicksilver and I don't know what. What the hell happened to youse lot? You all look like you've been on the receiving end of a right tonking. What did Nimue do to you?'

The girls looked to their lady, and all Faith could manage was to lift a hand and make a vague gesture; it was Sapphire who broke the silence.

'They went above and beyond the call of duty. Nimue can be a harsh mistress when the mood takes her. Are you getting a lift, Victoria?'

'It's Vicky, and yes. Reluctantly. Head down the drive and go to the right. And don't worry about driving over Scout: he likes to play chicken with slow-moving vehicles. He thinks if he can get you to stop, he's won the game. Daft dog.'

The bus headlights cut through the darkness to show a tree-lined drive, then the view opened out for a second, showing a house even bigger than Elvenham Grange. Before Alicia could understand it, they were round the side between parked cars and old outbuildings.

'Leave the bus here for now,' said Victoria. She opened the door, stepped down and pointed to a door next to a small brick add-on. 'This way. Scout! Come here. No one let that dog in the house.'

'Arff!' said Scout with an aggrieved look on his face.

They shambled off the bus and followed Victoria through the door. The brick building outside turned out to be a huge kennel, judging by the luxury dog bed, food bowls and scattering of well-chewed toys. Had that always been its purpose? Alicia was too tired to speculate. She shuffled through a cloakroom and into a big kitchen. Victoria was leaning on one of those always-on stoves whose name she couldn't remember.

'Right. I'm ga'n back to bed for a bit. There's some airbeds through there that you can put down by the Aga.' (*Aga! That's the one!*) 'Sorry, but we're a bit full upstairs, and Mina says to tell you that it's not a mark of disrespect.' She paused, then remembered that there were four extra guests, not three. 'Oh. Sapphire. Erm, do you snore?'

The Daughter gave the Seer a hard stare. 'I have already told the Princess that I am not my husband, and still less do I share his bad habits.'

'Ooh! There's a story there, I'll bet. I was only joking, pet. Honest. You come upstairs, and you can sleep in my bed. With me, of course. It's big enough.' She looked at the three People. 'Evie will be up first, I'm sure. About seven o'clock. If you genuinely need longer to recover, I'd kip down in the drawing room. Second on the left down the corridor.'

Faith bowed. 'This will be perfect, thank you.'

'Then I'll see you later. This way, Sapphire.'

Sapphire followed the Mage, and Alicia heard her say, 'Do I snore! At least you didn't ask me if I was bisexual before offering to share a bed.'

'Why? Are you?'

'No idea. And I'm too tired to find out.'

Their voices faded, and the Princess slumped onto a kitchen chair.

'Can you get the beds, Thistle?' She blew out air and waited until Thistle had manhandled three airbeds into the space before the Aga and returned with blankets. 'You both did well tonight, girls. Very well. I'm hoping that tomorrow will be less of a trial. Alicia? Will you undress me?'

'An honour, my lady.'

Chapter Twenty-Seven

Alicia was down to the last hen. The young Squire felt a lot better for having rested for a couple of hours, and things were going well. She had wrestled Saffron's beautiful white hair and got it tamed under a sky-blue hat. She had managed to address Evie Mason's 'bang average' hair while telling her stories about the People. She had used Fire to weave in Lucy's extensions in record time, making her look wild and carefree in her sunflower yellow dress. She had even made Tamsin look old enough not to be challenged about her age at the bar. And now their lord's sister Rachael had arrived and was sitting in the chair.

Rachael's hair was wet from the shower and she was busy putting on her foundation. 'Are you sure I can do this while you dry it?' she asked.

'Course,' Alicia replied, sorting her hair into strands. It really was the healthiest and glossiest of all the hens'. Except Mina's, of course, and that was being worked on in another room by the Princess, with Thistle assisting.

'Are you looking forward to the weekend?' she asked her client. 'I've heard all sorts of stories about what mortals do on these trips. They can't be true.'

'Why not? When you only live once, you grab your fun while you can. And you can talk, Alicia. What about all these Fae parties? No holds barred there, according to Ez.'

Alicia kept working on the hair, grouping the strands that would cascade down the front in elegant extended curls. 'I've never attended one since I dropped my wings, and I'd be serving drinks if I did. I'm only a Squire. In fact, this is the closest to any action I've ever been.'

Rachael put down the sponge. 'What? You're not telling me…? You are! You're a Fae and you're a virgin!'

Alicia had emerged from her Matching with a new understanding of many things. Fork-pain had become clearer, for example, because mortals have only a finite time to make choices. Bloodrise was clearer, too, and they had so many words for it; her favourite was mortified.

When she still had her wings, Alicia had often felt blood rush with her anger when she failed at something or when Lady Agnes was displeased with her. Mortals, it seemed, felt it differently. Alicia was still figuring this out, and trying to separate anger from embarrassment. If that were possible.

To Alicia, the fact that she was unpractised in bed meant little. She couldn't drive or fly the Smurf, either, and no one was taking delight in that. She decided to deflect that one, because she wasn't going to tell Rachael about Robbie. Oh no. He was her secret.

'Talk to Thistle. She was put to the couch, and she told me that she preferred it to cleaning the ovens. Do you want to finish your foundation? It's a bit streaky on the left side.'

'I … Yeah. Better had.'

Rachael picked up the sponge, and Alicia made the Ink for Fire. The Ink came alive, and she remembered to dial it down; she did not want her client going up in smoke. She fluffed the strands dry and twisted them into hanging curls as the water flew away. It would only need a little setting and shining to be finished. Perfect. 'Let me do your eyes. I'm much quicker.'

'What about my hair?'

'Done. Dry.'

Rachael was silent for a second, then she fingered a strand. 'It's so soft and silky. That is incredible. You must have commanded the water molecules without heating the hair. Just how did you do that? Every time I ask Sofía how she makes the rabbit turn green, she just shrugs and says something like, "You do the same with blowing air to cool your tea, but you use Lux and blow light." Totally not helpful.'

Alicia had picked up an eyeshadow brush. She waved it around. 'I dunno. I just call the Fire to the water, like you call to Scout. The difference is that the water always comes and doesn't demand a treat.'

'Right. I thought Sofía could do some serious shit, but this is beyond that. You really have no idea what you're doing?'

There was a story for this: how Princess Aylesbury mated with the bishop and lived to tell the tale. And the profit? When it comes to Ink, always change the subject.

Alicia dabbed the brush into the palette and tilted Rachael's head to start work. When there is an implement in the region of your eyeball, even a soft one, clients soon calm down. Even the Wolves.

She brushed the shadow over the top lids and used a little Fire to smooth them out, then said, 'How come Sofía's not here?'

'Good question. As soon as dates started getting bandied around, she said that she had to go out to some godforsaken place in the middle of nowhere on Fridays for Herbalism tutorials and that there are exams coming up.'

Rachael's brows were already shaped and dyed to perfection, so Alicia picked up a pencil and got ready to add some drama to her eyes. 'Her cannabis is pretty awesome already, especially when Myfanwy grows it for her. Does she need to learn opium and cocaine?'

Rachael's eyes stayed perfectly still while her lips curved upwards. 'Don't say that to anyone else, Alicia. It would get so many people in so much shit if that was even mentioned. Unless it's Tamsin, of course. You can say anything about her you like.'

'I have told Tamsin that you are a good person, my lady, and that you deserve to be loved. She said something strange and I had to look it up. I still don't understand it.'

'Go on. What did the mad bitch say?'

'She is not mad.'

'Okay, okay. The Bodysnatcher is not mad. What did she say about me being deserving of love?'

'She said that she would take it under advisement. I didn't think the law interfered in love, but what do I know?'

'We'll have to work on that one, Alicia. You and me both. Shame you're not coming with us on any of the hen events. I reckon you'd be the perfect wing-woman. And even if we don't score with the men, I've scored some of Sofía's finest weed. Don't tell anyone, and I'll pass you a joint or two later.'

A little shiver ran down Alicia's spine. That would be a treat indeed. 'Do you not see much of Sofía with rehearsals for your Fire Games?'

'I did. Not so much since Easter because she really wants to pass her first year Fellowship exams and be accepted as an Apothecary. She's also suddenly busy at the weekends. I reckon she's got a boyfriend she's keeping quiet about, but Ez thinks she's got a job.'

'You mortal girls talk about things all the time,' said Alicia, risking a confidence. 'So do we, you know. Why would Sofía keep her boyfriend secret?'

'When your brother is the Deputy Constable and your sister is friends with your tutor, you need a bit of privacy. You don't tell everything to Faith, do you?'

'I do not,' said Alicia emphatically. She finished the right eye, stood back to check her work, then snapped the pencil in half when someone stuck a dagger through her mind.

'Owww!'

'Shit! Alicia, are you okay?'

The Squire bent double and clutched her head. The pain had gone, but its echo was loud and sore. She looked closely at herself and it was the Key to Middlebarrow, which she'd hung on to when they crossed the Wards. While she had rested and slept, the key had morphed and detached itself from the Artefact to become its own little bit of Ink on her body, and it had just told her something had happened.

Alicia nearly lost control of her bladder when she realised that the Middlebarrow Ink was trying to bind her. She moved to Encircle it and keep it penned in, and when it calmed down, she saw that it had been triggered by something. Someone. An arrival.

'The Anointed Guardian is here!' she exclaimed.

'Who? Oh, you mean Hannah Rothman,' said Rachael. 'Why have you just torn your leggings to bits and drawn that weird shape on your leg?'

Alicia looked down. More Bloodrise, and this time it was justified: she had directly shown the Ways to a mundane mortal. When she had corralled the key, she'd still had the eyebrow pencil in her hand, and she'd drawn the Ink, just like Thistle had told her not to do, and there it was on her leg in a visible manifestation. She licked her fingers and smeared the cosmetic shape she'd created, making it unrecognisable as anything magickal.

She'd also ripped her leggings apart without realising, and both girls were suddenly staring at Alicia's underwear. 'Those better not be your lucky pants,' said Rachael. 'I didn't know you could get unicorn knickers in adult sizes. Not that I've looked for them. Hang on, they look custom made!'

'Cathy was bored one night. She hates knitting and is learning to sew.'

'You are not going to get lucky wearing those. Unless your lot can make magick pants. Can they?'

'Erm, yes. For … Never mind.'

Rachael arched her eyebrows, then dropped them. 'Didn't Vix say that she was bringing Hannah up here via the back staircase? What's that all about?'

Alicia froze. She couldn't cope. She was caught between the wolf outside and the spider within, and that story never ended well.

'Earth to planet Alicia? What's up?'

'I … I can't speak of it.'

'Yes, you can. Secrets of the salon goes both ways, you know.'

Alicia couldn't help herself. She didn't know what to do. 'I haven't finished your eyes and the Anointed Guardian cannot see me like this! It would be a shame on the sídhe.'

'Don't move.'

With speed that was almost magickal, Rachael sprang from the chair and slipped out of the door, leaving Alicia alone with the churning Ink in her body.

She trembled at what had been happening to her: Nimue had done a lot more than unload surplus Quicksilver into Alicia's veins. All over her skin, Memories, Charms, Works and wholly alien Vortices of magick were flickering in and out of focus, and then there was the business of the Key to Middlebarrow. What should she do? Before she could even start to think, Rachael slipped back in and thrust a pair of athletic leggings patterned in bright red, black and white into her hands.

'Told you I'd be quick. Get 'em on.'

Alicia ripped off what was left of the old pair, pulling up the new pair with surprising ease. 'They fit!'

'Yah. Didn't think you'd get into mine, so I nicked some of Evie's. She's near enough your size. Right. Focus, Alicia. Eyes.'

There was a discreet tap on the door, and Alicia smelled her Sister. 'Come in, Thistle.'

The Squire stuck her head into the room. 'Are you done? Vicky wants to bring the Anointed Guardian straight up.'

Alicia touched Rachael's shoulder and spoke under Silence. 'Do you trust me?'

'Of course I do, Alicia.' She reached up and put her hand on Alicia's arm, accidentally doubling the Silence. For a brief moment they could hear each other's heartbeats, and that was way too intimate for a first date. Not that they were on a date...

Alicia released Rachael's shoulder. 'By the time the Anointed Guardian has been to the loo, I'll be completely finished.'

Rachael raised an eyebrow. 'You're good, but you're not that good.'

Alicia held up what was left of the eyebrow pencil. 'Look at the pencil and relax. That's it. Now, listen carefully...'

Rachael's mind surrendered before Alicia had sung even the first verse of the Fairy Lullaby (as Alicia never called it). She put Fire in her hands and finished Rachael's make-up in less than a minute, and she was applying the last strokes of lip-liner when Rachael blinked back into focus.

'There! See?'

'Bloody hellfire. You are good.'

There was a knock at the door, more formal this time, and Vicky came straight in, the Anointed Guardian right behind her.

Ink crawled over Alicia's body, worst in her left armpit. The Anointed Guardian blinked twice and scratched herself in exactly the same place. That could not be a coincidence.

Alicia bowed to cover her confusion. 'Guardian, it is an honour.'

'Come on, Raitch,' said Vicky. 'Let's leave 'em to it. By, she's done a good job with your cheekbones. You never did tell me what you were wearing today...'

The door closed, and Alicia was alone with the Guardian. 'Well met, Squire. What's your name? Just the short version.'

'Alicia, if it pleases you.'

The Guardian paused, and Alicia felt herself being stripped naked under the mortal's gaze. It only lasted a second, but it was enough for her short life to have been laid bare, and she felt more exposed than if she'd been standing without her leggings and unicorn pants.

'You're a surprise package,' observed the Guardian. 'There's more to you than hair and beauty, that's for certain.' She looked at a slim gold watch on her wrist. 'You've got five minutes. Turn around and close your eyes. All of them.'

Alicia did as she was ordered, closing down every sense except hearing. It would be amazing to look at such a legendary mortal and see what lurked under the skin. Fatal, too.

She heard a zip opening, a few grunts and then, 'Ready.' She turned around and was glad she'd set her face beforehand.

The Anointed Guardian had a jumpsuit over one arm and she lifted a finger to point it right at Alicia's heart. 'What we are about to do must never be disclosed under any circumstances. Understand?'

'It is as my lady wishes.'

'Good. This is what I want.'

The rain which had lashed over Alicia when she practised the Ways last night hadn't been as heavy in Cheshire, and it had stopped in the early hours. It was a mild spring morning, perfect for Ladies Day. Except for the field outside the Manse.

The Smurf was in the pasture, and not only was the grass long and untrimmed, it was also rather soggy underneath. Not good for heels and trouser hems, and there were two options: matting or carriage. They had no matting, so carriage it was.

'Where's this carriage?' said Lucy Berardi when she came back from poking her head outside.

The hens and helpers were milling around the kitchen, finishing the last of the Prosecco and checking their phones while they waited for the bride and her handmaiden to appear.

'I'm here,' said Alicia.

'Eh?'

'Faith and I will link hands and carry you across the field to the Smurf. It's how our noble ladies keep their shoes and skirts dry.'

Vicky turned to Sapphire. 'You! No pictures of that bit, okay?'

Sapphire was hitching a lift with them, and the pilot had been convinced to fly her up to Ambleside after dropping the hens at Aintree. After all, their slot at the VIP Helipad was limited, so the Smurf would have to wait for them somewhere else anyway.

Sapphire lifted her mug of tea and grinned over the top of it. 'Just the one? Mina Desai being carried in the style to which she has become accustomed?'

'Shut your face. Now.'

A cheer and applause broke out from the edge of the group, and the hens parted to reveal the bride.

'Wow, she looks amazing,' said Alicia. Mina was wearing a lilac dress with a slit to the thigh and sleeves which formed a cape. Amid the shimmering pastel fabric, gold glinted and magick swirled, adding to the impact. 'That really suits her.'

Alicia jumped when Rachael touched her arm and leaned towards her. Without thinking, Alicia made a Silence, and Rachael responded, 'Of course it suits her. We had to send pictures of our outfits to Vicky and anything in lilac was vetoed. That's why I'm sporting bottle green.'

Mina did a twirl to applause, then their pilot, Leah Kershaw, coughed. 'We'd better get going. I'll go and complete the checks. If you could make your way up to the LZ? Sapphire, if you come first and give me a hand, that'll save five minutes.'

Mina offered her arm to the Anointed Guardian, to test whether the layered Glamour Alicia had helped make could survive proximity to Mina's Artefacts (it could), and the bride and her Matron of Honour led the party out of the kitchen and up the drive.

Alicia fell in at the back with Faith and Thistle, and she watched to see how the hair and hats would survive contact with the wind. It was looking good, until Faith spoke quietly in the People's tongue.

'Taking Sapphire home was my idea, and I've paid Leah to fly to Birk Fell before Ambleside because I need Amrita. When we get to the gates, you two will have to make the carriage. I don't think I have the strength.'

'My lady!'

'Shh.'

Saskia Mason was waiting for them at the end of the drive, looking a lot happier than she had at four o'clock in the morning. She went up to her daughter and beamed, giving Evie a hug and holding her hands. Saskia was here to see her daughter, yes, and to wish them all good sport, yes, but also to collect the tokens from those who'd needed them.

'Arff!'

And to stop Scout sneaking out of the Haven grounds.

'You're first, Saff,' said Vicky.

Alicia and Thistle linked hands and slid them under Saffron's bum while she placed her arms on their shoulders. The Squires engaged some extra life and strode off.

The hens thought it was hilarious, and started pretending to whip the Squires like horses and telling them to 'giddy-up!' They did giddy-up for Tamsin, who loved it. When they carried Evie, though, they got a different message. 'Why are you wearing my new compression leggings, Alicia?'

'I'm sorry. Another accident, I'm afraid. I shall return them in perfect condition.'

'Ew. No thanks. You can keep them, but they cost me a fortune. I got them for my new personal trainer. He's well fit.'

'How about I weave a Glamour to ... to give you the *after* look?'

'What are you trying to say about the *before* look?'

'Nothing, my lady.'

Evie snorted. 'Yeah. Right. If you can produce leggings that really make me look thinner, then great.'

After dropping Evie, they jogged back, and Thistle said, 'Who's going tae do that wi' the pants? You cannae.'

'The Anointed Guardian just taught me how to. She is a rather different shape to this Ahearn mortal, so there was a lot of work in the butt department.'

'Neat. Who's next?'

'Erin.'

'Right. Soon be all aboard.'

Chapter Twenty-Eight

The hens had been loaded, as had the trunk with the cordless GHDs and the emergency repair kit. Just in case. This wasn't Alicia's first flight, and she wasn't nervous. At least not about the flight. It was their Princess who worried her.

Faith slumped against Alicia when they took off and kept her eyes closed all through the short journey. Alicia had to shake her as the engines slowed down.

Passengers usually de-planed with the rotors going (at great risk to their hair), but their hostess had somehow got permission for the Smurf to shut down completely. Thistle opened the door and stood ready to hand the bride down, and Alicia peered out of the window. Coming across the LZ was their hostess, the noble Princess Birkdale, allegedly the sworn enemy of their lady, and here they were, right at their enemy's hearth. Faith would have a plan. She must have a plan. And a backup plan for when she was weak. Surely. Alicia zipped her lips and tried not to think such thoughts. She also tried to remember that Princess Birkdale was to be called 'Tara Doyle' today.

The other hens had dismounted the Smurf, with the Anointed Guardian last, and the way was clear for Alicia and Faith to leave. 'Give me your hand,' said Faith.

Their lady was weak, really weak. *How* weak only became clear when Faith had to put most of her weight on Alicia's shoulder. The hens and Tara Doyle's party were mingling and air-kissing and looking very excited. Alicia craned her neck and saw that Kelly Kirkham had obviously spent some of Mina's bounty going to a *proper* salon. The auburn highlights gave her a real touch of class. Alicia breathed a sigh of relief: her job was done, and as soon as they'd bowed to Tara Doyle, she could help her lady back onto the Smurf.

Through a break in the crowd, Alicia saw Sapphire Gibson talking to Tara Doyle and holding up her camera. Words were exchanged in Silence, and suddenly Tara took charge. She waved over one of her household and started arranging the hens before taking hold of Mina and Lucy.

'Hurry up, you bitch,' muttered Faith. 'And fuck *you*, Sapphire Gibson, *and* your fucking camera and your borrowed eyes.'

Alicia had the urge to run and grab Birkdale because she could see Faith's flame starting to flicker. What was the worst thing that could happen? And then she knew exactly what the worst thing was. As the mortals said, *where there's life…*

Finally the hens were in order, and Sapphire herself made some minor adjustments while talking to Tara's PA. There was another pause. Pictures were taken, and Sapphire bowed again before going into a huddle with the assistant.

From within the hens, Tara's voice rang out. 'My God, that picture is *so* amazing, Sapphire. Just give us a sec, Mina, yeah? Just wanna say hello to me new friend Faith.'

The hens gave Tara some space and she strode towards the Smurf. Alicia tried to give strength to Faith, but it was blocked for some reason, and Faith couldn't manage more than a head-bow.

'Well met,' said Tara. She paused, and the expected welcome did not come from her lips. Instead, she switched to the People's tongue and made the People's smile. 'It's always nice to welcome strangers, and this is Common Ground today. Enjoy the sights, Princess. They'll be your last, I reckon.'

Alicia stiffened. Surely her lady couldn't be *that* bad? No wonder Princess Birkdale looked so pleased. Faith rallied a little. 'I regret the pleasure will be fleeting. I must repair to Lakeland.'

Birkdale opened her jaws fully, then closed them completely and switched to English. 'There's no rush. That Daughter of the Earth is just working with my PA to sell her picture to *Celebrity Enquirer*. Air Traffic Control won't kick you off for a good half an hour yet. I've seen to that.'

Faith sank even harder onto Alicia's shoulder. 'Why? I am no threat to you. I can smell your Hlæfdige from here. A little Amrita from her and I would put myself in your debt for a generation. There is room for both of us, Tara. The mortals of Lancashire are unguarded and rich.'

Alicia was appalled. Her lady was coming as close to begging as the People ever got. Even the Sainted Queen of Asaph had been more circumspect when she begged from the Dwarf.

A voice shouted over. 'Do you want some fizz, Tara?'

'Sounds good. Stay there and I'll join you in a minute,' she replied, commanding her household to hold their positions. Then she dropped her voice and whispered. 'I won't see you later, Faith.'

Faith had no strength left at all, and Alicia was taking all of her weight. She shuffled her hip to give more support, and Faith swung round clumsily to hold her hand up. With almost the last of her strength, her lady spoke in power. 'Wait and witness,' she commanded Princess Birkdale.

'Oh yeah? Hurry up and die, will you.'

Faith's breaths were ragged now. 'What name would you give me, Leesha, if I became Queen?'

'What? My lady! Let me force the mortal to fly us to Birk Fell now. There is still time.'

'Like fuck there is. What name, Leesha? *What name!*'

Alicia tried to keep her lady engaged and fighting. 'Right now it would be the Luckless Queen, but you can do better than that. You *will* do better than that!'

'Thistle! Come here!'

Princess Birkdale frowned, unsure of what was going on but too proud to speak. After all, she had said her final word, and she had spoken on Common Ground. To go back now would be *utter* humiliation.

'Yes, my lady?' said Thistle, who looked as distraught as Alicia felt.

'I dub you Saerdam Thistle Lightfinger. There. You're a Knight now, so Proclaim me. Here and now. You heard Alicia. Do it!'

This was as wrong as wrong could be. Nothing here was in any story that Alicia had ever come across. Ever. And even in the moment, she couldn't find it in herself to be angry that Thistle had been Knighted before her. Then again, she herself was all that stood between their lady and a return to Mother Nature. If Thistle spoke the words in power, Alicia would be holding a Queen Proclaimed. What a story *that* would be!

It was something they did in the nest when they had wings: playing at Proclaiming. Apparently mortal girls played in the same way at becoming a bride. Thistle looked at Princess Birkdale and at Princess Faith, then she dropped to her knees, drew strength and prepared to speak with power.

Faith had some final words for Alicia, and each one was a sharp blade edged with n'Haeval. 'I hope Thistle's worth it, Leesha. If you'd let me eat her by the lake and draw on the river of Lux, I wouldn't be about to die in your arms.'

No one would *blame* Alicia if Faith died. No one would hold her to account and punish her. It was simply that no one would ever speak to her again. Ever. 'You will not die in my arms,' said Alicia as she lowered Faith to the ground.

Hurt bloomed in Faith's eyes, and Thistle stopped her preparations in confusion. As Alicia scanned the group, desperate for help, Faith spoke bitterly. 'Carry on, Thistle.'

Who could Alicia turn to? Who could persuade Birkdale to intervene? Lucy? Mina? No. Neither would twist the Princess's ear hard enough, and that left only one. The only one who had real skin in the Lakeland game. Alicia sprang forwards and grabbed Sapphire Gibson's arm.

'Faith is dying, and Tara is letting her.' She pointed to the PA, standing next to them and masking every feeling on her face. 'This one is a Hlæfdige. She can save Faith.'

Sapphire's eyes went dark, as dark as a First Mine, then they blazed with blue fire. 'Tend to your lady, Alicia. I will get help.'

Alicia dashed back and gathered Faith once more into her arms, and her lips moved along as Thistle spoke the words. 'As it is written in the Book of the Great Queen, I Proclaim you here. Princess Faithful of Staveley you were—'

'Stop!' commanded the vision of Irish beauty who was actually the Anointed Guardian. How in the mother's name was she keeping that Construction going while also radiating the power of Nimue, and who was the Daughter talking to on her phone?

Sapphire held out her mobile to Princess Birkdale. 'The Red Queen would speak with you, honoured lady. She says that you should "Remember Accrington" before you decline her call.'

Birkdale looked as if she were caught in the most violent fork-pain known to the People, and for a moment, her fingers reached out to Princess Faith, then she turned, grabbed the phone from Sapphire's hand and made a Silence.

In Alicia's arms, Faith had fainted. Whatever game she was playing with Thistle's Proclamation was gone forever. Alicia drew more Fire from her bones and pressed her lips to her lady's neck, desperate to breathe a little more life into her in any way she could. As she fumbled the magick to her mouth, one of the new Memories swirled out of her skin and into her head.

It was a vision of water and of trees. A vision of sunlight bathing the leaves with warmth and giving them life while the roots soaked up the water of the lake. In one of the trees dwelt a Spirit, stretched from the lowest root to the highest bud and pulsing purple as it drank the light and water, its existence barely a whisper of twigs moving in the breeze.

As the vision faded, Alicia's lips shifted slightly, moving out of the mortal world and dropping into the shared space of Faith's neck. 'Become the tree,' Alicia whispered, and somehow Faith's flickering life drew a tiny drop of Alicia's essence. Enough for Faith to rally and for Alicia to slip into the darkness.

She awoke with the hard metal of helicopter wheels pressed into her back and – of all creatures – the Digger's Daughter pressing a plastic cup of hot, sweet tea to her lips.

'I don't know what you did, but by the Mother you saved Faith's life.'

Alicia's eyes darted around the Aintree LZ, and they were alone. 'What...?'

'Can you stand?'

'I can try. More tea?'

Alicia took the cup and spilled some of it down her chin as her hand shook. She ignored the burning and let it rip down her throat to nourish her. 'A hand, my lady?'

Sapphire stood and helped Alicia to her feet, then shouted, 'Coming!'

A thin whine broke through the hubbub of pleasure as the mighty engines of the Smurf woke up once more. With Sapphire's hand on her back, Alicia stumbled to the door and stopped when she saw the scene inside.

Faith was bleeding again, her pelvis propped up on more towels, her head supported by Thistle. Was it a dream or was Alicia's Sister now *Saerdam Thistle Lightfinger*? If so, then they were Sisters no longer.

And perhaps strangest was Princess Birkdale's topless Lady sitting above Faith, her face rigid with fury and hatred.

'In you get,' said the Daughter, heaving Alicia's bum over the threshold and propelling her into the forward passenger seats. Sapphire leaned in, and with a wicked grin took in the Hlæfdige's blouse, jacket and scarf. 'Thanks for these. I do love Chanel, and tweed goes a treat with these jeans. I'll take the VIP pass, too.'

She held out a hand, and the Lady slapped a laminated pass against Sapphire's fingers.

'Good luck, everyone. See you later.' Sapphire backed out of the door as the wash from the rotors started to drive the race-goers further away from the LZ. She slammed the door closed and jogged out of sight. Alicia turned to her Princess and dropped to her knees to crawl closer.

Faith took Alicia's fingers and massaged them. 'Thank you, Leesha. I have escaped death *and* seen new Ink, all in one morning, even if it was your fault I nearly died. Thank you for both. Let me feed, for we will be at Middlebarrow in moments.'

Alicia climbed back up and held on as the pilot lifted off and swung the helicopter away, towards the sea. They skirted the great city of Liverpool and followed the course of a river until Leah took them back inland and then dropped them back to earth. All the while, their lady feasted on short sips of Amrita. When the wheels touched the grass of Middlebarrow, Leah began the shutdown, and they waited until silence had returned. And then they waited while Leah tapped on a tablet. And then they waited while she sent a text message.

Finally, she turned and said, 'I'm going in for a cup of tea. When I get back, I'm flying Faith to Birk Fell, then back to Southport to drop whatshername off. I'll wait there until it's time to pick up the hens. Okay?'

'Thank you, Captain Kershaw,' said Princess Faith. 'Leesha and Thistle will be done in a moment.'

The pilot smiled. 'Thanks for the promotion. It won't make any difference if there's blood on the seats, though.' Then she jumped out and left the People to enjoy an awkward silence.

'Move me,' said Faith. 'I can lean on the wall now.'

Thistle lifted their lady's shoulders, and Alicia shuffled the towels along; she was pleased to see that there was no longer any bleeding.

'Alicia, give your T-shirt and bra to the Hlæfdige for later. I would not be accused of sending her naked into the world.' Faith turned to the Lady. 'I need you to wait outside for a moment, and the path here is public.'

Alicia took off her salon tunic (thank the Morrigan she didn't have to surrender *that*) and passed over what was underneath. The Birkdale Hlæfdige accepted the clothes without a word, dumping the bra on a seat and pulling the T-shirt over her head. She left the cabin and went to stand well away from the helicopter.

'I have no idea why Birkdale has a Hlæfdige as her close confidante and PA, but that's her choice. Today was apparently a reward, and that's why she has a face like a constipated baboon.'

'My lady!' said Alicia. 'You live. What happened?'

'C'mere, Leesha.'

Alicia came and knelt, and her lady gently took her hand, and it was the Princess who kissed the Squire's fingers. So wrong yet so right.

'Would you keep your name?' said Faith.

'Only until I am made Countess. I—'

'That could be a while, I'm afraid. First things first, though. I dub you Saerdam Alicia Lake and appoint you my handmaiden. You have served me beyond words, and I will make today's story the first told in the Staveley Sídhe, both the good and the ill.'

'My lady.'

'And this is yours. You'll need it.' Faith fumbled under the seat and pulled out her phone. Alicia took it with a lump in her throat, fear biting her insides. 'You are in charge of Shear Magic for the rest of the hen party. I know you'll do a brilliant job, too.'

'For you and for Mina, I will give what I can.'

'Thistle, you may go. I have a final word for my bonded handmaiden.'

Thistle couldn't go without giving Alicia a big hug. When the door closed behind her, Faith's eyes saddened. 'And now for the bad news.' The Princess's fingers came alive with the Ways of Binding and hovered inches from Alicia. Somehow, her lady dragged up the strength to make a Geas and placed her middle finger on Alicia's Third Eye.

'I place this Binding on you, Saerdam Alicia: that you speak not of these matters until the marriage is over. Do your duty to Rani Mina and walk in my steps as her handmaiden. And when the ceremony is done, I will release you from my household to answer to Princess Birkdale for what you did. It was the price of my life.'

The Geas was sealed, and the Princess dropped her hand. Alicia was bewildered. *How can she release me when I have done this? Where was the profit in that?*

But the Princess was not finished and she was taking no chances, gripping Alicia's hand and making a Silence so profound that even the Ravens of Godshome wouldn't hear their words. When the Silence was around them, the Princess told her handmaiden one more story, a story which shocked Alicia to the core, a story which gave the newly Knighted handmaiden both hope and despair.

Editor's Note: I have no idea what the story was that Faith told to Alicia in the helicopter, and when I asked Corrib why Birkdale should 'Remember Accrington', I was told that it was none of my business.
Evie Mason

Part Five — Confidentiality of the Salon

Alicia stepped down from the Smurf and the Hlæfdige of Princess Birkdale almost barged her out of the way as they swapped places. Thistle was waiting at the gates to the Middlebarrow Manse, and she had unloaded the beauty cases. Alicia and Thistle embraced long and hard before crossing through the Wards and walking hand-in-hand down to the house.

'That was a lucky escape and no mistake,' said Thistle. 'To think that our lady nearly died as the Luckless Queen. Could you no think of something better, love?'

'That's the only thing which bothers you?'

'Aye, well, it's easier to think aboot than the rest of today.'

Alicia laughed. 'As Lowri the Wolf would say, *If the Westmorland People are going to rely on Alicia Lake for deep thinking, we're doomed before we're named.*'

'What did you do, Leesha? How did you bring our lady back from the brink of the final crossing?'

Alicia shrugged. 'Not sure. It just came to me. Maybe Nimue read the waters and saw that I would have need.'

'So you'll no be needing my help with the Ways now, will you? Bonded handmaiden and Saviour all in one morning. Get you.'

'Thistle, I'm going to need all the help I can get. Starting with the rest of the hen weekend.'

'Don't fret. I've got your back.'

Yes, Alicia was both of those things – handmaiden and Saviour – and she was also due to be cast to the wolves in less than two months. Alicia and Thistle arrived at the back door, and there was a ferocious barking. Scout emerged from his luxury lean-to, or emerged as far as he could with a long rope attached to his harness. The rope was unusual and spoke of ignorance or cruelty. No one at the Manse was cruel, but it certainly looked as though someone was ignorant: Scout looked on all forms of rope as a challenge, not a restraint.

They went through the cloakroom to the kitchen, where Warden Saskia was about to take away a tray laden with refreshments, and the ignorance was explained: the Warden had brought the lesser dog, Benji, with her. Lesser than Scout, that is. The Warden smiled at the girls and said, 'I'm entertaining Leah Kershaw in the drawing room. Help yourselves to whatever. Come on, Benji. Stop sniffing.'

'I need meat,' said Alicia. She went through to the scullery and cracked open the chest freezer. She rummaged around and pulled out some ice-encrusted prehistoric packages which wouldn't be missed and dumped them in the butler's sink. She ran some hot water and left them to thaw, then rested with her back to the wall before deciding it was too much effort to stand.

She let her feet slide from under her until her bum hit the floor. She stretched out her legs, then opened her arms and looked at Thistle. Her (former?) Sister got onto her hands and knees. She came closer and bent her head level with Alicia's ankles. She laid her cheek to the concrete floor and reached her arms forwards to touch Alicia's knees, and magick came alive between them.

Ink swirled over both their bodies as they sought the bond which had once made them Sisters. Alicia felt a stab in her heart as the fork-pain gripped her. Did she even want to be bonded to Thistle? Would it mean more pain to come?

Some of what she felt must have transferred to Thistle, because the hands on Alicia's knees moved to the inside of her thighs, and Thistle's expression mixed pleading with the promise of delights to come.

The Ink which marked their bond was still there and it floated between them, fragile and ready to uncurl its meshed sigils if not renewed. Thistle opened her jaws and re-Inked her part of the bond with her tongue. *Neatly done.*

Alicia lowered her head and brought up her finger – it would be a long time before she did anything magickal with her tongue – and as she Inked her portion, a fleeting vision crossed her Third Eye: *a dark room. Candles and torches. A mortal woman, red of hair and wearing nothing but a gown. She picks up a candle and walks towards the doors…*

The Ink of the People blew the vision away like a cobweb in the wind, and it was done: Alicia and Thistle were Sisters still, and there was no doubt that Thistle was now firmly the younger sibling. Whatever that meant.

Thistle let go of Alicia's legs and rolled away. 'What do you need the meat for?'

'Fetch my Heartstone.'

Thistle returned in a moment and carefully offered Alicia the hairbrush. Alicia motioned for Thistle to hang on to it and said, 'There's a spiral in there, close to the handle. I would have you use it on me.'

Thistle examined the brush. 'Jings! So that's how you did it. Lift your head away from the wall.'

With long and gentle strokes, Thistle started brushing Alicia's hair. 'You were amazing today, and I'll keep saying it until the story is Inked. For a Squire to save a life like that … I cannae believe it.' She paused to rearrange her hair. 'Does that really mean you'll no be needin' me to teach you the Ways now?'

'I will always need you, Sister. I don't know what's happening to me. It just … it just came from the Nymph's donation. A whole paella of Ink that I don't understand.'

'A *paella?* Where did *that* come from? You'll work it out. And while you're at it, you can work on a better name for our lady for when we Proclaim her for real. *Luckless Queen*. I ask you. She'd ha' died of embarrassment with that moniker, never mind bleeding to death.'

Alicia gave a little smile. 'I already have the true name for her, Sister, for she has many strands to her greatness. Perhaps I'll get to use it one day.'

'You're Eclipsed, you are. Nae doubt.' Thistle laughed and carried on brushing Alicia's hair off until there was none left. Thistle gathered it into a skein and placed on Alicia's lap.

'Thank you, Sister,' said Alicia. 'I think I can manage to grow a short bob before the girls get back from the races. Pass me some of the meat.'

The hens spilled out of the Smurf while the rotors were still slowing down, laughing and clutching their hats to their heads. Two of them were still clutching bottles of champagne, too, and all of them looked like they'd had the time of their lives. Even the Anointed Guardian had a slight wobble to her walk. On days like today, the revels of mortals are not so different from the People's revels.

Alicia felt fork-pain: whether to be thrilled that the hens were all safely returned, or heart-sore that Faith was no longer here to lead Shear Magic? As the hens got closer to the gateway, she heard the Seer talking to the Bodysnatcher. 'I canna believe you photobombed that lass from *Loose Women*.'

'She gets right up my nose. And not in a good way. Is there anything left in that bottle?'

'Nah, but you don't litter the Smurf.' The Seer stopped at the threshold. 'By the gods, Alicia, what's happened to your hair? I canna believe it! Mind, it suits you.'

'Thank you, my lady.'

The Seer turned. And stumbled. She grabbed the Bodysnatcher for support and yelled, 'Right, ladies, let's go through to the drawing room and I'll do me best Uncle Conrad impersonation.'

The Enscriber belched. 'You mean you're gonna take the dog and go for a walk in the rain?'

'Ha ha. No. I am gonna give you a militarily style briefing on tonight's mission. And then I think we might all gan lie down for an hour.'

The hens staggered, lurched and sang their way down the drive. Alicia and Thistle ran ahead and diverted them to the side so that they could bypass the kitchen and go straight to the dining room. After all, there was no point in encouraging Evie to suddenly remember that the Manse had a large wine fridge.

The younger girls gathered together for mutual support like the poles of a tepee, and now that they were back here, their mortalness, their *humanity* reasserted itself; Alicia felt a stirring in the Ink of her right shoulder as the Seer became Victoria Robson once more.

Vicky looked at the coffee table and tried to hitch up her skirt. Alicia cringed. Thistle gasped. The material stretched over Vicky's thighs but it refused to go any higher, and just when it was on the verge of splitting, Vicky abandoned the idea of climbing up to Conrad's height.

'Right, listen up you lot. Tonight, by special invitation, we are heading into Manchester for …. Wait for it, wait for it … Ladies' night at the Fairy Gardens!'

A big cheer broke out from everyone except for Sapphire Gibson and the Constable who were standing together at the back. Sapphire frowned and whispered to the Matron of Honour, who shrugged and whispered something back.

When the cheering subsided, Vicky added, 'And we haven't seen the last of Tara Doyle, neither. She's not joining us, but she will be there to make sure we have the best time. And get more photies for those on Insta. So, time for a lie-down, I reckon.' She peered into the champagne bottle. 'Unless—'

'Thistle and I will escort you to your rooms!' said Alicia smoothly. 'Shear Magic will be in business in the dining room from six o'clock. And, please, leave your bottles behind and take a little libation to help you on your way.'

Thistle held a tray of shot glasses filled with a murky brown liquid, and she dispensed them to the hens as they passed by. The bride-to-be was last; Mina was as unsteady on her feet as the others, but somehow seemed to carry it off. 'Where's Faith?' she asked.

Thistle took Rani Mina's hand and led her towards the door. 'About that, hen. There's been a bit of a change of plan…'

Chapter Thirty

The libation in the shot glasses was something the People rarely shared, mostly because it had to be distilled from a tincture of Amrita. It *smelled* of alcohol, and it burned the girls' tongues, but it was actually a purgative and when they drifted back a couple of hours later, they were almost sober. Except for Sapphire Gibson, who was completely sober and had some bad news.

Alicia was busy setting up shop in the dining room so that she could work on several hens at once and supervise Thistle at the same time; her Sister was no master of GHDs, but she could be trusted with an eyebrow pencil. Alicia sensed a presence and looked up, expecting Thistle. No, it was the Digger's Daughter, still wearing the Hlæfdige's Chanel jacket.

'Good evening, my lady. Are you staying here tonight?'

Sapphire's eyes flashed in the shadows, away from the collection of standard lamps which Alicia had arranged around the chairs. 'I've come to help. You need a driver.'

'I don't need…' Alicia stopped. *She* didn't need a driver, but the hens did. 'Will not the Warden do it?'

'Saskia has no interest in driving a bunch of tanked-up hens into Manchester. And her daughter has even less interest in being driven to a nightclub by her mother.'

Alicia swallowed hard. This was a decision way beyond her. 'I shall call Birk Fell.'

Sapphire lifted her phone. 'Already done it. Cathy said that Faith was out for the count.'

'I…'

'Let me help, Alicia. You were happy to ask for it at Aintree, and you want the hen party to be a success, don't you?'

The stories were flooding into Alicia's mind now. *Beware the Digger who shows you the hand with the diamond and has an axe behind their back.* 'What's it to you?'

'I want pictures, including the ones I've already taken. And you really do need to provide a driver.'

'It is agreed.'

'Good. I'll be ready at seven thirty.'

Alicia put the matter out of her mind as the hens drifted in to be prepped for the evening, to be complimented on their shimmering creations, and to take pictures of each other. Except two, one of whom arrived after the others had adjourned elsewhere.

'I hear that congratulations are in order,' said Rachael Clarke when she'd sat down. 'That new hair is totally right for you, and Thistle says that you've both been made Knights. Is that the right term?'

It was something Alicia really didn't want to talk about, given the burden laid upon her. 'I don't think we need to do much with this, do we?' she observed, trailing the silky chestnut curls through her fingers.

'Don't change the subject, Alicia. Some serious shit went down at the racecourse this morning.'

Alicia went round to stand in front of Rachael. 'Faith has been through a lot. She was forced to retire, and it was a sign of respect to you all that we were made Knights. A bridal party should not be attended by Squires.'

'So you're Saerdam Alicia now?'

'I am! Not that you need to call me that. I hear you were the only one who took money away from the bookmakers. What's your secret?'

'I called Eseld and asked her for tips. She knows a man who knows these things.'

'Do you want me to do something special with your eyes? Something fitting for the Midnight Gardens?'

'Why not? So long as you don't make me look like a drag queen.'

'Impossible. You're totally the most naturally feminine hen.'

'Flatterer.'

'Yes. I'm going to go for blue on blue here. Trust me on this one.' Alicia picked up an unused palette and clean brush and leaned in. 'Talking of Eseld, I'm gobsmacked she's going on the stag.'

'Technically she's escorting them, but yeah, it would have been a shame if she'd missed out completely on the stag and hen. She's been a great friend to me.'

'Eyes closed. And is her little house party at Clerkswell all set up? Jules played ball, did she?'

'How do you know about that?'

'I was there, remember? In the stables.'

'Yah. Not gonna forget that day in a hurry. Faith told me not to worry and swore blind that she'd, like, wipe your memories or something. Makes me wonder what else she lied about.'

'Hold still. She didn't lie.' Alicia swapped palettes and moved to something extreme glittery. 'She thought she had. I think. If you see what I mean.'

'My eyes are closed, Alicia, so I'm not seeing too much right now. Even if they were open and I hadn't had a bottle of Bolly this afternoon, you still wouldn't be making much sense.'

Alicia didn't have any problem keeping her hands still, even though she was shaking inside. What Rachael had said explained a lot, including the reason that Faith had plied her with marijuana at Elvenham Grange: to stop her Inking Memories. What else had been kept from her? 'It's complicated and hard to put in mortal words. Is everything sorted?'

'Yep. Jules and Stephen are staying in Winchcombe for the duration. And Fiadh Ahearn is bringing a friend, apparently. Have you heard of the Countess Portarra/Corrib from Ireland?'

'Of course. I know *The Hound of Gloucester* by heart.'

'Right. Well, Portarra is representing the Queen of Galway. Erin says the protocol for that is going to be interesting. Does Team Faith just hide in the background?'

Yesterday morning, the wedding had seemed easy in comparison to the hen party. Not any more. Alicia was beginning to think she wouldn't live to see beyond it. 'We'll see, shall we?'

Now that Rachael's eyes were open, she was staring at Alicia. 'Have I got this right? You and Thistle are the first nobles in Faith's household?'

'We are not nobles. That's complicated.'

'Right. And who gets to be Prince and Princess? I assume that Queen Faith will need them.'

'Our lady will choose who is elevated to Princess-in-sídhe, but the Prince…' Alicia paused, dreaming of what was to come. 'After the first clutch is laid, there will be a Swarming. Princes will come from all over the lands and beyond the sea to compete for our lady's favour and a place at the top of her court. The first Prince must not be of the same People as the Queen, and there will be singing and dancing and fighting and hunting and a final judging in the royal bower.'

'Sounds amazing. You know where to send the invite.' She grinned. 'Joke, Alicia. Joke. Hang on, though, if the first Prince comes *after* the first clutch, then where does the first clutch come from?'

'It will be a special one, because your brother will provide the First Seed on coronation day.'

The room went quiet as Rachael digested what Alicia had just said and Alicia thought about stabbing herself with her sharpest scissors. There were *so* many reasons to just disappear into a puddle of jelly right now, and the fact that she had now told the Dragonslayer's brood-sister that he would be in the royal bower was actually the least of them.

'First Seed,' said Rachael thoughtfully. 'And is that First Seed provided in person or in a turkey baster?'

'What's a turkey baster?'

'Never mind that. Just tell me this: *will Conrad be shagging Faith, and does Mina know about it?*'

Alicia sighed inwardly with relief. 'Oh yes. It was one of the conditions of the peace. The Red Queen insisted, and Rani said that she wouldn't object.'

The silence returned until there was a cough from the doorway, and the only member of the party who hadn't yet come to the salon spoke out. 'You look amazing, Rachael. Shame there won't be many men there tonight.'

It was the Anointed Guardian. Alicia glanced from Rachael's black sequinned mini-dress to the Guardian's modest skirt, boots, blouse and headscarf. The new Knight bowed. 'Did you have a good day, Constable?'

'Best in years, thank you. I can't find Vicky, and in Faith's absence, I wondered who was driving me to Prestwich? I don't somehow think that Sapphire will want to miss the action at the Midnight Gardens.'

Oh. Alicia had forgotten about that, too. How had Faith managed to ride so many horses at once? Alicia had needed Sapphire to remind her about the minibus, and Thistle to remind her about snacks – and because Shear Magic didn't have to do any work on the Anointed Guardian, Alicia had forgotten that Hannah's God had forbidden her from enjoying herself on Friday nights. Someone needed to deliver Hannah to … to … some relative. Human families were *so* complicated.

'I'll do it,' said Rachael. 'If I pass the test.'

'What test?' said Alicia. 'Can you take a driving test on a Friday night? I will need to learn soon.'

'Not quite,' said Rachael. 'Can you summon Thistle telepathically?'

'No. I'm totally rubbish at Air magick, and only Queens have even half a chance. We use the royal register.'

'Wait!' said the Guardian. 'If you're going to use ultrasonics, let me put a Silence on. We don't want Rachael to end up as deaf as her brother, do we?'

The Guardian came over and touched Rachael, and Alicia called her Sister. It didn't take long before Thistle skidded into the room, slaloming in her socks over the parquet floor.

'Aye, Sister?'

'Miss Clarke has a mission for you,' Alicia told her.

Rachael smiled the mortal smile at something which went right over Alicia's head, then said, 'Find Leah Kershaw and ask her where the portable breathalyser is. It's probably in the Smurf.' Thistle ran off, and Rachael looked up at Alicia. 'It will tell us if I've had too much to drink. If I haven't, I can drive Hannah to Moshe Kaplan's cousin and meet the others at the Gardens. Won't take long.'

'Oh no,' said the Guardian. 'I'll get an Uber from town.'

'Honestly, it's no bother. They're only going for pre-drinks first. The show doesn't start until nine o'clock.'

Thistle came back, along with Lucy Berardi. 'Erm, bit of an accident,' said Lucy, slurring her words slightly. In one hand she held half her hair extensions, and her head now looked *very* lopsided. Short of the Morrigan herself stepping through the door and asking for a Goddess Braid, Alicia didn't think this could get any worse.

Thistle was holding the breathalyser device, Lucy was holding half her hair, and Alicia was holding an eyebrow pencil. What to do next? What did Princess Nancy do when faced with all her enemies and her back to the sea? She did what she could and let others sort out the rest.

'I'm done, Rachael. Lucy, sit yourself down and I'll have that fixed before you can say *prestidigitation*.'

Lucy flopped into the chair. 'You've got plenty of time, then. Is that even a word?'

Alicia relieved the little mortal of her hairy burden. 'It is, and I can't wait to meet Sofía, because she's a mistress of it. Now, let's see.'

As she worked, the others sorted things out. Rachael was (just) fit to drive; Lucy had driven her own car here last night and was quite glad to lend it to her.

As Alicia smoothed out the last stray extension, she spoke up. 'Do *not* attempt to brush these again, okay?'

Rachael smiled at them. 'Why don't you come with us, Alicia? I could use the company, and I don't want to walk through the city centre on my own.'

'Hey!' said Lucy. 'Manchester's quite safe! Especially where we're going.'

Rachael put her arm around Alicia, and Alicia stiffened with anticipation. The mortal put her weight on Alicia's shoulder and leaned down to take off her shoe. 'Alicia will come with us, and she will carry my shoes. I'm sure I'd be fine walking in them, but I'm not wearing these bad boys a minute longer than I have to, and certainly not on t'cobbled streets. Besides, I want to talk to her about my brother and his future donations … to charity.'

Alicia could have said no. She *should* have said no. 'Of course. It will be an adventure.'

Chapter Thirty-One

Transcript of a telephone conversation between
Francesca Somerton and Rachael Clarke

- Hi, Rachael. I wanted to talk to you about Alicia's story, particularly the part about the visit to the Midnight Gardens. For some reason, it was sealed and keyed to your Imprint. I wondered if…
- No way, Francesca.
- But, Rachael, you're the only one who really knows what happened that night.
- God, no. I'm taking the Fifth.
- Do you think that will satisfy Conrad? Or Tom?
- Lucy will tell Tom it's not worth the bother, and I'll tell Conrad to mind his own business.
- [Sigh] What about Mina? If she doesn't believe that there's an answer sealed away in the safe, she'll never let it rest.
- [Pause] That's a low blow, Francesca. You shouldn't threaten people with Mina unless it's a matter of life and death. And one old Skoda is not a matter of life and death.
- [Pause] I've seen the police report, you know.
- No, I didn't know. And I don't think I care. Once the Feds were happy that poor Serendipity Colquhoon of Gosforth had nothing to do with it, they gave up. I mean, who calls their child *Serendipity*, for fuck's sake.
- Language, Rachael.
- [Pause] I am not your daughter, Francesca.
- No, thank the gods. There was more than one statement in the police report, Rachael. As well as Serendipity, they also spoke to Zachariah Brown. [Shuffling of paper.] Mister Brown's aliases include 'Red Zach' and 'Ziggy Zach'. 'ZigZag', too. Perhaps I can track him down. Or Elaine Fraser could.
- You wouldn't.
- Try me.
- [Longer pause] What if I give you my word, as a Clarke, that if you send it to me, I'll edit it and leave in all the gory details and then return it with the stipulation that it's only to be opened with my permission or after my death?
- That will do nicely. Thank you, Rachael. I look forward to receiving it. And that brings me neatly to the matter of Mina and the stripper. Alicia wasn't there for that part, so…
- Ha Ha, Fran. Ha ha. I'll add a postscript, and that's all you're going to get

from *this* hen.

➤ [Pause] Then I shall have to be content with that. Thank you, Rachael.

Alicia's Story
(Edited and Revised by Rachael Clarke)

Look, I'm not proud of it, okay? Let's get that clear from the start. It wasn't funny, and I never meant for it to happen. I have apologised to Lucy and she has forgiven me, and now that I've read … this, I realise that I owe an even bigger apology to Alicia. All I can say is that I had no idea. None. Until I read this, I'd taken her word for what happened, and I am truly sorry.

Anyway, this is what Alicia said. I haven't changed what happened at all, because – well, you'll see why, so the only real difference is the names and stuff like that. I mean, who goes around calling Hannah 'The Anointed Guardian', I ask you?

I hope Evie did the same for the rest of it is all I'm saying…
Rachael Clarke

Lucy stood by her car and waved her impeccably manicured fingers helplessly at the contents of the boot. 'Sorry about that. I'm so used to running stuff between branches that I forgot to clean it out. Someone should be able to sit on the back seat if they move the disposable cups…'

'OMG, Lucy, what's that smell?' said Rachael.

Alicia sniffed and scrunched up her nose. 'Did a cow die in there? How did you fit it in? Because there's not much room…'

Rachael gave Alicia a look which said *Really?* Out loud, she said, 'Nice. Just what I wanted to hear.'

'Oh yeah. Sorry. I've got used to it,' said Lucy, blushing through her make-up. 'It's Bridget's ice cream. I took twenty litres to Garstang wrapped in a blanket and totally forgot about it.'

'Better than entrails, I suppose. We'll cope,' said Rachael. 'Alicia, could you squeeze in there? I'm not going to make the Constable sit in the back, obvs. Here she comes. See you later, Luce.'

Lucy backed away and took the last seat on the minibus. Sapphire already had the engine running and left straight away. Hannah smiled serenely at Rachael and Alicia, then climbed into the front; Rachael shrugged and Alicia folded herself into the space behind the passenger seat. She also suppressed the pain in her knees.

Ten minutes into the journey, and just after they had joined the motorway, Rachael said to Hannah, 'So what's this *Erev* we're going to?'

'Erev is the night before Shabbos. We're going to the Eruv,' replied Hannah. 'It's…'

Alicia didn't understand the explanation, and she didn't think Google would like the question *Why does Jehovah make so many rules?* So she watched the landscape change as they approached the city, then tuned back in when they got to talking about Hannah's sister's husband's family. You never knew when this information will be useful, not that she could keep track of most of the names or relationships. *So* complicated. She did Ink the name of one of them when she heard that he had been involved as a lawyer in one of Tom Morton's cases, because it was the case where he'd met Lucy, and that needed recording.

Alicia looked up again when Hannah added, 'He's nice enough, considering that he's betrayed the faith.'

'You mean he married a *shiksa*?' said Rachael.

'No. Much worse. He supports Trafford Rangers.'

'So does Lucy.'

'But Lucy *is* a shiksa. Who cares which team she supports?'

Rachael paused. 'You wouldn't be winding me up, would you?'

'Yes. I find that when dealing with the Clarke family, it's best to get your retaliation in first.' She paused, as if waiting for Rachael to say something, then added, 'It's as much fun as I get these days.'

Rachael glanced over her shoulder. 'Alicia, could you arrange some fun for the Constable?'

Alicia sat up straight, cricked her knee and banged her head on the roof. She was excited, though. 'Of course I can, Rachael. Hmm. Guardian, would you prefer Robbie or Thistle? Or both? Faith can send them over on Sunday.'

'See?' said Hannah. 'Always best to get in first. Have you ever been invited to a Friday night dinner, Rachael?'

Not much later, they arrived outside a very neat house among many other neat houses surrounded by roads which contained more neat houses than Alicia could keep track of. When Hannah got out and waved goodbye, Rachael asked Alicia to get in the front and she nearly cried with pleasure. She *did* cry with pain when she collapsed onto the grass because her leg wasn't working properly. Not to worry. Soon fixed.

They stopped just round the corner. Alicia had barely fastened her seat belt, and was mystified that their destination was so close. 'That was a very short journey. Is the Guardian not allowed to walk? And where are the

Midnight Gardens?'

'The Midnight Gardens are miles away. I have never driven round Manchester and have zero interest in learning how to. Hannah got us here, but I have no idea where *here* is. Don't take this the wrong way, but can you use the satnav app on your phone?'

'I'm using Faith's phone. Is it difficult?'

'Unlock it and pass it to me.'

Rachael was about to set the coordinates for the secure car park which Lucy had recommended when there was an incoming message, which she read (shamelessly in Alicia's opinion, but she loved Rachael, so that was okay). She started keying the information in and muttered, 'Traitors.'

'Why? What have they done?' asked Alicia.

'Message from Vicky. They've gone straight to the Gardens without waiting in the bar. Never mind ... should only take twenty minutes. There you are – just let the nice voice tell us where to go.'

Alicia stared at the screen. 'How does this work? How does it know so much?'

'I have no idea and I don't care. Ask Conrad next time you see him, and he'll bore the unicorn pants off you with a detailed explanation involving specific relativity and trilateration. Right, look out Manchester, here we come. And on the way, you're going to tell me about what my brother's going to be doing for Faith.'

Me and my big *mouth*. Alicia squirmed in the seat and found that she couldn't get any further away from Rachael, no matter how hard she tried. She loved Rachael, and more than that, she liked her. There was only one option. She had to lie. Why hadn't she thought of this before?

'I was just winding you up, Raitch. It's a *symbolic* donation. That's all.'

There. Done. Rachael would be happy and they could move on.

Wrong. Rachael burst out laughing and held out her hand. 'Tissue, quick, before all your hard work on my eyes starts to run.' They stopped at the first of *many* traffic lights, and Rachael dabbed her eyes. 'It was me winding *you* up, Alicia. Do you seriously think I want to talk about my brother's sex life? It's bad enough seeing the glow on Mina's face some mornings, never mind discussing inter-species fertilisation rituals. But I do have one question: will there be magick pants involved?'

'Mmmm. Mmmm.'

'Fair enough. I get the picture, even though I'd prefer not to.'

There was quiet and Alicia breathed out. Conrad had a favourite saying (a favourite saying which annoyed Mina immensely). It came in two parts and the first part went like this: *There's light at the end of the tunnel.* 'So you won't want to talk to the others about it?'

'Ew. No. No chance'

Alicia smiled to herself. There *was* light at the end of the tunnel.

Rachael smirked. 'I won't forget it, though.'

And the second part of Conrad's saying went like this: *Let's just hope it's not an oncoming giant mole.* Alicia struggled with that part of the saying (never having met a giant mole), and it looked like she would have to struggle with Rachael knowing something which she shouldn't know. Perhaps there was a way round this. If she used the same magick as Faith had done … Now where was that Ink?

Alicia was still searching for the answer when Rachael interrupted her. 'Are you okay, kid? Now I know that you're not communing telepathically, what's going on when you zone out like this? Is it my company?'

The stories were very clear on this. Every single one. When a mortal asks awkward questions about the Ways of the People, change the subject. The only problem was that she could see a clear benefit in saying *something* that would answer Rachael's question. She reached a hand towards the steering wheel, and her heart did a spin when Rachael took her fingers and, just for a second, gave them a squeeze. Alicia withdrew her hand and decided to tell a new story. A story of her own.

'In a way, that's exactly what I *am* doing, Raitch. I'm communing telepathically, only the other person is inside me and I talk to my Memories. Like Tamsin does when she sits and meditates. You know? Oh. You don't, do you?'

'Yah. Tamsin is not my BFF, Alicia, and never will be. I have no plans to go to hot yoga or Vedic breathing classes with her at any point in the future.'

'Oh. Sorry.'

'Nah. I'm not going to let Tamsin spoil the moment, and thank you for telling me. I look forward to getting an explanation which makes more sense one day, preferably a day when I'm not about to destroy even more of my brain cells with alcohol.'

Alcohol! That was the key. Alicia was going to search her Memories again, then paused, not wanting to be seen as rude.

'Nearly there,' said Rachael.

They were at rest by one of the huge glass clad buildings which Alicia had seen from Prestwich but hadn't believed could really be *that* big. She lowered the window and stared up at them.

'What's up? Dragon overhead?'

'Oh no. It's just that I've seen Manhattan in films, but these buildings are just so … huge.

'They are. Monstrous, some people would say.'

'I say that they are a mirror.'

'Eh? You mean the glass walls?'

'Yes, and more. This city makes me understand one of your words: *alien.* It makes me realise how alien you are to me and, like a mirror, if this is alien to me, I must be to you.'

'Bloody hell, Alicia. I was hoping to get drunk and have fun tonight, not get an insight into Fae philosophy. Every day's a school day in the world of magick, eh? Here we go.'

Alicia surveyed the rather dark corner in which Rachael had parked the car and tried to see the surrounding buildings as trees made of bricks, telling herself that this was just like the forests around the Lakeland sídhes. She failed. This was *nothing* like Birk Fell or Sprint or Staveley.

'Come on, dreamer,' said Rachael, opening the door. 'I wonder which way it is to the Gardens?'

'That way,' said Alicia. 'I can smell it.'

'Tidy. Alain says I can sniff out a bargain in the bond market, but the ability to smell *nightclubs* would be so much more useful.'

They set off towards the nightclub. Rachael gestured to her Manolo Blahnik patent leather pumps that Alicia was carrying. 'You can put those in your tote if you want. There's no need to walk along as if you were actually my lady's maid, you know.'

'I don't want to scratch them. There are lots of sharp things in here.'

'And there you go again. Lady's maid and bodyguard. I could get used to this. In fact, you take the car keys because they're huge and I won't need them again. Are you going to do a Glamour thingy?'

'What for, Raitch? Can I call you that?'

'You already have. Several times. In fact, you should aim for a ratio of twenty *Raitch*es to one *my lady* and zero *brood-sister*. How's about that?'

Alicia was being wound up, but she didn't have a clue how. There was *nothing* in the stories about that one, and then she remembered something. 'You do numbers even better than Rani Mina, don't you?'

Rachael stopped. 'Actually, no. Mina does numbers much better than me. She can spot a rogue debit like you can smell nightclubs, but I can do maths, and that is strictly off tonight's agenda. You still haven't told me if you're doing a Glamour. Those leggings suit you but they don't exactly fit the dress code for the Gardens.'

'Oh no. I have no desire to enter there. I shall explore and await you.'

Rachael looked as if she were going to challenge Alicia's plans and then she spotted something around a corner that led away from their destination. 'But you could get in if you wanted to?'

That didn't sound good to Alicia. She didn't want to put so much as a shoelace on Princess Birkdale's ground. But if Rachael needed her for something… 'If it was necessary, I could use the staff entrance. It's back there and Warded.'

'And you can keep a secret? Just you and me?'

'Confidentiality of the salon.'

'See that guy down there? The one with the Trafford Rangers top?'

'I do.'

'He's got *dealer* written all over him in even bigger letters than the shirt sponsor. And why is a law firm sponsoring a major football club? Whatever.'

Alicia guessed that Rachael meant *drug dealer*. She wasn't sure where this was going, but if Rachael needed her to make a citizen's arrest, she'd be happy to help. 'What would you like me to do?'

Rachael opened her tiny clutch and pulled out a wad of folded banknotes. 'Today's winnings. Why not use them to spread a little joy? Can you score a couple of grams off him? And don't pay more than a hundred a gram.'

'A couple of grams of what?'

'Coke. We'll keep it simple for tonight.'

That was not good. There were several universes where this was not good, and none that she could think of where buying illegal drugs for the Dragonslayer's sister was a good idea. 'Are you sure?'

'Absolutely.' Rachael paused with the money in her hand. 'Can you tell how pure it is with magick?'

That was easy. 'Yes. It tastes like wormwood.'

'I'll take your word for that, and also how you know what wormwood tastes like.'

Rachael held out the money, but Alicia was not keen to take it. Perhaps if she kept her new friend talking, the dealer would go away. 'Lady Agnes told us one day when she was warning us about ketamine, which the Hlæfdigan keep well locked up. Do you think the dealer might sell me some? I've often wondered whether it's more powerful than Sofía's weed.'

'There's a whole world of wonder in that statement, Alicia. Just get me two grams equivalent of coke and we'll explore other options later, eh?'

Alicia took the money with a sigh. 'I won't be long.'

'And I'm not hanging around here when the party's already started. If you don't want to be seen, bring it through the back door and text me. I'll meet you behind the stage or something.'

'You don't have your phone.'

'But you have Tara Doyle's number in Faith's phone. Lucy told me. You'll think of something.'

Alicia's shoulders slumped. 'Right.'

'Shoes?'

'Oh. Sorry. Here.'

Rachael swapped her trainers for the strappy pumps and clattered off with an over-the-shoulder wave.

With a heavy heart, Alicia retraced her steps and saw two men slink out of the alley where the dealer was lurking. The men glanced at her and moved on, not giving a second thought to what she was doing here. Was she losing her touch? Every other time she'd been on her own, a good proportion of the males had shown clear bodylonging, especially when they saw her from behind for some reason.

How was she going to do this? There were no stories whatsoever about approaching mortals to break the mundane laws. Well, there were, but it was usually about buying and selling children, and that was not a job for Squires. *Oh, hang on, I'm a Knight. I can do this.*

When she rounded the corner, the dealer took one look at her and scanned several shady spots nearby, probably checking for a fast exit. He took his hands out of his pockets and stepped away from the wall, then said. 'Help you?'

'I've come to strike a bargain.'

The words slipped out because she'd been waiting for something better to appear, and they were all she had. Ouch.

'Who sent you?'

Who indeed. There was only one person this dealer might have heard of, so… 'Prin … Tara Doyle. She sent me.'

'No, she didn't.'

'Yes, she did. I come on a commission for her.'

'Not in Holly Nugent leggings, you don't. She makes all her skivvies wear her own gear.' He pulled at his red shirt. 'I had to get permission to wear this.'

Alicia was lost. Again. The mortal was talking riddles. 'Why?'

He ignored her. 'Who really sent you?'

Fork-pain. Again. Should she disappoint Rachael or should she risk upsetting Princess Birkdale even further? She reflected for the blink of an eye, then got out her phone. The Geas placed on her really didn't leave much room for manoeuvre, did it? And Princess Birkdale couldn't get any angrier, could she? 'What's your name?' she asked the dealer.

'ZigZag. Hey, who are you calling?'

'Tara Doyle.'

He started backing away as the phone was answered by the wrong voice.

'Tara Doyle's phone,' said the Hlæfdige last seen wearing Alicia's bra and top. 'What the fuck do you want?'

The People's tongue was incomprehensible over mobile phones, so Alicia had to stick to English. 'For favour from your lady. I need to buy from ZigZag.'

'Who for?'

'Secret of the salon.'

Princess Birkdale must have been in the room, because the broken, half-syllables of the corrupted People's tongue came down the line. The only word Alicia heard clearly was her own name. Beyond her, ZigZag had retreated but not run away.

'Tell ZigZag that Tara says he should deal fairly but expect a tip. A *big* tip.'

Alicia kept the line open and repeated the Hlæfdige's words; ZigZag did not look convinced and asked, 'What was last week's password at the Well?'

Alicia opened her mouth to repeat the question, but Tara's voice cut her off. 'Tell him *cherry brandy* and you report to me when you've scored, understand?'

'Yes, my lady.' The line went dead straight away, and Alicia looked up. 'Cherry brandy.'

ZigZag's eyes glinted. 'What do you want?'

'Two grams of pure cocaine. Or equivalent.'

'I don't have that here, and I don't want to do the other in a back alley, neither. You got transport?'

Alicia remembered Lucy's car keys. 'Yes! But I can't drive.'

'No problem. You'll be busy warming me up. Come on, where is it?'

'This way.'

The dealer caught up with her and looked down at her crotch. Then his hand went to her buttock, and he gave it a squeeze, and that was *nothing* like she had imagined it would be.

'Nice,' he said. 'What's your name, sweetcheeks? Now that we're going to be getting to know each other...'

'Alicia.'

'Where are you from?'

'Lakeland.'

'No wonder you look lost. Isn't that place full of sheep? What are you doing here, sweetcheeks, and who are you really buying for? Maybe I know them?'

Alicia doubted that very much. 'No one you know.'

'So you do have some brains up there? Never mind.'

'Here. That one.'

'The Skoda? I was expecting something better than that. Never mind. Never mind. Give us the keys.'

She did, and ZigZag fumbled with the button then got in without a word. Alicia was still trying to do her seat belt when he shot out of the car park and screeched round the corner. 'Where are we going?' she asked.

'Salford Quays. Only takes ten minutes at this time of night, especially as we don't have to mind the traffic cameras, do we?'

'We don't?'

'Not my car, is it?'

He put his hand on the horn and shot past two cyclists and through a red light. 'Wa-hey! Here we go!' He span the wheel and the tyres screeched as he threw the car around a roundabout, emerging onto an elevated road on stilts. 'Have a feel.'

'Of what?'

'What do you think? Give me your hand.' He grabbed her hand and pressed it onto his groin. Under the jeans, she felt it hardening. 'Keep it going, sweetcheeks. You're in for a treat when we get to my flat.'

Alicia was not stupid. Princess Birkdale had stitched her up like a loose-lipped Squire in the laundry. *Tell him to expect a big tip.* She was not doing *that*. She withdrew her hand. 'I don't think so, ZigZag.'

He shot her a furious glare. 'We'll see about that.'

He slowed down only to exit the expressway, then threw the car into three tight turns on narrow streets before skidding to a halt. 'I don't care who you are or who you're buying for, but when Tara Doyle promises, she always delivers. Or gets someone else to deliver. So are you gonna give me what I'm owed or am I gonna dump you here?'

It was Coniston Water all over again: she was going to be abandoned in an alien wilderness. But that was then and this was now, and ZigZag was not Imogen. He was a mortal, and his plan had more holes than Gertha the Spider had legs.

She looked up. 'Is this your flat, here in the abandoned building?'

'Course. It's all modern inside. Nothing but the best for Tara's friends. Look, I've got some real shit up there. That'll make us *both* happy.'

'If that's your real flat, you might want to drive off before the police stop you. Don't want to give anything away, do we?'

'What police? What are you fucking talking about?'

'Have a look,' she said, pointing to the driving mirror.

ZigZag hadn't bothered adjusting the mirror when he got in, and it was easy for Alicia to put the image of blue flashing lights on the glass when he turned it to look behind the car.

'Shit! Bastards.'

He slammed the car into gear and shot off, and Alicia braced herself to take action. She waited for him to turn into the wide open space with the café in it, then she grabbed the wheel and turned it towards the café. That would make him slow down. But why was the café moving towards them?

'Fucking tram!'

Alicia had already turned the wheel a little, and ZigZag turned it more. He put his foot down to shoot in front of the tram (which looked *very* much like a café), and that was why he couldn't stop at the kerb. The car bounced into the air, through the light chains and into the water.

Chapter Thirty-Three

As they shot through the air, Alicia just had time to punch out the rear windscreen and make a Glamour of Lucy's car stopping at the kerb. That should buy them some time. Then they hit the water and there was a loud *bang* as a huge bag burst in ZigZag's face and the mortal bounced back. Water was pouring in through the shattered window. Perhaps that wasn't such a good idea, then.

Alicia burned through her seat belt with a small flame and said, 'I think we'll leave the cocaine, ZigZag.'

Only he didn't respond, because he was unconscious, and suddenly they hit the bottom of the canal. Alicia breathed deeply and tried to decide where the profit was: leave him to drown or drag him out. Clearly this mortal had dealings of many kinds with Tara Doyle, so…

'Nrguuh,' said the dealer.

There was a tiny pocket of air trapped in the car. For now. 'I will save you if you promise to keep quiet,' she told him.

'I can't move me legs! Help!'

She grabbed his arm. And twisted. 'Promise.'

'Whatever! Just get me out of here, you mad bitch.'

'One moment. I don't want my bag to get wet.'

She thought for a blink about what to do, then used the strap of her tote to make a deflection. That pleased her enormously. She punched the door out just as the water filled the whole interior. ZigZag started thrashing madly, so she punched him as well. That shut him up.

She had to struggle to get him free from the balloon, then it was easy enough to drag him to the surface. The burst of air shocked him back to life.

'Can you swim? Good. I'll pull you out in a moment.'

She chucked her bag onto the dock and hauled herself out, then offered him a hand, because there was quite a drop. 'Now, shhh. I need to think.'

The mortal lay on the cobbles, groaning and trying to do something to his shoulder and, just to be sure, she put her foot on his back and pressed. Hard.

Ooh, that squelched. Not nice. She started Fire on her body, easing it out to the fabric and setting the water to steam away. Then she got out her phone and sighed. Who was going to sort this out for her? She had no choice really, did she? And so for the second time that day, she called on Sapphire Gibson to get her out of a very deep hole.

There was a full-on reception committee waiting for Alicia behind a red velvet rope when she arrived back at the Midnight Gardens (the front entrance). As well as a distraught and horrified Sapphire Gibson, there was a huge Knight in a tuxedo and a thin, shadowy mortal woman in a grey dress that looked more like a uniform than anything and had Tara Doyle's florid signature stitched in purple up the left side-seam. At least it fitted the woman's body.

Alicia bowed to the Knight, and he said something into the sleeve of his jacket before giving the tiniest nod of the head to show that he wasn't about to eviscerate Alicia on the pavement.

'Hey!' shouted a voice from her right. 'How come she gets in wearing *that*?'

Alicia glanced to her right, and there must have been a hundred hens … no, they weren't all hens. They weren't even all females, but they were all waiting in a big queue. The Knight turned his face to them, and suddenly they were quiet at the front, though further down the line someone shouted, 'Can I have a piece of the bouncer with me mojito? There's enough to go around.'

Sapphire swung her leg over the rope and came up to Alicia. 'How in the mother's name did you get here so quickly?'

'Fire, Shadows and satnav. It's not just useful for cars. I am deep in your debt, honoured Daughter.'

'You're not joking, Alice, and you're also in deep shit with Tara Doyle. When I went to see her, she said that you and Faith were going to account for tonight, because it was nothing to do with the hens.'

'But…'

'Yes?'

It was everything to do with the hens. Or one of them: Rachael Bloody Clarke. There. She was angry with her new friend, but it was the anger of love, not revenge. And Alicia had let Rachael down. At least Sapphire hadn't asked *what were you doing in a car with one of Birkdale's mortals?*

'Nothing. What must I do?'

'Go with Stacey. I'll see you later. The show's due to finish around one o'clock.'

Sapphire stood aside, and Alicia climbed over the rope. As she passed, the Knight took her arm in a grip that would have impressed Robbie. He also made a Silence and whispered in the People's tongue. 'Just so you know, I'd have taken the gear off you anyway. Strictly no drugs inside here since the change of management.' His grip relaxed a fraction, then tightened again. 'Oh, and Stacey isn't Entangled. And she's one of Mina Desai's former cellmates, so try to be less stupid than your Ink is telling me you are.'

He released her, and Alicia tried to smile at Stacey – unsuccessfully, judging by the flash of fear in the mortal's eyes. Stacey went to step back, then rallied and said, 'Come with me.'

Alicia followed the pinch-thin woman through the entrance and through the cloakroom to a dark passage which skirted the club. Music throbbed through the walls, and of the many terrible smells assaulting Alicia's nose, the only natural ones were sweat and sex; everything else had come out of a bottle or a canister.

She was scared. More scared than she'd been since the Borrowdale Sídhe, and all she could think of to say was, 'I like your highlights. They've been put in well.'

Stacey frowned. 'Are you *really* a hairdresser? I thought that was a code name.'

'Shear Magic Hair and Beauty. That's me.'

'Oh. Then thanks. They cost me enough.'

She stopped at an unmarked door and knocked. Lux flashed as a minor Ward was broken and they were invited in.

Tara Doyle was leaning against a substantial desk, her bare feet crossed at the ankle and her arms folded. There was no one behind the desk and no one else in the room, though Alicia had needed her nose to tell her that because the only light came from a green-shaded banker's lamp behind the Princess.

'Alicia Lake, Tara,' said Stacey, then instead of leaving them she went to stand at the side, disappearing into the shadows.

Alicia forced herself to remember that Stacey was not Entangled, so gave the barest of nods to acknowledge who was in charge here.

'You haven't half caused me some grief today, you useless peasant,' began the Princess. 'Stace, how's Ziggy doing, and is everything squared away now?'

'He has a dislocated shoulder and they've had to pump his stomach. He'll recover. The police have already put it to the bottom of the pile. Now that they know there is only one real person called Serendipity Colquhoon and that she was at home in Newcastle, they've lost interest. Why on earth did you give them that moniker as a false name? Whatever. Our officer came through for us and the police have bumped it to the insurers. There'll be a big bill for recovering the vehicle, though.'

'Not my problem. How much do we owe our friend in blue?'

'A thousand quid and tickets to the next Fiesta.'

'I don't suppose you have the cash on you, peasant?'

Alicia opened her bag and took Rachael's winnings out. 'This is all I have.'

'Give it to Stacey.'

Alicia handed over the cash, and it was counted with lightning fingers. To Alicia's surprise, she was handed some back. Rachael was either incredibly lucky at the races or she routinely carried more money than Alicia had been told was wise.

'Good. Thanks, Stace.'

The mortal slipped outside, and Tara waved the Ward back onto the door, locking them away in Silence. And there was silence in the room as she stared at Alicia.

Alicia knew that she was doomed to something bad. Her lady was going to release her, and the Princess would have her revenge. Somehow. Until then, Alicia was still Knighted and still a handmaiden to a future Queen, so she lifted her head and returned the stare, despite fear running down her back like the ice water in the canal.

Tara unfolded her arms and rested them on the edge of the desk. 'I have no idea what Faith sees in you, especially now you've lost Mina's hair. I reckon my PA's right: you are *totally* Eclipsed. A complete liability. You and that bedmaid, Thistle, will attend the hens in Blackpool tomorrow, and you'll learn your fate then. Now get out of my sight.'

Alicia nodded and left the room.

Stacey was waiting for her, and ushered Alicia further into the depths of the Gardens. 'Are you alright?' said Stacey, with more sympathy than Alicia had expected or thought she deserved. 'Fancy a brew before I kick you out?'

'That would be a mercy, but I would not put you to so much trouble.'

'It's my break. I've got a few minutes.'

They went into a tiny room, not much bigger than the staffroom at Caffè Milano where, on a much happier day, Alicia had done Lucy and Kelly's hair. Stacey put teabags into mugs and filled the mugs from some sort of magic tap that seemed to run with boiling water. With her back still to the room, she said, 'Did Ziggy try it on with you?'

'He expected sexual favours, if that's what you mean.'

'Bastard. You should have left him to drown. World would be a better place without him.'

That was a shock. How did *that* work? And did the Princess know that her people were being disloyal like this? Alicia didn't want to go there, so she said, 'Do the hens know what happened?'

Stacey started squeezing teabags and adding milk. 'Luckily they weren't too drunk when I got the news, just drunk enough to believe any old bullshit. I've told Lucy that we asked to borrow her car so that one of the barmen could fetch supplies, and you went because you were bored. Then, in a moment of madness, he tried to give you a driving lesson. She didn't seem too bothered.'

'Thank you. That was a kindness I didn't deserve.'

'You didn't deserve to be assaulted by that bastard, either.' Stacey turned round and stood in front of Alicia, holding the mugs up but not handing them over. 'Just give me one honest answer, Alicia. Just one. Was it Mina or Kelly who got you to score off Ziggy?'

'No. I give you my word.'

'Then here you go. Biscuit?'

Afterword

Yeah, I was shitting myself when Stacey slipped up to Lucy and whispered something in her ear. When Luce said, 'You'll never guess what! My car's in the Manchester Ship Canal!' everyone else burst out laughing and Erin said, 'Goodbye heap of shhh.'

I pretended not to have heard and said, 'What's up, Lucy?' and she said, 'Alicia's gone off on one again and tried to learn to drive. Not to worry though. Tara's sorted it all out, and I can have a new car!'

'To new cars,' said Kelly. 'May we all get one. Especially me!' and that was that as far as the hens were concerned. When we staggered out of the Gardens, Alicia was waiting for me. Poor kid. She did a Silence and said how sorry she was and that the idiot dealer had tried to rob her, hence the accident, and that she'd had to bribe some Fed to make it all go away. I gave her a hug and told her it was my fault, and did anyone else know? She said it was going to be our secret. If only she'd told me the truth, but sometimes you can be too good a friend.

Oh, and as for Mina and the stripper, NO ONE knows who took the picture, okay? And if you want to know how she ended up like that, I have only two things to say: the camera doesn't lie, and a picture really can be worth a thousand words.

Rachael Clarke

Chapter Thirty-Four

They travelled to Blackpool in the minibus because there wasn't enough room in the Smurf and because the hens had a *lot* of luggage, not including the two suitcases which the Anointed Guardian had locked, sealed and Warded, labelled *For Saturday night. Hands OFF!*

While the hens were chivvied and poked into life by Sapphire and Rachael (who hadn't drunk as much as the others for some reason), Alicia and Thistle started to load the bus, assisted by Scout.

'What is it with you and canines?' said Thistle. 'Ye have all the Wolves and that damned dog eating out of your hand. Literally. If you pick up a case, he opens the door with his nose, but if I pick up a case, he tries to bite ma ankles.'

Thistle knew nothing about what ZigZag had done to Alicia. The humiliation of admitting she had been deceived and the pain of betraying Rachael was too much, so Alicia had pretended to have been stupid rather than naive, and Thistle had shrugged and said, 'Learning the Ways is harder than learning to drive, or so I'm told. You're doing much better with magick, so handling a car should be nae problem. *If you listen to your teacher.*'

Alicia pointed to Scout. 'He recognises a fellow Lunatic. Him and me, we're both Eclipsed, and we all know what Lady Moon does to the Wolves.'

'Aye, right enough,' said Thistle. 'Are you no gonna answer the phone?'

Alicia had been trying to ignore it, but she would have to face the music at some point so she wandered off and accepted the call from the Birk Fell landline. 'Tell me it's not true,' said Faith. 'Please tell me I do not have to buy Lucy a new car on top of everything else.'

'Is there no insurance, my lady?'

'Yes, Little One, there is insurance. For *accidents*. Not for unauthorised drivers who have given false names. I mean, *Serendipity*? Seriously?'

'I am pleased that my lady sounds in better health.'

The Princess sighed. 'I know you are. And I know you're lying about something, but I don't care. Just make sure the rest of the hen party goes smoothly and, Alicia, *stay out of trouble!*'

'Yes, my lady.'

Vicky emerged, still in her Hartsford Hall dressing gown (now where had Alicia heard *that* name before?), and she was accompanied by a very fragile-looking Saffron Hawkins. 'Have you recovered from last night, Leesha? I know I haven't, and I dread to think what Tara's gonna do to us today.'

'I am quite recovered, thank you,' said Alicia, and in yet another attempt to change the subject, she continued, 'unlike Evie's leggings. It is hard to erase the smell of Manchester Ship Canal without a proper laundry.'

'You're telling me. The back of the bus stank to high heaven last night, and talking of smells, did you actually go into the Gardens?'

Alicia glanced at Sapphire, who would have no reason to lie if asked, so Alicia said, 'Yes. Briefly.'

'Aye. Look, I can get Conrad to make this official, but tell me, did you smell Fairy Dust anywhere?'

'Forest Manna,' added Saffron, using the People's preferred term.

It was a shocking question, and Alicia had no problem in answering honestly. 'No, Honoured Guardian, I did not. Nothing but sweat and sex. You didn't…?'

'Hey! Less of your lip, pet. You're right about the sweat, though. Thanks, Leesha. See you at the Blackwell Hotel.'

'What was that about?' said Thistle.

'The Seer suspects Princess Birkdale of using Forest Manna on her customers. Or something.'

'She'd no be so stupid. Are we done?'

'Yes.'

'You deal with the dog, and I'll tell them we're off. Oh, and we mustn't forget to call at the lodge and hand in the tokens.'

'I'll drive us up the Golden Mile,' said Sapphire when they left the motorway. 'We've plenty of time, and if you've never seen it before, it's something else.'

Alicia and Thistle got to sit at the front all the way, and by not thinking about Princess Birkdale at *all*, Alicia restored some balance and began to enjoy herself. While it lasted.

Blackpool was yet another revelation to her, and to Thistle as well. When they turned onto a road next the sea, with the great tower in front, they were suddenly amid a throng of mortals. All of them seemed to be eating or drinking, and many of them seemed to have made a great habit of both, judging by their size. Strange.

'I'd say that's a sídhe,' said Thistle, pointing ahead to their left, 'but it's over the sea, and that doesnae make sense.'

'It's a pier. P-I-E-R,' said Sapphire. 'Somewhere to go and have fun. From another age.'

'You're not joking. Are we going there? Is that where the fun happens?'

'You are in the British epicentre of fun,' said Sapphire. 'More fun to be had per square metre in Blackpool than almost anywhere on earth. Except Las Vegas.'

'At the next junction, turn right,' said Sapphire's phone. Sapphire did just that, and they were soon driving up to an impressive old building which seemed to be the child that Elvenham Grange would have produced if it had mated with the old warehouse where ZigZag claimed to live. Above the portico, the name Blackwell Hotel and Spa gleamed in gilt letters.

'You two unload while I check us in and sort the keys, then I'll head to the airport and wait for the Smurf,' said Sapphire. 'They should be expecting us inside.'

They were expecting them, and two young men rushed to pile the cases onto luggage carts. They carefully attached labels with the hens' names on them to each case, promising to deliver them to the right rooms. Alicia smiled and wondered if the hotel were copying the Borrowdale Sídhe or vice versa. The only thing she wouldn't let them take was her beauty trolley, because she hadn't had the chance to Ward it.

Inside the lobby, a woman was standing with a fistful of room keys. 'I'll get ours,' said Thistle. 'You mind your case, cos I don't look strong enough to pick it up on my own.'

The woman smiled and asked Thistle's name, then shuffled through the cards. 'You're sharing with Ms Lake, yes?'

'Under protest, but yes.'

'There's plenty of room,' said the woman.

And then Alicia noticed that the woman's dress was very familiar: grey and fitted, and with *Blackwell* embroidered on the breast in the same purple thread as seen on Stacey's outfit. No wonder Princess Birkdale was so powerful.

Sapphire returned from the main desk holding a piece of paper, and asked if they were sorted.

'Aye,' said Thistle. 'What's next?'

'All I know is that you have to get the hens into their gym gear and down to the fitness studio at eleven o'clock. Not even Faith knows what's on the agenda for today. Here's a list of names and rooms.' She looked down at Alicia's case. 'That includes you two, and you won't be needing the case until later.'

'I love surprises,' said Thistle. 'Not. So long as there's no paintballing involved, I'll live with it, and so will Alicia, 'cos she wouldn't want tae get paint oot of everyone's hair.'

Chapter Thirty-Five

Despite Sapphire's words, Alicia was indeed called to action – by Mina. The hotel woman had not lied. Alicia and Thistle had plenty of room, and three beds to choose from (although they couldn't see the sea, which *was* a shame). Shortly after opening their cases, Alicia got a text from Rani: *Come to the bridal suite and bring your A Game for up-dos. Mina. XXX*

The bridal suite was huge. Way too big for one small Indian woman (as the bride-to-be described herself). 'It makes me realise how much I'm missing Conrad to see all this. I wonder what the stags are up to today.'

Alicia parked her trolley near the dressing table and sat on the bed. 'I know what they are doing.'

'Really?'

'Yes. Would you like to know?'

'Go on. I hope it involves pain and humiliation, then I will know that he is suffering, too.'

'They have gone to a watercolour landscape painting class, my lady.'

Mina's eyebrows shot up, then she burst out laughing. 'I don't know who told you that, but they were winding you up, Leesha. No way are those boys going to sit down and *paint*. Paintball, yes, but watercolours…? I don't think so.' She paused. 'But I have been hearing strange things about school reports, and they must play *some* part. Whatever.'

Alicia wasn't surprised that she had been lied to again, so she just forgot about it. 'What does my lady want?'

'I want you to stop calling me that, for a start. Unlike the stags – allegedly – we will be burning a *lot* of calories today. It's going to be a surprise to everyone, including Vicky, because I've arranged it with Tara Doyle. Via Hannah.' She checked her phone. 'Priya hasn't messaged. I hope she's okay.'

'Priya?'

'Has Faith shown you the wardrobe list for the wedding day?'

'Briefly.'

'Well, after the final ceremony, we are getting changed for Indian dancing, and Priya is coming specially today to run us through some routines. She is a trained teacher, and very good. I want you to do my hair up at the front, down at the back and restrained so that it doesn't get in my face. Okay?'

'Of course, Mina. I'll have it done in two sh— two seconds. Bear with!'

She set to and was soon braiding and combing and using magick for the extra hand, as she'd been taught when making the Goddess Braid, until Mina asked, 'What really happened last night, Leesha?'

'I was foolish, my lady. Do not worry, Lucy will not be out of pocket.'

'It's you I'm worried about. You have taken on a hell of a lot with Faith so ill. I remember how you looked at me in the Broadwater Sídhe, you know.

You were so little and so vulnerable and so scared, and I know you're a big girl now, but that was only weeks ago. Are you sure you're okay? Is there anything I can do?'

'Enjoy yourself. That is your only duty this weekend.'

'If you're sure, then I shall do my best. Seems to have worked so far.'

'Good. Will Priya mind if I wear these?' asked Alicia, pointing at the jeans she'd been forced to wear now that so much of her clothing was bloodstained or waterlogged. 'I seem to have run out of options.'

'Why? Are *you* involved? Brilliant! Don't worry, Tara is bringing some freebies. There's bound to be something in your size. And your timing is excellent, by the way, getting rid of that *mane* of my hair yesterday. The new bob is perfect. What are your long-term plans for it?'

Alicia ended up going down with Mina and some of the hens they'd collected along the way. Thistle rounded up the rest.

Alicia's fears were realised when she saw what was in the corner of the superbly finished gym studio. The large space, complete with sprung floor, mirrored walls and barre, was empty apart from a speaker stack, a crate of sparkling water and a pile of *MerseyFit by Tara Doyle* athletic clothing. *Be your best self* said the packet. Alicia felt tears welling up as she pulled out a pair of size large purple leggings and slipped off her jeans. She was now going to dance in front of her enemy with her enemy's name scribed all the way up her leg in a mockery of the way her true Name was Inked into her arm.

To complete her humiliation, she was still pulling them up (and wondering if she could get away with size medium) when Lucy came over. There was no avoiding her.

'I am so sorry…'

'Forget it,' said Lucy emphatically. 'Water under the bridge. As it were.' She looked at Alicia's half-covered legs. 'The Holly Nugent ones suited you much better, to be honest.'

Alicia pulled them off and took a medium pair instead. 'Forgive me, my lady, but who *is* Holly Nugent, and why does Tara Doyle dislike her?'

'I thought you were up on celebrities, Leesha. Oh, I suppose Holly *has* been keeping a low profile since … since the business in 7Bridge. Holly was years ahead of Tara in having her own range of athleisure wear, and Holly, of course, is married to John Nugent, and to be fair to Tara, she's *very* loyal to her husband.'

Much better, thought Alicia. These were actually well cut and a good fit. Not as good as the Holly Nugent ones, though. Those ones had support in the places that *needed* support. 'I'm sorry, Lucy, but who is John Nugent and what does he have to do with Conan Doyle?'

Lucy's mouth dropped open and she shook her head. 'I'll explain later. Or Vicky will. Why is everyone looking at the door?'

Everyone was looking at the door, even if not everyone knew why. Lucy,

Mina and Rachael were looking because the others were, and the others were looking because a wave of magick was coming down the covered walkway that separated the gym and spa from the main hotel building, and leading the wave was the imperious figure of Princess Birkdale. But who – or what – was that following in her wake?

The doors opened before her, and Tara swept in, then stood aside and the wave of Lux collapsed, revealing … in the name of the Morrigan! What was *that?*

A Dual-Natured creature, for certain, with a low, slithering form flickering in and out of existence and hinged to a body with a ripe female form, native brown skin and hair in a *very* similar arrangement to Mina's. The hinge was a brightly glowing ruby in the centre of its forehead. And the creature was heading towards the bride…

Alicia wasn't the only one to step forwards with Ink or copper magick at her fingertips. Vicky was, too, as was Saffron and even Tammy. The creature stopped before Mina and bowed, then lowered itself (herself) to one knee in submission.

'Please forgive the surprise, honoured lady. I am Damini, daughter of Pramiti, and I am sent by Lord Ganesh to bless your wedding.'

'A Nāgin,' said Vicky. 'That's all we effing need.'

Mina did not look happy. 'You are very early. My wedding is not for another four weeks.'

'I bring more than one blessing. I am also here to help with the dance. She is embarrassed to admit it, but like your handmaiden Faith, Priya is indisposed.'

'How did you get into the country?' asked Vicky, with a face like a Dwarf whose beer has been stolen.

'Please, let me withdraw a moment while you call your Deputy Constable. That's Drummond-sahib, not the Dragonslayer.' Damini gave Vicky a smile. 'I would ask for you to call the constable, but she told me that if I arrived on Shabbos then Drummond-sahib would vouch for me. And rest assured that I will work with Joshi-sahib as befits a humble woman priest.'

'I have never heard so much shit in all my life,' said Tammy. 'I was there when your mother got her marching orders.'

'I am not my mother,' said Damini. 'I believe that I will not be the only one at the wedding who wants to distance themselves from their ancestors. Living or dead.'

The hens looked from one to another, waiting for Mina who had lowered her head as if her hair might hide her, but Alicia had done her job too well. 'I see,' said Rani. 'Ganesh sent you personally?'

The Nāgin touched the jewel in her forehead. 'This jewel is blessed by our lord, and what he bids me do, I am commanded.'

'Then wait outside.'

Tara Doyle cleared her throat. 'I'll go, too. I need a word with Thistle and Leesha as well. Come on, girls.'

With heavy legs, Alicia followed her Sister outside, taking a good look at the Nāgin on the way. Alicia could see the snake form more clearly now, until Damini shook herself and folded some magick around her to make the separation more defined. There was also a question nagging at her which hadn't seemed to bother the hens: how and why had Damini come into the orbit of Princess Birkdale? Because Damini already had the complete signature outfit (in fuchsia pink), and the food stains hadn't got there from walking down the corridor.

Before Alicia could worry about that, the Princess wove Silence and smiled the People's smile, though she stuck to the mortal tongue. 'Listen carefully, you two. You will put your heart and lack of soul into this dance. You will memorise every step and when the wedding party assembles, it's down to you two to get them rehearsing. Clear?'

'We will not let Rani down,' said Alicia, meeting the royal enemy's gaze.

'Good. And there's something else. When Princess Flopsy releases you, Leesha, I will be snagging you and handing you over to Damini here. She is having *terrible* trouble getting servants.'

Alicia's head was still reeling when Thistle exploded into the People's tongue. 'What the arse are you talking about? *Release Alicia?* It's you who's Eclipsed if you think that's going to happen.'

'Tell her,' said Tara. 'Oops, you can't, can you? I spy a Geas. Shame. It would be nice to make you say the words.'

'No!' said Thistle, grabbing Alicia's arm and feeling the Ink.

'Aanh,' said Alicia, the pain forcing a sound past her sealed lips.

Thistle's eyes had gone into shock when she found the Geas, and Alicia's silence could only mean one thing: she couldn't deny what Princess Birkdale was saying.

The Princess smiled again, her jaws almost fully out. 'I am going to enjoy that so much. How many do you think will stand at Flopsy's side when she can't even hang on to a hairdresser? Not a single Squire will flock to her once word gets round about what she's done and what I'm planning. Oh, and before I pass you on to my new friend, we'll have a little chat about what Princess Flopsy's been up to, shall we? Under force of truth, of course. I'll look forward to that. Assuming she doesn't kill you first. That would be good, wouldn't it? Release her Squire and then hack her down at the wedding.'

Alicia was bemazed and humiliated, and destined for bondage *to a snake*. Even Thistle had taken a step away from her. All she had left was her hairbrush and the hope in her heart that she could live long enough to perform the bridal dance. 'You'll have to catch me,' she said to Princess Birkdale.

'Oh, I've already caught you,' she replied. 'It's just a question of reeling you in.'

'What are you three wittering about?' asked Damini. 'It looks like the hens have reached an agreement.'

They had, and Alicia dragged herself back into the studio. Damini stood by the barre and clapped her hands. 'Right, ladies, shoes off. In India we like to keep ourselves grounded. And if your heads are a bit sore after last night, don't worry. I will soon have your bodies aching so much you'll beg for your hangovers to come back.'

'Oh joy,' said Vicky. 'Whose flipping idea was this, and can I kill them now?'

'I know I'm grateful for her doing the driving and all that, but seriously, if that video of me with me face bright purple and me eyes bulging goes *anywhere*, there may be violence. Once I've got me breath back.'

'And once you've actually got up off the floor.'

'That too. Thistle, can you fetch an ice bucket with a bottle of Sambuca and a siphon hose?'

All of the mortals had collapsed onto the floor when Damini finally announced that she was satisfied with their performance and swept out of the studio with Tara Doyle, leaving Alicia and Thistle to survey the wreckage. Not that they were much better off.

'I'm not fetching nothing for nobody until ma legs stop burning like they're on the spit.'

'Another image to savour,' said Lucy. 'Is there such a thing as post-Fae Stress Disorder? If there isn't, I think I may be the first sufferer.'

'Waaater?' said Evie plaintively.

Alicia pushed herself off the barre and collected bottles of water, putting one by the head of each hen.

'How come you can move?' whined Mina. 'You were still dancing like Damini when the rest of us had lost the will to live, and don't tell me it was magick, because Thistle and Tara were taking it easy by then.'

'I run through the woods being chased by Wolves. It's good exercise. And you worked harder than anyone, Rani. You had to practise your solo while the others rested.'

'Traitor,' said Rachael. 'You're supposed to be sympathetic to *all* of us.'

'Please tell me there's afternoon tea, Alicia,' said Vicky.

Alicia panicked. 'My lady?'

'Hannah gave the rest of the agenda for today to Faith. I haven't a Scooby what's next.'

'Erm…'

'In her luggage,' said Thistle. 'I saw the Anointed Guardian hand over a Parchment, and our lady put it in her luggage … you have still got it, haven't you?'

'Yes. I shall be as fast as I can.'

Alicia ran from the studio and across to the hotel, and used what was left of her Fire to run up the emergency staircase. Back in her room was all of Faith's luggage as well as theirs and the two sealed cases left by the Guardian. She dived into Faith's suitcase and wondered whether her lady would mind if she borrowed some of her clothes. She did *not* want to spend another minute with *Tara Doyle* scrawled up her leg.

At the bottom of the case was a sealed Parchment, and Alicia slumped onto the bed. She was torn. She needed to make Memories of the afternoon, and seeing Lucy trying to teach Saffron the shimmy was worth keeping for several generations. Unlike the prophecies of Princess Birkdale. Then again, if you do not know what the boiling copper will be like, you cannot choose the fire as a better option. With great delight, she manifested her claws and ripped the leggings open, then after the barest Reflection, she Inked the Memories into her thighs and breathed out.

She picked up the scroll again and saw that there was hardly any magick holding the seal and that it had already been opened once and re-sealed, presumably by their lady. She was about to read it when Thistle appeared at the door.

'By the gods of the sea, what are ye doing? Do you know how much those things *cost?* I wish our lady would give me enough to throw away good clothes.'

Alicia looked up. 'There is more than one way to measure *cost*, Sister.'

'You poor thing,' said Thistle in the mortal's tongue. 'I'd ask you to tell me it's a lie, but it's written all over your body.' She came in, closed the door and joined Alicia on the bed, switching back to the People's tongue and whispering, 'Was this the price of becoming our lady's Saviour?'

Alicia's mute pain confirmed that she was bound to say nothing of the bargain. Thistle took her Sister in her arms. 'And me?' Alicia shook her head. There would be no repercussions for Thistle. 'Then we do what the People have always done. We endure and we prepare. We've three weeks to get you at least on speaking terms with the Ways.'

'Thank you.'

'Good. Now, what's going on with the hens, hen?'

Alicia fumbled to open the scroll. 'The dance studio is booked until eight of the clock. We are to assemble the hens at seven and hand out their costumes, dressing the bride first, and then finish the preparations.'

'Costumes?'

'In the cases, I suppose.'

'What does the rest say? I need to practise reading as much as you need to practise the Ways. Our Anointed Guardian's handwriting is awf'y strange.'

'She says that we should provide alcohol and accompany them on their revels. For safety.'

'That's a Kraken's breakfast, that is. What are we gonna do?'

'We have no choice. I shall accompany them, and you will follow in the shadows.'

'Great. Let's see if we can go one better than a car in the canal. How aboot all diving off that pier thingy and trying to swim to Norway?'

'Ireland. And there is a postscriptum in even worse writing. It says, *Don't worry, Faith, you won't have to wear a seashell bra. I wouldn't be that cruel.*'

'What in the name of the Morrigan does *that* mean?'

Alicia stroked her Sister's arm. 'I somehow think that it's the least of my worries. We'd better get back to the studio and tell them the good news—'

The hotel phone was ringing, and Alicia jumped to answer it. Or tried to. Sitting down had let her muscles stiffen so much that she collapsed in a heap and had to crawl to the bedside cabinet. 'Hello?'

'Can you bring the phones, pet?' asked Vicky. 'If you don't mind. I wanna see what Sapphire really puts on the shared folder.'

The Daughter of the Earth had taken a few short videos of the warm-ups, then retired for a couple of hours until Damini had drilled the hens (and hen helpers) on the routine they would be performing at the wedding. Sapphire had then filmed the full routine a few times and said that she would edit it and share it so the hens could practise at home. It had not been a universally popular idea, and now Sapphire had gone back to Lakeland for the night and they wouldn't see her until tomorrow afternoon.

'Of course. Immediately.'

'And order a selection of sandwiches to the dance studio ASAP or you'll be calling an ambulance with those phones. I don't care about the cost.'

Alicia grabbed the locked box with the phones and turned to go.

'Aren't you forgetting something?' said Thistle.

'Sorry?'

'Clothes would be good. Here, this is too young for our lady's current skin.'

Thistle was holding up a short denim skirt that might have belonged to one of the Wolves. Why had Faith packed *that?* Whatever. Alicia tore off what was left of Tara Doyle's Lycra shackles and slipped the skirt on. Oops. Definitely one of the SheWolves. *Breathe in!*

'Sister, order sandwiches for the hens. They are faint from lack of food.'

'Lack of alcohol, more like. Nae bother. I'll go to the kitchens and sort something out myself if I have to.'

Alicia paused. She wasn't sure that the hotel kitchens were ready for a rampaging schoolgirl. The last time she had been faced with so many decisions, she had recalled Princess Nancy with her back to the sea. This time, she adopted the Enscriber's motto: *Sod that. Not my problem.*

In the dance studio, Vicky unsealed the box and took her own device, then Alicia passed around the others'. By the time Alicia got to Evie's (who still had sweat dripping off her nose), Vicky was waving her arms around.

'Hey! Hey! Have you seen these pictures of Alain? He's only gone and got himself a new French bird. *And* she's a stunner.'

'Is that her in the leather outfit?' said Tamsin. 'I might have to up my game.'

'Why?' said Lucy. 'You're not after him, are you?'

'Given the shortage of men in my life, I'm considering all options that don't involve living underground. And Alain must have *something*.'

'Says the woman who somehow fell for the most boring man in Salomon's House,' said Vicky. 'I mean, Tammy, you've not got a lot to compare Alain with, have you?'

'I shall say this once and once only,' intoned Tammy in a strange voice. Then she giggled. 'The next time you look at Chris – or up to him, depending on how close you're standing – just remember this: all of him is in proportion.'

'Nooo,' said Lucy. 'Is there a spell you can cast to un-say that? Please?'

'Too late,' said Rachael. 'Some of us have had to carry the burden of knowing for a while.'

Alicia felt the temperature drop from sauna to plunge pool in a heartbeat as she realised that Rachael was referring to Eseld. Thankfully, Mina had been looking at other things and dissolved the tension. 'Leesha! I owe you an apology. It seems that the boys really *are* doing watercolours in the French countryside.'

'Eh? Tom can barely use a fingerprint brush, never mind a paintbrush,' said Lucy. 'Oh my God, you're right!'

'After what we've been through, I actually feel jealous,' said Vicky. 'And I bet they had more for lunch than a few energy bars. Where's them sandwiches?'

There was almost an armed rebellion when Alicia told them the arrangements for the evening. In fact, if Thistle hadn't turned up with an entire trolley load of sandwiches, coffee and cake, there was no telling what might have happened. When they'd eaten, it started all over again.

Alicia's Sister stood in front of her and wagged her fingers. 'Do you lot no ken what a *Geas* is? Heh? Well, she's way too nice to say it, but Leesha is bound to obey this one. You will get your outfits when she says so, and not a moment sooner.'

'Whoa! Where did that come from?' said Rachael.

Thistle folded her arms. 'I've had enough stick in my time to know how to put it about if I have to.'

'Is she speaking literally or metaphorically?' asked Lucy.

'Literally,' said Saffron.

'Aye,' said Thistle. 'A beating from a besom of gorse is a great stimulant.'

'I think I'll stick to coffee, thanks,' said Lucy. 'And talking of coffee, this stuff wouldn't put a fire under Guy Fawkes. I am *so* going to open a branch in Blackpool.'

'How about this?' said Alicia, now that the rebellion had been postponed. 'You have showers and come down here, and I'll dry everyone's hair *and* make sure there's a crate of Prosecco waiting.'

'Now you're talking. So long as somebody does something about those picture windows out to the courtyard,' said Mina. 'Right, who's going to give me a hand up?'

The hens limped out, and Alicia started to clear up. 'Thanks for getting the food. I'll take the trolley back. And we need to get some chairs for later.'

Thistle was stuffing a sausage roll into her mouth and chewing frantically. 'You leave that to me. Both bits. This is what you're gonna do.' She moved to the pile of Merseyfit clothing and scooped it all up. 'You're gonna take this lot and put it in a case, and when we get haem, you're gonna give it to Lowri. You're ever so tight with her, aren't ye?'

'I am, but I don't think that seeing the Pack wear it is any better. Besides, they don't like restrictive clothing, for when they…'

'I know, I know, and I try not to think about it. It gives me terrible visions, and now I've to try and stop thinking about yer snake woman, too. I mean…' She shuddered and pinched her nose. 'No. Lowri runs the Pack eBay account. With help, obviously, but this lot can go on there as unwanted gifts. Which they are. Now scoot.'

Alicia grabbed some food, the leisurewear and a bottle of water. With some re-packing and sorting, she found something to wear. After a shower and some rest, she felt much better. She was putting on Faith's midi dress when Thistle, still dressed for the gym, finally reappeared.

'Sorted. Finally. I had to raid the spa to get some chairs, but it's sorted. You can go set up and I'll see you in a bit.'

And she was gone into the bathroom before Alicia could get her mouth open. 'Thank you, Sister,' she shouted, then started wheeling cases towards the lift.

She was still trying to figure out the Wards on the Anointed Guardian's gift when a damp Thistle bounced in and headed for the Prosecco. 'I need a glass o' this. Dry my hair, would you?'

Alicia was surprised that the spa had relinquished so many of their salon chairs. They must be overstocked in there. Never mind. She set to, and Thistle said, 'You are so good at this. I know you were great before, but this is awesome. Was it something to do with the Nymph?'

'Perhaps.' She stopped brushing. 'I feel like I want to burp Ink sometimes. The Nymph's gift tastes funny.'

Thistle rotated her head. 'You scare me. Just remember who your Sister is, eh? If you feel like you're gonna explode Quicksilver everywhere, try and give me a warning. Here comes the Chief Bridesmaid.'

Vicky had abandoned her Hartsford Hall dressing gown in favour of one from the hotel. She went straight to the Warded cases. 'Shit. These must be keyed to Faith, 'cos I can't open them.'

Of course! Why hadn't Alicia realised? When the Guardian locked them, she had no idea that anyone but Faith would be in charge. That should be a simple matter.

'Let Alicia worry about that,' said Thistle. 'You make yoursel' at home and I'll get you a glass.'

'You've talked me into it.'

The other hens drifted in, and Alicia busied herself. It struck her as odd that the only one to ask after her lady was Tammy. 'Have you actually spoken to Faith today, Leesha?'

'No. Cathy says that she is deep in a recovery slumber and that she ate well this morning.'

'That's good.'

By half past seven the studio was filled with laughter, perfume and smiles. And then Tara Doyle walked in.

'Hiya, girls! Looks like you've made yourselves right at home here.'

There was a suppressed anger in her voice which put Alicia and Thistle on red alert and made even Vicky's ears prick up. The Seer tightened her dressing gown and said, 'According to the boss, the studio's booked till eight.'

'It is,' said the Princess brightly. 'But the chairs aren't. There's a queue waiting for mani-pedis in the spa and nowhere to sit down.'

Everyone turned to look at Alicia, and it was all she could do not to dive through the now-covered picture windows. She thought, for a second, about putting the blame fairly and squarely where it belonged: on Thistle's shoulders. But where was the profit in that? Blaming her Sister wouldn't change her future for the better.

'Forgive me, my lady. Is there any way I can fix this?'

'There's a couple of benches going spare in the gym. I'll give you a hand swapping them back. I've even brought a trolley.'

'Don't panic,' said Tammy. 'I'll take over on Prosecco duty.'

Princess Birkdale used Fire to lift the sturdiest chairs outside, then they worked as mortals to get them onto the trolley. The Princess happily enlisted two men from the gym to carry the benches. 'But leave them outside the studio, yeah? There's a hen party going on in there.'

'Couldn't they use some company?' said one of the men, flexing his abs (a neat trick, and one which Alicia would have *loved* to see Robbie attempt…).

Tara stroked his arm. 'They'd eat you alive and come back for more. How about a selfie? You and me, when you've finished?'

And the bright face was kept up until the game of musical benches was done, then the Princess showed them her teeth. She knew exactly who to blame, pointing her finger at Thistle. 'I have lost a kitchen apprentice thanks to you. Poor kid actually wet himself when you breezed in demanding food.' She stepped closer and jabbed each word into Thistle's chest. 'You. Do. Not. Do. That. Here. Understood?'

'My lady is wise,' said Thistle. 'Would you have me serve in his place? Once the wedding is over?'

'I wouldn't have you in my kitchens if the whole of Blackpool was booked in for a buffet. Tell Princess Flopsy to make amends in gold. Not too much, though. We were gonna fire him anyway.'

They lifted the benches into the studio. 'Why did those guys stop outside?' asked Tammy. 'The one with the dark hair was well fit.'

'Don't want to ruin your appetite for later, do we?' said Tara. 'So what's goin' on now?'

Alicia scampered to the Warded cases and saw that one of them was labelled *This one first*. She laid it on its back and used Faith's Name to open it, trying not to think about how the Guardian knew her lady's Name in the first place.

Once she'd unzipped the lid, two bulky brown paper packets sat next to each other. One said *Faith – for you to dress Mina*. Alicia knew that she must fulfil Faith's role, so she passed the other packet to Thistle and said, 'Wait a moment, Sister. We must examine this first.' She looked down, and there was a second, even bulkier packet labelled *Mina Part Two*. 'And this also.'

'What do you reckon, girls?' said Evie. 'Mina has to go out in double denim?'

'I know what she truly hates,' said Erin. 'I've heard it often enough. I reckon the first parcel is an old Barbour jacket, bought off a dairy farmer, and the second parcel is an inflatable Border collie on a stick.'

'You're proper weird,' said Evie. 'I dread to think what you and Barney get up to in the bedroom. I mean, what you did to that singer last night…'

'Shall I open it?' said Alicia quickly.

She tore the paper and a cascade of brown fabric and leather tipped out, along with a collarless white linen shirt and a pair of pink fluffy socks.

'I hope that fits,' said Mina. 'Hannah-ji took all my measurements, but…'

'What's in the other parcel?' said Tammy.

Alicia opened it to reveal some rustic knee boots … and two curved short-swords in scabbards attached to a leather harness. And they did not look the plastic toys the cubs sometimes played with.

'Ooh,' said Saffron. 'The potential for chaos has just gone into overdrive.'

'A ninja!' said Tammy. 'You're going to be a ninja!'

'I think not,' said Mina serenely. 'Given that I am not Japanese, that is unlikely.' She turned and gave the hens the most mortal smile Alicia had seen, complete with a twinkle in her eye that no amount of magick could fake. 'You lot have been calling me Rani for long enough.'

'To be fair, it's what you call yourself,' said Vicky. 'Only saying.'

'Well, tonight, I think I am going to be a *warrior* princess. I can't wait to find out what you lot are going to be.'

Alicia had been sorting through the garments – woollen leggings, leather girdle, leather bracers and a woollen cloak with crossover leather fastenings. Should Alicia ever feel like attacking a hunting party, she would *definitely* dress like this.

'Shall we start with the shirt, my lady?'

'And I'll see what's in here,' said Thistle, staring at the packet for a second, then shrugging and ripping it open.

'Ooh, what's that—' began Evie.

'Boring!' said Tammy. 'And weird. Since when did a warrior princess lead a troop of elite trolley dollies?'

The air crackled with magick. 'Say that again,' said Princess Birkdale, with an edge to her voice sharper than a broken bottle.

Tammy frowned. 'They're—'

'No, they're not!' said Lucy. 'It's a mistake. You're seeing things, Tammy. Here. Let me.' She barrelled Thistle out of the way and started grabbing the slippery polyester of the bright red fancy dress uniforms.

Desperate for something to defuse the tension, Alicia raised her voice. 'Let's see what else there is, shall we?' She grabbed the zip and almost ripped the other oversized suitcase in half getting it open. Inside were more carefully wrapped brown paper parcels. The top one said *SAFFRON* in large letters, and then in much smaller writing, *Tell her I couldn't resist it. Not that I'm stereotyping or anything.*

Had Gertha the Spider written this? Because Alicia couldn't see any way in which Albion's Anointed Guardian had been responsible. Never mind. 'Ladies! We have more, and first up is my lady Saffron,' she announced.

She passed the parcel to her, and Saffron read the message aloud. When she carefully peeled back the tape, Alicia recognised the blue dress straight away: exactly the same one was hanging up in the Pack Hall. 'Elsa!'

'Eh?' said Saffron.

'It's an Elsa costume, and you won't need a wi—'

'Leesha, you have an amazing knack of saying the wrong thing,' said Tammy. 'Though it's a fair point. You may have your work cut out on the cheekbones, though.'

Saffron held up a long white blonde ponytail which would attach perfectly to her own hair. 'Well, we've got one warrior princess and one ice queen so far, Tammy, so I'd wait until you know *your* character before having a go. Who's next?'

Thistle had been helping Mina, and the bride-to-be was suddenly a fierce warrior, especially when she drew two sharp steel blades. 'This is entirely too much fun,' she declared. 'And I think the sight of a warrior princess with her harem is something Blackpool has been waiting for.' A semicircle of open mouths greeted her, and then she grinned. 'What? Too much?'

'Erm, Sister?' said Thistle. 'Do we think letting the girls out with edged weapons is a guid idea?'

The hens' faces held an octave of responses, the bass disapproval of Vicky at one end and the high C of excitement from Tammy at the top. Tara Doyle capped them all by saying, 'Now that I *would* like to see.'

Alicia's first thought was something which Princess Faith said to her on her bad days, the sort of bad days when Alicia curdled the milk or fed chocolate to the Wolves after they'd Exchanged, and it was all she could do not to say it out loud. *Why do I always have to be the grown-up?*

'They will look magnificent in the pictures, Mina,' she said instead. 'We can put a background Glamour on those curtains when you're all dressed, and then perhaps Thistle can hold them for you when we go out?'

'Great. Sorted,' said Vicky. 'Who's next?'

'Why, you are. Here. Perhaps you can read Guardian Hannah's writing better than me.'

The Chief Bridesmaid accepted her parcel and read aloud: '*Victoria. I thought it was about time that Saffron got to play the big sister.* Why do I have a bad feeling about this?' She tore the paper and peered inside with a groan. 'Why do I have to be Anna? I'm gonna boil in this.'

Saffron grinned. 'I am *so* looking forward to the karaoke.'

'Karaoke?' said Rachael. 'Who said anything about karaoke?'

'It was an executive decision,' said Vicky, 'even though I'm starting to regret it now. I think we had enough of strippers and drag queens last night, so Tara's recommended The Five-Leaf Clover Irish karaoke bar.'

'Irish karaoke?'

'Don't panic,' said Tara. 'In Blackpool, you have to cover all the bases. I've told them to make sure your names are always top of the list.'

Another property belonging to the Princess. Alicia shook her head and said, 'Tamsin. You're next.'

'*If you don't recognise her, ask your daughter,*' read Tammy. A huge gown of yellow nylon exploded from the package.

'Oh, that is *priceless*,' said Tara, who clearly watched Disney with her children – unlike Tammy, who frowned, knowing she'd been made fun of but not knowing why. Tara picked up the yellow evening gloves which had fallen out and handed them over. 'It's Belle. As in *Beauty and the Beast*. Sounds about right for your ex. Enjoy.'

'I didn't have Chris down as a *beast*,' said Evie. 'Until you told us about his proportions.'

'Oh yeah,' said Tara. 'Now this I must hear.'

'Erin!' said Alicia. 'I wonder who you are?'

'Rumpelstiltskin, probably,' said Erin. 'Hand it over. Ah. Apparently mine is *symbolic*, according to the Peculier Constable.' She peered inside. 'I'm loving the blonde wig. Who's the pink princess again?'

'Aurora. The Sleeping Beauty. Pricked her finger in the forest and went to sleep. How is that symbolic?' asked Alicia.'

'Don't ask,' said Vicky. No, not Vicky. Wow.

Alicia stared open-mouthed at the transformation. Anna swung her skirts and made cow eyes at Elsa. 'You'll save me, won't you?'

'That was so creepy,' said Saffron. 'You are way too good at that.'

Vicky curtsied. 'Why thank you. Shame I can't keep it up after a bottle of Prosecco, talking of which…'

'Let's get dressed first,' said Alicia, motioning for Thistle to intercept the open bottle. 'Lucy and Rachael. Here you go.'

'Mine says *Don't take it personally. Actually, do take it personally*,' said Lucy.

'And mine says *Not all towers are made of ivory*. What the hell?'

Lucy examined the package. 'Snow White. Ha ha ha.'

'Rapunzel,' said Rachael. 'And there is at least eight foot of coiled wig to go with it.'

'Which leaves two,' said Thistle. 'Evie, there you go, and Alicia, yours was made for Faith. Hope it fits you.'

Evie read her label. 'Very funny. *You shall go to the hen party!* Must be Cinderella. So long as I don't actually have to wear glass slippers. Ooh! I like the waist cincher. Gonna need a hand with that.'

Rachael had slipped over to Alicia. 'Go on then, kiddo, what you got?'

Alicia relaxed inside. If the Guardian had chosen this costume for Faith, it couldn't be *that* bad. Could it? And then she twigged. 'I think it's Ariel. The Little Mermaid,' she told Rachael. 'With no seashell bra.'

She peeled it open, and Rachael called to the group. 'Hey, this isn't fair. Alicia here has got a custom costume from Etsy. *Steampunk Ariel*.'

'Aye, well, what'd you expect?' said Vicky. 'She's our chaperone. Never know when she might need to fight off the guys. Mind you, with this get-up we'll be a fetish magnet and no mistake.'

There was hair and make-up to do and Prosecco to be poured, then they were ready to strike some poses.

'As Sapphire's tiddled off home, I'll take the group shot,' said Tara. 'And a few pairs, while you're still sober. Got to have Anna and Elsa together.'

After many pictures and much posting to Instagram, they were getting ready to go. Then Mina spoke up: 'I need a picture of me and Leesha.'

'What for?' said Tara.

Mina flinched, then handed over her phone and said, 'If you wouldn't mind?'

Tara smiled, the tiniest glimpse of teeth visible, then took the picture.

Then she had to wait while Erin threw a Glamour of a beach scene onto the curtains and re-posed the shot.

After considering Alicia's Steampunk Ariel look, complete with vermilion wig, Erin (aka Aurora) observed, 'That red suits you, Leesha. Not saying you shouldn't have a natural colour, and I am totally not saying you should be ginger—'

'Definitely not,' said Rachael loudly.

'But I'm not sure about the blonde, neither,' concluded Erin. 'You have to remember that some are born blonde, some achieve blondeness, and others have it thrust upon them.'

'You should totally *not* remember that,' said Mina, putting her arm around Alicia. 'Now give Tara a big smile for the camera. Not too big, though. We don't want to scare Instagram to death, do we?'

Mina AirDropped the picture to Alicia, and Alicia was smiling with a full heart when Princess Birkdale walked past her and said in the People's tongue but with a mortal accent, 'I'd make a Memory of that if I were you, 'cos where you're going there won't be phones or fun.'

While Alicia shook with fear, Tara wished the hens a great night. The Princess lowered her voice and told Thistle to make sure that the benches were taken back to the gym, and then she walked over to a corner where the forgotten cabin crew uniforms were piled in a heap. 'I think I'll take these, thanks. Never know when I might need to return the favour.'

Tammy had been very quiet for the last five minutes, but as soon as the Princess was beyond hearing, she picked up some wrapping paper and waved it at the door. 'You idiot, Alicia. You totally fuckbrained idiot.'

The rest of the group froze, and Alicia stepped backwards. 'My lady?'

'This,' said Tammy, thrusting the paper at her. 'The package with the trolley dolly outfits. It says very clearly *Do not let Tara see these.*' She turned to Lucy. 'And you seem to know what's going on. What's the Princess's problem with cabin crew?'

Lucy had gone red, even redder than the rouge on her Snow White cheeks. She swallowed and took a breath. 'It's not cabin crew in general. It's these uniforms. They were the actual ones worn by the wives of the Octet. The Gnomes who killed the Count of Canal Street. Hannah must have gathered them up and kept them as a joke.'

'Ooh, no wonder Tara was upset,' said Vicky.

'Yeah. Ouch and no mistake,' said Saffron.

Tammy threw the paper at Alicia's feet. 'Un-fucking-believable. You have dumped so much shit on Faith this weekend, Alicia. First at Rydal Water, then Lucy's car in the canal with Tara's friend. And now this. Princess Birkdale is *not* someone you should be getting on the wrong side of. No wonder they call you *Littleworm.*'

Rachael was still standing near Alicia. She picked up the wrapping and peered at it, then she raised her eyebrows at Alicia with a pointed look towards Thistle. Clearly Rachael had spotted that reading was not Thistle's strong point. Alicia felt a burning inside her, starting somewhere near her gut where the leather corset (in Faith's size) was doing something unpleasant to her diaphragm.

She nodded to show Rachael that she was right, then shook her head to close it down and turned to walk away. As she did, Rachael gave her a squeeze round the middle which was well intentioned but *very* painful. Alicia groaned and everyone thought it was embarrassment.

'Leave Leesha alone, Tammy,' said Vicky. 'She's only a bairn, and she's doing her best.'

'She is,' added Mina. 'And I hereby appoint Alicia as the judge for tonight's karaoke.'

Like the hug from Rachael, Vicky and Mina's support was well intentioned but useless. In the end, Alicia's future did not lie in the hands of these mortals. It lay in the curved talons of Princess Birkdale and the cobra fangs of Damini.

Chapter Thirty-Eight

By the time that the last bottle of Prosecco had been drained, the hens' thoughts had turned to karaoke, and soon Vicky was leading them through Blackwell Hotel lobby and onwards to The Five-Leaf Clover, with Alicia bringing up the rear and keeping her eyes (all of them) wide open. The hens were attracting a *lot* of attention.

It took about twenty minutes to walk there, and ten of those included Evie moaning that the bloody slippers might as well have been made of glass and could somebody carry her because her feet were killing her?

Vicky stopped the party with a raised hand and pointed at Evie. 'Shoe size?'

'Seven.'

'Hah! You told me *six*, you daft 'nana. No wonder your feet hurt. Serves you right. Onwards, ladies!'

Rachael was in the middle of the gaggle, and just as the lurid green frontage of the Irish bar came into view, she stood on her Rapunzel hair and nearly tripped over. The nylon braid detached itself and flopped all over the pavement. 'You go on and get me something green and alcoholic,' she said. 'Alicia will need a bit of privacy to fix this.'

'You didn't think we were going to wait, did you?' said Erin. 'I'm like a dying man in the desert with the oasis just in view. I haven't had a drink for … ooh, at least twenty minutes.'

The hens surged on, and Evie called out, 'Something green and alcoholic? I'll get you a leprechaun, Raitch.'

Rachael stepped into an alley and dusted off her Rapunzel hair. Alicia rushed to help. She had just started to undo the ribbons which performed the heavy lifting on the eight-foot braid when Rachael closed her hands around Alicia's and said, 'What's going on, Alicia? I saw you and Thistle having a strip torn off by Tara Doyle earlier, and it must have been serious because Tara's face blurred out. She was showing you her teeth, wasn't she?'

'It was nothing, Raitch. I'm just not used to things running away from me.'

'Are you in trouble? And is it my fault?'

'Nothing I can't handle.'

Alicia felt Thistle detach herself from the darkness. 'It's no your fault, Rachael, but Leesha's in the deepest shit possible. Deeper than your worst nightmares.'

'Is this true, Alicia?'

'She can't answer you. She's been bound to say nothing. I haven't, though.'

'What's going on? And why aren't you bound as well?'

Thistle touched them both to make a three-way Silence. 'I only know because Princess Birkdale has a mouth like the Mersey tunnel and couldn't wait to gloat. The price for Birkdale saving our lady's life yesterday was Alicia. When the wedding is over, my Sister will be released from Faith's household. Completely cut off and beyond her protection, and Birkdale will be standing waiting. She'll take Leesha, put her to the question then hand her over to Damini.'

'What? This is—'

Thistle cut her off. 'Aye, but you dinnae ken the worst. I got out of Tiree's service because I was patient and because I got my chance. Once you've been put into the service of an immortal who's not one of us, then that's it. No escape. Ever.'

Alicia felt stabs of pain all over herself. The corset squeezed her ribs, tears stung her eyes and her heart was as chained in her chest as she would soon be chained to the Nāgin's will. Unless…

Alicia peeled Rachael's hands away, gently but firmly, and tried to be conversational. 'There is another option. Knights who are released can go roving.'

'Pish,' said Thistle. 'That'll just make it worse when she catches you. And if you *did* escape, what then?'

'Yeah, that's not rhetorical,' said Rachael. 'There wasn't a chapter on *roving* in the book I read.'

'Because we keep quiet aboot it, and you'll do the same,' said Thistle. Then she waited.

Alicia started re-fastening the blonde braid, and Rachael realised that a response was needed. 'Of course. Confidentiality of the salon.'

Thistle gave Alicia a strange look, as if she wanted to pursue that idea, then shook her head. 'A Knight released cannae re-join the same household. If they prove themselves in some way, they can join another. Faith will be on the lookout for a few like that when she's Proclaimed, but no one will have Alicia 'cos there'll be a great target on her back. So she'll have to live among mortals.'

Rachael frowned. 'But don't you need the Water of Life or whatever it's called?'

Alicia gave a tug on the ribbons and stepped back. Job done. 'We do. A year without bathing in the pool or drinking the Water of Life and we start to fade, and once it starts…' She shrugged. It was a fact of life. 'I can tell you many stories of the People who have gone to live with mortals. For love, among other things. We should go.'

Rachael had her back to the road, an effective barrier. Her eyes darted from Alicia to Thistle and back again. 'And this is all about Faith being ill? Not about … Alicia's adventure last night?'

'Our Queen-to-be wasnae ill, lady Rachael,' said Thistle. 'She was nearly dead until Alicia got the Red Queen to intervene and brought Faith back from the brink. Birkdale would have let her die.'

'But … But why?'

'To remove a rival,' said Thistle, rolling the alliteration with more relish than was fitting for such a deadly manoeuvre. 'Anyways, why are you so bothered about wee Lucy's car? What's it to you?'

'What does "put to the question" mean?'

'Ask your brother,' said Alicia. 'I think we should be going, because they've been in the bar on their own for long enough to get in trouble. And your leprechaun will be going flat.'

'You're more than Eclipsed,' said Thistle. 'It was a joke, hen.'

'No, it wasn't. I checked. It's a cocktail. Not one that I would drink, but I'm not a young mortal on a wild night out.'

'Unlike me,' said Rachael, finally heading towards the bar. 'Are you really going to judge the karaoke, Alicia?'

'I shall be harsh but fair, especially about your future sister-in-law. It's such a shame that one so beautiful, one who can dance so well, is also such a threat to the eardrums.'

Rapunzel put her arm around Ariel. 'I've got a spare key to Mowbray House, you know. You could hide there. Anyone who's willing to tell Mina she can't sing has a great future somewhere.'

Ariel brushed the glowing nylon hair back from her face. The love pouring out to Rapunzel didn't slow, but it did have to divert around a rock: the thought of going into the house of the mortal who'd made *those* Wards around the Grange was enough to make you sticky. And not in a good way.

'And the winner is … Lucy!'

'What's the prize? What's the prize? Another round of Tipsy Nuns?'

'I think we've had enough Tipsy Nuns,' said Vicky. 'How about you get to choose the group finale?'

Away from the still-immaculate Disney princesses, Alicia watched the rotund and sweating Knight of the Alderley People hold his breath. He had dashed around the bar pandering to the Elvenham hens. He had managed to stop two fights, appease another group of hens who thought they were being short-changed on karaoke (which they probably were), and then helped Alicia talk Erin out of a shot-drinking competition. And now…

'Gotta be "Sweet Caroline",' said Lucy.

The Knight cringed, and Alicia almost felt sorry for him when a tear crept out of the corner of his eye.

Ten minutes later, they staggered into the street and the sea air hit them hard. So hard that Cinderella made a dash for the nearest litter bin; Aurora followed, holding on to her wig.

'I don't think Cinders is gonna be invited to many balls looking like that,' said Anna. She lurched sideways and grabbed Elsa for support 'Hey, Leesha, how come we didn't win with our amazing duet of "Let it Go"?'

'Yeah, how come?' echoed Elsa, who then made the mistake of trying to pirouette.

Alicia picked them off the floor and secured their arms. She saw Thistle watching out for Cinderella and Aurora and left them to it. She started marching the *Frozen* sisters towards the hotel and said, 'Because you used magick.'

'And your point is?'

'Ooh! Look!' said Elsa. 'Is that Raitch being arrested up ahead? Where's my phone? I *have* to get a picture of this!'

'So who was it?' asked Thistle when they finally got back to their room, having split the hens up and taken half of them each to make sure they got to bed safely.

'Take this corset off and I'll tell you,' replied Alicia. She collapsed onto the edge of the bed and started working her feet out of the boots.

Instead of coming over to help, Thistle peeled off her own clothes with lightning speed and threw them into a corner. Then she turned off the main light and picked up Alicia's Heartstone from the dressing table. She came over to the bed and climbed behind Alicia, putting her naked legs around her Sister and resting her cute little feet on Alicia's thighs. She started brushing Alicia's hair and whispered, 'In a minute. What did I miss?'

Alicia sighed. Or tried to. She was going to have to make a Healing on her abdomen when the corset was finally released. 'Well, they *were* police officers, but they were also a stag party. I think. Anyway, Rachael was the one who approached *them* and asked to be handcuffed.'

Thistle put the brush aside and set her fingers to work on the leather straps on the corset. But only for a second, to work out what was needed, and then her fingers were round the front, exploring beneath the bottom edge, where the leather finished. 'I think it's about time someone cheered you up, Alicia. You've waited long enough, and if you wait for Robbie, the mortals will all be in Heaven before he comes to you. Not that any of this lot are going *anywhere* near Heaven.'

Alicia felt the stirrings. And why not? After all, she was in the hands of a master.

Chapter Thirty-Nine

'It makes sense now,' said Alicia, unwrapping the parcel before breakfast. It was labelled *For Sunday morning* and contained eight pairs of sunglasses. 'If their hangovers are in proportion to last night, they may never take these off. I shall start gathering them.'

The last portion of the hen party was taking place in Blackwell Spa Retreat, and the hens had been given the services of no less than three staff for restorative treatments, relaxing therapies and whatever they wanted from the rejuvenating menu. In fact, all Alicia had to do was hand out the sunglasses and sniff the girls on the way in to make sure that there was no alcohol under their spa robes.

When the last hen had fumbled their way to the juice bar, Alicia and Thistle turned to look at each other. 'Thank you for last night,' said Alicia. 'It was more than favour.'

Thistle grinned. 'It's been a while. Good to know I've still got the touch.'

The places inside and outside Alicia which had been *touched* sent shivers of thanks, and she wondered why Lord Tiree had been happy to sacrifice such a practised bedmaid. 'What shall we do?'

'I'm for a sauna,' said Thistle. 'Judging by the marks I saw on you from that torture device, I'd have thought a massage was the bare minimum.'

'Perhaps, but I'll have to join the queue. Can I trust you to keep order? I think a walk by the sea might be a learning.'

'Knock yoursel' out. When you've lived all your days on an island the size of Windermere, the sea's no so much of a novelty.'

Alicia took a coat so that she could blend in and changed into a very short and rather tight skirt (because she wanted access to her skin), and then set off to walk down the Golden Mile. It was quiet today, mostly occupied by young families with pushchairs – nothing like the crowds who'd thronged the road and pavements last night. She drank deeply of the sea air; at least the smell was better in daylight. The mortals' taste in evening food matched their choice of liquor.

Sapphire Gibson was right: she was surrounded by *fun*, and rising above it all, just to the south, was the great tower. It was made of iron, which made her feel slightly ill, but the mortals could not have chosen a better beacon to draw in the crowds. They even had a funfair, though she'd been corrected that *amusement park* was the preferred mortal term. Just in case there was residual doubt, they'd even called it the Pleasure Beach. Blackpool left very little to the imagination, and there were ways to have fun and spend money *everywhere*. And where that happened, magick was sure to follow.

She'd seen enough Lux flickering from inside bars and glimmering from down alleyways to know that there were a number of players in the seaside game. There was Princess Birkdale, of course, and at least two other large properties with the People's Ink on them. She'd even seen one building marked with Mother Earth's Red, though she couldn't tell whether that was meant to protect one of the Daughters or if it signified a bigger Clan presence. No matter.

She bought a coffee and went to sit on an empty bench with a view of one of the piers. There was much to think about and many Memories to Ink from last night, some bitter but most as sweet as honey on the tongue. It was a good job that Thistle couldn't see her out here, putting her finger to bare flesh to make the Memories.

'Mind if I join you?' said a wobbly voice. 'Are you all on your own, love?' It was a mortal nearing the end of her days, wearing a thick coat and a big silk scarf.

'No. I mean, yes. Please sit down and I will leave you.'

'No point in that,' said the woman, who sat down anyway. 'I chose this bench 'cos there might be someone to talk to. All the young families are so wrapped up in themselves they don't want to talk to an old dear like me. *Are* you on your own?'

Alicia considered the question. There were several answers, and she didn't want to get it wrong. 'In what way, my lady?'

'I saw you last night with that bunch of drunken Witches.'

Alicia blinked and tried to see if the mortal had magick, but something was wrong with the woman's aura. The woman was looking right back at her. 'You're so fresh I can still smell the paint,' she told Alicia.

'I don't know what you mean.'

The woman rolled her eyes in a gesture that could have come from Evie. Was the older skin a *Glamour*? Surely not.

'I mean, you're not five minutes out of the nest and here you are playing nursemaid to some very powerful people. Are you in Bowland's service?'

And now Alicia was at sea again. 'Who?'

'Haven't got the sense you were hatched with. I didn't realise you were one of *them* until I got close. Thought I might tempt you with a reading, but that would be like trying to sell rock to the Dwarves.'

She was at sea, and the pier was receding into the distance. Where was Thistle when she needed her? 'My lady is wise,' said Alicia. That usually worked.

'Less of your cheek! *My lady* indeed. *Can* I interest you in a reading? Best in Blackpool, I am.'

'You see the future?'

The woman inclined her head gracefully. 'I do.'

Alicia smiled. 'You are kind, but I'm afraid that I know my future, and the only light in the tunnel is an oncoming giant mole.'

The woman – the Diviner – snorted. 'Don't you try to riddle me. I'm the one who weaves riddles round here. Scared, are you? Frightened that I might know something you don't?'

Alicia didn't feel at sea any more. She felt very uneasy. And trapped. But how could she be trapped by a mortal, no matter how mysterious her magick? What did the stories have to say about *this*? They said nothing, so Alicia had nothing to fall back on. And perhaps *that* was the problem.

'I have much to learn. Anything you can tell me about the future would be a boon.'

'Then shift yourself up to the café. Not the one where you bought that muck you've got there. Go down the road next to the lap dancing club and you'll find Gino's. Tell them you want one of Jorrow's fortune telling teas and one of her hot chocolates, and if I were you I'd get a cappuccino for yourself and throw that rubbish in the bin.'

'Are you coming?'

'Whatever for? Your legs are much younger than mine, so I'll wait here and watch the world go by. Go on then. Hurry up.'

Alicia walked as fast as her certifiably young legs would let her, which wasn't that quickly because the skirt was both too tight and too short for running (though she'd swerved the unicorn pants today. Faith had *much* nicer underwear.). She found the café and stopped outside to carefully look in. There was no magick that she could see, but the Diviner (Mrs Jorrow?) had fooled her, too. And it was very dark inside. She glanced around, then pushed open the door.

Alicia shifted uneasily when she found that not only was the interior *dark*, it was unlit by mundane light. Who would come here? The mortal behind the counter looked like what she seemed so, based on today's results, she almost certainly wasn't. *Get a grip*, Alicia said to herself.

'Good morning. I am to ask for one of Mrs Jorrow's special teas, a hot chocolate for her and also a cappuccino for me.'

'Oh yes,' said the woman, not moving. 'And who sent you?'

'I don't know. I thought it was Mrs Jorrow herself.'

'She doesn't work Sundays, and it's just Jorrow, not Mrs Jorrow.' She frowned. 'Wasn't an old dear with a red silk scarf, was it?'

'Yes. Who is she?'

'Jorrow's sister. Jorrow has a little place up the road and *never* works the front. You can have the stuff, but I'll have to ask for a ten pound deposit for the teacup. Once bitten, twice shy.'

'Why?'

'You can't read tea leaves without a china cup, and we've had a few go missing. Up to you.'

You can't read the future from tea leaves no matter what sort of vessel they're brewed in, thought Alicia. Unless you put them in a scrying bowl, of course. She tittered at the thought of such sacrilege, and nearly walked away until she remembered that Saerdam Michael had only prospered because he took every chance to learn that came his way. 'Yes, please.'

'Indian or China tea? We buy bancha tea for Jorrow, what with her being Japanese and all that, but I think her sister sends people back to get large leaf Indian.'

It was clearly an omen, and Rani Mina would have no hesitation here. 'Indian, please.'

'Coming up. Can I tempt you to a pastry?'

Alicia wasn't hungry in the least, but food with the drink would be a better offering. 'Thank you. Your choice.'

The woman turned her back to make the drinks, and Alicia shoved the bag with the pastries into her tote so that she could somehow balance a china cup and saucer along with two takeout cups, one of which was piled high with marshmallows.

'What took you so long?' said Jorrow's sister when Alicia returned. If that's who the woman was, because she didn't look in the least Japanese. Alicia had seen plenty of Japanese tourists in the Lakes, worshipping at the shrine to Beatrix Potter. There was even a story that the Red Queen had once produced a clutch after mating with a Samurai, but there were a lot of stories like that, and the Diviner sitting next to Alicia on the bench looked and sounded like any other mortal who hailed from Albion.

Alicia smiled. 'What do I do now?'

'Put your coffee down and cross my palm with silver, of course, and I mean *actual* silver, not cash.'

'Oh. I … One moment.'

Alicia put down her coffee and unhooked an earring. The earrings were nothing special, just stylised daffodils in silver with a gold centre. The daffodil was the Red Queen's flower, and until Princess Faith chose something different, the daffodil was also Alicia's flower. The Diviner held out a hand, and Alicia dropped the earring into it.

The woman grunted. 'That'll have to do. Slowly sip your tea while you think of your question, and stop when there's a dessert spoonful of water left. I'll be busy with this. And thank you for the pastry.'

The tea was cool enough to drink without magick so Alicia settled back to think about the future while she sipped, and while the Diviner attacked her own overflowing cup.

Princess Faith would release Alicia at some point *after* the bride's dance, that much was certain. Not straight away, obviously. Perhaps an hour later, when everyone was drunk, dancing or dozing off. Princess Birkdale would have to be there to witness it, but it would not be in the wedding tent or within the Grange, so … How in all the stars was she to escape from that?

'Wake up, dreamer,' said the woman. 'Are you done?'

'Forgive me. I am.'

'Then listen carefully. Hold the cup in sinister, swirl it thrice widdershins, then *carefully* upend it onto the saucer and turn it thrice more. Finish with the handle pointing to the south. And *don't* use magick. Of any kind. Let the Sympathetic Echo guide the leaves.'

Alicia did as she was bid, and just as she placed the cup and saucer down on the bench, her phone rang. She scrabbled into her bag and saw that it was the landline at Birk Fell calling.

'Excuse me,' she said, rising from the bench and stepping away. 'Cathy? Is all well with our lady?'

'Our lady is on her way to you. Alex has taken her across the lake to meet the Digger's Daughter. You should prepare to receive her.'

'Is she well?'

'She is, but I am afraid.'

'What's wrong?'

'She's been talking to Guardian Karina, and I think our lady has a new plan.'

'Thank you. I will go and shake Thistle.'

She turned back to the bench, but the Diviner was gone. Alicia scanned the growing numbers of mortals for any sign of the red scarf, but there was nothing. Nothing except a swirl of Ink disappearing down a narrow crack between the lap dancing club and a sports bar. With trembling fingers, she turned over the cup. Also nothing. The rich black leaves were all gone, the surface swept clean and her future was gone, too. Blank. She had been deceived, tricked and taken for a fool. Again.

She sighed bitterly. It didn't really matter. Nothing really mattered any more. Short of *actually* throwing herself off the pier, she might as well carry on. What else was there? She picked up the cup and saucer. Underneath, neatly folded, was the paper bag which had contained the pastries. Alicia was going to throw it into the handily placed recycling bin when she felt something hard inside it.

She peered into the bag and there was her earring – or what her earring had become. Instead of a daffodil, the gold and silver had been re-formed into a five-leaf clover. What was she to make of *that*? She had never heard talk of such a thing, not once in any of the stories.

The earring had also been transformed from a hook to a stud, and Alicia didn't have a back to fix it in place, so she put it safely in her purse and went to reclaim her ten pound deposit.

When she got to the darkened windows of Gino's café, she hesitated again, dimly aware that she was being watched. It would be a weakness to stand and stare with nothing to focus on, so she pushed the door open and crossed the threshold.

There were patrons in the café now. She could smell them, even if she couldn't see them, and there must be magick at work because all that tickled her nostrils was a floral scent and musky cologne; of the creatures' essence, she could discern nothing. Again, it would be a weakness to linger, so she put the china on the counter.

'Here you are.'

'Thanks. I'll get your tenner.'

As the woman opened an old tin marked *tips*, Alicia said, 'You say that the one with the premises is called Jorrow?'

'Something like that. Jorro-gummy. No one can get it right, so she's happy with Jorrow.'

'Her sister does not seem Japanese, by nature or nurture.'

'I know, and whatever the story is, they're not telling. Ten pounds. Did you like what you heard? Any tall dark handsome strangers in your future?'

'If only. I'm afraid that my future is nothing but a blank.' She tucked the note into her purse and felt the five-leaf clover. 'Do you know what Jorrow's sister calls herself?'

'Gertha.' She looked over Alicia's shoulder at a new customer. 'What can I get you, love?'

Alicia rushed back to the Blackwell Hotel as fast as her legs and her skirt would let her. She arrived in the lobby and hesitated, looking at the corridor to the spa. No. It would not do. She flew up the stairs, the last Ink of her wings pulsing on her back as she used Fire to lift herself. Evie's leggings were hanging over the shower rail, still dripping, and Alicia forced them on, making heat to start the drying, then she took herself to the spa and found Thistle where she said she'd be, in the sauna. With Tammy.

Thistle's hand was stroking Tammy's abdomen with feather fingers, and Tammy jumped up with a start, losing her balance and going even redder. Thistle just frowned. 'What the hell ye doing here, Leesha?'

Alicia was regretting getting changed. The People can absorb a *lot* of heat, but a *sauna*… She ignored it. 'I have been tricked by Gertha the Spider.'

'You've lost the plot,' said Tammy. 'You need to get out of here and I am going to get Faith to put you to the pool and check. You are definitely Eclipsed. An egg hatched in the shadow of the moon. Now get out.'

'Hey,' said Thistle. 'That's neen o'yours. C'mon, hen.'

The lithe and glowing form of Alicia's Sister turned her back on Tammy and an arm came around Alicia's waist. 'What ails you, Sister?' asked Thistle in the People's tongue. She glanced around the corridor. 'Changing room's this way.'

Alicia allowed herself to be led into the relatively cooler tiled space. All her senses told her they were alone. She grabbed Thistle's hand. 'I was visited. My future was read by Gertha, and it is blank. And now our lady approaches.'

'And I'm naked, which is fine in the sídhe. Less so here. C'mon.'

Thistle opened a locker and grabbed her dress and a pair of flip flops, ignoring her underwear. She pulled the dress over her head. 'Let's start with the end. What do you mean about Faith? And take a *deep* breath before you answer.'

Alicia inflated her chest all the way, drawing air through her nose and holding it, then releasing both the breath and a little Calming through her system.

'Cathy called me. Our lady is coming with the Digger's Daughter, and she has been making plans with the Archer.'

Thistle took her hands. 'Good. That actually makes sense. Even better, she must have healed greatly overnight. Now that's good news.'

Alicia took another breath, mostly to enjoy feeling Thistle's fingers interlace with her own. 'It is.'

Thistle smiled. 'And the rest?'

Alicia adored *Line of Duty*. It was one of her favourite shows, and she couldn't wait for next week's episode. She thought of how these *real* police officers did things and sorted her thoughts, like Tarot cards, into the correct order. 'I was approached by a creature in the form of a mortal female, powerful enough to mask their true nature. The creature knew what I was, but did not know me for who I am. She offered to tell my future through tasseography, and I agreed.'

'You what?' interrupted Thistle. 'Tassywho?'

'Tasseography. Divination by tea leaves.'

Thistle laughed. 'Maybe the Bodysnatcher's right. Agreeing to that was what wee Lucy calls a totalbonkers brainfart. Not saying it was wrong, though. What did she see?'

'I do not know. She erased the reading while I spoke to Cathy.'

'Who do you think she is really? 'Cos your pal Gertha doesn't strike me as one to lurk around the Golden Mile.'

'An independent witness identified her as the sister of a Japanese Diviner who uses the name Jorrow. The sister calls herself Gertha.'

Thistle patted her hand. 'Old?' Alicia nodded. 'Then she's been around the block, and the Lakes are a spit from here. She went there, probably for revels in the Derwent Sídhe, and she has a good ear for stories. Coincidence.'

'Thank you. You have eased my mind.'

'For favour, you're going to the kitchens, 'cos I'm barred, and you're going to organise a late lunch for our lady and Sapphire. I am going to talk the Bodysnatcher down from her high horse.'

Alicia frowned. 'What led to you to giving her pleasure?'

'She was curious, that's all. Never tried it before. She'd tried to get the other hens to play a game, ranking their men by their manhood and stamina, but Mina put her foot down. Said that would only encourage some of them and traumatise the others, and that without Myfanwy the Druid and Anna Flint's testimony, it was all pointless. I think Rani just wanted a bit of peace and Tammy wanted to milk every moment away from her weans.'

Alicia stood. She needed to get to a cool spot and start drying out again, and now there was food to organise. It was only when she was outside and the sea breeze lifted some of the damp hair away from her neck that she remembered the earring. Later would be soon enough to share that.

Alicia didn't just organise a late lunch; she also organised one of the meeting rooms for her lady and Sapphire to eat it in, for which she received much praise and an invitation to wait on them. 'We'll do business later,' said Faith under Silence. 'And I want Thistle to hear it, too.'

Princess Faith looked much restored. Better even. Her skin was glowing again, and there was a bounce to her hair which had been sadly lacking for a couple of weeks, a point which Alicia made when she served dessert and was then graciously invited to join them.

'Alright for some,' said Sapphire. 'I got my two youngest dumped on me last night while George went to a Clan meeting. Bloody typical. He *knows* that's the nanny's regular night off, and unlike some, we can't just whistle down to the laundry for extra hands.'

'Quite,' said Faith, then she looked troubled. 'Enjoy them while you can, Sapphire. There's a saying of ours: *Mortal parents' troubles end when their children leave the nest, and that's where ours begin.* Alicia here is a case in point.'

Alicia looked down at her cheesecake. 'Forgive me, my lady. I have let you down.'

Faith reached out a finger and lifted Alicia's chin. 'You are my Saviour, Leesha, and I will never forget that, nor will the girls. I've seen the videos of last night. And the dance rehearsal. Even a picture of Erin with a seaweed face mask from this morning. The girls have had an awesome time thanks to you.' And in the People's tongue: 'You are the only one who has suffered, and Gertha does not have you in her clutches yet.'

Alicia flinched. *How did Faith know?*

A knock at the door, and in came Thistle. And Tammy. And it was Tammy who rushed over to Faith, dropping to her knee and putting her arm around the Princess.

'Faith! Why didn't you tell me you were coming? I've been so worried.' She looked at Alicia. 'How come I had to find out from Thistle?'

'Oh good,' said Faith. 'You need to be here for part of this. Have you had enough, Sapphire?'

'In other words, fuck off, *Daughter.*' Her sapphire eyes sparkled with mischief. 'Delicious, thanks, Alicia. See you later, guys. And Tammy, fasten your robe, will you?'

She twinkled her fingers and left them, and Tammy flushed almost as red as she had in the sauna.

'I need the loo,' said Faith, rising and putting her plate on the trolley. 'Why don't you throw some clothes on, Tammy, and I'll be back in two secs for a coffee.'

When she'd gone, Tammy stood up and glared at Alicia. She was about to say something until Thistle intervened. 'I was just telling Tamsin that what happened in the sauna is most *definitely* covered by the confidentiality of the salon. That right, Alicia?'

It was a favour indeed. 'Of course,' said Alicia. 'I swear by my Heartstone that what happens in Blackpool stays in Blackpool.'

Tammy nodded and left; the girls finished clearing and pouring coffee, and then Faith was back with a surprise for Alicia. She held out a box with the Apple logo and said, 'Swap. You're going to need a decent phone. It's last year's but Sapphire is *way* too generous with her brood. She had it lying in the cupboard. And there's more: the Clan will have a mundane identity for you next week. Birth certificate, driving licence, the lot. You can open a bank account next time you're in Penrith. It may come in very handy. Just send

Sapphire a picture when you've decided on your new look. I'm loving the blonde, by the way, and that bob suits you.'

Alicia handed over Faith's phone and accepted her new device with a bow. 'My lady is kind.'

'There's more, too. You can be first to learn to drive. When you have time.'

Tammy returned before Alicia could express herself fully, and Faith smiled at them all. 'There's been a lot going on while you've been having fun. In fact, it was lucky I *did* spend the weekend at Birk Fell. Once I'd woken up.'

'And you're fully recovered?' said Tammy insistently.

'For now. The next phase will begin in a couple of weeks. That meeting Sapphire was complaining about was good news for us. It seems that the fallout from the collapse of the mortal Ripleys is a gift that keeps on giving. They had Skelwith Construction booked for a big job starting next week and they can't afford it, so the full crew are coming to Staveley tomorrow. They're going to start digging out the lower levels, and I'm moving in to supervise.'

'You're leaving the Pack?' blurted Alicia. This was *very* troubling, because Sir Conrad had mandated Faith's presence at Birk Fell.

Tammy frowned at Alicia, then beamed at their lady. 'That's *awesome*, Faith.'

Faith gave a quick smile to the mortal but spoke to Alicia. 'This morning, Guardian Karina pronounced herself satisfied with the Pack, and made it very clear that *you* were responsible for that. So long as I go at weekends to do the grown-up stuff like take them to craft fairs and drive to Sainsbury's, then Karina's happy with you looking after the day-to-day running, and so are the Pack. You're quite a hit with them.' She turned to Thistle and added, 'With your help. I know you don't like the Wolves, but Leesha can't do it on her own. Cathy, of course, will be coming with me. And I'll have to do my own hair for a while. I'll live.'

Alicia didn't know whether to burst with pride or cry at being separated from Faith, so she said what she'd said to the Diviner. 'My lady is wise.'

'Possibly,' said Faith. 'Only time will answer that question. It's a shame we don't know a decent Diviner, because life would be so much easier if we knew the future.' She frowned. 'Why have you only got one earring in, Alicia?'

'Erm, have I?'

'Yes. Bloody daffodils. Such a cliché. I'd choose a thistle if the northern Queens hadn't cornered that particular market, and I've got my own personal Thistle, haven't I?'

'What will you choose?' said Tammy.

'Blue and blue have always been my colours, but I have given zero thought to all the other trappings, especially flowers. What's that flower on the Westmorland flag? Anyone?'

'Apple blossom,' said Sapphire. 'For Appleby.'

Faith tilted her head. 'And we have the river Eden. Seems like an omen. Apple blossom it is, though whether Adam and Eve will make an appearance is doubtful. Talking of making an appearance, do you reckon I've got time for a massage before we go home?'

Part Six — Good Friends, Bad Sisters

Chapter Forty-One

Long term, Alicia was still unsure. Part of her felt born blonde, and if she wasn't about to be chained to Damini for eternity, then she might have continued to experiment and discover whether she *had* been born blonde. For the present, though, she had heeded Erin's advice.

Alicia's bob was now heading past her shoulders and had been dyed to match her emerging new colour: a glossy chestnut brown, inspired by Kelly Kirkham. Alicia was *so* looking forward to showing it to Thistle, and she was looking forward even more to seeing what her Sister had become after three days in the pool.

In one week's time, they were leaving for Clerkswell and the beginning of the wedding buildup, but today they were having a different sort of feast – one to honour the full moon and the Wolves, and Faith was coming back from Staveley to Birk Fell especially. That alone was a great favour, and more than made up for the other guests.

Alicia was still trying to juggle the sleeping arrangements and work out if they could avoid using the workshop when she heard a car horn from the gate. One of the cubs ran to open it, and Alicia was thrilled to see the battered pickup from Sprint Stables waiting to be let in ... but where was Thistle? All she could see was Sophie in the driving seat.

Sophie hopped out, and for once she was dressed in clean clothes that had been nowhere near a horse.

'Hiya, Alicia,' she said. 'Are you ready?'

'For what? And where's Thistle?'

Sophie frowned. 'Didn't you get the messages?'

'No. I gave my phone to Lottie so that she could look for dresses. She's in a terrible panic now that she has to pretend to be human at the wedding. And...'

'And Mannwolves can't read. Yeah. Better get it back before we go.'

'Go where? And what's going on?'

Sophie pinched her nose. 'Let's see if I've got this right. First, Lady Morag comes out of the pit and says Thistle won't be ready in time to come with me. Then this Becca says she'll cook for you tonight, but only if we get some shopping. Then Erin says we have to get the posh Prosecco from Booths and not the cheap stuff from Sainsbury's. Then Faith says that I have to help you open a bank account, and finally she tells me that I'm to let you drive to Pooley Bridge. If I wanted a job as a bloody PA, I'd have gone to Kendal College, not Myerscough.'

'What? Me? Drive?'

'Yeah. Get your phone and your coat and prepare for the shock of your life.'

Alicia was fairly sure that the pickup couldn't give her a bigger shock than diving into Nimue's Vortex had done, but as it wasn't her place to say, she did what Sophie asked, glancing at her phone on the way to the passenger door.

'You missed one part,' Alicia told her. 'We are to meet one of the Clan at Rheged.'

'Oh yeah. That too. I'll drive us onto the lane, then we'll start your first lesson. And how does Lottie look for dresses if she can't read?'

'I Google *girls' party dresses* and let her look at the pictures.'

Lottie herself was waiting to let them out. Sophie drove a little further so that no one could see them. 'That was a favour,' Alicia told her.

'No, it wasn't. It was common *human* decency. Right, I'll go round and you can climb over, what with you having rubber bones.'

'Whatever gave—' Alicia began, but the door had slammed and she had to contort herself over the obstacle course that lay between her and the driver's seat.

When Sophie had fastened her seat belt, she put her hands on her knees and said, 'Right. Robbie says the magic words are "Make a Memory of this". I'm going to tell you once, and you have to remember.'

'If nothing else, I know how to make Memories.'

'Good. Right foot: accelerator and brake. Left foot: clutch. Left hand: gear lever and handbrake. Right hand: hold on tight. Got that?'

'Yes, even if it means nothing.'

And Alicia *had* got it – she Inked those new words into herself without ruining yet another pair of leggings. Progress.

'Now for the biggest shock of your life. You cannot use magick to drive a car. You have to do it all with your hands and feet.'

'I … But … Oh. I see what you mean.'

'Erin says that may change one day. Today is not that day.'

'So how does it feel to exist as a legal person?' asked Sophie when they exited Praed's bank. 'To go with your legal hair. I keep doing a double-take, wondering where Mina's sister has got to.'

'I am not a legal person, Sophie. Alicia Lake is the legal person, and she does not exist.'

Sophie grinned. 'I love talking to you. Let's grab a coffee and pastry to celebrate being in the real world.'

Alicia had enough paper in her hands to make a small fire. She stared at the myriad glossy booklets, including the printed *Personalised Recommendations Summary* and *Introduction to the Financial Conduct Authority*. 'Do I have to read these and make Memories?'

'Fuck no. Shove 'em in the nearest recycling bin. Oh, except for *that* one. You'll need that to set up online banking. Is Costa Coffee okay? I'm starving.'

Alicia separated the *Welcome to Your Current Account* leaflet, folded it carefully and put it in the strong brown envelope she'd collected from the Digger in Rheged, and then ran to catch Sophie before she disappeared round the corner.

While she waited for Sophie to be served, she took out the envelope again and couldn't resist admiring the picture of herself in the passport they'd supplied. It was like looking at the twin sister you never knew you had (and that would be very strange for one of the People as the People couldn't have twins). The creature – the *person* – in the photograph looked like Alicia, but was not her. Not really. Not with that lack of expression on her face.

Sophie placed two coffees and a big plate of Danish delicacies on the table. 'Tuck in. How's things? Been ages since I saw you.'

'Good, thanks,' said Alicia automatically. Well, she didn't have much choice, did she? Not with a Geas on her.

'Come on then. I'm dying to hear all about the hen party. Especially what Erin got up to.'

'What happens in Blackpool stays in Blackpool. Especially the reason that Erin had to run round the paddock at Aintree barefoot.'

'No. How come?'

Alicia zipped her lip. 'Sorry, Soph. When I've been ordered to keep quiet, I've got no choice.' She leaned forwards and whispered, 'You're going to the ceremony in Derwent, right? The one at the full moon after the wedding? You'll find out then.'

'Spoilsport. And don't call me Soph again. Not if I have to pronounce every syllable in *Alicia*.'

Alicia felt a stab of guilt. 'I am sorry. Please forgive me.'

Sophie waved a hand of dismissal then turned the wave into a swoop as she grabbed the vanilla crown. 'Mine, I think. You know what. I've been thinking. About what you said.'

Alicia was feeling delicious fork-pain between the croissant and the pain au raisin, so Sophie's words took a moment to register. 'Me? What can I have said that's worthy of thought? Oh – your hair. It is looking much better.'

'I have to look good for Robbie. Well, not for him as such, more that I actually feel like I have a social life for a change. We went to Carlisle last weekend on a proper date. Thanks for the tips, but I meant what you said about goodness and the gods and such. I can't get my head round it.'

Alicia decided on the pain au raisin. 'It's simple: without the gods to tell you what was *good*, how would you know?'

'You call that *simple*? I call it bonkers. We all know what good and evil is without gods to tell us.'

Alicia was puzzled, and lowered the pastry. 'Do you? How?' She wasn't *that* puzzled though, so she took a big bite. 'You know what? This isn't good. I don't think it is from today's batch. I must tell Lucy to open a shop in Penrith as well as Blackpool.'

Sophie chewed over both the pastry and Alicia's question. 'This is fresh enough. Much better than you get from Morrisons, anyway. *Good* is when you do something for other people, and *evil* is when you hurt them, right?'

Alicia shrugged. 'How should I know? Coffee's not bad.'

In distress, Sophie put down her pastry. 'You *really* don't have goodness? What about evil?' She pointed her finger at the disappearing pain au raisin. 'You said that's "not good" and the coffee's "not bad". How does that work?'

Alicia thought about this, and she very quickly bumped into parts of the story she didn't want to think about at *all*. The part where it told of the first Eclipsed egg. No, no, no. Not that. She retreated from the Memory and scanned her Ink for something useful to say, because Sophie was entitled to an answer. Aah. There. And there.

'We have different words for it. We say a word closer to *quality* for coffee. Seriously. And for what you call goodness, we use the word *goodness*, too. See?'

'Of course I don't. I get the thing about quality coffee versus what Flora makes, but using our word for good and evil is just a cop out.'

Alicia looked around the busy café. It was clean and bright and nowhere near as nice as the branch of Caffè Milano in Garstang. In the opposite corner were a man and a woman in deep conversation, eyes locked and postures mirroring each other. Sex looked like a strong possibility at some point, and that gave Alicia the answer she needed.

'Rachael Clarke says that Eseld Mowbray is a good person. Tamsin Pike says that you cannot be a good person if you go around shagging someone else's husband. They can't both be right, can they? And if they can, what does that say about *goodness*? You need to talk to a mortal about this. A wise one.'

Sophie grinned. 'In other words, *not* Erin Slater.'

'Erin is a friend of the People, so no, not her. One second, I am just getting used to my new phone.' She flicked through the screens. 'Here. I am going to AirDrop the contact details.'

Sophie accepted the transfer and stared at the screen. 'Francesca Somerton. Hang on, she's Perci's great aunt, isn't she? And some mega important Mage. Or was. Librarian?'

'Yes. She is incredibly wise. For a mortal. You should talk to her.'

'Like she's totally gonna take calls from a stable girl.'

'You are a friend of Perci, and Francesca is bored. I heard her say so myself.'

'I don't know whether to laugh or cry. Seriously, I don't. What's gonna happen? I go, like, "Hi Fran, can you tell me what good and evil are and why the Fae don't have them?" No chance, Alicia.'

Alicia drank her coffee. 'If it bothers you, call her. How else will you learn?'

'I … I give up. I'll stick to horses. They're *all* good. Shall we go and buy a lake of Prosecco?'

They bought the Prosecco and some delicacies from Booths, then the rest of the list from Sainsbury's. Sophie sent Alicia to the checkout and disappeared into the make-up section before paying for whatever it was she bought out of her own money. Alicia wouldn't have remembered this if it hadn't been for what happened when they got back to the car park.

'There you go,' said Sophie when Alicia had finished loading the bags and tying down the tarpaulin. 'Round here.'

'Why have you got a white lipstick in your hand? You haven't put it on yourself, so…?'

Sophie walked backwards with a grin and pointed to the near-side wing. A white ring had been drawn around a deep dent, and underneath was written *Alicia's first bump, 15/4*. 'Do you wanna sign it? Prove to Saerdam Felix that it wasn't me?'

Alicia froze, Bloodrise fighting with tears and … yes, laughter. She held out her hand. 'Of course. It's what friends do for each other.'

'Yeah, well, that's open to debate. Here you go.'

Alicia signed her name under the dent (which had taught her the true meaning of *blind spot*), then she added some Ink to the lipstick and drew an arrow to a big scrape over the wheel arch. Then she wrote *And this is Sophie's*.

'There.'

Sophie snorted laughter. 'Yep. That's totally what friends do for each other.' She took a tissue and started wiping. 'Why won't this come off? Don't tell me you used magick.'

'Of course I did. Shall I drive back? I enjoyed finding second gear on my own.'

Sophie snatched the lipstick back. 'You just wait. This is not the end. Get in. *That* side. I do not have a death wish, thank you.'

Where did the young mortal get it from? Now that Alicia had felt the power throbbing through the machine for herself, she couldn't understand where Sophie got the confidence and courage to point all that iron at a stream of other vehicles and *put her foot down*. This was going to be a lot harder than learning to ride the aon-adharcach. And her friend voiced a series of questions about the hen party which Alicia found increasingly hard to bat away. Another skill she would have to practise. Along with finishing the new boards for Operation Barnet.

The wedding hair and beauty was a whole order of challenge greater than the hen party: several days of constant change, *so* many new girls to work with, and she had been left to look after the Pack on her own this week, too. At least she now had pictures of everyone (or almost everyone), and she had a list ready to delegate to Thistle and Cathy. She could do this. It was what she had been Matched for, and the gods had sent her the Heartstone to make sure that Rani's wedding day was fitting.

And it helped her stop thinking about what would happen when the bridal dance was over.

'Do you wanna drive from here?'

'No chance. I'll run and get the gate. The cubs don't always remember to stop the chickens escaping.'

There were two more vehicles in the yard now: Faith's BMW and Karina's little car. Alicia tried not to shudder. Not only was the Archer no friend of the People, she was also meticulous and demanding when it came to the Pack, and Alicia had been swanning around in Penrith while her work had been inspected. She gripped the gate. *There's nothing wrong. The Pack are in good health.* There. Sorted.

If only.

Sophie drove in and reversed, and this time there really was something to unload. They set to work as Lowri emerged from the Pack Hall.

'Were your ears burning, Leesha?' asked the SheWolf.

'Why? Where are they?'

'Guardian and Madreb are walking the Wards with Becca. The Bodysnatcher has gone to look at the Ley line with the king and Chantress. And that Cathy is in the house if you're bothered.' The aged Wolf came closer. 'And don't worry, Little Madreb. King Alex said that our fangs are sharper with you behind us. In fact, I think they've gone for a walk so that the Guardian can rip off the Madreb's ears for leaving you on your own.' She looked at the clinking cases. 'How many are coming tonight?'

'Six plus Erin.'

Lowri winked at her. 'Say no more.'

Faith and the mortals returned, as did the others, and Alicia was thrilled with the praise she received (a grunt from the Guardian and a short hymn from Becca). Becca was trying to explain what she was cooking when those with magickal hearing all looked towards the lane.

'Who's that?' said Faith. 'Have you ordered anything, Leesha?'

'No. Lottie! The gate!'

'That's the old count's car!' said Sophie. 'It must be Saerdam Felix.'

'Who's that with him?' said Becca.

'And what's he doing coming here?' said Karina. 'This is none of his business.'

The Land Rover bounced through the gate with a jerk that nearly wiped out Lottie, then screeched to a halt. The driver's door was flung open and the furious Knight stomped round to the back to swing open the tailgate. He reached in and dragged out a female form, bound at the wrists and completely naked. He turned the girl towards the astounded group and gave her a firm kick to the backside. Alicia groaned. 'It's Thistle.'

'You what?' said Sophie. 'She … no way!'

Alicia's Sister was two inches taller than on Monday, and had gone blonde and taken the curls out of her hair. Much of the softness was gone from her face, and her nose now looked average rather than cute. If anything, now that she looked older she was even hotter. Or she would be when the bruises and wounds had healed. Alicia wasn't sure that this is what their lord had wanted when he told Thistle to grow up a bit.

'Princess Staveley,' said Saerdam Felix. 'This is yours, I think.'

'It is,' said Faith. 'And why have you bound my Knight, Saerdam?'

'Because she emerged from the sídhe this morning, made a Construction and proceeded to rut with your Guard.'

'Ooh,' said Becca. 'Does that mean what I think it means? This sounds good.'

It did not sound good to Alicia. 'Tell me you didn't,' she said to Thistle in the People's tongue.

'Course I did,' said her Sister. 'Showed him what he was missing.'

Sophie looked confused. In a moment, her head was going to join the dots between *Construction, rut* and *your Guard*. Alicia wanted to grab her and break it to her gently, and she would have done if Faith hadn't stepped forwards.

'And what is it to you, Felix, that you treat my people thus?'

The Red Queen's Knight was not the biggest or most striking of the People. He was quick, though. 'There's a mortal saying, my lady. *Don't frighten the horses*. These two were rutting in the stables. Not only frightening for the beasts, but a distinct distraction to *my* grooms. Good day.'

Faith's lips pressed together and she gave the Knight a bare nod to show that the conversation was done. He returned to the Discovery, and Alicia held up a finger to her lady, risking her wrath. She grabbed Sophie, who tried to flinch away, but Alicia's hold was iron. She made Silence and said, 'I knew nothing of this. I swear. Nothing.' She took a quick breath. 'Thistle was lying. She wanted you out of the way so that she could take your shape and seduce Robbie, and she chose to do it where everyone would know about it.'

She let go, and Sophie staggered back. 'No. No way. He wouldn't. He can't have.'

Wolves were emerging from the Pack Hall. Becca caught on and dragged Karina away from the growing confrontation. Everyone followed her example and moved away, bar Tamsin. She licked her lips.

'You. Silence. On your knees,' said Faith to Thistle. 'I'm sorry, Sophie. Was Robbie sworn to you?'

Sophie was blinking back tears. 'I dunno. We never said nothing. Didn't seem to be any point up there. There's only him and me.' She quailed at the sight of Faith's anger and turned to Alicia. 'You must have known! That's why you didn't answer any messages.'

'I didn't! Tell her, Thistle.'

Thistle winked at Alicia, and Alicia was furious. So furious that she turned to Faith. 'My lady, let me administer the punishment to prove my word.'

'As you wish.'

Alicia turned to Sophie. 'Do you have a whip in the pickup? We don't have one here.'

Sophie's head nearly spun off its neck as she looked from Thistle to Faith to Alicia. 'You're gonna *beat* her?'

'Soundly. It will be my first time.'

'No! That's wrong. That's what evil is, Leesha. No beatings. Can I go, Boss?'

'Of course, Sophie. One second.' Faith pointed at Thistle, glistening with magick. 'You are forbidden Robbie's bed until after the wedding.'

'Thanks,' said Sophie. She turned, avoiding everyone's eyes as she got into the pickup and started the engine.

Faith was still glowing as she continued to speak to Thistle in the People's tongue. 'No beatings for you. I have a better idea. I will give your punishment … later. Now get dressed and go to the kitchen.'

Chapter Forty-Three

Alicia was miserable. She was furious with her Sister and she was scared to message Sophie in case she had been blocked and deleted. And she had to accompany Karina on a tour of the Wards.

'I really am sorry,' she said for the umpteenth time.

'You don't get it, do you?' said Karina. 'The resident Madreb or her deputy *must* check *and* maintain the Wards on a daily basis. If you don't learn how to do it by Sunday, Faith will have to move back in.'

'Thistle is here now.'

'No, she isn't. She's confined to the kitchen.'

'But…'

'We are leaving at eleven tomorrow morning. If she has shown me that she can do it and Faith orders her to remain here, then I will be content. Now, let's see about that beck. I'm not sure that encouraging the cubs to learn to build dams is a good idea.'

'Perhaps you could talk Becca into letting us have beavers.'

Karina gave her a dark look, then stopped. 'You can ask her yourself. I hear they're coming to the Lowther Estate.'

'Thank you, Guardian. And the Pack are still asking about archery, you know. They really enjoyed that.'

Karina sighed. 'And so did I.' She looked as if she were going to continue, then turned and marched towards the beck. 'How did this damn dam business start, anyway?'

'Oh, one of the boys said they wanted to play at being Diggers. I'm told it's quite common.'

'Small children of both sexes playing *with* diggers is quite common. Playing at being Gnomes is not.'

'Guardian? I hear the howl. We are summoned.'

'Good. I'm hungry. Just don't flood the mundane path. Okay?'

'Of course.'

They gathered in the amphitheatre, and Alicia was given a seat at the table (Thistle and Cathy were not). Erin had arrived in their absence, and the Wolves took up seats beyond them; the Wolves would be eating later. If the hunt was successful.

Thistle, now dressed, brought food down from the house with help from Cathy and with Becca bringing up the rear. 'Spring lamb with farm potatoes and early broccoli,' announced the Witch. 'From the Coven's flock. A gift in return for the haunches of venison. Enjoy.'

They did enjoy, and as the sun dropped towards the lake, Becca said to Karina, 'You happy now, love? All Pack-shaped and Bristol fashion?'

'Oi,' said Erin. 'What's Bristol got to do with it?'

'Nothing,' said Karina hastily. 'Subject to the Ward inspection tomorrow, then yes, I am. The Pack is in good health.' And then she went quiet and looked at her scarlet-haired partner, who Alicia knew could talk for the whole Coven, never mind just her girlfriend.

Becca looked at the Princess. 'I know it's a long time off, Faith, but I've got to ask: are you planning to split the Pack and take some to Staveley?'

Faith frowned and anger flickered across her eyes. She looked at the mortals and the Wolves; this was neither the time nor the place.

'I don't know.'

'You promised,' said Maria from the shadows.

Faith's head snapped round. 'Who gave—'

'I did,' said Karina firmly. 'While I am Guardian, the Pack will speak with their own voices. You don't have to like it, but you do have to listen.'

Faith went still for a moment, then blinked. 'Maria, Lottie and Daniel are welcome to my protection when I am Proclaimed.'

'Where you gonna get the rest from?' said Erin. 'Three Wolves do not a Pack make.'

'Precisely,' said Becca, jumping in before Faith could answer. 'Alicia, what happened on Tuesday evening?'

Alicia was on the spot again, almost certainly her least favourite place in the world. 'Erm...'

'Tell her,' urged Becca.

Alicia looked at an empty spot, normally filled by one of the older SheWolves. 'There was a miscarrying. I did my best.'

'No one could have done more,' said King Alex. 'That's not the problem.'

'Then what is the problem?' frowned Faith.

'Blood lines,' said Becca. 'Genetics, if you prefer.' She looked at the Wolves. 'It's always a tragedy, of course, but when a Wolf miscarries like this, it's a sign of crossed lines.'

Faith nodded to show that she understood and accepted the Witch's word. 'What do you suggest?'

'Conrad has enough on his plate right now, but he needs to be told before the autumn. And it's not just here – I've spoken to Omnira at Harprigg and she's got issues, too. There needs to be a Wolfmoot. With four Packs minimum. Five if you really want your own, Faith. Birkfell and Derwent, obviously, and the Bowland Pack—'

'No,' said Faith sharply. 'There will be no Wolfmoot with Bowland.'

'What's a Wolfmoot?' said Tammy. 'I've never heard of them.'

'Neither had I until I met Karina,' said Becca. 'A lifetime in the Circles and not a dickybird. Amazing what you pick up when you broaden your horizons. Until she met me, Karina had never heard of chocolate-flavoured—'

'The Wolfmoot!' said Karina, trying to give Becca a meaningful glare.

'Basically a big hunt. Huge. Three Packs are the fewest you can get away with. Needs a couple of hundred square miles at least. And access to the Fae Realm. On the full moon before Yuletide, all the Wolves gather together and the Protectors wait at the other end of the chase. There's a hunt, and, well … shall we say it can get a bit red in tooth and claw. At the end the King and Queen, or the *new* King and Queen, lead a recombined Pack to their Protector.'

Faith sighed. 'I think a quote from our lord is appropriate here. "You haven't half opened a can of curried worms." '

'I'm sorry?' said Becca. '*Curried* worms?'

Faith waved a hand. 'Did you speak to Omnira only?'

'Yeah, well, that's another problem isn't it? Apparently Prince Harprigg isn't flavour of the month in the Derwent Sídhe, and he's not taking calls from the likes of me.'

'There's more to it than that,' said Faith. 'First, Omnira only told you part of the story, because the last Wolfmoot was sixty years ago, and I was there. We – the People – run or ride with the Wolves, and at dawn someone is going to end up with a smaller Pack than they had at sunset. It has been known for *no* Wolves to return to their Protector, which can be seen as a slight. The blood that flows in a Wolfmoot is oft tinged with Quicksilver.'

'Oh,' said Becca. 'I wonder why Omnira didn't mention that?'

'If I know her, it's because she's hoping this will land in the lap of the Pack's Lord Protector. Have you forgotten the Dual-Natured Commission that Conrad must hold?'

'Karina?' said Becca plaintively.

Karina shrugged. 'He keeps putting it off.'

'I am no mortal Mage,' said Faith. 'Tammy? Tell me this: what will the human members of the Commission say when the chairman reveals that a crucial part of Pack health is a blood-soaked hunt with duels to the death?'

'Ouch,' said Tammy. 'If the new Warden's crew get a whiff of that, they'll insist on a complete ban and replace it with supervised genetic matching.'

'I hadn't thought of that,' said Becca.

Faith pinched her nose. 'You know, Alicia, life was so much easier when I was the spare Princess. All I had to do was exercise the Royal Unicorns and help Her Grace choose lingerie for mating. You want to bear that in mind before you climb any higher up the greasy pole.' She shook her head like a dog. 'Well, Becca Lewis, something else you haven't thought of is what the People will say if the Warden tries to trample on our traditions.'

There was silence for a moment as the company digested this. From the lengthening shadows, Lowri spoke. 'Guardian? May I speak for the Pack?'

'Of course,' said Karina.

'We did not follow much of what you said between you. Perhaps the Little Madreb will tell us. Whatever it was, we in the Pack know that at the *first* Wolfmoot, Great Fang was triumphant, and that when he submitted to the

Morrigan's Protection, she made him King of *all* Wolves. Past, present and future.'

'Thank you,' said Karina. 'Of course Alicia will explain.'

Lowri stood up. Her silver hair had a glow of magick to it. Alicia allowed herself a fleeting smile: she had given the crippled SheWolf the best look of any Pack Elder in Albion. 'There is a time for talk,' said Lowri, 'and a time to hunt. The time for talking is over.'

'I'll top up the glasses,' said Erin. 'Well, mine anyway.'

The Wolves dispersed, and the Single-Natured wandered up to the yard. In moments, the naked Pack surrounded them and looked to Karina for her blessing, eager to Exchange.

'Hold my glass, Leesha,' said Faith.

Alicia took her lady's drink and was about to say something when Faith strode over and reached round Cathy to grab Thistle's ear. 'Come here, you.' She dragged the newly skinned Knight before Alex and Cara. 'You saw what she did. I pronounce her tonight's lure. Try not to damage her too much.'

'My lady? No! I beg you!' screamed Thistle, twisting in Faith's grip until her own ear was almost wrenched off.

And then Faith spoke to the Wolves in the People's tongue, a short phrase which Wolf ears could understand and which had been passed down by the Elders. 'Go with Great Fang and rejoice in your nature, for it is twice blessed.'

'Stop,' said Karina. 'I will not—'

The rest of her words were drowned out by howls from the Pack and Thistle's screams as they Exchanged. Faith released her ear, and Thistle put Fire into her legs, vanishing into the darkness. The king greeted the full moon in the Wolf's tongue, and then the Pack slipped soundlessly out of the yard on Thistle's trail.

'How dare you,' said Karina, her face rigid with fury.

'Tell her, Alicia. Tell her why the Pack think you're the bees knees all of a sudden. It's not because you do their hair, is it?'

'Me?' squeaked Alicia. She tried to shuffle away from the spotlight. Twice in one day was twice too much.

'Tell her what Lowri asked you.'

'Erm. She said that free hunting was the best, but the Pack needed to train to the lure. If all they can follow is wild animals, they lose their purpose.'

Karina considered her words. When she spoke, she addressed Faith. 'The Pack are not bloodhounds. Neither the Chief nor I want that.'

'No,' said Faith. 'But they are a potential target. If they can't follow individual scents, especially ones masked by magick, they can't protect themselves properly or give accurate reports. Most of it is instinct, and Lowri brought the rest of the knowledge with her. With all due respect, Guardian, humans can't train them to the lure. You don't have the powers.'

'*Teach* them. We don't *train* the Pack, Faith, we *teach* them. Neither do we set them to maul people.'

Faith raised an eyebrow. 'How else do they learn not to kill? If I choose to use it as punishment, that's my business. It won't happen often. Not once word gets around. Or are you going to turn tattletale and tell Conrad?'

'Hey, Faith. No need to get arsey,' said Erin, stepping between the Princess and the Guardian. 'That was bang out of order, that. You should have asked Karina first. Show her some respect, eh?'

When Erin didn't move, Faith worked her jaw, fighting to keep her teeth restrained. Finally, she bowed. 'Forgive me, Guardian. It came to me on the spur, and I should not have proceeded without your consent.'

Alicia had been watching Karina. Her hands had flexed as if they wanted to grip something. Like a bow. When Faith apologised, they relaxed. A little. Her words were still angry, though. 'Apology accepted, Faith. You should have thought it through, though, because Thistle won't be maintaining the Wards, will she? Not with Healing to do. You can remain here until the wedding rather than delegate the hard work to Alicia. And no, I won't be telling tales to the Chief. Not until he visits. He *does* need to know.'

She turned to Becca. 'I think I've had enough. Shall we go back to your place and return at dawn to greet the Pack?'

'Yeah. Perhaps that would be a good idea.'

'Thank you for the meal,' said Faith. 'It was made with love and received with gratitude.'

'You're welcome,' said Becca. 'That's quite a compliment coming from someone who's eaten at the best restaurants. I always say that—'

'You always say too much,' said Karina. 'Let's go.'

There were bows and handshakes, then the humans walked off. As the lights on Karina's car flashed, Cathy turned to Faith. 'You could have waited until Thistle had done the washing up. You should see what Becca's done to the griddle. One thing's for certain: it won't be me who cleans it.'

'Leesha?' said Faith.

Alicia sighed and rolled up her sleeves. Metaphorically speaking. Hairdressers never wear long sleeves. 'Can you at least dry and put away?' she asked Cathy.

Chapter Forty-Four

Cathy was right about the griddle. Ugh. And the cottage only had one tiny sink in the kitchen. Ludicrous. Alicia finally got the last traces removed and put it on the draining board for Cathy. The Hlæfdige had helped deal with the plates and then abandoned Alicia to the heavy pans, saying, 'I'm allowed a drink tonight, and I'm going to make the most of it. I'll finish up in the morning.'

Alicia wandered around the cottage checking and re-arranging the beds now that the Guardian and her woman would not need the second bedroom. She was carrying a duvet upstairs when she got a message from Faith: Aren't you done yet? Come down to the fire. We have business to sort.

She hastily dumped the bedding and dashed down to the fire pit where Lowri, fresh from the hunt, had joined Faith, Erin, Tammy and Cathy, and had a glass of wine in her hand. Now that was totally unheard of at Harprigg – the Prince would never let a Wolf join in their revels. It looked as if Faith was having a re-think about the way she treated the Pack.

That wasn't all that shocked Alicia. Naturally, she moved as quietly as possible. The People always do at night, and that's why Tammy didn't see her coming. She was sitting next to Faith on the end log, and she had her arm around their lady's waist. Alicia retreated, coughed, and walked noisily towards the roaring fire; Tammy's arm withdrew as if it had been burned.

'Yes, my lady?'

Faith stood up. 'Lowri tells me that Thistle would appreciate a hand getting back. She didn't get very far, so she should be easy to find. Grab a sheet for bandages and I'll see you by the gate when I've had a pee. Oh, and Erin, there'd better be some of the good stuff left when we get back.'

They met at the gate, and Faith said, 'Apparently she's up the slope from the LZ. Give me your hand, Leesha.'

'My lady.'

They walked off, following the track, and Faith slowed the pace right down. 'I am so sorry, Alicia. I wish it could be different. I am going to miss you when you are gone. As the mortals say, it took a near-death experience to make me realise just what I got when Fortune put you in my household.'

Alicia trembled inside, love for her Princess fighting with the pain to come so that she couldn't even manage a basic thank you.

The Queen-to-be continued. 'I've done my best. I'm going to make sure that the well is off-limits once the Grange is open to all-comers. I'll say that it's a security risk to have the villagers trampling near the Homewood Oak and the sacred yew. You'll have all sorts of options to escape then.'

This time Alicia managed to stammer, 'My lady is wise and kind.'

'I do my best. There's more. You know why I got you that mundane identity?'

'Umm. So that I could do the online ordering?'

'We're going to the wedding in a week. You'll barely have time to get your account verified. No. I wanted you to be able to pass through the mortal world safely and quickly. If you escape, that is. Here we are.'

They were at the foot of the path to the LZ, and Faith took her hand out of Alicia's. 'Get your phone out.'

She did so, and Faith AirDropped a series of notes and contacts. None of them meant anything to Alicia.

'I don't want you to waste your life in the mortal world,' said Faith.

Alicia bowed her head. 'There is much pleasure and infinite wonder to be found there.'

Faith put her hands on Alicia's shoulders and stroked her hair. 'I love this new look, and it pains me to think that you have learned more from my head groom and from the Dragonslayer's sister than you have from me.'

'I am lucky to have come so close to you so soon after hatching.'

'And I have had more from you than I deserved. There will be one final service that only you can perform. On the day before the wedding.'

'Whatever my lady needs is hers to take.'

Faith lifted Alicia's chin. 'Listen. Thistle told me about Damini, and about Blowhard Birkdale's threats. That changes everything.'

'How so, my lady?'

Faith shook her head. 'I can't say, but it does. Mina and Tammy have given me all the details about Pramiti's little visit here last summer. There is one place you are guaranteed sanctuary. Pramiti wanted vengeance on the Duke of Ashford, and her daughter will want that, too. I have given you the contact details for the Duke and some of his nobles. Get to them, and they will take you in. And if they ever tire of you, then you are welcome back here.'

'My lady! I—'

'Hush. The south of England is different. You may love it. Who knows what might happen. Use the next two weeks to plan your escape, and when the time comes, you will go with my love.'

They found Thistle propped against a tree. She had a few minor wounds which had stopped bleeding, but she was holding closed a nasty gash on her thigh.

'You got off lightly,' said Faith.

'Bloody cubs,' said Thistle. 'The adults held back, but the weans couldna help themselves. I was sparring, my lady. Knocked a couple across the snouts, then Lowri called them off.'

Faith peered closely. 'That's not a bite on your leg.'

Thistle shifted uncomfortably. 'Aye. Well. I tripped and hit a sharp rock.

That's how they caught me.'

'Let me bind it,' said Alicia, stooping to check the rest of her Sister's wounds. She pointed to one on her abdomen. 'This one needs a compress because it will open up when you move.'

As Alicia tore a sheet and prepared to bandage the leg, Thistle made Silence and said, 'You were going to beat the truth out of me before. Well done, hen. You're learning.'

Alicia smiled to show she understood Thistle's words, but inside she was completely unsure what she had learned that day. Except for how to use the accelerator, brake and clutch. That was fixed forever. The rest though…

It didn't take long for them to get back to the yard and the fireplace. Alicia eased Thistle down and saw that Erin had lined up three full glasses on the table log. The Enscriber stood up and offered two of the glasses, one to Faith and one to Alicia who accepted hers gratefully.

Erin took the third and held it towards Thistle but out of reach. 'You are so lucky I was late getting here. If I'd been around when you rolled up from Sprint Stables, it would have been you on the griddle, not the spring lamb.'

Alicia nearly choked on her Prosecco. *This was outrageous!* Mortals do *not* threaten the People and live. Yet … in that moment, something about their lord clicked into place. Alicia had often wondered how Conrad Bloody Clarke had managed to have *two* Queens bend the knee to him, and part of her wanted to say that it was the work of the Gallows God, because the alternative – that the Red Queen and her Queen-to-be had been outwitted – was too terrible to contemplate. Only they hadn't been, had they?

Reviewing all of their lord's intercourse with the People, it suddenly struck Alicia that he had never once threatened. He either struck with his blade of n'Haeval or he offered them a choice of deals. She blinked and wondered if Erin Slater had learned the same lesson.

Thistle glanced at Faith, having absorbed Erin's words. Something in the Princess's gaze held her back from responding, and the much-changed Knight stilled herself. Waiting.

'Sophie Guest is a *child*,' said Erin. 'A kid, just learning about herself and the world, and you pull that stunt, Thistle. In mortal eyes, it makes you a bully, not a trickster, and that is not a good look.'

'She's got a point,' said Faith. 'We do not throw our weight around.'

'Yes, my lady. What will be my punishment?'

'I have punished you for upsetting my head groom. That is finished. The rest is up to Erin.'

Erin must have learned *something* because her next words were cunning itself. She was still holding the glass of fizz, and stretched it an inch closer to the prone Thistle. 'If you wish to close this, you will apologise to Sophie and tell her that you are barred from approaching Robbie's bed. And you'll do it tomorrow. I'll take you there myself and watch.'

Thistle knew when she was beaten. In all senses of the word. She groaned, levered herself up and accepted the glass. 'So mote it be.' She drank a sip, as did Erin, then Thistle looked beseechingly at her Princess. 'Will someone bring me back, or will I have to walk like Alicia did from Coniston?'

'Finish healing your leg in the pool, then take one of the stable bicycles. You'll be back in time to cook supper.'

A flash of the old Thistle flickered across her eyes. 'A midnight feast, you mean. I cannae see Erin getting out of bed before noon.'

'Guilty,' said Erin. 'Especially if we stay up until the hunt is finished.'

It was actually Sunday morning before Thistle returned. Erin drank so much on the Friday night that Tammy wouldn't let her drive Thistle to Sprint Stables until the Saturday afternoon, then Thistle left Sprint Stables the next day as the fingers of dawn stroked the summit of Force Ghyll.

Alicia was still in bed when her Sister crawled in next to her. 'Hush,' said Thistle. They embraced for a moment, then Thistle whispered, 'Can I have a rest?'

'Of course. I'll get up and start work. Was Erin satisfied?'

'Aye. And Sophie. You know why Erin insisted on going? So that she could stop me playing the sympathy card. Never mind. I'll get ma own back on Erin at the wedding. After you've been released, of course. And I'll fight fair wi' Sophie, too. Robbie will be mine one day.'

Alicia kissed Thistle and slipped out of bed. They had less than a week before they left for the wedding, and there was a *lot* to do.

Worrying about what happens when you are gone has never been part of the People's make-up. When they seek to see the future, that is never a question they ask. Alicia grabbed her clothes and headed for the kitchen to make a special vat of porridge with rat. Thistle would love that.

Part Seven — Beltane

Chapter Forty-Five

Where was I? Oh yes. The hen party. Moving swiftly on…

I didn't have much to do with the Manor while I was growing up. Nothing sinister. Just a question of timing. Stephen is about fifteen years older than me so there was no crossover, and they never had things like garden parties, so I had no reason to go there. Didn't even need to scrump apples. Not when we had our own.

Oh, and don't get me wrong – they did plenty for the village. More than Dad did, tbh. Doesn't excuse what happened, though.

Conrad really is a lucky great lump, you know. I mean, who arranges a whole load of outdoor events *in England* and then gets unremittingly good weather? If anything ever happens to Mina and he gets remarried, he could pay for the whole thing by holding it at the Glastonbury Festival. I mean, they'd pay *millions* to have guaranteed sunshine. And he could go and see the Sisters for an extra blessing. Or is it the Daughters? Whatever.

I saw him briefly on the Wednesday (or T-Minus Five as he was calling it on WhatsApp), and he came straight out and asked me if I were going to the Manor for dinner, and if so, what the fuck was going on?

'Ethan has some business he wants to discuss with Stephen.'

'Really? What on earth could they have in common?'

'I guess we'll find out tonight. Or you could ask Eseld…'

'Already have. She told me not to push it, and I respect her, so I thought I'd push you instead.'

'You have totally summed up my entire life in one sentence. See you tomorrow.'

I'd already been extensively grilled about tonight by Ez, before I left London. I'd made a promise to Jules that I'd leave all the crap out, so I told Eseld that they should all relax and that the dress code was firmly in the midi-dress-and-trainers category. I got a few supplementary questions from Cador, and one of them was genuine. The others were just him trying to line up getting me in bed at some point over the wedding. I'm used to that.

We walked up from the Inkwell in a good impression of a royal walkabout, with Princess Morwenna in the middle and the rest of us acting like ladies in waiting and security guards. Kenver is going to have to let his sister live her own life soon or she'll get fed up and leave him. I must talk to Ez about that.

They met us at the front door and I made the introductions, then stood back to let Ethan take over. Naturally we waited several heartbeats before he cottoned on and spoke up. Even though he's the Staff King of Kernow, he always assumes that someone else will take the lead in social situations. The hardest part is training yourself not to go first.

'Beautiful house, Stephen. Are they your arms over the door?'

Stephen laughed. 'No. That's the old squires of Clerkswell. My dad wanted to put ours up, until I pointed out that we don't have a coat of arms and that we're only looking after this house for future generations. He came round eventually.'

'Yeah, when he found out how much it cost to get your own,' added Juliet. 'Down, Floss!'

'What a gorgeous dog,' said Ez, fussing over the admittedly very cute golden Labrador.

'Come in, please, there's champagne getting warm in here. And freshly squeezed juice for Morwenna.'

Clerkswell Manor has several distinguishing features. To start with, it's *really* old in the middle. We think maybe fifteenth century or early sixteenth, with most of the building only a hundred years newer. It looks way more impressive on the outside than the Grange does, and if you like linenfold panelling, then it's even better inside.

There is one problem though. Until you get to the Edwardian garden room at the back, there isn't a single door that Conrad could walk through without banging his head. Good job he hadn't been invited. Or Chris.

'Shh!' said Ez when I suggested this. 'The thought of Chris seeing my family in full muster is something I can't cope with yet.'

We'd drifted to the back of the group, and I added, 'Will you *ever* be able to cope with that?'

'Ooh! Is that glass for me? Thanks.'

And so it went. Everyone played their part, even me. With help from Lena, I forced Ethan into a corner so that Stephen could make his pitch, and Cador made sure that Ethan was listening. When Stephen rattled off the names of several Cornish stonemasons and asked if he'd thought about granite sourced from Kellysporth Coombe, Ethan actually looked impressed.

And Juliet's beef Wellington was beautiful, and I'm not just saying that because I was suffering from beef withdrawal (although I was).

Did I notice that anything was wrong? Well, Stephen was messaging someone for a start. And he even showed some of the texts to Juliet, so it can't have been his mistress. If he has one. I also heard the name Chloë

Greenwood for the first time.

'Who's she?'

'My assistant,' said Juliet. 'It was her who recommended that Stephen bid for the marina project.'

Did my antennae twitch? Did they ever. 'Is she Cornish?'

'Oh, no. She says that a friend of her girlfriend knows them. Not sure of the details.'

A friend of a friend. That said *Mage* to me. 'Is she coming?'

'No. It's a shame, but she's got a family do on tonight, and of course we're off to Tenerife tomorrow.'

I didn't have probable cause to ask for the girlfriend's name, so all I could do was ask Eseld later, and then Vicky and Saffron, if they knew a Chloë Greenwood. Naturally they came up blank.

We didn't outstay our welcome. After all, the Mowbrays were moving in tomorrow morning, and the Bloxhams needed time to clear up and finish packing.

'And where are you going to go, eh?' Ez asked Floss.

Being a dog, Floss had to let Jules answer for her.

'She's going to my mother's, or you're welcome to look after her if you want. Mum collected the kids earlier, and if you look after Floss, it'll save her another trip back and the hassle. I think she's coming into season, and I'm not sure Mum's prepared for that. There's loads of food in the cupboard.'

'Would you like to stay with me, Floss?'

You can usually predict how much Ez is going to drink: it's in inverse proportion to her level of responsibility. That's one of the reasons she's my friend – I can take her to lots of unimportant events and we can get smashed. Win-win.

Naturally she'd had plenty to drink tonight, and that was why she was trying to hold a conversation with a dog. 'She's not Scout,' I told her. 'So don't expect her to answer.'

'I speak Labrador tail,' said Ez. 'And this tail is telling me she wants to stay *here*. Don't you, Flossy?'

'I think Morwenna's tired,' said Kenver. 'Shall we?'

'I shall see you tomorrow, gorgeous girl,' said Ez to Floss

'And I look forward to video-conferencing with the human inhabitants,' said Cador. 'I'll get our estate manager to look over the documents. He knows they'll be in his inbox in the morning.'

'This is a gorgeous house,' said Lena. 'You have given me much to think about, Juliet.'

At least Eseld waited until we were out of earshot before she said, 'Who's for a nightcap? Nah, too early for that. Let's see whether the Inkwell's wine cellar matches their beer cellar. You coming, Raitch?'

I wasn't going to say no to that, was I?

They met in Chloë's rented house the next morning. Or the house which Juliet had rented to Chloë, if you prefer to look at it that way.

'We can't stay long,' said Stephen. 'The taxi's coming at eleven to take us to the *airport*.'

'Where are you *actually* staying?' asked Chloë.

'Mallory Court in Leamington Spa,' said Stephen. 'Close enough for access but way out of the gossip circle. And their food is excellent. Not that I'm hungry after last night. You did brilliantly, Jules.'

Juliet gave a brief smile but said nothing.

'I'll come over when they video-call you,' said Chloë. She was desperate that the Bloxhams didn't just write their loss down to experience.

Stephen thought for a moment. 'Maybe. Now budge up.'

Stephen sat on the sofa, way too near for Chloë's comfort. She would have got up and moved, but he opened his laptop and moved even closer. His thigh was now touching hers. Ugh.

'Right,' he began. 'That poor kid only said around three things last night, and one of them was that she wished Harry could see his babies grow up.'

'You mean Morwenna?'

'I do. And Lena said something about Uncle Matt, and Cador made a crack about Matt Eldridge being even more tassety than Ethan.'

'*Taciturn*,' said Juliet. 'Strong and silent. Unlike you, Stephen.'

'Whatever. So I followed up on her story. Harry Eldridge was murdered up in the Lake District, apparently. And after I opened the second bottle of port, Eseld says that their father was murdered, too, but that's not what it says on the *Western Morning News* website. According to them, he died suddenly. Mind you, being murdered counts as fairly sudden. I'm going to ask you again, Chloë: *who are these people?* And have you asked me to bid for a contract with some bunch of drug barons?'

'Don't be silly, I—'

Stephen's hand slammed the lid on the laptop down, bending the casing alarmingly. 'I will *not* have my family at risk. Do you know how often I've kicked a project to the kerb because I could smell the money being laundered?'

'Stephen!' said Jules pleadingly. 'Let's not look for conspiracies.'

'Well?' he asked Chloë.

'I don't know!' she protested. 'I've never heard of Harry Eldridge, and the Mowbrays are *not* drug lords. I swear.'

She licked her lips. It was true about Harry, but she was going to have to lie about Arthur Mowbray because she knew fine well that he *had* been murdered. 'I think Eseld blames their doctor. Undiagnosed heart condition. And Morwenna was pretty much the black sheep of the family.'

'Red sheep, more like.' He got up. 'We'll see, shall we?'

Chloë remembered something. 'You have sorted an IP address for Tenerife, haven't you?'

'No. Why? We're staying in the new block, so one hotel room looks pretty much like another, and we've packed a studio portrait of the family to put up on the wall behind us.'

'I wouldn't put it past them to have people tracing you. That's something I can double check for you if I come over tonight. I really do know how to do that.'

Stephen got her meaning and nodded. 'I'll message you when they've sent me a time. Takes about forty minutes from here.'

'Do you think you'll hear from them today?'

'Why?' said Stephen. 'Another "family event"?'

Juliet gave him a nudge. 'Come on. That taxi will be here.'

<h1 style="text-align:center">Chapter Forty-Six</h1>

It took the Mowbrays ten seconds to rule out the Bloxhams, and they did it over breakfast on Thursday, to which I'd been invited. The conversation went like this:

Cador: Are you seriously going to invite them to tender?

Ethan: When Kenver owns fifty per cent of a development company his father set up? It would be cruel to give them hope. We'll do it tonight.

Only *tonight* was a problem. For some reason the Bloxhams couldn't get their video link sorted, so it had been re-arranged for Friday. 'Do you want me there?' I asked hopefully.

'Thanks, but we don't need you.'

'Can't you hear the pleading in her voice?' said Eseld. 'It's Friday night dinner at the Grange, and she knows we've got a chef coming in.'

'Yeah, and it would be great to catch up with Fiadh.'

Ethan grunted; Lena rolled her eyes. 'It would be good to have you here. I keep forgetting that you were in Ireland with Conrad and Eseld. I'm surprised you remember it fondly.'

'The part where a Fae Queen dubbed my brother "Lord of Death" is not something I dwell on. But Fiadh's good craic.'

'What's your ulterior motive?' said Eseld. You can always rely on her as a friend. 'Apart from the food, of course. Would it involve Fiadh's travelling companion, by any chance?'

I gave a start. How did she…? Oh. Play it cool, Rachael. 'Busted. I want to see if Portarra has any news from the Noble Queen. I didn't leave my card with her for no reason.'

Ethan and Cador shook their heads, almost perfectly in sync; Ethan left Cador to answer. 'Portarra won't be there, but you're more than welcome, Rachael.'

'Thank you.'

And that's how I came to be at Clerkswell Manor again, for what I'm calling 'The Gloucester Getaway of the Red-headed League'. I mean, there were three of them! Four if you count the dog: believe me, Floss has distinct ginger tendencies.

It didn't take long for me to realise why I'd been invited: I didn't care one iota about their problem. Conrad is both more and less of a friend to them than I am, but he'd have had an angle on it. He'd be thinking two steps ahead and wondering if there'd be anyone to kill round the corner. Or to save. He's flexible when it comes to violence.

The heart of their issue goes back … oooh. Ages. Before I was born, anyway, so therefore ancient history. Fairytale territory.

Once upon a time there was a poor family who lived in Galway called the Ahearns. They were blessed with magick but often cursed by their choice of friends. Some might say that they were also cursed with additional copies of the MC1R gene, and some might say that they were blessed with it. As I said, this is a fairytale.

In those days, two mighty Queens of the Fae were battling it out for control of the west coast of Ireland, and the Fair Queen was slowly but surely squeezing the life out of the Noble Queen and her human allies. And then one day the Fair Queen pounced, besieging and conquering a castle and then holding a mass beheading on the dock.

That's the part where it stops being a fairytale.

The Ahearn family were split in two. Some stuck with the Fair Queen, others with the Noble. Over the years, the stranglehold tightened. Poor Fiadh was trapped in a pub for fifteen years, and when she was first confined to the Market Tavern, *there was no internet shopping.* How did she stay sane?

The branch who stuck with the Fair Queen broke up and then disappeared. Aisling Ahearn moved to Cornwall and married Arthur Mowbray, becoming mother to Morwenna and Kenver, and then getting herself killed by a magickal octopus. Aisling's mother, Clíodhna, and Aisling's sister, Éimear, were last seen in Scotland, and that brings us to dessert.

The brought-in chef was good, and he possessed the most important quality of all: not being me. Whenever someone else cooks, I am always in awe. He had a lad from Cheltenham with him (who peered down Lena's dress when he served her), and when the lad had deposited the lemon possets, the chef appeared for a round of applause and then they got in their van, taking the pots and pans with them. The ones they'd brought, that is. As far as I know, they didn't steal anything.

As soon as Lena had returned from waving them off, the Mowbray-Ahearns got down to what they thought was the real argument. My brother didn't go to Ireland to kill the Fair Queen but he did set in motion the train of events which led to her death, and following the complete shift in the balance of power over there, the question was this: should the Ahearns go looking for Clíodhna and Éimear?

'We absolutely have to,' said Cathal.

'I agree,' said Oighrig. 'We'll never have a clearer path than we do now.'

Fiadh agreed. 'I'm in favour, because there's one of us out there doing who knows what, and I'd like to find out. What do you reckon, Kenver?'

And now we came to what *I* thought was the real problem. Kenver may not have the red hair, but he's a potent mixture of Mowbray and Ahearn magick. Some say the sky's the limit for his potential. And he idolises the mother he never knew, whose last act before being eaten was, allegedly, to throw her children out of the octopus tank and save their lives.

It was touch and go for Morwenna, and the eight-armed beasties robbed her of whatever future in magick she might have had. Now back where she started, pregnant and almost mute, Morwenna shook her head and placed her hands protectively over her bump. No one was going to argue with that.

Kenver, though, was fair game, and the Ahearns seemed to have appointed Fiadh as their hunter-in-chief. She'd had lots of practice at wheedling things out of people.

'Kenver, do you not think there's unanswered questions about your ma?' she began. 'I'd want to know if I were in your shoes.'

'Yes, I'd love to know,' he said. 'Someone cleared up after her, and Dad always said it was Clíodhna.'

'Then let's find out! Road trip, eh? And I'm not just saying that because I want to ride around in the Smurf.'

'You'd be doing the whole family a great favour,' said Oighrig. 'If you do go, then I'll be right beside you, Salomon's House or no Salomon's House. After all, Fiadh needs someone to keep her out of trouble.'

The Mowbrays who *aren't* related to the Ahearns were keeping quiet: Ethan, Cador and Eseld didn't exactly fold their arms and stare, but it was awfully quiet at their end of the table. Even Lena was keeping her lips zipped, and she can normally be relied on to make the humanitarian case for anything.

Kenver nodded sympathetically, and then he said, 'Éimear and her mother, if she's alive, are welcome at Pellacombe.'

There was a pause.

'Is that it?' said Fiadh. 'Are you not in the slightest bit curious? Would you not like to dig a bit deeper?'

Kenver gave a rather inadequate shrug. 'I've got a lot on. I won three contracts for Ley line repair last week.'

I'm afraid that it got a bit personal after that, and when I thought that Fiadh might be about to call Kenver a *wee boy*, I stepped in. 'Are you in a rush to go back, Fi? How long is Portarra staying in England? And *where* is she staying?'

'She's staying at some swanky hotel in Cheltenham,' said Oighrig. 'As you'd expect.'

'She was a bit vague about her plans,' said Fiadh. 'I know they don't include me, though.'

Damn. Damn and shit. I *really* needed to see her.

'How about London, Fi?' I said. 'If I ask Ez nicely, I'm sure she'll give you a room at Mowbray House, and I'll show you some of the mundane sights.'

'What? Like the Tower of London?' said Fiadh, slightly bemused.

'If you like. There's also Club Justine, for starters…'

'Now you're talking.' Fiadh looked at Ez. 'There's no need to—'

'Yes, there is,' I said. 'Give us a hand making the coffee, Fi, and we'll let her think about it.'

'No need,' said Ez. 'If you actually *do* make the coffee, Raitch, I'll give everyone a room who wants one.'

After no one else got up to help me, Fiadh looked slightly guilty and followed me into the kitchen. I just came straight out with it: 'Look, Fi, I'm on Schul duty tomorrow, so I could meet her then, but I haven't got her number.'

'What the feck is *Schul?*'

Well, why should she know? 'Synagogue. I'm taking the Peculier Constable to the synagogue for Shabbos.'

'Really? Whatever for?'

'Well, she's not going to drive herself, is she? Long story. Biblically long. Would you mind sharing Portarra's number?'

'Course. I've left me phone in there, though. Remind me later. Will you be away all day?'

'No. Hannah's only going to the early service, and we have to be back for the cricket match.'

'Fecking cricket! I couldn't believe it when Ethan said we have to go and watch a *cricket* match. And then he said there was a "three line whip" on it, which got me excited until Cador explained what it was. Mixing politics and cricket in the same sentence ought to be against the law.'

'Watch yourself, Fi. Mrs Clarke's Folly has a bigger congregation than St Michael's.'

While we waited for the kettle to boil, I lined up the cafetieres and Fiadh started opening cupboards. 'Cups or mugs?'

'Cups, but not the best ones. In there, I think.'

'Grand. Was that really why you brought me in here, or were you trying to stop me calling Kenver a wee little nodding dog who does what the big boys tell him?'

'I'm a woman, Fi. I can multi-task. Where are those chocolates you brought?'

'I'm not sure they deserve them.'

'Give him a year. For goodness sake, *visit* him. In Kernow. I'll swap you Jane Kershaw's number for Portarra's and you can plan your visit for when he's there on his own.'

'Now that's a plan,' she replied, cheering up. 'You're almost as devious as your brother, so you are— Ow! What did I say?'

'You'll learn. Chocolates. Now.'

'Fucking typical,' said Stephen, after he'd double-checked that the connection had ended. 'These families think they're sharks when they're just carp in a fishpond.'

Chloë blinked at that metaphor and nearly lost her place in the script. She caught up before Juliet could interrupt.

'And we all know why it happened, don't we? Rachael Bloody Clarke. You could see her in the background, and to think they did it from your own house.' She shook her head. 'What did I tell you?'

'I don't think it had anything to do with Rachael,' said Juliet.

'How else did they find out about the Hereford Cathedral business?' said Stephen peevishly. It had not been his finest hour.

'Google?' said Juliet.

Chloë did just that: Googled *Bloxham Properties* and showed them the results. There was no mention of the Cathedral Close redevelopment on the first or second pages.

'See?' said Stephen.

'The Clarkes owe you big time now,' said Chloë.

'Rachael said she'd be fair, and we've no reason to believe she hasn't been,' said Juliet.

Chloë countered with, 'Other than Hereford. And that was enough.' She looked at Stephen and raised her eyebrows. 'Well? Are you up for a bit of payback or not?'

'What's going on?' said Juliet.

Her husband looked a little guilty, but mostly defiant. 'Chloë has been spinning you a bit of a yarn, Jules. Turns out she has about as much time for the Clarkes as I do.'

Juliet flinched away from Chloë. 'What do you mean?'

Chloë gritted her teeth. If Stephen dropped her right in it, Juliet would veto the whole project, and it looked like Stephen had read the same runes. 'Chloë applied for the University of Gloucester deliberately,' he began. So far, so good. 'She wanted to find out if the legend of her family was true: that the Clarkes still lived in Elvenham and the old well was still there. When she found out that her landlord's husband had a bit of history with them, we got talking.'

'You and Chloë?'

'Yes. Turns out that the old squires of Clerkswell weren't the first victims.'

Juliet's head flicked back and forth between Chloë and her husband. Was that a scintilla of doubt? Did she suspect something else had been going on between them, or was she just confused? She opted for a neutral question. 'What do you mean?'

'Stephen and I both have something at the Grange which we're interested in,' said Chloë. 'I said that if the Clarkes stitched you up again over the Mowbray deal, I'd help you get it back in return for your help with our problem.'

Juliet sighed. 'Is that why you insisted in staying here instead of going to Tenerife, Stephen?'

'Yes. We'll never get a better time to wander into the Grange than when *everyone* will be at the wedding.'

'There is an alternative. We could actually go to the wedding and forget all about this. Not only is it dangerous, what on earth are you going to do if we find this bloody safe? Break it open with your head?'

'That's where I come in,' said Chloë smoothly. 'Have you done what I asked, Stephen?'

'It's in the wardrobe.'

Chloë quickly stepped over to the wardrobe and flung open the doors. There on the right was the hotel safe, the standard four-digit PIN model. She completely ignored it, and with an *oof*, she picked up the portable Victorian strongbox which Stephen had sourced from an antique shop. She brought it over to the table and said to Juliet, 'The Grange safe is old, right? You try to open this while I get my universal key.'

Juliet hesitated. Chloë knew she was aware that if she started to play along, she might not be able to stop.

'Go on,' said Stephen. 'If this doesn't work, then I'm out, too. Chloë's promised us something truly magical.'

It had taken days of practice before Chloë had been able to trigger the unfolding Work in the Artefact, and it had cost their Principal a *lot* of money. Universal keys which can be operated by the Ungifted are hard to find, and a box of thirty would have bought the house Chloë was living in at Allington. It was a good job she'd only burned through twenty before she got the hang of it.

Showing more confidence than she felt, Chloë slid in the metal probe and made the mental picture which would unfold the Work. *Click*. Done. 'There you go.'

'Bloody hell,' said Stephen, and it was his reaction which convinced Juliet. Stephen might have a good poker face when it came to his own bluffs, but when it was someone else's, he always gave the game away. 'Where did you learn to do that?'

It hadn't been the question Chloë was expecting, and she was so nervous that she made another slip with her answer. 'At the Akademia Club.'

'A club that teaches breaking and entering?'

'A club that teaches women how to do anything that men can do and to do it better.'

Juliet sighed and surrendered. 'What are you after, Chloë?'

'Buried treasure.'

'I'm struggling to see you with a spade, or with time to dig anything up during the wedding.'

'Which is why I'll be with Stephen. Beth and Anita from the Akademia club will be climbing down the well and crawling along the tunnel.'

It was Stephen's turn to have doubts. 'In my book, the one going for the bigger prize would be the one most deserving of it, and you'll be with me? Another white lie, Chloë? This is your girlfriend's game, not yours, isn't it?'

She gave in straight away. 'Yeah, but we're engaged, so strictly speaking it's *our* game. She got a full-time job after uni, so I said I'd see what I could find.'

'And this *Anita* woman?'

'Beth's an apprentice at the Akademia, so Anita is more like her supervisor. I'm only an associate member.'

'You won't just be with Stephen,' said Juliet. 'You'll be with me, too. If nothing else, I can be the lookout. Let's hear the details.'

Chloë rubbed her hands on her jeans. 'We thought it would go like this…'

'You look amazing,' Alicia told Maria. 'Totally. The other team won't know where to look.'

The women of Elvenham Grange were all gathered in the driveway, waiting for the signal to process up Elven Lane, past the House of the Crucified God and onto Mrs Clarke's Folly for Saturday's cricket match. Maria would be leading the parade in the guise of a cheerleader. They'd even been practising a chant: 'Go Wizards, go Wizards, go Wizards go!' Despite Maria's protestations, the cheerleader outfit was only a part-Construction: the Pack had refused to fork out for yet another costume for the dressing-up box.

Alicia stepped away and joined Thistle and Faith at the back of the party.

'If Rachael Bloody Clarke doesn't show up soon, we're going anyway,' muttered Faith. 'If we're going to do this, we need maximum impact.'

'Car!' said Alicia. 'A very loud car.'

Alicia winced as Rachael drove Lucy's brand new Mini through the gates of the Grange, missing the stone pillar by a Wolf's whisker. Sitting in the passenger seat and smiling serenely was the Anointed Guardian, fresh from her devotions at her temple.

Faith sighed with relief. 'Right. Let's get this circus on the road. Leesha? Will you get Myfanwy and Anna? And take care while we're gone, okay?'

Alicia skipped into the house and summoned the pregnant mortals from their seats: they were being driven to the match, and Alicia was being left alone to have a *good* look around the Grange ahead of Monday, when her future would come to an end, just like the tea leaves had predicted it would.

She stood on the steps and waved everyone off, then pulled the doors closed behind her and set off round the side of the house. That way, she could avoid the other job she'd been left to sort out.

Elvenham Grange was now transformed beyond belief compared to her first visit, and not just because of the marquee pitched outside the back of the house and the event matting laid in the meadow beyond the stables. The People (and the Wolves) had been here for a week now, and every day they had cooked, cleaned, moved furniture, put up decorations and made up more and more extra beds as the wedding party started to gather. The men had moved out on Thursday (thank goodness), and now the People (and the Wolves) were all sharing the stable where Alicia had practised for Shear Magic (except for Robbie, who was in a tent beyond the fence).

A stable was not fitting for a Queen-to-be. Not at all. However, if Faith minded this, she had said nothing beyond making some remark about a stable being fit for the Crucified God. That one had gone right over Alicia's head.

She zig-zagged through the grounds, checking that Scout was still in his luxury kennel (he was), and that the temporary Wards at the fence were in place (they were), and then she walked slowly through the gardens towards the well. When she got there, she realised that she was holding her breath. *What power! What history! What stories!*

As well as a bi-planar oak tree, there was a cutting of the Morrigan's tears growing here (or trying to), and that was before you got to the well itself. Alicia strained all her senses, and saw the sharp vertical rise from the well to the realm above where the sídhe was located. Beyond that, she could only sense darkness. It was time to find out whether there was an escape route for her on the higher plane.

Five turns later, she was sweating and frustrated. *It shouldn't be this hard.* There was something – or some*one* – blocking her, and they must have had a lot of practice, because no matter how hard she twisted and turned, there was no way up. If only she'd practised more!

She was trying to move through the Void using her native magick, just as she'd done every day when she was a Sprite – up to the Gallops or down to the sídhe without even thinking after the first time. Even the transition at the new Staveley Sídhe hadn't been that much of a challenge, and that was still under construction. She sighed, lifted her top and brought up long buried Ink.

And then felt very uncomfortable, because there was a tiny worm crawling around the spiral which aligned her with the different levels. *It must have come from the Nymph*, she thought. *So what do I do with it?*

She anchored the spiral with her left fingers and caught the worm-like Ink with her right hand. Should she attach it or make a fork in the spiral? If she attached it, the magick would become part of her, but a fork might unravel the Ink like a split thread of wool. She closed her eyes, felt the Ink on her skin, and twisted the worm to the spiral. And then ran to the bushes to bring up her breakfast.

The *thing* crawling over her skin reminded her of the day she had left the Sprint Sídhe, the first day she'd worn a bra. It just felt *wrong* (though, yes, she'd discovered that Lady Morag hadn't given her the correct cup size). Alicia twisted and twined her limbs, trying to settle the sensation, and then she broke into the wedding dance, just to move and bring some control back to her arms and legs.

Five minutes later, she was out of breath and feeling a little better. A little more her again. And she had been step-perfect, too, something which could *not* be said of all the girls who were going to take part. There had been rehearsals over the last few days; both Saffron and Vicky would be in trouble if they didn't shape up.

She controlled her breathing, and without consciously summoning the Ink, she launched herself *up* and into the realm of the Elvenham Sídhe. *Oh my!*

The well was beautifully co-located here, with only the mundane water pump missing, and the oak sapling was almost a young tree. No sign of the Morrigan's tears, though. She looked around at the healthy woods, and then she noticed that the door to the sídhe was both intact and *locked*. Who had done this? Her lady had not been here since they arrived, so had Princess Birkdale sent spies ahead of her? Had traps been laid?

Alicia looked around and considered the prospect. This was an isolated realm, with no way to elsewhere unless you could walk the Void, and as Alicia would never have that power, that left the sídhe. She sidled closer to the door and examined the fastenings. Apart from a whiff of sulphur, she got nothing. The door was fastened from the inside. What alarmed her, though, was the sense that it was *occupied*. By something or someone.

She felt around the wooden beams that made up the door, then jerked her hands away. There was *copper* in there! Some human had re-worked the Quicksilver of the door into a simple fastening and then put their own lock on it. And they'd locked it from the inside.

Some of the People can work copper magick. At a price. Alicia didn't know where to start, so it looked like there was no easy exit this way. With a sigh, she returned to the mortal realm and went to do the washing up.

Mina had been as good as her word. As soon as the bridal party had returned from Mrs Clarke's Folly, the People had been stood down from their duties, for tonight was Beltane Eve and the People were to be honoured on this night, not sent to the kitchens to wait on mortals.

'Was it good sport?' Alicia asked when they went upstairs to change. 'Everyone seems full of good spirits.'

'It was, actually,' said Faith. 'Lots to eat, lots to drink, and lots of gossip. And our lord was one of the heroes of the game.' She grinned. 'Thankfully our home is too hilly to accommodate a cricket pitch. What are you wearing tonight? And don't wear white, Leesha. Don't forget there's a bonfire afterwards.'

'No, my lady. I shall wear red. It will be an honour to share my first Beltane feast with you.'

It had taken days before the feast to sort out the order of precedence for the parade, and whether *all* the Clarkes should go first or just the host and hostess. In the end, the People were put just behind the Dragonslayer's *other* sister, Sofia, and Lord Alfred's one-time mistress, Mercedes – not that they were allowed to call Mercedes that. Oh no. She was *Sofía's mother, and don't you forget it.*

At the well, Myfanwy led a dignified tribute to Mother Nature, to the Goddess, to the seasons, and to the continuing favour of the People. Alicia felt warm and loved and close to all the life around her, mortal or otherwise. She even smiled at the Diggers. Briefly. And then it was time for their host and hostess to honour the Morrigan. Alicia knelt on the ground in fear as Conrad filled a vessel and drank to the dread goddess. In a whoosh of air, Faith was gone from Alicia's side.

'Stone me, that was quick,' said Lloyd.

'Where's Myvvy?' said her man, Ben.

'And Faith,' said Robbie.

'Don't worry,' said Tamsin serenely. The way that she had swept the offerings to the higher realm had been effortless and stylish. No wonder Faith was happy to share her bed with a mortal woman, for now. The Bodysnatcher stepped into the circle. 'Conrad, Mina, Faith and Myfanwy have gone to the old sídhe. It's very pleasant up there, and they're not alone. If you didn't catch the scent of battle, the Morrigan is now with them.'

'Are you sure?' asked Ben.

'No doubt about it,' said Lloyd. 'You can smell her like a far— Ow! Anna! That hurt.'

Tamsin spoke again. 'I suggest we make ourselves comfortable for a while. The time gradient up there isn't huge, but they could be a while.'

Some of the older mortals sat on the well, others talked and Alicia was about to address Robbie when the air to her left shimmered. She whipped her head round, and the Void appeared around the cutting of the Morrigan's tears, and from the Void came Faith's hand. *A tunnel through the Void? How can this be?*

There was more. More dread and more fear, and a darkness hinted at. Faith had not just made a tunnel from the grass around the well; she had tunnelled through somewhere else. Before Alicia could draw breath to cry out, Faith's hand had reached through the soil and plucked the cutting out of the mortal realm and away from her sight.

'Here we go,' said Robbie. He had disappeared when the Morrigan made her presence felt, and now he was back, carrying two cases of San Miguel beer. 'Thought these might help to pass the time.'

When Alicia tried to have a discussion with Thistle about what she'd seen, she might as well have been talking about hair relaxing lotion for all that Thistle cared. Her Sister had been diligent since they arrived, cooking and preparing all manner of amazing dishes, even the strange ones for Friday night, but when not in the kitchen, she only had eyes for Robbie. She might have been forbidden his bed, but there was no stopping her campaign to win him over, and now she had rushed to his side to help hand out the beer.

And so, alone, Alicia waited, and she was the only one really looking when two things happened in quick succession. First, both Faith and Myfanwy stepped down from the sídhe. Second, the giant form of the dread goddess materialised in front of Faith and swept her up into her arms like she was a child and swept her away back to that place of darkness. The one *up there* somewhere. Alicia opened her mouth to exclaim, but Myfanwy had the floor.

'You'll never guess what! Conrad and Mina have just had a greenwood marriage!'

'No!'

'Ooh-er!'

'What's that?'

'And now they're consummating it!' said the Druid with an evil grin.

'Perhaps we should get changed for the bonfire,' said Ben. 'They could be quite a while, and it's getting a bit chilly. I don't think Mina would welcome us hanging around to give them a round of applause either.'

'Shame we can't watch,' said Lloyd. 'We could give them marks out of ten when they're finished.'

'How do you put up with him?' asked the Digger's very pregnant wife plaintively. It was a tone which Faith had used about Alicia on more than one occasion.

'He's just saying what most of the blokes are thinking,' said Eseld. 'You have no idea what it was like on the stag party. When I get back to Salomon's House, I'm gonna ask Heidi Marston to create a gag that only works on Gnomes.'

'Truly, the world would be a better place if you did,' said Saffron. 'Ben's right, we don't need to hang around.'

'I will wait for Faith,' said Alicia.

And so it was that Alicia was on her own when her lady returned, naked and glowing with the brightest Quicksilver leaking out of her pores.

'It is done,' said Faith. 'I have drunk of the *uisce bethu*, and I am a Queen-becoming.' And then she collapsed to the ground.

Alicia used the royal register. 'Robbie! Look to our lady!'

Everyone took turns to place something in the wicker man. 'No plastic!' shouted Myfanwy to Lucy. 'Has to be biodegradable and combustible!'

The People had gone first, placing something they wished to be rid of into the hollow chest of the giant figure. Alicia had been racking her brains for weeks trying to think of something: in forty-eight hours she was going to be released, and she was quite attached to everything in her life. As the mortals might say, she'd only been alive five minutes, so what could she want to get rid of? The inspiration had finally come from the strangest place: Sofía.

With the men (and the Mowbray-Ahearns) staying elsewhere, Sofía was the only smoker at the Grange. This morning, she had greeted Alicia as she headed for the smoking shelter. 'What are you doing with Scout?' she asked.

'I'm trying to get him to hunt rats, but either Myfanwy has got rid of them all or we've been feeding him too much. He's not interested.'

'How you do that?' Sofía paused. 'Better still, *why* you doing that?'

'Comfort food. Porridge with rat is my go-to comfort food.'

'Bleurgh. Why?'

'It's what Lady Agnes made for us in the nest. When we were Sprites.' She cast a wistful glance at the field, where Robbie was finishing tonight's wicker man, having already built a huge bonfire. 'I used to make it for Robbie when he was 2nd.'

Sofía went slightly green. 'You are all grown up now, I think. Maybe it's time to find a new comfort food. Like bacon sandwiches, no?'

And so on that Beltane Eve, Alicia placed a dead rat (from the woods) into the wicker man, and watched it go up in flames. Whether she was enslaved by Damini or escaped to the Duke of Ashford, she was putting nursery food behind her.

Faith only made it for an hour, despite saying it was one of the best mortal parties that she'd ever been to. 'It's the Inkwell Bitter,' she explained. 'And don't you even think of looking after me. That's Cathy's job. You get out there and enjoy yourself.'

Alicia tried. She really tried, but everywhere she looked, mortals were standing in groups with their backs to her. She could sit on one of the thrones, of course, and a team of tapsters was on hand to supply the People with whatever they desired (without knowing why, of course, because many of the crowd knew nothing of magick). Alicia did not desire food or drink, though. She desired company. She was about to disobey an order and check on Faith when Rachael appeared, dragging a slightly older woman who looked slightly bewildered.

'There you are! Alicia, this is my BFF since Oxford, Carole Thewlis, who is also Ben's sister but we'll forgive her for that. Caro, this is Alicia, the truly creative genius from Shear Magic.'

'This is awesome,' said Carole. 'It's like a film set, there's so much going on.' She paused, then added, 'Level with me, Raitch. Do you sometimes think that your brother's gone a bit overboard on the new-agey stuff?'

'Carole, you don't know the half of it. I'm going to blame Myfanwy. But don't forget, without this *new-agey* stuff, there wouldn't be a women-and-children-only party tomorrow, would there, so let's drink to that, and Alicia will tell you why you need a bob and that that eyeshadow doesn't suit you.'

Carole looked afraid for a second, and Rachael laughed. 'They don't call her the Ninja Hairdresser for nothing.'

Later, as the stars bid them welcome to the night, the three friends ended up as part of a larger circle where several big fat joints were circulating. 'It's an offering to the Fae,' said Rachael. 'And as there aren't any *actual* police officers here … oh. Hang on, yeah. Tom Morton's one.'

Carole peered around the group. 'Lucy's boyfriend? The one who's passed out next to the hog roast?'

'No. That's Lloyd, Anna's husband. I think Tom was over there, but I can't focus anymore.'

'That's because it's gone dark,' said Carole with a snort.

'Oh yeah. Hey! Alice … Alicey. Sia.'

'You can call me Alice if you want, Raitchy-Raitch. It's allowed for mortals. I mean the mortally stoned.'

'Alice. Why are you taking your knickers off?'

Alicia stood up and swayed, so she sat down again. 'I want to make tonight a memorabubble one.'

And then Alicia joined Lloyd in the lad of nod, and Rachael performed the office of getting her to bed. 'We have to serve the servants tonight,' she told Carole. 'It is an hobligoblination. Holy obligation. Whatever.'

'Why? I don't mind putting your new friend to bed, but why *was* everyone running round after Robbie and Thistle and Cathy? I mean, I'd run round after Robbie, but why the other two?'

'You know what, Caro? I've completely forgotten.'

Chapter Forty-Eight

'Where's Conrad when you need him?' said Rachael the next morning. 'He may be otherwise useless, but he can do cooked breakfasts like no one else I know. Pass me … no, don't. You'll get grease on your dress.'

'Watch me,' said Alicia. She went to the griddle and put a shield up in front of herself, then used a gentle warm breeze to slide the bacon onto a plate.

'Impressive,' said Sofía.

'The dress?' said Rachael.

'No. The magick she just did. I like the dress also.'

'So do I, but why do you suddenly look like a model from the Boden catalogue, Alice?'

'Because in one hour I must stand at the gate and perform a great service for my lady.'

'Faith or Mina?'

'Oh, Faith.'

'What service?'

'I must, at all costs, stop Marcia Bracewell from meeting Victoria Robson until she has first met Faith.'

Rachael's eyes bulged. 'That is the weirdest thing I've heard on the weirdest weekend of my life. Good luck. Enjoy your breakfast.'

Alicia did enjoy the breakfast, and she also enjoyed the special sunshine of Beltane as she went to help Anika Ben's daughters master the intricacies of the Maypole dance. So much so that afterwards, she had to get to the front of the Grange via the road and put Fire in her legs to arrive at the main gate before the judge's Uber arrived.

'Allow me, my lady,' she said, having skidded to a halt on the gravel.

'Thank you.' The judge frowned. 'Aren't you…?'

'One of the People. Yes. Alicia, handmaiden to Princess Faith. If my lady would greet the dragon?'

'Sorry?'

'House rule. You have to say hello to the carving. I'll take your bags.'

The Senior Justice of the Cloister Court, Mrs Justice Bracewell, stared at the ancient block of limestone and gave it a curt, 'Good morning.'

Alicia also stared, as she had several times over the last week. On their first visit, both she and Faith had assumed that it was an m'Ghenz, the keystone of a dragon's nest. It still *looked* like one. Didn't smell like one, though. Was that another whiff of sulphur, like she'd had at the door to the well sídhe?

Oops! The judge was wandering off.

'My lady. This way, please.'

Alicia hurried to shepherd the judge away from the gardens and through the main doors. Once inside, Alicia once more felt deep love for Rachael Clarke, because her friend was standing at the bottom of the stairs with one finger to her lips and another pointing at the drawing room. Once Alicia had got the message, Rachael pointed upstairs with a grin and a wink. Then she went to stand by the drawing room doors, ready to lay down her life to keep the Seer away.

Well, perhaps not lay down her life. That would be a waste.

'Is there a ladies' room nearby?' said the judge.

'Oh, just upstairs, next to where you're staying. After you, my lady.'

Alicia showed the judge into the bathroom and stood on guard outside. From here, she could hear that no one had emerged from the drawing room, but someone did emerge from along the landing. Faith. And she did not look happy.

'What have you done?' she said in the People's tongue. 'I get myself sorted and then Rachael Bloody Clarke comes and says she's there to help you with your *mission*! We do not sell our secrets cheaply, Leesha. Still less do we give them away for nothing.'

Perhaps it was the universe ticking down the seconds on her life. Perhaps it was the lies. Whatever it was, Alicia didn't simply bow her head and apologise. No. She nodded, then looked at her Princess, her Becoming-Queen. 'You told me no secret, my lady. You merely gave me orders which I did not understand.'

'I … never mind. But mark this: whatever you learn today is *not* for any ears. None at all until I give the word.'

'Yes, my lady.'

'I'll be in the Sunset Room.'

It was the smallest bedroom, originally intended for the Anointed Guardian alone, but now shared with the Keeper for reasons of 'logistics' which escaped Alicia completely. The new guest emerged from the bathroom, and Alicia ushered her down the hall.

'I hear it's a bit crowded at the moment,' said the judge. 'I told Victoria that I'd be happy to stay at the pub, but she insisted. Something to do with tattoos.'

'In here, my lady.'

Alicia opened the door, and the judge walked in; Alicia followed and closed the door, making Silence around the room and securing the lock. When Faith separated herself from the shadows, the judge flinched and raised her hand to her chest but she did not cry out.

'What is this?' she demanded.

Princess Faith bowed deeply. 'Forgive me. I will explain.'

'This had better be good. Who are you, anyway? Oh, I know. You're that new Queen from the Particular.'

'I am.'

'If you're going to threaten me, you're wasting your time. If you're after free legal advice, you can forget that too.'

Faith was almost as weak as she had been after the trip to Rydal Water, and it clearly cost her a lot to kneel before the judge. 'I have something to tell you. Something to tell you, *Mélisande*.'

The judge gasped. 'How dare you use my name!'

'I am Princess Faith, but I was once Princess Mielle.'

The effect on the judge was electric. 'You! You're my mother!' It was instinctive and raw – a first reaction that went to the heart of where the judge had come from. The words which followed, once she'd seen the Princess nod her confirmation, were both considered and red with anger. 'Or rather, I should say that you're the person who gave birth to me and gave me away. I already have a mother, thank you.'

'I know. And she has done everything I could have wanted. Better than I could have done for you.'

The judge – Mélisande – frowned. 'Are you telling me that a Princess of the Derwent People couldn't have brought up a child?'

'No.'

'Then why not?'

Faith wiped her face. 'Do you know of my Shaming?'

'No. Nor do I particularly care.'

Faith was pained. Her face showed many wounds, inside and out, all fighting to inflict the most damage. 'It was less than a week after I'd ... after you were born. The Red Queen lost a bet, and you were demanded as the forfeit. For a Changeling.'

It was Mélisande's turn to have many hurts cutting her. 'A Changeling. To be sacrificed for my ovaries. It makes me sick.'

'I refused.'

'Not enough money?'

Faith shook her head. 'We do not breed Changelings. The Radiant Queen's line has never done so, but that's not why I refused. I wanted you to be loved, Mélisande, and if I could not do it, then someone else should have the charge.'

'Get up.'

Alicia risked her lady's anger by darting to her side and helping her to stand. Job done, she tried to vanish again.

Mélisande had been thinking. 'Am I your *Shame*?'

'No. Never. You were my first source of pride, Mélisande. The Red Queen was merciful. I had to give you away, and I was sent to the kitchens. And branded. A small price to pay. And I was forced never to acknowledge you or allow you to discover who I was. I still cared, though. I used what little following I had to make sure that you were safe and prospering.'

'How closely?'

'Closely enough to know that your daughter was not in danger of interbreeding with her husband.'

'I did worry about that. Good to know. I'm not going to thank you for it, though. What has changed? Why now?'

'The obligations dissolved when I submitted to the Dragonslayer, but that's not why I asked Leesha to intercept you today. I would have preferred something less dramatic.'

'That sounds unlike the Fae.'

'Perhaps. Have you heard the story of Sofía Torres's first arrival here?'

Realisation dawned. 'Victoria! It's one thing to be in court, and another to be forced into a social setting. She'd have seen it, wouldn't she?'

'She would. I can tell her, or you can. Whichever you prefer.'

'That was thoughtful, and you can tell her. And extract suitable promises to never, ever mention it to anyone. One more question: who is my biological father? I presume you do actually know.'

Faith took an envelope out of her pocket. 'He was from a mundane family with no connection to the world of magick. Sadly, he suffered a heart attack and passed away several years ago. His name and details are in here, should you wish to discover them.'

Mélisande stared at the envelope, then accepted it. 'Thank you. Is this my room? It looks rather occupied already.'

'Forgive me once more,' said Faith with suppressed emotion. 'Your room is actually at Allington Rectory, with Dean Hardisty and her family. If you have no objections. Alicia will show you to Myfanwy's room so that you can get changed, and we have organised transport to and from Allington whenever you wish.'

'Fine.'

She turned, and Alicia rushed to unlock the door. 'This way, my lady.'

'Why were you in there, Saerdam?' asked Mélisande as they left the room.

'To bear witness. Last night my lady was made Queen-becoming.'

'So?'

'She may not be Proclaimed or Enthroned, but she must run her household as if she were a Queen.' Alicia glanced at the judge. 'Though it hang by a shoestring. This is Myfanwy's room.'

Mélisande shook her head. 'I don't know which would have been worse – for her to have been killed and me never to know, or for me to know the truth. Wait here and stop anyone coming in. I need to make a phone call.'

Alicia was still standing outside the room when Faith reappeared, her eyes swollen and scrunched up. There was a crude but effective Silence emanating from the room where the judge was making her call. 'What did she say?' asked Faith.

'She has fork-pain of the past, whether it would have been better to know or not know.'

'Yeah. I wonder whether she dreamed that her mother was a queen when she was a little girl? I doubt she ever dreamed that I was a Fae Princess.' She shook her head. 'She loves her foundling mother. And that is what I hoped for.'

'And we love you, my lady. And if the Dragonslayer did not love you, he would not have saved your life so that you could tell this tale.'

The Princess cheered up a little, and made her I'm-the-grown-up face. 'Is that what you think, Little One?'

Alicia was thrown into confusion. Yes, there was the rebellion to sort out, but Faith had been teaching their lord the blade and weaving her web for a long time before the attack at the Gallops. 'My lady? Surely it is so.'

'Listen carefully, Alicia. If it had been personal, me against Galleny, then our precious lord would have stood to one side and watched one of us die. Conrad Bloody Clarke made me an offer for one reason and one reason only: to keep his version of the peace. With me on board, he could force the Red Queen to submit, and then have her stand at his side while he faced down the Greening-Ripley assault. *That's* why I'm alive. Ask him about his biggest historical inspiration one day, but don't do it when Mina's around.'

Alicia didn't know where to put herself. *Surely not* was her first thought. And second.

Before she could try for a third, Faith straightened her spine, tipped her head from side to side and said, 'Right. Time to dance the Maypole.'

'I think Alicia should finish it off,' said Mina. 'She's the one who's done all the hard work.'

'Yeah, right. Like she totally prepped your skin and drew all the designs,' responded Erin.

Mina gave the Enscriber an airy wave. 'Did I see you up to your arms in the sink, covered in henna paste? I don't think so.' Then she grinned. 'But Shear Magic *has* played a part, Erin, even if you are most definitely the artist.'

'You are such a wind-up merchant, Mina Clarke-to-be.'

'Leesha?'

There was one tiny space left on Mina's left arm, just below the copper-filled tattoo scar which did weird things to her magick and which Alicia didn't understand at all. On every other square and rounded inch of flesh were the most intricate designs in henna, some abstract, some figurative, some with magick and some mundane.

The largest single section had been completed by Mary Clarke, a gift from the groom's mother and a sign of their future together – or it would be if Mina were moving into the Clarke home and Mary didn't live in a different country. Mary was meticulous in following Erin's designs and didn't make a single mistake, unlike Lucy who had insisted that she could do it freehand. 'I do chocolate art on cappuccinos all the time,' she had declared, but it seemed that human arms were more of a challenge.

Alicia approached the centre of the circle where Mina was enthroned and surrounded by the women, girls, Wolves and cubs who were preparing her for marriage. Some of the children were asleep, and Lottie the cub was fighting to keep her eyes open. It had been a big day for everyone.

Alicia had spent Beltane torn between wanting to help and constantly being told that she was being honoured. In the end, when not needed to supervise the Maypole, she had opted to walk around the pasture and listen. It was always interesting to know what mortals said when they thought they couldn't be heard.

She had nearly shouted a protest when two women with poorly behaved children complained that there was no bouncy castle, and several times she had heard comments like 'how can she afford this?' or 'very lady-of-the-manor' and 'does she think she can buy the village?' Alicia made Memories of these so that she could think on them in the future and balance them against the equally positive comments, most of which seemed to focus on Myfanwy rather than Mina. Why some of the village should favour the Druid over the princess was something she didn't understand and which she might never know, because there would be no time to ask. Not with the mehndi party tonight and her doom to face on the morrow.

After the Mayday/Beltane celebrations, the women and children of Clerkswell had dispersed and Robbie had resumed his duties as Guard to Elvenham Grange, and the bridal party had gathered in the drawing room for Mina's last night as a single woman. In theory. In practice, there had been a lot of comments about having already consummated the greenwood marriage, followed by a lot of backtracking when talking to Mina's sister-in-law, Saanvi. Once the Prosecco had been opened, several people kept forgetting that there were non-Entangled guests of honour.

Since the arrival of Saanvi and an elder from the village called Miss Parkes, there had been a constant shuffle between different rooms to make sure that the magickally enriched parts of the mehndi party were performed away from un-Entangled eyes.

Mina had begun the ceremony in her bedroom, and it was Cathy who had performed the first part. The First Lady of Staveley had grown in many ways since their lord had dragged her out of the Sprint Sídhe to keep Scout quiet in the helicopter. Thrust into a leading role, the barely mature Hlæfdige had almost buckled at first, then gritted her teeth. She had never let down their Queen-to-be. One thing hadn't changed, though. She still much preferred sewing to cooking, and had thanked the Morrigan profusely for sending Thistle to Birk Fell. Cathy had worked on some of the flower girls' dresses, so this was her moment in the spotlight, with both her breasts and her needle required.

'I've expressed this. We don't want to get too symbolic, do we?' said the dark-haired Cathy. She handed Mina a small goblet of Amrita laced with anaesthetic and continued: 'Drink a small sip, then rub it on your nose.'

Mina drank and dabbed, Alicia took her lady's head tenderly in her hands, and Faith plunged the room into darkness, a darkness which the People could see through easily. Then Cathy struck.

'Ow! That still hurt!' said Mina.

'Done,' said Cathy.

'Mirror,' said Mina. 'I can feel blood running down.'

Alicia held up a mirror, and Mina calmed herself: the 'blood' was just Amrita dripping from the glinting new stud in Mina's nose, pierced and threaded by Cathy.

'Perfect,' said Mina.

'Well, she did have a big target to aim at,' said Vicky.

Mina gave Vicky a death stare, and Vicky burst out laughing.

'Shall we move on?' said Faith diplomatically. 'Erin?'

The Enscriber took Mina's arms and began laying down magick and sketching the designs for the mehndi, and then Mina descended to the drawing room where the women queued up to take their turn. Much love had flowed, but the mehndi required more magick to be complete.

Alicia saw her Sister bump into Saanvi, and as befitted her new name, Saerdam Thistle Lightfinger extracted Saanvi's phone and then disappeared. A few seconds later, Vicky nodded to Sofía, and the Dragonslayer's younger sister made the Glamour of a phone ringing in the kitchen with music from some Bollywood film.

'Isn't that yours?' said Anika.

'Oh damn,' said Saanvi. 'I must have left it in the kitchen. I'd better go in case it's my mother.'

They should be safe for a moment. Once reunited with her phone, even after the shortest separation, Saanvi would sit down and triple-check every app and notification. Alicia knelt and sneaked a quick glance at the Ink which Thistle had shown her earlier. She breathed out, blinked, and drew four lines into a knot of magick, then attached them to the scar and wove them together. To mundane eyes, they would present as a Celtic triskele.

'There. Done. Try it.'

'What do I do?'

'Touch your finger lightly to your tongue – very lightly – then draw it down from the tattoo with your eyes closed.'

Mina licked her lips, dabbed her finger and made the connection. She winced with pain and said, 'Ow. That was like an ice cream headache. Wow! It worked.'

The henna was still there, but now it was invisible. 'Why did you want this, my lady?' asked Alicia. 'Do you not want to show it off?'

'I do, but with the extra bonding agents, this will last for *weeks*. I might need to hide it. When you are marrying Conrad Clarke, you never know what's around the corner.'

'Now try it backwards,' urged Erin.

The henna revealed itself once more, and Mina stood up, showing her arms to a huge round of applause from the room.

'Let's grab something to eat before the show,' said Vicky.

The Anointed Guardian and the judge had been sitting on the edge of the group, and Mélisande asked Hannah, 'What show is this?'

'A child-friendly blend of illusion and sleight of hand, suitable for a mundane audience. Featuring Sofía as La Gitana and Rachael Clarke as her beautiful assistant.'

'Shame,' said Mélisande. 'I was hoping for a proper Fête du Feu.'

Vicky heard this and shook her head vigorously. 'You're joking, aren't you, ma'am? After what happened the first two times?'

Mélisande grinned. 'That's exactly what I was hoping for.'

Vicky gave the judge a dark look. 'Aye, well, it's not always funny to have your secrets revealed. Onion bhajis, anyone?'

Part Eight — Tying Knots

Chapter Forty-Nine

Alicia had to stand on a stool for the last part of the dressing. Reaching the top of Mina's head had become a real challenge since Mina had put on her enormous heels, and Faith had entrusted Alicia with the crowning glory.

The tiara had come from the royal treasury in the Derwent Sídhe, and that was the *borrowed* part of Mina's ensemble. The silver fretwork was exquisite, fine and airy, made by the People's best silversmiths in centuries gone by. It was studded with emeralds, and new earrings had been forged with matching stones. The earrings were a gift from the Queen.

Alicia placed the tiara on Mina's head, tied the finest black silk thread through Mina's hair to secure it, then hopped off the stool and stood back. 'My lady, you are ready.'

'I don't think I'll ever be ready for this,' said Mina. 'But let's have a look.'

Alicia cast a Mirror onto the door of the en suite and stood aside. 'You are beautiful,' she told the bride.

'Not gonna lie, you're a knockout,' added Faith. 'And this is only the *first* time today you're going to be the best-looking woman in Clerkswell.'

The three paused as Mina swayed her hips, watching the ivory silk flow like water. 'Thank you. Both of you. All I need to do now is avoid falling over in these heels.'

Faith nodded to Alicia, and Alicia cancelled the Mirror. 'They're waiting,' said Faith. 'Leesha, the door?'

Alicia opened the bedroom door and held it wide.

'Wish me luck,' said Mina, and with that she swayed out of the room and down the corridor to the staircase. When Shear Magic heard the cheers and applause, they knew that she was descending the steps in triumph and that Rani was no longer in their keeping.

'I'm going straight to the stables,' said Faith. 'See them off then send Cathy to attend me.'

'My lady.'

Faith turned left, towards the steep back stairs, and Alicia went down the front stairs after checking that everyone had left. The bridal party was either climbing into a minibus for the short trip up Elven Lane or setting off to walk, depending on their age and how tight their shoes were. Cathy and Thistle were lurking in the shadows, and Alicia sent Cathy to attend their lady then joined her Sister to wait for the wedding carriage.

Rani was erect and poised on the steps, flanked by the Seer and the Anointed Guardian and now clutching a bouquet of flowers which had been gathered at dawn and tied with a blessing by Myfanwy.

'Here she comes,' said Thistle.

Alicia had been working on the bridesmaids since first thing, while Faith had focused on Mina and Thistle brought food and drink to everyone. A low loader had rumbled down the lane with the bridal transport, and then horses had been delivered. And more flowers, more food, gifts and last minute remedies must have all arrived but throughout all this Alicia had been oblivious, focused on reconciling the *actual* outfits brought by the bridesmaids with what they *said* they'd be bringing.

And then there was what Faith had called the 'elephant in the room': Lottie's dress, which had most definitely *not* been sewn by Cathy, given that it was made from the boudoir shift of the Fair Queen of Galway. None of the People would touch it, and it turned out that Lottie's growth spurt had been *over*estimated, and the dress needed taking up by an inch, and not a single guest knew one end of the needle from another. Eventually Saanvi got down on her hands and knees with a loud complaint about the beauticians being 'too damned picky'.

Iron-shod hooves struck the road, then wheels crunched over the gravel and Alicia got her first glimpse of the much-maligned Mage, Eseld Mowbray.

'You have to be fucking kidding me,' said Vicky, from the step. 'She's got bigger balls than Chris, that's for certain.'

'*Wha's the problem*?' hissed Thistle.

'Eseld will be driving Mina to her marriage in a farm cart with actual hay bales,' said Alicia. 'Covered in rugs and silks of Mowbray-blue, of course, to keep the straw off the dress. The generosity of this cannot be denied, so Mina cannot refuse. Neat. It could almost have been thought up by one of us.'

'If I know Rani, she'll get her back.'

'Oh yes. Probably with a few well-chosen words.'

The wagon drew to a halt by the steps and an older woman in a Mowbray-blue tailcoat jumped down. 'You look gorgeous, Mina. Hang on while I get the steps.'

'Thank you, Maggie.'

While they fussed around getting Mina into the back of the wagon, Alicia stared at the carriage driver. Eseld's dark hair was up and under a blue top hat, and under her matching tailcoat and white jodhpurs was both power and strength. 'What do you reckon?' she asked Thistle.

'Aboot what?'

'Whether you'd go for Eseld or Tamsin if you were Chris Kelly.'

'As I've never met the guy, I dinnae ken. If it were me, I'd take Tammy. Why is a dog on a lead tied to the cart?'

'It's Floss. The Bloxhams' dog. Remember?'

Alicia was about to add that Floss was in season and that it was a good job that Scout wasn't here to wish the bride good luck, but Thistle continued: 'On second thoughts, I enjoy being a bottom occasionally, and La Mowbray's got *top* written all over her today.'

'Thistle! Shh!'

The bride was settled in state, the bridesmaids made comfortable and the steps removed. Maggie climbed onto the driving seat and Eseld took the brake off.

'Walk on,' she commanded, and the giant workhorses shuffled into life.

'Good luck,' whispered Alicia. 'I hope that both of us get what we want today, but if only one of us is blessed, let it be you, my lady.'

'You're Eclipsed,' said Thistle. 'Totally. What are we doing first? Finishing the marquee or doing the mandap thingy?'

As the marquee was near Robbie, Thistle would no doubt prefer to work on that, so Alicia ordered her to finish the garlands for the mandap. 'We haven't got long, and I don't want you distracted,' she told her Sister.

'We haven't got long,' said Chloë to the Bloxhams, 'and I don't want you distracted.'

'But I want to see her,' said Juliet. 'Come on – a quick glimpse won't hurt.'

Chloë was desperate. They were across the lane, down from the Grange but ahead of the entrance to the pasture, and she knew that they had a tiny window to act now that the minibus and guests had headed up to St Michael's.

'We need to follow the carriage into the grounds and skirt around the house,' said Chloë, 'not stand around admiring the bride.'

'Well, I must say that Eseld Mowbray scrubs up nicely,' said Juliet.

'For a Mowbray,' said her husband.

The farm cart/carriage was opposite them, the horses snorting impatiently and Eseld commanding them with her back ramrod straight and a long whip in hand. When the last of the shouts and laughter had faded up the lane, Eseld ordered the horses forwards, and the raiding party emerged from behind a hedge heavy with May blossom then crossed the road.

Chloë was nervous, terrified and guilty. She was about to lead the

Bloxhams into potential danger, and she was beginning to wonder just how much her devotion to Beth was reciprocated, because this was the shittiest thing she'd ever been asked to do.

The carriage turned into the drive. Chloë held up her hand for a second, then urged the others forwards. When they were through the gates, they turned left instead of right, heading for the narrow gap between house and wall … and walked straight into a rusty iron gate, secured by an equally rusty padlock.

'Shit,' hissed Chloë. 'Why didn't you tell me about this?'

'Because I didn't know it was here!' said Jules. 'No one ever comes round here. As you can see.'

They had run right in front of the study windows and no one had said anything, so Juliet went back and peered around a pillar. 'Wow. She looks amazing.'

'Sod that. What are we going to do?' said Stephen. 'Your lot are waiting on our signal.'

They were. Beth and Anita had been working their way slowly down the path through the woods and were now in position above the well. Chloë risked standing next to Juliet and peering round the pillar. The carriage drew away, and once it was gone, two young women emerged from the house and drifted off round the side. Perfect.

'They've left the front doors open,' she said. 'Quick. You go in, and I'll give the signal.'

The *signal* was a text message, soon sent, and Chloë dashed along the border, avoiding the gravel, to catch the Bloxhams.

They were standing in a large hall with a substantial staircase and several rooms off it. Stephen pointed down a passageway. 'I still think it's down there. If the safe's built in, there can't be anywhere else it could be.'

'But we've looked down there,' said Juliet. 'If you're so certain, you look down there, and I'll try the study. If ever there was a room that would have a hidden passage or safe, it's that one.'

'Fine. Be quick about it.'

'And I'll check the back,' said Chloë.

She headed past Stephen who was busy tapping on the panelling, and found herself in a beautifully cosy kitchen. A kitchen with a view of the gardens. Good.

Five minutes passed. Nothing. Then a bloody dog started barking and howling, and one of the women, the blonde one, came out of the marquee and disappeared from sight. Chloë leaned on the sink and peered round. She had been sweating already but now it was a river. She glanced into the scullery and saw many, many bunches of flowers in water. She grabbed one just as a Border collie bounded into the house and launched himself at her.

'Down, Scout,' came a voice with a thick Scottish accent, followed by the woman. She frowned when she saw Chloë, and said, 'Help you?'

Chloë showed her the flowers. 'Last minute delivery. There was one missing from the order we delivered earlier. My fault.'

'Oh, aye? Is that why you're wearing Distraction Shades, eh? To see the flowers better? Who the fuck are you?'

Suddenly there was a knife in the girl's hand, and Chloë knew that she was both in the presence of magick and severely out of her depth. Even the dog looked like it was about to turn on her. She retreated a step.

'Hello there,' said Stephen, coming down the passage behind Chloë. 'It's just me. One of the neighbours. Came round to leave a present. There's no need for a knife.'

Before Chloë could stop him, Stephen pushed past to stand between her and the knife-wielding Mage. This had the potential to go very wrong very quickly.

'Who are ye?'

'Who are you?' said Stephen.

'Stephen, I … Oh,' said Juliet, joining the stand-off. She took in the girl, and her husband, and the knife. 'Are you with Shear Magic?' she asked, pointing to the girl's polo shirt. 'I met your colleagues Faith and Alicia recently.'

'Oh, aye?'

'Yes. I'm Juliet Bloxham. This is my husband, Stephen. We just—'

'Oh right! I've heard all about youse lot, and if you're here then you've mischief on your minds. Let's have a bit of fun finding out what you're up to, shall we?'

A new voice with a Cornish accent echoed from outside, approaching quickly. 'Hi there, Thistle! It's just me, Maggie Pearce. Gotta pop to the loo. I … Aargh!'

The female footman from the carriage had appeared behind the girl, and she had turned to see what was going on. Big mistake, because Stephen took the opportunity to make a heroic grab for her knife hand. Even bigger mistake.

The girl allowed him to grab her, then she clamped her other hand onto his wrist and squeezed – but that wasn't the worst thing. Her face contorted, her jaw opened wider than humanly possible and *a whole set of extra teeth appeared*. Stephen cried out in pain, Juliet screamed in utter terror, and Maggie Pearce ran off, pulling her phone out of her jodhpurs.

Chloë turned and ran. She had to get round to the well and warn the others. There was a tremendous '*eurghh*' of pain from behind her. The girl must have kicked Stephen in the balls. Chloë hurtled through the hall and outside, skidding on the gravel and heading for the path to the gardens. Weird sounds in a strange language pierced her ears.

She shot through the gate but then stopped, unsure of where to go next.

Since her first brief glimpse of the Grange, it had all changed, with a giant marquee, tents and pavilions now sprouting everywhere. *The well. Where is it?* She turned left, round a rockery, and saw the other beautician hurtling towards her, then past her and round the fire pit at an inhuman speed. Ahead of Chloë, disaster was unfolding.

The Mowbray footman was on the phone, and Eseld Mowbray was approaching, whip in hand. Emerging from the stables was the Fae bitch-queen. *How had Beth got it so wrong? Had she really imagined that Elvenham Grange would be unprotected?*

She had barely registered this thought when a huge man (or not-man) ran through the gate from the pasture with the Bloxhams' Labrador on his heels, which provoked an immediate response from the back door of the house: the Border collie shot out and made a beeline for the Labrador with only one thing on his mind, and it looked like she was very much in agreement.

Chloë thought about heading for the well to help her girlfriend, but sod it: Beth had got herself into this mess, and she could get herself out of it. Chloë made it as far as the gates before the huge man appeared in front of her and held up a sword.

'That's far enough,' he said. 'Back you go.'

Chapter Fifty

Alicia and Thistle went round to the gardens, still discussing how Mina had looked as she'd driven off and whether Mina had made the right decision in not forcing her bridesmaids to wear matching dresses. Of particular concern were the Chief Bridesmaid and the Matron of Honour. 'Do you think it was a compromise?' asked Alicia. 'I mean, to wear lilac, and with that headscarf!'

Thistle shook her head. 'That's beyond me.'

'Perhaps they can Photoshop the pictures.'

'What is it needs doing again?' asked Thistle as she contemplated the mandap – the Hindu wedding canopy.

'Mister Joshi, the priest, said that it was a little bare in some places, according to Vicky. He said that when it comes to weddings in India, more is definitely more. There are some leftover flowers, I think. They're the ones in the sink. And more ribbon would be good.'

'What about you?' Thistle turned to the kennel, where Scout was on a long lead and serenading them with increasingly desperate howls. 'Will you no shut up, you mad dog!'

'I'm going to prepare the barrels for tapping and take the glasses out of the boxes.'

Thistle frowned. She was much less cute now that she had a normal nose that didn't wrinkle up when she frowned or pouted. 'How come you're on beer and I'm on decoration? Should it no be the other way round?'

'Listen! That's the carriage. Why is it coming back? It's heading for the pasture.'

'It's heading at a fair clip. They probably forgot something. Like Mowbray's cigarettes.'

'I'll stay and see what they want.'

Thistle sighed. 'I'll go get some ribbon and flowers. Look, put a Ward on the hotplates and I'll let the dog loose else he makes me remove his vocal cords.'

Alicia headed into the marquee and stared at the hotplates and warmers, already loaded with Indian snacks ready to feed the guests in the gap between the weddings – 'two rings of the circus', as Mary Clarke had put it. Alicia put her hands on her hips and wondered what sort of Ward would deter a hungry Border collie but not the mundane guests. She glanced at her Sister. Scout was following Thistle inside; it seemed that he wanted to explore the kitchen first.

From the pasture, she heard Maggie the footman say, 'Stable toilet's busy. I'll just nip to the scullery.' Then she jogged past, and from the scullery door said, 'Hi there, Thistle! It's just me, Maggie Pearce. Gotta pop to the loo. I … Aargh!' She ran out, reaching for her phone.

Something's badly wrong! What has Thistle done to her?

Alicia hurtled towards the house, and immediately sensed intruders. Human intruders. And then the lightest breeze brought something else: a whiff of sulphur. She wheeled around and stared towards the well. Was that an extra glow? From the far side of the house came another intruder, running at full speed. *We'll see who can run faster.*

She put Fire in her legs and shot past the intruder, noting that it was a human female with powerful Distraction magick in her glasses. As she approached the well, Alicia engaged the worm of ink without thinking and transitioned to the glade above the well. And there she found two more mortals, very different ones, trying to break down the door to the sídhe.

She could tell almost nothing about them except that they were female and clearly Mages. The layers of Glamour and Distraction they had woven around themselves told Alicia that they must be enemies, for only an enemy would arrive in such obvious camouflage. And then they saw her.

'Cockroach,' said one, the slightly bigger one.

'Shit,' said the smaller, and now obviously younger, one.

Alicia grabbed her scissors from her belt and stepped towards them.

'It's only a handmaiden,' said the older one. 'You deal with her, I'll get this door open. We can lock her out.'

Only a handmaiden! She'd show them. She approached the younger one, who took out a dagger. It was no Great Fang in size or edge, but it shared something worse with Conrad's blade: an edge of n'Haeval. Alicia glanced around, but no one was coming to help her. She would have to face this on her own.

There is only one thing to do when faced with Dwarven Death, and that is to bring down the Night. Alicia steeled herself, but she couldn't do it. She couldn't bring herself to dig down to where the deepest, darkest Ink lurked within her. She was not ready. She couldn't do it. *There must be some other way.*

She dodged forwards, slashed with her scissors, then stepped back. The girl backed off, missing her chance for a riposte, and that told Alicia her opponent was no master of the blade. It didn't change Alicia's situation, though, and the girl still advanced.

Alicia tried to weave a pattern and stepped to the right. 'We can keep this up all day, if you like,' she told the girl. 'When the Queen's Guard has finished with your friends in the Grange, he'll be coming for you. Or perhaps my lady will be first, and she will see you for who you really are.'

'Ignore her,' said the older intruder. 'I'm nearly there.'

The younger one hesitated and looked at her colleague. Alicia took the chance to close in and slashed at her left arm, striking then dodging back with blood flowing on her scissors. Got you.

'Ow! She's fucking cut me,' said the invader.

'You finish here. I'll get her,' said the older one, pulling out a sword of n'Haeval and taking a stance that looked like she meant business. Her colleague took her place at the door.

Alicia had no choice but to engage, and was relieved when the riposte came so slowly that she had no trouble dodging it, unlike the feint which followed. That was close.

'I've got it!' shouted the younger one. 'I ... oh, shit!'

Alicia was far enough away for the older invader to glance around safely, and she lowered her blade a fraction when she saw what had happened. Alicia would have gone for a stab if she hadn't also been transfixed by the sight which greeted her. The younger Mage had fallen, sprawling on the grass, and in the doorway to the sídhe stood the most eldritch figure Alicia had ever seen.

He was human to look at, but not to smell or sense. Tall, with light brown hair in a ponytail and half a beard of stubble. And he was weirdly familiar in some way, despite the even more weirdly assorted outfit he was sporting. Unless Alicia was being Eclipsed, the figure in front of them was wearing one of Rachael's baggy old sweatshirts in blue (Gloucester Tennis on Tour), coupled with a pair of Myfanwy's maternity leggings in red (Hot Mamma round the waistband).

The blue eyes of the figure looked first at the younger Mage, then at the older, then they bored into Alicia. She bowed her head, remembering one of the stories from the Grange. Before Alicia could ask anything, the young invader scrabbled to her feet and declared, 'I'm outta here.'

The older one slashed the air, then both of them disappeared to the mortal realm. Alicia wanted to follow, but as the others would surely intercept them, she addressed the figure. 'Are you Spectre Thomas returned?' she asked.

'Hunh,' he grunted – more of a growl than a grunt. Could he even speak one of the tongues?

'Well met, sir.'

'Thought today would be quiet. Go away and say nothing,' he commanded in a gravelly voice that sounded a little like Lloyd Flint. And with that, he retreated through the sídhe door and slammed it behind him.

'Egg and wings, what was that?' she said out loud. And why did he have the Elvenham dragon tattooed on his forearm? Nothing else, just the dragon.

If that wasn't enough strangeness, Alicia's tongue had now been bound more tightly on the subject of this apparition than it had been about her forthcoming fate. She bowed again and dropped down to follow the invaders.

The invading Mages had headed not for the front gate but to the woods, and they were now disappearing up the hill and through the trees. Alicia was set to pursue them when she was called by Cathy in the People's tongue, a great shout from away at the house. 'Leesha! Attend us here.'

Alicia flew on feet of Fire towards the group of three: Cathy, Eseld and Robbie. She glanced at the pasture and squinted for better sight. Was that…? *Egg and wings!* Maggie the Mowbray footman was standing about ten feet from Scout and Floss as if wondering whether she should interrupt their mating. Alicia shook her head and braked hard in front of Cathy, but it was Eseld who took the lead.

'What a fucking mess,' she said. 'Someone is going to be in so much shit.'

'What's happened?' said Alicia. 'Has Thistle killed the intruders?'

'No, thank the gods, but Maggie's called the cops and they'll be here in less than two minutes. I've got to intercept them. Faith's having a crisis and Cathy needs to heal her. I'm going to stand in the road, and when I bring the cops inside, I need you to keep this under wraps. Understand?'

'Me?' said Alicia with a squeak.'

'Faith said you're creative when it comes to mortals. Don't let me down.'

Eseld jogged towards the front gates, and Cathy gave Alicia's arm a squeeze before heading to the stables. So why was Alicia in charge and not the Queen's Guard? She looked up at Robbie, and saw fierce determination on his face and a sword in his hand. Oh. That's why.

'Two more intruders,' she told him. 'Escaped through the woods. Go and track them down.'

'On it!' he shot back, and then he shot off in pursuit.

Alicia went into the house and found three mortals penned in by a hungry looking Thistle, who had already bound their arms to their sides with red ribbon. One of them was the intruder with the Distraction glasses, another was Juliet Bloxham and the third must be Juliet's husband, currently slumped to the floor, unconscious.

'What have you done to him?'

'I've done nothing bar kicking him in the balls! Looks like he has more in common with Alfred Clarke than he thought: he's blind to magick, and his brain sparked out as soon as I showed them my nature.'

Eseld had told Alicia to keep things under wraps. Of course!

'Thistle, finish binding them, but make sure their mouths are closed. I will talk to the police.'

'You've got blood all over you,' observed Thistle. 'The polis dinnae like that.'

'Whose blood? What have you done?' said the unknown mortal.

Alicia stepped forwards decisively and took off the Distraction Shades. She folded them and put them in her apron, then studied the girl, who was now bug-eyed with fear. 'I will know you again,' she told her. Then she licked the blood off her scissors. 'As I will know this one. She lives, by the way. Now hush.'

Alicia and Thistle pricked up their ears. Sirens.

'Quickly, Sister. You have done great work already. I must go.' Alicia ran out of the house and past Scout, who was heading in and looked *very* pleased with himself.

It soon became clear that Alicia was going to be kept away from their lord. Eseld had taken the decision to blame everything on *her* for some reason, and Faith had been quick to agree: after all, Alicia would be disappearing soon. Even Mina was on board, although she didn't know about Alicia's impending doom.

'We have to keep Conrad in the dark,' Rani told her as Alicia checked the bridal gown for any damage or stains. 'If he thinks it's under control, he will wait until later. Tomorrow will do. After all, if I cannot distract my husband on our wedding day, I'm not much of a bride. Husband! Can you believe it? I will be a married woman again.'

The other women who had streamed upstairs to prepare for the Hindu ceremony were all agog to hear about the intruders, but were easily distracted once they realised that the hairdresser's lips were sealed. The intruders themselves had fled the moment the police left, with the Bloxhams going up the lane and the girl heading for the woods. Robbie, it seemed, had been unsuccessful in catching the Mage invaders. After all, he was the Royal Guard, not the Royal Huntsman. If only they'd had a Wolf...

The bridal party were crowding around Mina and drinking champagne and swapping stories when Faith got a message. 'Tara Doyle is approaching. Lucy, can you escort her to the drawing room? We need to do a ... thing with her. Tell Conrad that it's Alicia's fault. We're blaming her for everything today.'

'Right.'

Lucy dashed down the stairs, followed by Faith and Alicia. When Lucy opened the front doors, they caught a glimpse of Conrad outside, on duty to greet the VIP guests. 'Come on,' said Faith. 'Soon be over with.'

Gravel crunched. Voices warbled happily outside. Inside the drawing room, Alicia sweated into her clean tunic. Lucy's voice grew louder. A new child's voice was heard saying in wonder that this house was nice but *so old*, and then it stopped as Princess Birkdale swept into the drawing room. She halted inside the door and sniffed the air.

'Ah, look at you, eh? The Morrigan's been, hasn't she?'

'I am a Queen-becoming,' said Faith in the People's tongue.

Birkdale slowly bowed her head. Instead of being the one with seniority, she was now junior. Fractionally. Power, though, was a different matter. 'My lady,' said the junior noble. 'Congratulations. I look forward to you fulfilling your vows.'

'In time,' responded Faith. 'For now, let us all focus on the *real* queen for the day.'

'Of course.'

Princess Birkdale shook herself. With a grin, she raised her voice and shouted, 'Did someone say *champagne?*'

The theme of *Mina first* had continued throughout the day. Even when Damini the Serpent-woman arrived, the business of making sure that Rani was queen for the day took top priority. The snake even managed to compliment Alicia during the final rehearsal for the bridal dance.

'If all you had practised as assiduously as Leesha, we would not be in this mess!'

Focusing on Mina wasn't the only reason for peace prevailing, though. When Damini had finished her encounter with Conrad, she had not entered the Grange alone: everyone could see that she bore the blessing of Ganesh.

Well, not *everyone*. In fact, it was only the People and a couple of the Mages who could see *that*, but it was there, and although Alicia was being eaten away by the ticking clock, the rest of the company had other things on their minds.

At least, that's what she thought until Rachael Clarke brought a glass of something beautifully golden into the Sunset Room, where Alicia was carefully sorting clothing discarded by the bridal party when they had changed into their sarees.

'We're nearly ready,' said Rachael. 'Shame you can't walk down the red carpet with the rest of us.'

'No more than I could attend the House of the Crucified God.'

'So how come Princess Birkdale gets to lead the parade?'

'She has submitted to Damini for the day, and Portarra has our lord ... I mean *your brother's* favour. We are just servants.' Alicia forced a smile. 'You look gorgeous, Raitch. Red really suits you.'

'Here. This is the last of Dad's special stock of brandy. I'll go and tap Conrad up for some more. Did you know that my sneaky brother has *two* hip flasks in that outfit of his?'

'Thank you. This is a favour.'

'Least you deserve. You've been working flat out all day. And I want to hear all about what the Bloxhams were up to, okay?'

'In time, I'm sure you will.'

Sofía's voice came from the landing, calling Rachael away. She put down the brandy, gave Alicia a hug, then wafted out of the room in a cloud of spiced perfume.

Alicia downed the brandy in one, enjoying the taste, and picked up the Anointed Guardian's unfortunately chosen trouser suit.

Faith, Cathy, Thistle and Alicia watched the ceremony from the morning room, and as soon as Ganesh's blessing had been laid upon the happy couple, they hurried out to help. Faith was acting as assistant Maître d', Thistle and Cathy were on drinks, and Alicia was acting as photographer's assistant to the Digger's Daughter.

As the moment of the bridal dance approached, Alicia started hallucinating. Or she thought she was hallucinating or something, because Thistle approached her from the side without her feeling a thing. Normally even her Sister's presence would have her aware. Thistle handed her a red headband and moved away.

And then Alicia realised that her world was shrinking, her senses focusing only on what was in front of her, because despite the joy and love and fireworks spreading all around the Grange, she had no future here. With a sigh, she squeezed herself into her crop top and adjusted her boobs. She pulled up her skirt and shed her shoes, ready for the dance. In less than an hour, it would all be over. Or that's what she thought. The gods, it seemed, had other ideas.

Chapter Fifty-One

When the bridal dance was finished, Alicia felt like she'd been hollowed out. Her head was floating away on a cloud of drums, music and cheers from the wedding crowd; her heart was a lump of lead, and there was nothing left of *her* in between the triumph and the looming disaster. Thistle skipped back towards the stables to get changed, and Alicia followed with feet that had seconds ago been dancing but which could now barely move.

When Alicia got to their room at the stables (which still smelled of horses from next door), Thistle had already discarded the dance costume and thrown a floral mini-dress over her head, and was now shoving her feet into orange trainers. 'I'll get back to it and work twice as hard. No one will know you're missing.' She paused, threw her arms around Alicia's neck and whispered, 'Know that you go with my love, Sister.'

Alicia undressed and wiped herself with a towel before donning her getaway outfit. First she swapped the borrowed jewellery for just one item, a reminder of what she had to face. Then she pulled on her clothes: black running top, black fleece, new fell-running shoes and the leggings she'd inherited from Evie Mason. Wearing something with Holly Nugent's name as she stood before Tara Doyle would be Alicia's last act of defiance. And she'd had help from Cathy, too.

She took the pins out of her hair and put it in a high ponytail, then picked up her escape bag. Her last purchase with her new debit card had been a runner's rucksack, and it was all packed, except for two things. Alicia folded her Shear Magic tunic, put her Heartstone into the side pocket of the rucksack and placed the tunic on top before snapping the clasps. She put her sharpest scissors into one pocket of her leggings and her phone into the other. Done.

She walked across the gardens through the gathering darkness and stashed her rucksack near to the well, a quick Glamour hiding it from the wedding guests. Then she stopped and sniffed. *Wolves.* They were gathering outside the boundary, and they were *not* from the Birkfell Pack. And that wasn't all the bad news: the Wolves had minders with them. Then the full truth hit her: Tara Doyle's Pack was the Bowland Pack, lodged in the Forest of Bowland, barely thirty miles as the raven flies from Birk Fell, and now that remark about Princess Bowland made sense. When Tara Doyle drank the Water of Life, she would not become Queen of Birkdale, she would become Queen of the Bowland Forest, right on Faith's doorstep.

No wonder *Bowland* wanted to put Alicia to the question and drain her of every drop of knowledge about Faith's household and the new sídhe being built at Staveley. There was no way that her lady would allow her to give up that information, and Alicia came to new learning: to protect her People, Faith would have to kill Alicia as soon as she was released. It served her right, she supposed: if she had let their Princess consume Thistle at Rydal Water, Faith would not have fallen at Aintree, and would not have had to go into Tara Doyle's debt.

There was a while to go yet, and Alicia had duties to perform. She stepped up to the well, the bees from the new swarm coming to inspect her then flying home for the night. She ran her fingers over the stones and felt the magick throb deeply within. Shame she wouldn't get to answer the riddle of the strangely dressed Guardian. With a shrug she'd copied from Conrad, she headed back towards the Bollywoodmusic throbbing from the marquee. It stopped, and cries were heard: 'By the lords of Neverwhere! It cannot be!'

When Alicia arrived at the marquee, all the attention was focused at the other end, where Mina was putting on Thistle's trainers and a party of Mages was preparing to greet the Gallows God – for who else could it be?

Faith almost knocked Alicia over as she retreated. Tara Doyle wasn't far behind, then Thistle bumped into them as almost the entire village focused on the garden gate leading to the front door.

'We'll do it now,' said Faith in the People's tongue. 'You wanted Alicia released after the bridal dance, and at a time when the magick would not draw attention to us. There will be no better time.'

'Are you Eclipsed, Flopsy? That's the *Gallows God* out there!'

'And my lord bears his ring. I fear him not.'

'Then you *are* Eclipsed,' spat Tara.

'Come on, Leesha. Let's get this done. You don't have to join us, Tara. If you're a bit tired, why don't you go for a lie-down? I find it helps.'

Faith strode off towards the well, and the barefoot Thistle barged the Scouse Princess aside to follow. Hope leapt in Alicia's heart until she remembered a mortal saying: *It's the hope that kills you.* It wouldn't be hope that killed her, it would be Faith; of that she was certain. And she would have to *hope* that it was quick. She took a slight detour to grab her getaway bag. No sense in leaving it to be discovered by others.

Faith was in position by the well, and Alicia stood ready to escape to her death. She had decided that the invaders this morning had been on to a good thing – the path through the woods was hard but led to wide open country. She would go that way. If she had the chance.

Thistle stood on the path to the house and gave a Huntsman's whistle. What was that for? Whatever. Princess Birkdale arrived and reached behind her skirt.

'Shit,' she said, then looked around accusingly. 'Who's nicked me phone?'

'Lost something?' said Thistle sweetly, waving the device in the air. 'They dinnae call me Lightfinger for nothing.'

'Give that here, you poxy tart.'

'You can fight my Acting Chamberlain or you can watch the ceremony,' said Faith.

Tara Doyle gave a cry in the highest pitch of the People's tongue, and a little bit of Alicia's hope evaporated because the Princess's Guard came down the path from the trees, sword in hand and cutting off Alicia's escape route, and she was now too near to him for comfort.

Thistle nodded at Faith, and Faith turned to Alicia. 'Approach, Little One.'

Alicia turned and looked at Princess Birkdale, aka Princess Bowland, aka *Princess Blowhard.* She had one word for her, and she said it not loudly but clearly into the darkness. '*Braña_hoo*nah.* My lady.' She ran her fingers down the red stripe in her leggings and turned her back on the Princess.

She stepped up to her true lady and saw the love in her face. Alicia wouldn't run. No point. She'd offer her neck and let her Becoming-Queen take her life quickly. She knelt down and bowed her head.

'Saerdam Alicia-6th-Staveley-Redqueen-Iris-Nymph Child, I release you from the Staveley People to rove the earth or serve another as you see fit. Give me your Name.'

Head still bowed, Alicia lifted her arm and manifested the Ink of her name. Faith erased *Staveley.* It was done.

A great crash and clash of steel signalled the end of her life … so why was she still breathing?

'Run!' shrieked Faith.

Alicia lifted her head and rose to her feet. *Robbie!* Robbie was at blade with Birkdale's Guard, and Thistle had rugby-tackled the enemy Princess, but that wasn't the most important thing. Oh no. *Faith was letting her live!* The joy!

'Run, you Eclipsed creature!'

Alicia couldn't go through the woods now that they were blocked by blades, so she took the line leading towards the pasture, well away from the party. And then ran straight back, because the Bowland Pack were out there and closing in.

Magick was spread all around the Grange and its gardens, and the whole intricate web of Lux shuddered and the air rumbled. All eyes turned to the house as a great column of Lux burst into a rainbow. It was Alicia's only chance, and she took it, engaging the worm and flying up to the higher realm, where the evening light still shone on the well, on the new hive of the Morrigan's bees and on the old sídhe.

Sure enough, the column of rainbow magick was even brighter here, and the eldritch figure from within had come to see what was happening. Alicia drew breath and charged him.

He had barely noticed she was there, and only had time to raise his arm before she cannoned into his middle and threw him into the door – which didn't move. He'd shut it behind him.

As their flesh touched, Alicia smelled sulphur and … *apples?* His right arm was pinned to the floor, but his left hand grasped at her throat and squeezed. As he squeezed, she could feel copper leaching from his fingers and burning her skin. Her eyes bulged, her sight dimming until all she could see was the dragon tattoo. Her nose was filled with sulphur. She reached her left hand towards the wood and saw the last of Nimue's Ink on her skin, the one she'd never quite understood. Funny how things become clear as life leaves you: the dragon in the tattoo matched part of the Ink.

Matched!

She slumped for a fraction of a second, and he moved to finish her off. That was her chance. She brought up her knee until it connected with his groin. He spasmed and slackened his grip, which was enough for her to free her right arm and roll to her left. She placed her right palm on his tattoo and her left hand on the door. As her sight faded to stars, she brought up the Nymph's Ink and made the sign of the High Dragon. Done.

the man screamed as the backwash of Fae Ink burned his arm. They rolled apart, the door now ajar. Alicia could only crawl. She butted the door open with her head, desperately breathing air into her lungs. She was in. She drew life into her legs and staggered to her feet, then staggered down the passage into the sídhe.

Chapter Fifty-Two

The way was dark and poorly repaired, and sloped down, down into the hill then circled back towards the well. She could hear the dragon-man pursuing her, and she would have put Fire in her legs but there was nothing left.

They hadn't planned one for Staveley yet, but one thing that every sídhe *had to* have was a back door. There would be one here. Somewhere.

The stories said that the Elvenham Sídhe had only ever been the home of a Count, but there were Counts of all sizes. Had not the Count of Canal Street been more powerful than some Princes? There might even be *two* back doors. She staggered into a receiving room and stopped with her mouth open. *What is this?*

Old furniture lay scattered around, and in the corner was a bed, seemingly well used. A grand table dominated the room, and on the table was a magpie's collection of everyday mortal objects, *including the missing trophy!* Rachael had complained loudly that her second best tennis trophy was missing from the Grange attic when she had tried to show it to Alicia, and had accused her brother of throwing it away. There was food, too, including some of the Beltane offerings. Egg and wings, who *was* this creature?

She had no time to think further, because the Guardian was coming down the entrance passage and Alicia had to decide. There were three doorways, two made by the People and a third, broken through the wall as if by some giant burrowing creature, beyond which lay darkness deeper than the night. Alicia recoiled from it.

One of the sídhe passages would lead to the Count's chambers and contain the back door. The other would lead to the kitchens and no doubt the laundry and privies. There would be no exit that way – this was no grand sídhe.

If the People were like mortals, they would have placed helpful signs over one of the archways, but Fortune was laughing at Alicia today. She stood for seconds, transfixed by the fork-pain of a life choice, desperately searching for clues in the dilapidated fixings.

'Fret not,' came a voice from behind her that made her bum cheeks squeeze together with fear. 'The old Count's escape route is gone. Buried under earth.'

She turned slowly, reaching for her scissors. He was standing in the doorway, as shabby and rumpled as before. Those leggings really were designed for someone much larger in the waist. He was sucking on his arm where Alicia had gripped it, and he spat something out which glinted in the darkness.

Alicia remembered the stories of their lord and reached for the only thing she could find as an offering. She took the packet of curried worms and tossed it lightly towards the table, where it landed on a cracked plate covered with crumbs.

'My gift.'

He looked up and stepped aside from the tunnel. 'That is kind, but I have no fight with a swordmaiden of the Clarkes anyway. You may leave now that you've satisfied your knowing-hunger.' When she didn't move, he frowned. 'You may leave and you *must* leave. That is my word.'

'Forgive my hesitation, sir. My doom lies back that way, and I am in no hurry to meet it.'

'Is it so?'

'It is.'

He looked to the right, towards the gaping black tunnel. '*That* is the only other way but the spring is also guarded, and *that* Guardian has no love for anything but herself and a dead god whom none worship these days. Unless you're the battle-goddess. She may come and go.'

'Can I leave the sídhe that way?'

'Yes. I know not where it goes, but fresh air comes up, so…'

'Thank you, my lord. Forgive me for hurting you.'

The stubbled face inclined in acknowledgement, and Alicia turned away before his patience expired. As she approached the opening, she saw four signs stacked against the wall, all of them saying *Elvenham House*. The magpie guardian had been collecting them for *decades*. Centuries, even. She shuddered to have met such a creature, then crossed into darkness.

She shouldn't be afraid of the dark. She really shouldn't. It was supposed to be her native element. Where she was most at home. But Alicia had never felt more alien and alone than she did walking down the tunnel, a sharp curve quickly obliterating the light from the Guardian's parlour.

None of her eyes worked down here. Not the first and second, nor the Third, nor even the legendary *Fourth* Eye of the People could see through the blackness. For a second she hallucinated that there was a light ahead, and that it was the giant mole who'd dug the tunnel, then she blinked and it was gone, back to the depths of her imagination and memories. All was black again, and all she had as a guide were her trembling fingers trailing against the rock and her shaking feet reaching ahead for every step.

Down. Deeper. Below. Underneath all that was light and life until she was no longer below the earth but *within* it, at a depth which made her ears pop in the silence. Her hand slipped off the wall and one of her new trainers made a high-pitched scrape on the floor as the echoes shifted. She was in a cave, and a big one at that.

She should make light. It was obvious. She had the Ink at her fingertips and her scissors would make an excellent filament. She brought forth Lux, and the darkness drank it all away. Nothing came from her beacon except emptiness, sucking the life from her body.

She gripped the scissors tighter and closed her eyes, stilling her heart for a moment and letting the Lux flow to her ears, growing the tips to the royal shape and expanding the range. She heard the air moving, and then…

Skitter, skitter. Scherloop.

Her eyes flew open to see a light in the distance, a *column* of light, shining green and rising from the floor to a ceiling lost in darkness. If only that were all there was, because off to the right was a pair of rubies, winking and moving down the wall, then dropping like a stone and coming towards her. At head height. Eyes. The eyes of a spider…

'Gertha!' she hissed.

'Welcome, Daughter of the Morrigan,' said the spider. The light from the distant column gave no shape but shadow here, and then the great beast moved in front of the pillar and Alicia whimpered. *So big.*

'You are early. It is rare for one so young to drink from the Water of Life, and so soon after your own Queen.'

Gertha the Spider made no move to attack, when surely she could have devoured Alicia like Scout hoovered up his treats. And what did she mean, *Water of Life?* Could it be…?

'Come,' said the spider. 'The *uisce` bethu* is over there, where you'd expect it to be.' She pronounced *uisce` bethu* with the extra voice of the People, so there was no doubt about what she meant. Gertha was talking about the gift of the Morrigan which turns a Princess into a Queen, and the column of light must be … yes, it was! The column of light was *water.* It was the well, naked and stripped of rock, and at the bottom would be the spring where Faith had drunk only two days ago.

Gertha backed away a few steps – or a few dozen, given that she moved on eight legs not two. Her eyes moved back and forth, pointing out the way. Alicia moved one step, then another, and as she cleared the entrance to the tunnel, she felt the breeze caress her arm, bringing notes of May blossom and sweet bramble flowers. She followed the spider cautiously, and Gertha made no move to speed ahead.

Another few steps and the light showed her Gertha's shape, the eight hairy legs barely keeping the gross abdomen off the floor, and the eyes … there were *six* of them, two giant winking rubies and four more coals of fire, smaller and ranged up the sides of the head.

Alicia took some more steps. Wispy shadows higher in the cavern were faintly white. Gertha rose further up on her legs and her abdomen swayed as she walked away, with two tiny teats twitching at its end.

Teats.

Spinnerets.

Web-makers.

Gertha eats the ones who wander blindly into her lair. She eats the ones who mistake her honey-coated silken web for Amrita. Don't let that be you.

Lady Agnes's words burned into Alicia's skin, exactly where the breeze had touched it moments before, and Lady Agnes's words brought out the upper Guardian's warning: *She has no love for anything but herself and a dead god whom none worship these days. Unless you're the battle-goddess.*

Alicia pivoted and ran, back into the darkness and towards the source of the fresh air. In seconds she was ensnared by thick ropes of silk, and she banged her head into something large and hanging from the web, encased in more strands. *Spider's dinner.*

She tried to slash with her scissors, and they cut one rope, then more, but there were too many.

Skitter, skitter. Scherloop.

Gertha was above her. The spider twisted around and pointed her teats at Alicia, ready to entomb her in silk. Alicia wanted to reach inside herself, into the darkness, but the darkness around her was bad enough without bringing out *more*, and without that, she had nothing. None of Lady Agnes's words would help her now ... but something else might.

Alicia popped her right shoulder out of its socket, allowing her to reach into the side pocket of her rucksack, grabbing her Heartstone, Lady Agnes's final gift. She screamed as her shoulder popped back into place, and as the first silk descended from Gertha's abdomen, Alicia brought forth Fire from the hairbrush and swept it aside. She raked the spines of the brush down her arms, and above her she saw Gertha retreating up her own web.

Would she be back? How long did Alicia have to get out before the spider worked some magick? The slimy silk clung to her hair, her clothes and parts of her face. Even without Gertha's presence, the silk was contracting slowly, squeezing her as if it had a mind of its own. The deepest latrines wouldn't leave her feeling this icky.

Alicia started with her hair, fine-tuning the Ink in her Heartstone to burn through the silk without setting fire to herself. Satisfied, she picked up speed. *Take that, Gertha*, she thought as the worms of web flashed and turned to smoke.

Her arms, chest, head were all cleared of silk, and with the last of her strength, Alicia ignited the Ink which Cathy had sewn into her leggings, and the last restraints melted away, fizzling but not burning now. She staggered forwards, and the light from the well went out. She dropped to her hands and knees and crawled into the opening, rock biting into her palms and her Heartstone and scissors clutched in her jaws. She didn't look back. If Gertha pounced, then so be it. Further. Onwards.

Every time she reached a hand forwards, she was a little further away from the spider, and not just in distance. The tunnel was moving through the Void, taking her in a new direction. She *thought* it was down, back to the lowest realm, and she hoped the pinching rock around her wasn't heading to a dead end. Or worse, a spider's birthing chamber. The gods would most surely laugh at that.

Fresh air! Ahead! She kept crawling and felt the passage narrow around her as the wind grew stronger. Had she stood up, she'd have been knocked out, for the tunnel was tiny, barely big enough to crawl through. There was only one thing keeping her going now: *no silk in the tunnel.* Not surprising, really. Even with no bones to bend, Gertha would never have fitted in here.

The tunnel began to rise, faster but not as steeply as the passage down from the sídhe, then it broadened, and Alicia's eyes began to work again. Gouged rock walls, packed dirt floor. The most beautiful thing she'd ever seen. She stood up and dusted herself down, removing the last of the silk and replacing her Heartstone into her rucksack (without popping her shoulder this time).

She couldn't help it now: she had to glance back and check. There were no ruby eyes lurking in the darkness. After re-tying her ponytail, Alicia held her chin up and walked towards the starlight. She reached the liminal margin and stepped out of the higher realm and back to the mortal world.

And the first thing she heard was the howling.

Chapter Fifty-Three

The second thing Alicia heard – and felt – was her phone vibrating in her pocket. She whipped her head around her to see where she was, and the answer was clearly visible to her left – about three hundred yards from the Grange, and halfway up the scarp. She could smell Wolf on the wind, but the howls she'd heard were a gathering cry, not the howl of *scent found*, and there were none of Bowland's Hunters lurking in the brambles. As for spiders…

Safe for a moment, she checked her phone, both to see the message and confirm the time. The numerals jumped forward and agreed with what the stars had already told her: it was around one in the morning, the day after the three ring circus had played to packed audiences and much acclaim.

The Grange was only dimly visible, lights still shining but no music playing. She unlocked the phone and read several messages, ignoring those from mortals (no doubt wondering where she was) and focusing on the ones from Thistle. *We will seek you after midnight. Our Lady says you will not emerge before then.*

This was followed at half past midnight by: *Beware! The woods are full of Wolves. We are coming, Sister.*

Alicia thumbed a quick *I am gone*, then prepared to strike out on her own, through the woods and into the Cotswold uplands. There were railways stations to the north and west of Clerkswell, and that's where the net would be tightest. If she could put a few miles of open countryside between herself and the Grange, the circle would be too big for all but an army, and Princess Blowhard did not have one of those. Yet.

She dug down into her rucksack and found some food. She had barely eaten all day, and her struggles with the upper and lower Guardians had drained her. *What are the chances?* she thought. *What are the chances that our stories of Gertha were all about the Elven sídhe? How had that happened?*

As for the upper Guardian, the copper leaching out his hands screamed *human*, even if there was no mortal scent to him. And he was no Spectre if the crumbs and half-eaten dainties were any guide. Spectres *can* become fully corporeal. Once. And then they have to disperse before the cock crows. Or so the stories told her.

Alicia savoured the Indian snacks first, then bit down on an energy bar and was enjoying the sugar rush when the air was filled again with howling, and this time the words spoke of a quarry. And then her blood froze as new notes joined the music of the Wolves. *Maria. In distress. And Lottie!*

She shoved the rest of the bar in her mouth and shrugged on her backpack. The Bowland Wolves would finish the job and come looking for *her*. She set off through the trees towards the heights and ran straight up against a thicket of brambles, the nightmare of all woods. She was going to track left, but spun across the gap between two oaks was a spider's web, and in the centre were two glowing eyes.

Alicia's breath stopped in her throat. *How can this be? Gertha has no mortal children!* And then the nightmare spoke to her with the voice of her lady.

'I wanted you to be loved, and if I could not do it, then someone else should have the charge. You were my first source of pride, Mélisande.'

If Faith could endure decades of shame for a mortal child and was willing to risk her secrets in exchange for Alicia's life, did she not owe the same to the Wolves? No, she did not. They were Faith's to keep. And her lord's.

The spider spoke again, this time with the deep voice of Conrad Clarke. 'The King's Peace is for *all* creatures.'

Alicia was not an agent of the King's Peace – or anyone's peace except her own. What made her turn around and run as fast as she could towards the howling was the immortal voice of Lady Agnes. *'Where's the profit in that, Little One?'*

Alicia did not want to live in Kent. She wanted to live in Staveley, and if she left the Wolves to die, that would be denied to her forever.

She was late. Of course she was late. Alicia had been late for everything her whole miserable life. Lady Agnes had once told her she'd been so late to hatch that she'd nearly been eaten by a lynx. Or something like that. If she'd run towards the howling when she'd heard it, she might have been in time. Too late. And now her doom was coming full circle.

Four of the Birkfell Wolves were in a fighting ring, moving and darting widdershins to protect one who had fallen. The ring was made of Maria, who was in front of tiny little Lottie, and then Alex, Cara, and back to Maria in a constant round of growling, nipping forwards and darting back from the jaws of the Bowland Pack, who outnumbered them two to one and were all fully grown. And that was not the worst: beyond them, in the trees, two Huntsmen lurked, spears in hand and bows at their feet.

Alicia went as quiet and still as she could, putting every lesson she'd learned with the Birkfell Wolves to good use – no sight, no sound and *no smell*. It was draining her, but she could do it. She slipped from tree to tree, close enough to see who had fallen, and there, with a Wolf's kilt round her waist and two arrows in her back was Thistle. *My Sister, what have you done?*

Alicia was close enough now to see magick, and what she saw astounded her. Not only was the fighting ring a defensive manoeuvre, it was allowing Maria to use her magick to weave an Ancile. No wonder the Huntsmen had lowered their bows. And the Birkfell Wolves would not be protecting a corpse: Thistle must still live. For now.

The leading Huntsman called off the Bowland Wolves and called on her companion. You do not send Wolves in for the kill. That is the People's job. The Wolves would follow and pick off the remainders. Thistle and Gertha only knew how many of her Pack would die in a few moments, and Alicia could do nothing to stop it. Or would do nothing. Or was afraid of doing something, because in this wood, in this place and on this night there was only one thing left to do.

She stilled herself and dug for Memory. Lady Agnes was telling them one of their first stories, and when she spoke, her voice swelled with pride. *You are the People. You are born of the forest and of the Night. The wilderness is your home and the darkness your palace. Never, ever be afraid of the dark, because you* are *the dark.*

And mortal words, too, in the voice of the islands. 'You've got this, hen. You've got this.'

Alicia was too scared. She had fought against it since her Matching, had resisted it when face to face with the invaders in the glade, and she had turned away from it when trapped in Gertha's web. The fear could not be suppressed.

Never, ever be afraid of the dark, because you are *the dark.*

Lady Agnes's story finally made sense. *Ysgithyrwn, the wildest wild boar in the land.* The boar was but another name for fear, and though the fear could not be suppressed, it could be jumped over.

She shifted her being and brought forth the Lenses and the Construction, becoming the Night Warrior, the one the mortals called the *Nachtkrieger.* She moved past one more tree, then out of the darkness she leapt on the Huntsman.

The Huntsman's spear tangled in a bush and was lost. The two of them hit the forest floor, and Alicia scrabbled with her talons to tear open her opponent's armour, getting a punch in the face for her trouble. That didn't bother her, and she found an edge. Leather sliced open and the Huntsman's breasts broke free. Her enemy twisted, reaching for a dagger. The trees echoed with howling on all sides, and Alicia was rocked by a Wolf landing on her back.

She had not drawn her scissors because they were no use. Joining with the Night gave her only two weapons, claws and teeth. But what teeth! The Wolf tried to bite her but all they got was fleece. The Huntsman had her dagger drawn, and Alicia saw it glitter. She also saw the pale skin in front of her and plunged her enlarged jaw down, through flesh, through bone, and into the beating heart of her enemy. *Beware the Night Warrior, for she must feed.* And feed she did, until all of the Huntsman's life was flowing through her veins and she could feed no more.

She withdrew her jaw and her talons and rolled off her victim to see who was going to kill her. There had been quite a queue today.

Wolves will die to save their Protectors, but they will not avenge them. When the life had flowed into Alicia's jaws, the alien Wolves had withdrawn to stop the Birkfell Pack attacking the other Huntsman, and the Birkfell Pack were busy stopping him approaching Alicia, because vengeance was very much on *his* mind.'

Alicia jumped up, full of fight but empty of ideas. She did not fancy her scissors against a spear and she could not use Night to cloak her again. Should she call for help? What if she drew more of Blowhard's People and none of her own? She should run. Message Faith and draw the Pack away from Thistle. Alex could keep the other Huntsman at bay ... wait. Where *was* Alex? Lottie was standing watch by Thistle, but only Maria and Cara were with the Huntsman, and they were not enough to stop him. Alicia backed herself into a tree and waited. She would have one chance...

The Huntsman moved left to get a clear run at her, and Alicia dodged behind the tree. He advanced another pace and hefted his spear, choosing whether to cast it or close and stab.

Suddenly, the Huntsman dropped his spear and staggered away, clutching the arrow in his side. Alicia leapt forwards, grabbed the dagger from his fallen comrade and dropped to her knees by his head, blade raised, then she opened her arms wide in the sign of the cross and lowered them. *I am not here to kill*, her body said to the Wolves, and they responded, circling their Protector but not attacking.

'Leesha? Are you okay?' said Alex, padding towards her on bare feet, his naked form shining like his red hair and the Huntsman's bow in his hand.

'I am whole. What about Thistle?'

'Dying, but not dead. With help she'll live.'

Maria, sharpest eared of all the Wolves, howled a warning, and Alicia stood, placing her foot on the fallen Huntsman's side to keep him quiet. A shout. The crashing of clumsy feet through the woods. And here came ... Countess Portarra. Prince Corrib to be. *Egg and wings! Does the whole wedding party want to join the queue to kill me?*

'I will run like the wind,' she told the Countess. 'You will not catch me.' She gripped the dagger and prepared to put Fire in her legs.

'No! Stop!' cried a voice.

Rachael? What? A trap! It must be!

The clumsy crashing through the woods stopped, and Rachael rushed to the open space, her wedding finery exchanged for something more practical. She was joined by Eseld Mowbray.

Rachael raised her hands. 'Quick. I've done a deal. Submit to Finn and you will be safe.'

Alicia looked down at the grey-faced Huntsman. 'Him?'

'No, you great eejit,' said Portarra. 'Me. I'm taking the name Fionn, but yer pal here says that makes me sound like a girl, and I won't be one of them for long, so Finn it is.'

Alicia's jaw dropped open. *Submit to her?* It was too good to be true.

'Hurry up,' said Eseld. 'Not only is Tara on her way, I'm bursting for a pee. I've been out in the bliddy woods for an hour now, looking for you.'

Alicia looked from mortal to Wolf to Countess. She dropped the dagger and walked over to the squat warrior who did indeed smell rather strongly of manhood. She slipped off her rucksack and took out her Heartstone. She cradled the brush in her hands and took a knee.

'If it pleases my lady, may I join your household? To serve and support, to protect and to be protected, to add your name to my name, and my name to your People's. I do so willingly and freely and beg to become your handmaiden.'

'Yes. I will receive you. Willingly and freely. Got little use for a handmaiden, but I'll be needing a valet soon enough.' The squat and powerful Countess wasn't much taller than the kneeling Alicia, and peered at the side of her head, where her ears were still in hunting form. 'What's that earring?'

Egg and wings! She'd forgotten. Alicia almost ripped out the earring and showed it to Portarra. 'It came from the future.'

'Future? That's come from the past, that has. A five-leaf clover, eh? I'll take that as an offering.'

Alicia surrendered the tiny piece of silver gladly, and the Countess studied it, then shoved it in her pocket. 'Give me your chosen name.'

For the second time today, Alicia pulled back her fleece and raised her Name. 'May I ask a question?'

'So long as it's quick.'

'Are any names reserved in your People?'

'What? No. Unless you've a mind to be Oonagh. That wouldn't go down well.'

'Then I would become Alice.'

'Suit yourself.'

Portarra Inked her new Name, and signed it with a flourish just as Princess Birkdale broke through the trees and arrived at the scene. She took one look at Alice and said, 'Mine, I think.'

'Look to your Huntsman,' said Portarra. 'You've no other business here. Unless you've come to steal my valet, of course, and my blade would have something to say about that.'

There were more arrivals. Faith appeared with Robbie, and then Birkdale's Guard (who was minus his left hand).

Birkdale swept back her hair and let her eyes roam around the figures, those fallen and those still standing. 'That wasn't quite the ending I expected, but good sport nonetheless.' She turned to her Guard. 'Get the Wolves to take Rankin back to the transporter and you can all be on your way. I'll go and say goodbye to whoever's still awake at the party.' Her final words were for Portarra. 'If you are wise, this will be your only souvenir of Albion.'

'I think not, Princess. I've my eye on a couple more yet. Go well and in peace.'

'I go in peace. From you all.'

It was the bare minimum: Birkdale was leaving with no open quarrel but no promise that the dawn would not bring a new one. As Conrad Clarke would say, *It'll do for now.*

Chapter Fifty-Four

The Staveley People rushed to Thistle's side – and so did Alice, until she remembered that she was no longer of them, and she turned back to her lady. 'Your wishes?'

'I wish for one thing only, and that's another drink while it's still fresh. See to your Sister, Alice, and make your farewells. Your time is your own until dawn.'

'Thank you. You are merciful, my lady.'

'Don't call me that! It's *sir*. Understand?'

'Yes, sir. Until dawn. Are we off to Ireland then?'

'Oh no. Somewhere exotic and strange. Essex, it's called. You might want to get yourself a nurse's uniform for when we get there. Until the dawn.'

Portarra disappeared into the dark. Birkdale had already gone, and her People were swift in departure, too. Alice went to Thistle, and she arrived with Cathy, who promptly ordered everyone to give her some room. Alice stepped back and bumped into Maria, now in human form and with her arm protectively around Lottie.

'Here,' said Alice. 'I would not have you sneaking back to the Grange.' She pulled some clothes from her rucksack and handed them over. 'You should go back as heroes. Thistle will sing of you, and I will, too, if I am given a voice.'

Maria pressed her scarred and battered body to Alice. 'You go with our love. I hope I live to see your return.'

'Is it safe?' asked Eseld Mowbray.

'It is,' said Faith. 'Thank you. I am glad we finally met. I have heard *so* many bad things about you, Eseld, that I had become very curious.'

'Right.' The mortal shifted from foot to foot. 'Is it true that Tammy's moved in with you?'

'For now. It is not something I am broadcasting, though.'

A huge grin split Eseld's face. 'Good luck with that. You staying, Raitch?'

'Yeah.'

Eseld also vanished, and Faith lifted Alice's arm to inspect her Name. 'It's true,' said the Princess. 'They really do write things differently. Not seen much Ink from over the water.' She let go and smiled. 'For someone so self-effacing, *Alice*, you do have a habit of becoming the centre of attention.'

'I ... my lady, may I ask how you fared with Gertha?'

Faith shook her head. 'And you also talk in riddles. What the *feck* are you on about? Better get used to that word – I've a feeling you'll be hearing it a lot.'

'When you drank the Water of Life, was it not guarded by Gertha?'

Faith dodged round behind Alice with a laugh. 'Just checking to see if there's a hole in your head. Nope. And there was no giant spider at the spring. Or if there was, it gave the Morrigan a wide berth. Look, Thistle's awake.'

'And I hurt!'

'Shush,' said Cathy. 'One second … let me. There. You can sit up now.'

Thistle did just that, and she looked at the arrows Cathy had pulled from her back. 'Tha's cheating!' She threw them away in disgust. 'I *really* hurt, you ken?'

Cathy stood up and clipped Thistle round the head. 'And I'm out of Amrita. Just don't move for a couple of hours, that's all. I'm sure Alici— *Alice* will keep you company, and I'll have something for you in the morning. You have got *so* much washing up to do.'

'Of course I'll stay,' said Alice. 'And I will carry you back. It will be my last service. For now.'

Faith and Cathy left them, and Rachael Clarke emerged from behind a tree, pulling up her leggings. 'That's better,' she said. 'Whoa! Alice!'

The new valet had run and thrown herself on the Dragonslayer's sister. She kissed her on the lips and sent some love tingling through Rachael. 'Thank you, thank you, thank you. What did you do?'

'I asked around. Turns out that Princess Birkdale isn't as popular as she likes to think she is, and Damini is not popular *at all*. I made a few trades and Finn jumped at the chance to take you into his service. Her service. Whatever. Finn's off to grow a pair, and you'll be in his service until he returns to Galway, and *all* the secrets of the salon will stay secret. Win-win.'

Rachael was wearing a shell jacket with pockets, and from one of them she pulled her phone, then reached out to Alice's ear. 'And there's more.'

'How! That's awesome!'

Rachael Bloody Clarke suddenly had two fat joints in her hand. 'Are you allowed these, Thistle?'

'Just try and stop me.'

The three musketeers sat down and lit up. 'Tell us all about it,' said Rachael. 'What happened.'

Alice shook her head mournfully. 'I wish I could.'

'She's under a Geas,' said Thistle, drawing the smoke deeply. 'She cannae say a word.'

Rachael snorted. 'Bloody typical.' She laughed. 'Can you *write* it?'

'Not in the mortal tongue.'

'Then write it in Fae and get Portarra to translate it! It'll stop her climbing the walls when she's convalescing. And tell him no nookie until he's finished.'

'Nookie?'

'When the future Prince has all his equipment, he's going to want to try it out, isn't he? I wonder if there's always been a uniform fetish, or whether that's come with the testosterone?'

Alice coughed and tried not to think about that. 'Tell me of the wedding.

What did I miss?'

'A lot of dancing and a lot of drinking. Except by me. When Faith said you wouldn't reappear for hours, I nearly said *sod it.*' She nudged Alice. 'Nah. Just joking. There was a hell of a row between the princesses, though. Something to do with Robbie and Tara's bodyguard. Tara demanded access to Cathy for some reason.'

'Robbie cut off the Guard's hand,' said Thistle. 'He was awesome! Quicksilver fast, we call it. Birkdale wanted healing for her Guard, and Faith wouldn't agree until there was some sort of deal about some mortal Earl I've never heard of. And Birkdale's in the market for a new Guard. Obviously.'

Sofía/Myfanwy's special weed was special indeed. Rachael was halfway gone already. 'And I can tell you this,' she declared. 'There was the mother and father of fights over Mina's bouquet. Carnage. Guess who the next one to be married is?'

'Eseld,' said Alice.

'Nope. Erin caught it in the end.'

'Aye, but she'll no be marrying Barney until she's forgiven him,' chuckled Thistle.

'For what?'

'I got ma revenge for being forced to apologise.'

'Sister! What did you do?'

'I got Robbie to one side and said that his pudding-faced mortal was having second thoughts and she'd been talking to Erin, and Erin had been warning her off. That put Robbie in a spin, and when he ran over to find out, I went to Barney Rubble and dragged him to the dancefloor. He was well gone by then and it was easy to get him to hang on to me for support, so then I made sure that Rachael got a video of me nibbling his ear. Could come in very handy, that.'

While Alice's eyes were still bulging out on stalks, Rachael made things even worse. 'Yeah, but no one blames Thistle because she put on a Glamour of *you.*' When she spoke the word *you*, she gently poked Alice in the shoulder. 'Now there's a video of you nibbling at the Rubble. Naughty girl!' She gave Alice a squeeze. 'Don't worry, I'll put them right tomorrow.'

Alice shook her head in despair. 'I'm going to miss you, Sister.'

Thistle passed her the joint and kissed her fondly. 'Me too.' When their fingers touched, Thistle's eyes widened. 'Turn around!'

Alice twisted her spine and felt Thistle's fingers run down her back.

'They've gone,' said Thistle. 'Yer wing nubs have finally been absorbed. Must have been when you became one with the Night.'

Alice stood up and looked towards the Grange. She drew deeply on the smoke and held it in as long as she could. When she breathed out, she spoke to the sky, thanking everyone who'd help her escape her doom.

Rachael stood up too and put her arm around Alice. 'You forgot the most important person. Yourself. *You* did that, Alice. You ran, you hid, you fought and you escaped whatever monsters are allegedly lurking in Elvenham Grange. My brother needs to hear about that, by the way, and sooner rather than later.'

'I wonder where he and Rani Mina have gone, and whether they're happy?' said Alice.

'They're in Heaven. One way or another,' replied Rachael.

'Oh no. The Allfather knows the way to Heaven, and Conrad wouldn't get lost if he travelled on his own. I'm sure they've gone somewhere much nicer.'

'Nicer than Heaven?'

'I've heard mixed reports.'

'Okaaay. We'll just say they're in a paradise of their own making, and I hope it lasts for them. I really do.'

'Me too,' said Alice. 'Me too.'

Part Nine — Honeymoon in Valhalla

Chapter Fifty-Five

I let go of the troth ring and drew Mina close to me. She was shaking with terror. *I* was shaking with terror. It was also bloody freezing, even though we were indoors. That's it. I'll blame the shakes on the cold.

Instead of being a forearm's diameter and attached to the front door of Elvenham Grange, the troth ring was now a good yard across and fixed to a pillar of natural stone covered with intricate carvings and sitting at the centre of a substantial roundhouse. We huddled close to the stone and looked about us.

Odin had stepped back and was now about halfway to the doorless opening to the outside world. Was that *snow* out there? It was. Benches and trestles were stacked next to the wall, and a fourth person (of some sort) was lurking in the shadows by a low chest which could easily be a coffin. Not that I was worried or anything…

Odin looked into the shadows and beckoned to the lurking figure. The shadow turned into a woman who came over and lifted her heavy woollen dress in a curtsy to Mina. I was expecting a goddess of striking beauty when she looked up – and yes, she would stand out in a crowd for being tall and for the elaborate braids in her brown hair. The lines around her eyes spoke of a life lived, and the eyes themselves showed hesitation, as if a lifelong habit of fear was hard to shake. Her smile tried to be as reassuring as possible.

'I am Vya.' Her voice was warm and strong and had a slightly nasal twang, more Slavic than Germanic. 'Welcome to Asgard. You could say that I am a Valkyrie, and that will do.' She glanced at the Allfather with a look that acknowledged his power while asserting her independence. 'You could also say that I am Queen of Asgard, Odin's handmaiden, and every other female gender-specific title you can think of, because there's only me.'

Mina was still clinging to my waist and trying to burrow into my kurta, and she let me do the bowing. I cleared my throat ready to speak, but Vya came closer and said, 'You look frozen. Both of you. I have something warm over here. Come, Mina.'

She held out her hand, and Mina reluctantly detached herself from me and scuttled towards the chest/coffin, taking the long route around the troth pillar to avoid Odin.

I stepped towards him and bowed. I couldn't think of anything to say at first, so I waffled to buy myself some time. I pointed to the troth pillar and said, 'Has that always been located above Elvenham, or is it new?'

He nodded, showing something of approval in his shadowy face. 'A good question. No is the answer to both questions. Asgard is so elevated that my small home covers most of Northern Europe and part of North America. You could say that we are located above everywhere and nowhere. This ground where we stand is Bifrost, and before you ask, the Rainbow Bridge was always a metaphor. Bifrost is the easiest place from which to access Mittelgard, and vice versa.' He looked over my shoulder. 'It suits you.'

Mina was trying to fasten a leather belt around a white dress which was too long, and also trying to manage a fur coat which could probably eat her alive. Vya walked behind her, carrying more fur garments draped over her arms. She came to me and offered them up. 'Lord Guardian. Allow me.'

She stepped behind me and fitted a thick leather-lined fur cloak over my shoulders, then came round to fasten a chain at the front. She showed me how to draw the cloak around me for total body protection, and where the arm-holes were. I know little of fur, but I know wolf pelt when I see it. And when I feel it: the fine hairs were glossy. And warm.

Happy that she wasn't going to trip over or freeze to death, Mina came to my side and bowed to the Allfather. 'Vya tells me that these are gifts, my lord. You are very generous.' She paused. 'I doubt that I will get to wear them often, though.'

'A shame,' said the Allfather. 'Shall we go?'

Mina stood her ground. 'I am more honoured to be here than I have ever been in my life. You are the king of hosts, so you know that my absence means I am neglecting my guests. I hope that I can soon return and look after them.'

The Allfather's one eye fixed itself on Mina. When he does that to me, I have great difficulty in *not* running in the opposite direction and screaming; Mina looked like she was going to faint.

'It is not often that the Elderkind apologise, Lady Desai. I'm afraid that your guests have already gone to bed.' He cocked an ear to an unheard noise. 'I am told that they enjoyed themselves greatly.'

She looked at me. 'Really? He has dragged me from my wedding and now it is over?'

'I'm not surprised. Sorry, love.'

She sighed. 'Ah well.'

'Vya? Will you ready the sleigh?'

The Allfather's right-hand woman strode past us, saying, 'You can add chauffeuse and kennelmaid to your list.'

'Kennelmaid?' said Mina. 'Not … stable lass?'

'We will walk the first part,' said the Allfather. 'There is a path.'

We followed him outside, and I winced as raw sunlight bounced off snowdrifts and burned my eyes. All three of them. Not surprising that there should be so much Lux here, given how badly space had been warped. Mina felt it too, in her own way, and we instinctively slowed until we could see properly.

A stone-slabbed path led through snow piled deep on either side. The wind whipped some loose powder off the tops and swirled it in little eddies. After a short slope, the ground levelled and became less ... less hardcore polar. More Arctic. Trees and boulders were scattered across the ground, and grass was poking through in places.

'Why are those trees glowing, and why are they in leaf?' asked Mina. 'Even I know that they should be bare out here.'

'An Elven wood,' said Odin. 'Or what's left of it.' We stopped next to an area cleared of snow and covered in hard-packed fine black sand. There was a single-storey wooden building off to the left, and Vya was moving around outside it. The Allfather turned away from her and looked towards a low mound. 'When the Dwarf put me back together, he confined me below his Hall for his own safety and the world's. And mine, I suppose. When the madness had receded and my strength had grown, he helped me cross the Bifrost Bridge to Asgard, and I arrived at the troth ring as you did just now. It was once very different.'

He glanced down the way we'd come, and we instinctively followed his eye. From here, I could just make out the conical roof of wooden shingles protecting the Bifrost Troth Ring.

'That shelter is a poor thing,' said the King of Asgard. 'There was once an assembly hall around the Bifrost stone. The hall, the stone, the Rainbow Bridge: all together, they were a miracle of trans-planar engineering, as they would call it in Salomon's House. I found it in ruins. Blasted apart. In the snow, I saw the bones of my bondsmen. The ones who were too old or too frail to take the field at Vigriðr. Or who had been ordered to stay behind for a special reason. Come.'

He led us over the clearing to the low mound. His voice never rose in volume, but even with my dodgy hearing, every word was crystal-clear when he told his story. *Who?* I asked myself. After Ragnarok, *who* was left alive to come here, and what did they want?

I soon found my answer.

The low mound was clear of snow, and a smorgasbord of wild flowers bloomed from and within a carpet of emerald grass. 'Here lie the women and children of Asgard,' said Odin. 'My wife and my daughters and my granddaughters lie here, as do all the wives, mothers and little children of the Aesir who stayed behind. All the nurses, maids and elder-women. I found nothing left but their bones and rags. I carried them here and built their barrow with my bare hands.'

'All the women?' said Mina.

'The ones who stayed behind. The ones who died on the battlefield were ploughed into the ground. Those who could not fight or who stayed to keep the hearth warm are all buried here. And there were three more: Urðr, Verðandi, and Skuld. Drowned in their well.'

'The Norns,' said Mina to herself. 'Can the world turn without Wyrd?'

Odin made a grimace. 'It seems it can. Quite happily.' He glanced behind us, then back at the mound. 'There is no monument. Yet. We slew our enemies on Vigriðr. So who came here to do this?' He looked straight at me. 'At first I thought it was servants of the cross. Angels, you call them. That was until I found my wife's skull on the throne, upturned and used as a drinking cup. The Angels are capable of many things you would find terrifying, but they do not dishonour their victims. One day, I will find out who did this, and I will kill them and build the monument to the women and children of Asgard out of their killers' bones.' He looked back. 'Vya is getting impatient.'

'Oh my,' said Mina. 'We're going in *that*?'

'Of course we are,' I said cheerfully. 'Who needs a horse and cart when you can have a double-decker sleigh pulled by wolves?'

'They look hungry. Very hungry, Conrad.'

'I think a hungry wolf running amok is the least of our worries.'

'Not helping, husband.'

I took her hand and led her towards the black sleigh. As we got closer, I could make out gold tracery in the wood. Battle scenes and runic inscriptions flowed in Alchemical animation. Vya, now wearing leather leggings and a blood-red tunic, walked along the rope of wolves. Eight couple of grey and white canines were harnessed and ready to work. Or to hunt.

Odin held out his hand to help Mina into the back of the sleigh, and I levered myself in beside her, putting my arm around her shoulder and kissing the vermilion stripe in her hair.

'Is our wedding day over?' she asked.

'Not from where I'm sitting.'

'Good.'

The Elderkind (if Vya was of that species) got in below us, with Vya sitting and the Allfather gripping the rail. He shouted something incomprehensible and the wolves jerked the gangline taut, then we were off.

A snowy track led through the trees, and the wolves pulled hard to drag us up the slope. The running was smooth, the wind whipped our faces and the only thing I could hear was the howl of wolf and alien commands from the driver. We clung to each other as the sled swayed, banked and then crested a rise. As the ground levelled, the wolves picked up speed and shot across the snow with their paws barely touching the ground.

There were woods dotted across the plain glowing with Lux, and various mounds and ruined buildings, usually with only a stone chimney to mark the spot. Now that my senses weren't being overwhelmed by the sheer *otherness* of where we were, I risked changing my focus from my mundane sight to my Third Eye.

It was like being underwater, in Atlantis – or the Viking version of Atlantis – and just as water had replaced the atmosphere of that drowned city, Lux had replaced light as the medium of sight in Asgard. Except for our driver.

Vya the maybe-Valkyrie was a creature of Lux. Or a creature held together by Lux, or just infused with it. That didn't mean she couldn't also qualify as a person, just that she wasn't human in the way that my wife is human. Next to our hostess, our host looked as solid and ordinary in his overalls as Joe Kirkham did when I visited Ribblegate Farm. And that was so wrong.

Odin was hiding almost everything about his nature with a shield of the ordinary, and had been since we'd grasped the new troth ring hanging on our front door. There had been no mistaking him then, not if you've met him before, but now…

Why? Why did he need to shield his nature up here, in his home? And why had he *really* dragged us away from our wedding?

I looked up and looked ahead. On the top of a rise, I could see something black, but we went into a slight dip and it disappeared. The Master of Wolves ordered the team to slow down next to a cleared, flat piece of ground at the foot of the slope.

'Here stood the Hall of Heroes. Vast and great it was.' He gestured over the field and said, 'Hundreds of warriors lived here. Thousands. The Army of the Aesir. The Hall was vast and varied.' He turned his gaze to us. 'Forgive me. Their songs have yet to be fully sung, so I get carried away.'

'And he knows better than to go on to me,' added Vya. 'It's just that we don't get many visitors. Sorry.'

'As I was saying, there were many Valhallas on this ground, all of them stacked over one spot in Asgard and all of them present to the Aesir. All of them were built by the Spirits of the Slain, and all of them housed warriors waiting for war. Jousting and feasting, fighting and jesting were their days and nights. It's one of the reasons time runs so quickly here, compared to Mittelgard.

'When the horn blew and summoned them to battle, they took down their halls, timber by timber, and dragged them to the river where boats they made and oars they shaped. Flags and standards were sewn into sails. The second time that the horn was heard, they boarded their ships and they rowed into the night. Towards Vigriðr. Towards their second deaths.'

He stopped speaking and fixed his eye on somewhere else. The past, maybe, or some blood-soaked day yet to come. Vya put her hand gently on his arm. 'Enough for one day.'

He called to the wolves. They took up the slack and pulled us over the site of Valhalla and round to a hidden path which took a more gentle route to the top of the slope, winding through saplings and small trees. When we crested the rise, there was a ditch, a rampart and a bridge to take us into a compound that was invisible from the plain of Valhalla below.

The wolves slowed down without command and came to a stop next to another ruin with a chimney big enough to grace a blacksmith's forge. Around the blackened stack were the charred stumps of great timbers and chunks of half-demolished stone wall.

'My hall. My home. My hearth,' said the Allfather. It was a flat statement, designed to minimise what he felt while maximising ambiguity. Was it still his home? Would he rebuild it one day? After he'd let that sink in, he jumped off the sleigh and held out his hand for Mina to descend. 'How is your leg?' he said to me.

'I always take help when it's offered,' I said. Part of me didn't want to fall flat on my face in Asgard's white carpet, and part of me wanted to touch him and see what I felt.

When the Allfather's fingers touched mine, all I sensed was the strong, sinewy hand of a working man. Or a warrior. I got down carefully and shook my leg.

Vya came to us and smiled. 'We do have a home, you know. It's round the back, out of sight.' She glanced at the ruin of the High Hall. 'Mina, my lord would speak with your husband alone. You can wait or give me a hand.'

A complex web of smiles was playing over Vya's lips as she spoke. Mina is never one to dodge a social challenge, so she asked, 'Does your lord have any hidden talents? Making the perfect soufflé, perhaps?'

'Him? No. But he does do the washing up.'

'This I can't wait to see. Lead on.'

My new wife and the Allfather's Swiss Army Woman headed north, around the ruin of the High Hall; the Lord of Asgard turned south. 'Come.'

Chapter Fifty-Six

The Allfather led me towards the snowy top of the slope which runs down to the site of Valhalla. As we approached, the black object I'd seen from the sleigh resolved itself into a throne. If there was any doubt about *whose* throne it might be, the twin giant ravens perched on its shoulders were a bit of a giveaway.

Hugin and Munin flew off with a *Caw Caw!* They could probably be heard in Jotunheim. If there *is* a Jotunheim. It wasn't top of my list of questions. Then again, the throne grew exponentially larger the closer we got to it. Unless Odin grew with it, only a giant would be sitting up there today.

Two rough wooden chairs stood in front of the now five-metre-high throne, and the Allfather gestured to one of them. The seat was curved and the timbers mismatched, as if they'd been salvaged from something grander. Something consumed by fire, if the blackened edges were telling a true story.

And talking of stories, I had a feeling I was about to be spun another yarn. So long as it wasn't cut off prematurely, like the thread of the Norns, I was all ears.

I made myself comfortable, and from beneath his chair Odin produced two silver goblets and a leather flask. 'Vya made this,' he began. 'Since she joined me here, she has become something of an expert. What can you smell?'

He poured two generous measures of golden spirit and passed me a goblet. I paused to admire the intricate scrollwork around the rim. 'Arabic?' I suggested.

'Ottoman.'

I sniffed. Earthy. Rich with tropical flowers but not sweet. It smelled more like an imperial kitchen than a sultan's garden, and it reminded me of a short leave I once took in Dubai. 'Essence of Persia?'

'Very good. Vya says she got the recipe from Mesopotamia, but she was vague about who sold it to her. She calls it Uruk High for some reason. Health, long life and family.'

We raised our vessels and the promise of spice in my nose was backed with fire on my tongue. My eyes bulged and sweat started to form on my back. This was not for downing in one.

Odin took out two cigars and passed one to me; the paper band said *Havana.* He stretched out his thumb, just as he had on the first night of my life in magick, but instead of a gentle flame growing from his thumbnail, he palmed a Zippo lighter and clicked the wheel to bring it to life.

We settled back, and I thanked my host, adding, 'Mina will be jealous.'

'I'm sure Vya will have offered her something. They may even be having a tasting session.' He rested his cigar on the arm of his chair. 'I have a story that I'd like to tell to both of you, and I'd like to tell it in the right place, so that can wait until you are rested. For now, I have something personal.'

He picked up his cigar and drew it to life, then studied the end as if he were looking for auspices. 'I suspected it when I first knew about your family and your involvement with the codex. My suspicions grew when you were born, but I was not certain until I felt your Imprint under my fingers, that night by the well.'

'You don't look you're about to give me *bad* news, my lord.'

His smile was no less intimidating without his full presence to back it up. I felt the chair shift backwards as my body instinctively moved away from him.

'That depends on your point of view. Two things are certain, one is less so. One of the certainties is that we have a common ancestor.'

I inhaled the smoke by accident and coughed. I took a drink of Uruk High and coughed some more. Sweat was now soaking my back. 'My lord?'

He ignored my discomfort and dropped a second bombshell. 'The other certainty is that you are descended from Loki. Very, very distantly, but descended from him nonetheless.' His smile grew fangs of Lux. 'You can make of that what you will.'

And what did I make of that? Haven't a clue. Did I believe him? Why would he lie? Unless he was after something, of course.

Who am I kidding? Of course he was after something. Perhaps not today, but certainly one day.

'I hope you won't hold it against me, cousin,' I offered.

'Perhaps not, cousin. I told you that one thing was uncertain, and that is whether you are also descended from me. Loki's parentage was never ascertained, and many say that he was my bastard. He said it himself a few times.'

He went back to his cigar, leaving me digest his news. And after a couple of minutes, all I had was a swirl of possibilities and a tornado of uncertainty. It might mean absolutely nothing. After all, I had opted to clean up Spectre Thomas's mess for my own reasons and not because he was my certified eleven-times-great-grandfather.

There was one thing I needed to clear up straight away, though. I know how big a wolf is, and how long its fur is. I stroked the beautiful cloak I'd been given. 'Is this…?'

'Made from your great-uncle? Yes, it is. I can think of no better gift.'

I could think of several. Never mind. I won't tell Mina if you won't. 'Have you any idea when this happened?'

'I looked into it,' said Odin. 'Hugin and Munin flew far and wide, both in space and time. I cannot say for certain, though I did learn that William the Clerk never got to tell his own story. You know what that means, don't you?'

I grunted. 'It means that he may have murdered the French monk and stolen the codex, but he might have had a good reason for it.'

The Allfather stood. 'You would make a good skald,' he observed. 'Come, let us return.'

I stubbed my cigar out in the snow and drained the last of the Uruk High, then shook out my leg and limped past the epic and very solid black throne to catch up with the Allfather.

The sun had dipped a little since we arrived, but it was still bright day up here. When I drew level with him, Odin had something else to say.

'A second thing you should know is this: the Morrigan has made an offer to Mina, woman to woman, which your wife accepted.'

'Oh?' I tried to let my reaction imply *How do you know?*

'Because you both drank from the Morrigan's vessel, your daughters will be Mages. It was an offer Mina could not resist, I think.'

'Our daughters?'

'Precisely. I thought that I should even the playing field, so you have a choice: drink from the Ottoman cup in your bedroom, and the next child conceived will be a son. Drink again from the Morrigan's vessel, and you will have daughters. I like to give people choices.'

I didn't realise that I'd stopped in the snow until he disappeared round a ruined wall. He does like to give choices, and one of those choices was whether to tell Mina. She would be all ears when I told her about Loki, but would I tell her about my choice of children?

I hurried up and followed the Allfather's footprints to find his home.

Given the level of illusion, metamorphosis and general play-acting that was going on, I half expected a pair of semi-detached three-bed houses from Guildford, but no: the temporary High Hall of the Aesir was reassuringly traditional, with stone to hip height and timbers above.

Lamps of Lux lit the giant hammer beams of the roof, and a great hearth warmed the open space. Mina and Vya were seated at a long table with a whole selection of bottles in front of them, and they looked like they were halfway to solving the problems of the world. Or of one of the worlds. There are many which need their attention.

Vya rose to greet her lord, and Mina rose to give me a hug. She had discarded the furs and looked both warm and slightly flushed. 'This place is madness itself,' she whispered. 'And I do not know whether Vya is a person, a god, a Spirit or a cyborg. All seem possible.'

I gave her a squeeze and kissed her head.

Odin spoke up. 'You should rest; it has been a long day. But first, a toast.'

Vya brought four drinking horns in a grip that must have taken years of practice. Or magick. She passed them round, and the reassuring smell of well-hopped beer hit my nose.

'To Conrad and Mina, Lord and Lady of Elvenham,' said the Allfather. 'You and all your children will always be welcome in Asgard.' He paused, the horn almost to his lips. 'You will have to find your own way here next time. To you.'

Odin and Vya drank, and we drank in return. Vya whispered something to him, and he nodded. 'Goodnight,' he said. I glanced at Mina, and a ripple of Lux from my left told me that they were gone and that we were alone.

'Come,' said Mina.

She led me away from the hearth, into a darker corner of the High One's Hall and towards a raised platform covered with furs. 'We have a few hours to ourselves,' she told me.

I drained the rest of the beer and bent down, not to kiss the top of her head, but to put my lips lightly on the vermilion streak in her parting, and then down to kiss her lips. After that we did what newly married couples traditionally do on their wedding night.

Chapter Fifty-Seven

Vya coughed gently from the darkness, and Mina stirred next to me.
'Breakfast is ready when you are,' Vya told us.

I gathered my wife in my arms and kissed her fully awake.

'Mmm,' she responded. 'When I was undressing you last night, did I feel your phone in your pocket? Among other things?'

'You did,' I answered.

'Good. Your place is out to the left at the back of the fire. I am going to see how badly these furs have destroyed my make-up.' She lifted herself onto one elbow, and the furs slipped off her golden brown skin. She ran her finger down from my Third Eye to my nose and then to my lips. She lifted her finger, kissed it, then placed it back on my lips. 'Good morning, my lord. I will see you shortly.'

She slipped her naked body out of the bed and grabbed a fur coat, then skipped away into the darkness.

I flopped back onto the bed and sighed, a very happy man. The call of nature finally drove me to get up, grab my new cloak and explore what Mina had described as 'my place'. A half-open door sent me back for shoes, and when I went through the door, I found an earth closet and a steaming hot spring with an empty bowl beside it, a table and a folded towel. One of the benefits of having minimal hair is that you can tip water over yourself without worrying about having to dry your hair. There was no razor, so clearly no one expected me to shave. And that was it. Done. Ready. It's good to be a bloke sometimes.

I took advantage of the spare minutes to investigate a board laid with warm bread and a stone flask of fresh coffee. My kurta had pockets, unlike Mina's costume, and as well as my phone, I'd secreted my fags and another item. I poured myself a coffee and sat on a rock outside, staring across the whiteness and trying to get my head around what had been going on.

Part of me just wanted to luxuriate in an amazing wedding and the night which had followed, but the Allfather hadn't brought us here and laid on this show just because I've done him a few favours and we're distantly related. One day – maybe today, maybe when our children are older – I'll find out why. Like Odin himself, I can wait.

'There you are! Come on, we haven't got long.'

'Says the woman who's spent half an hour re-pinning her hair and raiding Vya's dressing table. Much longer and I'll be eligible to draw my pension when we get back. If we haven't been declared dead and our estates passed to our heirs.'

We stepped into the Hall. 'You are partly right, but only partly,' she declared. 'See?'

She had a new stone on a leather thong around her neck. She lifted it off and suddenly her face was as naked as nature, the tiny scars clear on her jawline. She dropped it back and pouted her painted lips. 'It's a loan. For the pictures.'

And so, after a simple breakfast, Vya showed that she was a dab hand with an iPhone as she took pictures with and without our borrowed robes on. I wonder what the location tags will say…

The Allfather didn't show up until Vya brought the sleigh round. Maybe he's camera shy. He greeted us and then mushed the wolves into action, heading away from the Hall and due north into fresh snow and ice.

Five minutes later, he slowed the team and we came to rest. He turned to Mina. 'Soon we will see the greatest thing in the higher realms. To get the full effect, you should sit far apart until you start to get a headache, Lady Desai. At that point you should close your eyes and hold your husband's hand.'

We looked at each other and shuffled as far apart as the sleigh would allow. I'd noticed that the way ahead appeared to be suffering from clouds and possibly a snowstorm. Not what you want to see, and my guess that it was another blind was right. The wolves strained at their harnesses to pull us up a slope, and I felt them pulling us to a different plane: not a higher one, just an adjacent one. At the summit we both gasped, and for once, Mina didn't exclaim in English.

'*Sri Akshaya Vata*,' is what I think she said.

I just stared, almost open-mouthed, because I was looking at Yggdrasil, the world tree. And it was growing out of the North Pole, and the only word I can come up with to describe it is *mountainous*. That's right. The next time you visit your parish churchyard, look at the yew tree and try to imagine it the size of Ben Nevis. And studded with red flowers that biologically have no place on an evergreen.

'Aagh,' said Mina, clutching her face with her left hand and fumbling for me with her right. I grabbed her and felt Lux flowing out of me faster than when I use my dowsing rod. I drew her close and kissed her forehead, breathing more life into her.

'Okay, it's okay now,' she said. I moved away and she opened her eyes, then squeezed my hand and swore again. 'Is this what you saw? A yew tree the size of Sagarmatha?'

'What did you see?'

'A banyan spreading all the way to Russia.'

Because of the scale, I hadn't realised that we were slowing down until Vya turned around. 'It's time to say goodbye. I'll be driving the sleigh back because it's easier to follow the Wanderer's footsteps from here.'

The sleigh drew to a halt, and Odin, still resplendent in his Wayland Ironworks overalls, jumped down and started speaking to the wolves. Mina signed for me to say goodbye, and I shook our hostess's hand, then left the women to embrace and share some final words.

When she stepped down and took my hand, Mina's face was glowing but free of cosmetics. This was something I should have paid more attention to, but in my defence, I was lost in the moment, staring at the tree whose tips touch the sky and whose roots reach down to feed themselves on Mother Earth's molten core.

'Look down and walk carefully in my footsteps,' said the Allfather. 'You should go last, Conrad.'

Mina hitched up her woollen dress and I watched carefully as her orange-trainered feet followed the Wanderer's workboots. 'Are we doing that thing?' she asked at one point.

'If you mean *are we Transitioning*, then yes, we are. Don't ask me how.'

A shadow fell over us from above, as if a cloud had finally passed over the sun after days of relentless light.

'You can look up,' said Odin.

It was no cloud. It was the regal branches of Yggdrasil, now forming a cathedral canopy above us. We were there.

'You cannot stay here long,' said our guide, 'and there is no longer any creature to offer hospitality, so you will have to make do with a final story.'

Mina bowed. 'I'm sure it will be nourishing.'

The Wanderer grinned. 'It should be. It has plenty of blood in it.' He turned to me. 'On our first night together, you asked me about the creation of the world. I told you that I remembered it, but that was only part of the truth. I *used* to remember it, but that memory faded at Vigriðr. The truth is this.'

He turned to face Yggdrasil. 'My earliest memory is wandering, alone, across the snow, until I found Yggdrasil and the Ladies at its base. They were here before me, and they whispered their wisdom into my ear. I climbed the branches and hung there, as it was said. What was not said was that it took a little longer than most stories tell you, even though they do not lie.' He grinned at me. 'As I'm sure you've guessed, Lord Navigator.'

Mina looked at me. 'Are you going to show off now?'

'The story says that my kinsman hung on the tree for nine days. What it doesn't mention is that the sun only sets and rises once a year at the North Pole.'

'Aah. I'll give you that.'

The first and last of the Aesir turned back to the tree. 'When I fell to the ground, Hugin and Munin flew from the branches and fed at my hand. I cut the haft of Gungnir from a branch and took a root with me to plant in Asgard. It is what allowed me to live after your great-uncle cut me in two.'

'Great-uncle?' said Mina. We had other things on our mind last night, so this was going to be news to her.

'Later, love. And did this root grow where your throne now stands?' I asked.

'It *is* my throne.' He reached into his overalls pocket and fetched out his phone. 'I had intended to gift you a cutting, but the Morrigan beat me to it. Don't tell anyone, but you already have Yggdrasil growing in your garden. Twice, because the Homewood Oak is also from here, as are all trees of magick, all around the world.'

He looked at Mina. 'Even the tree which shades Ganesh was cut from here. If you were to venture to Antarctica, you would find a smaller version. The North Star is not visible from Uluru.'

Mina let that pass, and pushed the envelope by asking, 'If Akshaya Vata was here before you, my lord, then who planted it?'

There is no doubt that the Lord of Gallows is more indulgent with Mina than he is with me. If I'd asked that question, he'd have given me the Elderkind equivalent of a clip round the ear. Instead, he gave Mina the Divine Raised Eyebrow. 'Who is to say that it did not grow of its own accord? Come. We cut Yggdrasil sparingly, but she does occasionally shed branches. Take this.'

He offered a slender wand, and I nearly dropped the bloody thing. It was made of iron, not wood.

He gave one final feral grin and unlocked his phone. 'Where to?'

On a whim, I suggested Tollsby Airfield in Lincolnshire.

'What!' said Mina. 'You can't—'

I never found out whether the *you* was aimed at the Allfather or me, because instead of standing in the shade of Yggdrasil, we were very suddenly in the depths of the British countryside. Probably. It was hard to tell, because it was pitch black and the middle of the night. It was even harder to tell when Mina followed in Vicky's footsteps by kicking my bad leg. And believe me, a wife kicks a lot harder than an honorary niece.

'OW! Aargh. That hurt!'

'That is only the *start*. We've been married less than a day, and you have magicked us to an airfield dressed like extras from *Game of Thrones* just so that you can look at your new toy! Aiee!'

'Not like extras. Like the King and Queen of the North. You look a—Woah!'

I managed to dodge the second kick and backed right away before there was a third. She wagged her finger at me and said, 'The Queen of the North would not travel without make-up. Or her phone.'

I didn't point out that the Queen of the North would have a raven to communicate with, not a phone. I didn't think that would go down well. And talking of phones, I'd had mine switched off in Asgard other than when the pictures were taken. I raised a hand to keep my homicidal bride at bay and powered it on. Mina made no move to attack, but she did fold her arms and give me a death stare.

'You'll be pleased to know that it's five past four on Wednesday the eighteenth of May. We've been gone sixteen days.'

'Really? Really and truly?'

I showed her the lock screen, which promptly went mad as sixteen days' worth of anxious, sarcastic, panicky and loving messages started to ping through.

'What do they say?' she asked, moving forwards and (I'm sure) preparing to make a grab for my phone.

'You can see for yourself in a second. I'm going to hand it over when I've sent one message.'

'Hurry up.'

I selected the *Family*, *Home*, *Irregulars* and *Merlyn's Tower* groups and sent a six-word message to all of them. *We're back. Will be in touch.* Then I handed over the phone.

'What are you going to do?' she asked suspiciously.

'Try to find my helicopter. There's a chance we may be able to fly out of here.'

'Won't it be locked?'

I showed the key triumphantly. 'So long as it's not been hangared and has had a recent service, we'll be good to go.'

The Allfather had landed us on the apron, between the buildings and the runway. I headed for the shadows to see what I could find. Sunrise was an hour away, but the stars and the pre-dawn light had been enough for Mina to aim a kick at me. My night vision allowed me to see more, but even that has its limits. I took out one of my dwindling supply of cigarettes and had a good look.

'Oh, you beauty!' It was a good job Mina wasn't with me, or there'd have been another kick for certain. I got closer and stroked the metal. She'd had the most amazing yellow and black paint job. She was gorgeous. Resprayed just for me? Possibly. Whether it was Eseld or Hannah or a previous owner who'd done it, there was only name for my new aerial chariot: the Wasp. 'Hello, girl. Are you ready to play?'

Helicopter doors don't have locks, so soon I was jogging back to Mina with a fistful of papers and in search of the torch function on my phone. If I could get it off her. Oh. That look on her face said there was serious news.

'The only person awake is Myfanwy. She's only been dozing for a week, and she'll be going into labour any day now. As far as she knows, everyone is fine, except for Tom. He's in York because his grandfather died the other day.'

'Poor Tom. They were incredibly close. He never talked much about his family, but whenever he did, it was usually some story about his childhood on Rooksnest Farm.'

'Lucy said much the same.'

'Can you shine the torch on these? Just for a second.'

She did. The Wasp had been prepared for use only a couple of days ago. Someone must have guessed I'd be coming soon and told them to get her ready. And then we both jumped when my phone played *The Magnificent Seven* theme. What else would you have for Sheriff Morton?

It turned out that Tom wasn't in York, he was up on the moors at a crime scene that sounded very magickal and very serious. You know what happened there, and what happened after, and the only thing you're missing from the story is that Mina proved her love for me by allowing me to stop at RAF HQ in Cranwell to draw two sets of combat uniforms: one in a women's small, and the other in Conrad-Bloody-Clarke size.

The last thing I did before we took off was to help her work the magick that suppressed the henna tattoos.

Chapter Fifty-Eight

Mina's Statement (Continued)

We all gave thanks to our gods when little Seren and Arthur were born so soon after our return and after what happened to Saffron in Yorkshire, when Conrad had left me to help solve the murder of poor Doctor Simon. The little ones filled the Grange with even more joy and love than I had thought possible. And it was a huge distraction to everyone. The reason I martyred myself by getting Conrad to drag me up the escarpment (as I would never call it) on the day that the twins were born is that what I had to say was too serious to be said indoors, where many guests might interrupt us and where the evil in my words would not be welcome. The things we do for love.

At one point, Scout stood above me on the precipitous incline and actually *laughed*. I looked up at him and said, 'You just wait! Your turn is coming.'

Conrad gave me a funny look and dragged me to a drier section, and then I was finally able to show that being ten years younger, several stones lighter and a non-smoker actually makes me quite nimble. Oh, that and the fact that my bone-substitutes are in my jaw, not my leg. When I got to the top, I took great delight in turning round and saying, 'What kept you?'

To which he replied, 'You, mostly. There's a great view just through that gate and round the corner.'

He was right. I could almost see the indentations from where he has repeatedly planted his backside when he comes to sit and think. I parked myself next to him and enjoyed the moment, the first truly peaceful moment since we became wife and husband. It was even quite warm now that we weren't surrounded by dark trees or sinking into damp ground. 'I love you,' I said. He replied with a squeeze and a kiss on the top of my head. I have never felt more at peace in my entire life.

'I wish we could stay here forever,' I told him. Then I thought about it. 'Well, I wish that this moment could last forever. I do not want to spend eternity on a hillside, no matter how far you can see. And don't tell me the names of all those places out there, because I don't care.'

'I know you don't care. I'll wait until our kids are old enough. They'll have no choice but to care if they want to get home for tea.'

'I see you've been reading the Clarke family manual on childcare. Especially the chapters written by your mother. No. Don't say anything. We both know that if *my* mother had written such a thing, it would need to be locked in a vault.'

He shifted slightly, pulling himself away. 'I wasn't going to say anything. I never met her, and all I can say is that if she produced you, she must have done something right.'

I sighed deeply. 'She also produced Arun. Which reminds me: he has made up his mind to take the job in Oxford. If they can confirm the funding.'

'Oh. Good.'

There was another moment of silence until I decided to break it. 'Look, Conrad, when I got home from Beckthorpe Abbey and turned my phone on, there was a very strange message from Eseld. She said that we had to talk urgently. Nothing about where you and I had disappeared to, or what you were up to with Tom – just that she and I had to talk. Now that is a very good way to get me hooked.'

I could see the fight in his face as he struggled not to immediately leap to Eseld's defence. 'And did you?' he finally said. 'Call her?'

'I did. And she was very upset, and feeling very guilty.' I held up a hand. 'When you saw her at the stables on our wedding day, she said that what she told you was true: that none of the human guests were in danger from the home invasion. It's just that she got her information from Faith and Thistle, and they only knew half of the story. And it gets worse: a *lot* happened after the Allfather whisked us away.'

He frowned. 'Tom would have said something. And I got no other messages.'

'That is because I asked everyone not to bother you when you were on an op. And because the only person who knows the whole truth is currently unavailable.'

His eyes narrowed. Just a millimetre. 'Are you saying that *Alicia* knows?'

'Yes. In fact, most of the questions you have can only be answered by her, and she is beyond our reach. She's not even called Alicia any more. She is now Alice.'

'Faith said she'd sent her to Ireland as some sort of finishing school.'

'Hah! I suppose there is some truth in that, and Faith has her own secrets to keep.' I shook my head. 'All I can say is that there was not one but *three* home invasions on our wedding day.'

His eyes narrowed another millimetre. 'Three.'

'Three. One of them happened after we left for Asgard and involved only the Fae. That one finished with Alicia leaving Faith's service and changing her name.'

'Okay.' He grinned. 'Pretend you're giving me an audit report and start at the beginning.'

I gave him a side eye, just so he knew his comment had been noted, then I did what he asked. Lives had been at stake and will be at stake again. 'The three burglars wrapped up in white ribbon were only part of one team.'

'But you know who got caught and wrapped up.'

I raised my eyebrows. 'Don't you?'

'I can guess at two of them: Stephen and Juliet Bloxham.'

'You're right. As for the third…' I shrugged. 'Alice is responsible for many of your questions, but she's not the only one. Rachael also had a hand in some of it.'

He laughed. 'Why am I not surprised?'

'It is going to be a long time before it all comes out. If ever. According to Rachael, Alice is writing it down in Fae because she cannot speak of it, and her words will be translated into English by her new lord and master. Only then will the Fae decide how few of their secrets they can give away while not denying the truth. Faith is adamant that you will learn what Alice knows when it comes to threats made on the Grange.'

'I should bloody well think so.'

'This is what I know so far. The Bloxhams were … suborned? Is that the word? Well, some *human* agent got them involved and wound them up, and she was the one caught in ribbon. And she was in disguise. Her two associates wanted to get into the Fairy House up there.' I pointed to the air above where this accursed well sits.

'Did they succeed?'

'Apparently not. We do know that they used serious magick to disguise themselves.'

'I'll get on to Ez. She's reactivated the Wards which keep out the Fae, but if there are others with an interest … That's serious. I'll also be on to Faith to ask why she didn't mention this after she slew Galwyddel.'

'Probably because she had a hole in her leg and you were about to drag her down to Furness to stand at your side with the Allfather. That may have been slightly higher in her thoughts.'

He grunted. 'And the third invasion?'

I was uneasy about this. I had had a long talk to Rachael about what had happened behind the scenes at the hen party and what had happened after we were abducted *from our own wedding*. Yes, it's going to take a long time before I get over that. I chose my words carefully. 'You know Faith has been taking time outs? For medical reasons?'

He nodded.

'It seems she was a lot sicker than she let on, and she needed help, and she fell out with Tara Doyle aka Princess Birkdale. The business with Alicia at the wedding was a bit of a proxy war, I think.'

'Great. And that explains something else: Tom Morton is determined to buy Tara Doyle out of Lucy's business. I'm going to ask Rachael to help out.'

'Thank Ganesh for that! Would you like me to deal with it?'

'Please.'

I shifted a little to have a better look at him. 'And there's something else you need to know. Another of the Elvenham men is going to become a father.'

Oh, it was priceless. The look on his face went through the biggest one-eighty I've ever seen, from shock and horror to love in the blink of an eye. And the love I saw is the reason I married him.

However, that does not excuse his choice of Lincolnshire as our return destination. He will be paying for that a *long* time. And the whole abduction thing. To put him out of his misery, I pointed to his reprobate, delinquent dog. 'Scout took advantage of the chaos to have his wicked way with Floss, the Bloxhams' dog. There's going to be a litter of Borador puppies in about six weeks.'

'*Borador?*'

'Border collie father and Labrador mother. Hopefully they will take after their mother. Like our children. When the time is right.'

He looked at Scout. 'You sneaky little so-and-so. I think we need to take action to avoid this happening again.'

'Arff!'

Conrad shook his head. 'Anything else you want to tell me?'

'Those are the headlines.' I paused, then lightened my voice. 'Now, tell me about what the Allfather said when you went for your manly bonding time. Is he a man, by the way?'

'Oh yes. Very much so. And don't change the subject. I want to know the truth about the stripper. Surely you're not going to blame Alicia for *that?*'

I tried to summon some dignity. 'I have nothing whatsoever to say on that subject.'

'Oh no? There's plenty who do. Why don't you give me your side of the story?'

I zipped my lips, paused then said, 'Odin. Spill.'

He took a deep breath. 'The Allfather is either my great-uncle or my great-grandfather. The exact relationship depends on whether Loki is his son or his nephew.'

I am used to sorting out relationships. It comes from belonging to an Indian family. I have also read some of the stories of the Aesir. 'Loki! You are descended from *Loki!* This explains much, Conrad Lokisson.'

It was his turn to give me a dark look. 'Very, very, very, very, very, *very* distantly descended. Way before William the Clerk.'

'Oh. Right. Was that all he said?'

'Isn't that enough?'

'I suppose.'

'What about Lucy's car in the Manchester Ship Canal?'

'Alice.'

'No. Seriously?'

'Totally.'

He lit a cigarette and thought for a moment. Given how much he'd just had to absorb, and how much he had on his hands as a result, his next question floored me completely.

'Do you think Dad would like a Borador puppy?'

Juliet couldn't avoid it any longer. She had to go home. There is only so long that you can keep two children away from their Playstations, even with McDonalds as a bribe. She told them they could have an hour's gaming and went to have a bath.

She set the taps running in the en-suite bathroom and went to start picking up discarded clothes around the bedroom. She'd been up and out at the crack of dawn every morning since she'd got the message: *They're back.* And she'd been dragging the kids to visit her mother. Or go out for treats. Anything so that they could be as late coming home as possible.

The laundry was in serious arrears. She made a start, then sighed and gave up, heading for the dressing table to take off her make-up.

She'd barely put on her Alice band to hold her hair back when a sound gripped her insides and froze her hand on its way to her bottle of cleanser. *Why has the bath water stopped running?*

And then another, much worse sound: the *snap* and *crump* of a Zippo lighter. And there he was in the mirror behind her. Conrad Bloody Clarke.

'Evening, Jules. Long time no see. We missed you at the match today. Ben made me skipper, because apparently Stephen is in Tenerife. Or Timbuctoo. Anywhere but Clerkswell. I wonder why that might be? Have you got an ashtray in here?'

She wheeled round. 'Of course I haven't got a fucking ashtray in here.' Her gaze darted around her bedroom. 'Is there one of those ... *things* with you? The ones with the teeth?'

He rubbed his leg and went into the bathroom, returning with a soap dish in one hand and a crystal tumbler in the other. 'Cheers. Stephen keeps a nice Scotch.' He sipped, drew on his cigarette and sat on the end of the bed. *Her* bed. 'No, I'm on my own.'

'What do you want?'

'First, and this is really petty, I wanted you to know what it feels like. I think you've got the message.'

She said nothing, because he'd triggered a wave of guilt which washed away her anger and left only fear behind. A huge castle of fear, and she was locked up inside.

'Second, and this is for both yours and Stephen's sakes, I'd do my best to forget Thistle, Alice and Faith if I were you.'

'Are they all like that? What are they?'

'They're from my world. The world I'm paid to keep away from *your* world. Let's just say that they're not *Homo sapiens*, shall we? They could be pre-human or post-human or just non-human. They won't bother you again if you don't bother them. I'm serious: if you stay out of my world, they'll stay out of yours. Understand?'

It was all she could do to nod, then she took a deep breath. 'What about Stephen? He seems to be in denial.'

'He is. It runs a bit deeper than that, though. His brain can't take it in. Once he knows you've made your peace, he'll literally forget about it. Just don't let him forget that he was caught burgling the house. Don't want him doing it again, do we?'

She shook her head. 'No.'

'Good. Now, about the third member of your little raiding party…'

'Chloë. But that's not her real name.'

'I didn't think it would be. We've already been through your phone records and isolated the number she used and the numbers her associates used. We might get something eventually, but the phones were dead ends in themselves.'

Her clothes felt transparent, as if he were staring at her naked. Her whole life was being stripped bare and laid before him. *And he said 'we'. Who else is in this?*

'We may need to search that rental property in Allington, Juliet. Hopefully not. Now, listen carefully. In a moment, there's going to be a knock on the door and two nice police officers are going to take you away and interview you off the record. The public record, that is. Just tell them everything. Tom Morton is a man of great integrity but incredible persistence, and Rick James is the same. And tell Stephen to get his sorry arse back here.'

'What about the children?'

'Your mother's on her way. A friend of a friend is bringing her, and don't worry, she knows you're in trouble, so she won't complain about the childminding.'

'And you? Is that it? You're just going to walk away and forget about it?'

He drained the Scotch and stubbed out his cigarette. 'I am going to the Inkwell to celebrate our narrow win today. Ben's coming to wet the babies' heads, as it were. Funny old tradition, that. And no, I won't forget, Jules, but the crap stops here. It's too dangerous. Other than that, it's back to normal. I'll take a couple of Floss's litter if you're struggling to give them away. Sorry about that. You're still in charge of the Clerkswell Coven and Stephen is still chair of the cricket club, and the only people who truly know what you did will never speak of it again.'

He limped out of the room. None of the creaky floorboards on the landing had anything to say about his passage along them. She was still digesting what had happened when the front doorbell rang out.

'I'll get it,' shouted her daughter.

Juliet took off her Alice band and got ready to face the music. It wouldn't be the first time she'd been questioned by the police, but it would be the first time her mother knew about it, and that was a reckoning she could happily put off for a long time. Team Elvenham might be powerful, but when it came to passing judgement, they had nothing on her mother.

From the top of the stairs, she heard DCI Morton introducing himself to her children using his rank and saying that his colleague was some sort of MI7 secret agent. Conrad Bloody Clarke could be a real bastard, but Juliet couldn't pretend that she hadn't brought all of this on herself.

Chapter Fifty-Nine

'He likes to meet my colleagues. Especially the dodgy ones.'

I wasn't sure I liked the label *dodgy*. I suppose she had a point though.

Detective Constable Elaine Fraser was going to be acting as my Police Liaison Officer now that Tom was taking up a post in the Cloister Court, and Elaine's husband wanted to accompany his wife on her first trip to Elvenham Grange. In his shoes I'd probably have felt exactly the same, except that my feet would have rattled round a bit in his shoes. Like Chris Kelly, Rob Fraser is a member of that extremely small group *People Who Are Taller Than Conrad Clarke*. Unlike Chris Kelly, Rob Fraser is built like an international rugby centre, and that's because he is one.

We shook hands on a beautifully sunny Sunday morning, standing on the Grange steps. 'Say hello to the dragon,' I said, as casually as I could, and I pointed upwards to make my meaning clear.

Rob and Elaine craned their necks and regarded the beast. 'Neat,' said Rob.

'Hi there,' said Elaine, having been briefed by Tom Morton.

Rob looked confused, because I was still standing in the way. His wife nudged him. 'Go on then. Say hello. It's a family tradition.'

'Hi?' he said, a slightly bewildered expression taking root on his ruggedly handsome Scottish face. If he was bewildered now, just imagine how the poor bloke was going to feel when he crossed the threshold and met the gang. He wouldn't know what had hit him.

Before that, he looked around again. 'What a beautiful house you have here. Stunning. Must take a lot to keep up.'

'Come inside and meet Myfanwy. When not breastfeeding the twins, she's in charge of keeping Elvenham Grange in order.'

We were having a big – huge – Sunday dinner, which featured not one but two enormous legs of Welsh lamb and had been fussed over endlessly by some of the many cooks in residence. I had made breakfast and loaded the dishwasher, and then beat a hasty retreat.

As well as the Frasers, my gorgeous wife and I were being joined at the big dining table by Myfanwy, Ben, Ben's Parents, Ben's sister (Carole), Rachael, Erin, Vicky, Tom, Lucy, Hannah, Rick James, Francesca, Miss Parkes, Nell Heath and the stars of the show … Seren and Arthur. It was very nice, but that's what you'd expect in a house full of good people all wanting to celebrate. Rob Fraser coped very well in the circumstances.

Oh, and the only ones you'd say were 'missing' were Sofía (exams) and Anna Flint (exhausted).

Rob and Elaine stopped and looked around the hall. A well-meant but frisky helium balloon saying *IT'S TWINS!!!!!* had escaped and floated well out of reach. 'Need a bow and arrow for that,' said Rob. Then he cringed. 'Sorry, love. Not the most tactful thing I've said.'

It had been an arrow in the leg which had introduced Elaine to the world of magick, not that she'd told Rob about the Mannwolves who'd also been about to attack her. Oh no. He was very much un-Entangled. Something I'd have to remember. Not that I would be seeing much of him – as far as I can tell, his life seems to be less adventurous than the average monk: training, matches, more training, off to the Six Nations championship, off on tour to Australia or somewhere. Elaine and him often see even less of each other than Mina and I did when she was in prison.

'Who's driving?' I asked, rather redundantly. Elaine was very much here on business.

'El is,' said Rob. 'For a change. Has your family really lived here since forever?'

'In this house? Since it was built. At Elvenham Grange, since the Black Death. Aah, here's Mina. And Tom and Lucy.'

During the introductions, Elaine came up to me and whispered, 'If you call me *El*, I will administer the punishment. The Sheriff was very clear that kicking your bad leg is almost expected.'

'No problem, Lainey … And you'll have to be quicker than that next time.'

Chapter Sixty

If you want to know what happened during dinner, ask one of the women to show you their phones. They certainly took enough pictures. It's what happened in the library afterwards that needs to be fully recorded.

Ben was taking Rob Fraser for a walk round the village (and possibly a pint in the Inkwell), while Carole spent some time with her nieces. In another room, Rachael, Mina and Lucy were discussing how to buy Tara Doyle out of her stake in Caffè Milano, and Ben's parents had been lumbered with the washing up.

We took a variety of chairs and a couple of card tables into the library, and I counted everyone off: seven. Hannah, Rick, Vicky, Tom, Elaine, Francesca and me. An auspicious number? According to the Fae, seven is the mortals number.

'Why are you looking under the table?' asked Elaine, a little more nervously than was warranted in my opinion.

'Checking to make sure Scout hasn't hidden himself in here.'

'Didn't I see Ben taking him for walk?'

'Means nothing. I'm sure that dog can co-locate if he thinks there may be biscuits. Let me know if you want a Borador puppy.'

'Erm, no. Not with him as the father. I'll just move my chair next to Tom's.'

'I wish you hadn't done that to Jules Bloxham,' Tom said to me as we gathered around the coffee pots. 'You're lucky she's a resilient woman. I mean, *sneaking into her bedroom.*'

'She's used to it. Stephen has snuck into more women's bedrooms than I ever have or ever will. Thank you for interviewing her, Tom.'

He gave a despairing shake of his head and took himself and his coffee cup to the far corner of the room, where he stood and stared into the blind eyes of Homer. Once everyone was sorted, Hannah called us together.

'Sorry to interrupt before you've even begun,' said Tom, 'but something important came out of my interview with Juliet Bloxham last night.'

'Oh?' said Hannah. 'Is this relevant?'

'I'm afraid so. Just before the wedding, Chloë let something slip. When the Bloxhams were having cold feet, she was desperately trying to talk them into her scheme and she said that the other two in her group were members of the Akademia. It can't be a coincidence.'

'What can't?' said Rick.

'When Douglas Geldart gave a false address to Kathy Metcalfe, he also said "Akademia". I think he wanted it to be something that was found if he didn't get the real letter away.'

'And it fits with the whole *Homer* identity,' added Francesca.

'Does it?' said Vicky, and her raised eyebrows were mirrored by Rick and Elaine.

'I wouldn't have been certain without the *k* in Akademia. It was a grove of trees in Athens where the world's first secular university was founded by Plato, after his teacher Socrates was executed. Aristotle was a pupil.'

Elaine and Vicky were already raising their hands, earning a smile from Francesca. 'No, you don't need to study philosophy for this. Unless you want to, like Sophie Guest.'

'Sophie?' I asked.

Francesca smiled. 'Erin called me while you were in Asgard and told me that Sophie was struggling with the question of good and evil. It often happens.'

'Not to Conrad, it doesn't,' said Vicky.

'Hey! That's not fair. What did you say to Erin?'

'I posted a copy of Plato's *Euthyphro* to Sophie. That should point her in the right direction.'

Vicky shook her head. Elaine looked as if she needed more coffee and even Hannah scratched underneath her headscarf. I think we may need to find Francesca something to do with her spare time now that she's retired. This was not like her at all.

Blissfully unaware of our reactions, the former Keeper moved serenely on. 'All you need to know is that Socrates, Plato and Aristotle were big hitters in their field, as my son-in-law would say. The rest is just window dressing.'

'So they're not still around? Like Conrad's ancestor?' asked Elaine.

'No. They ... never mind.'

'Thank you,' said Hannah. 'So, we have a group that was active forty years ago, and may still be active today. What can we definitely pin on them?'

'Raven,' I said. 'And whatever it was that Douglas Geldart meant by "Legacy". It was what he said just before he murdered his wife and took his own life. She confirmed that it was secure. And there's something Roly said,' I added, offering a sympathetic look to Francesca. 'He was imprisoned before Douglas's bindings were released, so when Roly warned me about Homer, he must have been speaking about something contemporary.'

Francesca frowned and gave me the *I'll see you later* look.

'Locations?' said Hannah.

'The Particular, for certain,' I said. 'Raven and Skylark Wilson were conceived there. Douglas fled to join Margot there before he was captured. And Cambridge can't be ruled out. His fake letter was addressed to the Akademia, care of Angel House.'

'Probably a blind,' said Hannah.

'I'm not so sure, ma'am. Margot Easterbrook came from there. I'm not saying the Akademia has an office in Angel House, but it was clearly bubbling away in his mind.'

'Hmm. Do we think the Fae are involved?'

'I think the Red Queen knew that *something* was going on. I'm certain that she knows nothing of anything today.'

'I'll have to take your word for that. Then there's the real person to whom he *actually* wrote a letter. The one who denounced him to his family. The one who didn't want him released, and that brings me to my conclusion.'

We all sat up a little straighter.

'Douglas Geldart's historical crimes are worth investigating, that's for certain, but we have no evidence that the Akademia or the new Homer pose any threat to the King's Peace. The fact that Douglas's correspondent wanted him kept quiet when they could easily have assassinated him suggests precisely that. What do you think?'

Those who spoke agreed with her. She left me until last.

I shifted in my seat and looked round. 'I know this is more personal for me – and for Saffron – but I have a bad feeling about this. I am definitely going to look at that sídhe above the well, and I don't think we should let the Akademia lie completely.'

The boss nodded in agreement. 'Elaine, this can be your first job. Do a full forensic analysis of Douglas Geldart and Margot Easterbrook. Don't be afraid to contact their relatives, but *not* in person. Not at this stage.' She paused to have another look at the young detective. 'I don't think you'll have any problems, but if you do, tell them that you'll get Conrad to come round with you. That should loosen a few tongues.'

Elaine was actually wearing a dress today. And her hair was down. First time for everything, I suppose. It's hard being Scarywoman 24/7. 'Yes, ma'am.'

Hannah turned to the Mages. 'Vicky, I want you to go and have a good sniff around East Anglia, starting with Angel House. Conrad, can you put Saffron on to the same job in the Particular when she's recovered?'

Vicky and I both said, 'Yes, ma'am,' and then Vicky added, 'If that's it, can I have a word with you and Conrad about the selection board for the new Watch Officers?'

'I thought that was all sorted,' said Hannah.

'Something's come up,' said Vicky, looking down at her notes. My admiration for her will never stop growing, but she's still a terrible liar.

'Why don't we take a walk to the well?' I suggested. 'It's a lovely day, and I'll need both your help to transition to the glade.'

'Fine. Rick, we're done if you want to get off.'

'Thanks.'

He stood up, and started saying his goodbyes. Tom offered to return the furniture, and I led Hannah and Vicky through the gardens towards the well, stopping at the fire pit. 'Any closer and we'll disturb the hive,' I said. 'Okay, Vicky, what's this bee in your bonnet?'

'My life, that's terrible, even by your standards,' said Vicky.

'Marriage has not improved his sense of humour,' added Hannah. 'He's not wrong, though, is he?'

We made ourselves comfortable, and Vicky looked like she was about to speak until she changed her mind, grabbed a wooden stool and came in close for a Silence. 'This is gonna hurt. I really, really hope it never gets out, but I've got to say something.'

Hannah and I glanced at each other. Vicky was really struggling here, which is most unlike her. Unless faced with tunnels or giant spiders.

'Of course,' said Hannah.

'It's like this. Remember when Georgina Gilpin dragged us to the First Roost and we met that Dæmon? To escape from it, I had to stop her heart.'

I wasn't there, but I'd heard all about it. Or almost all, because Vicky had clearly kept something back. If you haven't read that case file, it's the one attached to Vicky's first acquaintance with my sisters' Fire Games entertainment.

Vicky took a deep breath. 'Well, when you stop someone's heart and then re-start it, you have to get right inside their Imprint, and with my weird Third Eye I couldn't help seeing where she came from and why she really hates her mother.'

This was alarming on all sorts of levels. Georgina Gilpin – GG to most people – is already a freak of nature: as tall as me and as thin as Mina with wild hair and bottle-bottom glasses. She's a rich member of the Hawkins Clan and a skilled Artificer. Sadly, she has never learned to make a filter for that mouth of hers; it's thanks to GG that Chris Kelly's affair with Eseld became public knowledge.

'If Heidi Marston were my mother, I'd certainly find her hard to love,' said Hannah encouragingly.

'Aye, well, Heidi is George's mother *and* father. Georgina is a double-egg clone. That's impossible to mundane science, and should be impossible with magick, but it's true: Georgina's DNA is recombined from two of Heidi's eggs.'

'Oy vey!'

'Bugger me.'

'I know, and there's more: she didn't take the surname Gilpin because that's where she was conceived; it's because that's where she was *born*. Or where Heidi was staying when they called the ambulance. The Gilpin Lodge Hotel, right in the Particular, right around the time that Raven came along.'

Hannah shook her head in disbelief. As a police officer, she'd already become used to how low some people will sink. Becoming Peculier Constable had merely given her an insight into where people will go when given a magickal excavator to dig deeper.

'Someone needs to talk to Heidi,' said Vicky, making sure that we knew the *someone* doing the talking was not going to be her. 'And if George could be kept out of it, I would be *so* grateful. It's taken a lot for her to trust me.'

Hannah blinked, still digesting. I rubbed my chin, then had a brainwave. 'Leave it with me, Vic. I've got an idea. I might need your help, but I doubt that Heidi wants this broadcast.'

'Are you sure, Conrad?' asked Hannah.

'I'll work on it and run it past you.'

'Fine. Let's go and look at what those two Mage burglars were trying to do at your well. What did Tom say their cover names were?'

'Anita and Beth.'

When we got to the well, I discovered that Tamsin had been busy while I was in Asgard: there was a nice easy transitional step to get to the Fae Realm, suitable for heavily pregnant Druids and duffers like me.

The glade was as I'd last seen it on Beltane Eve, when Mina and I contracted a greenwood marriage. And consummated it, too. I tried hard not to stare at the grassy bank where it had happened. Unfortunately, Hannah knows me too well.

'Happy memories, eh, Conrad?'

'Oh, aye,' said Vicky. 'Was it over there?'

'Moving swiftly on,' I said, 'what do you make of the door, Vicky?'

We went over to what I thought was a long abandoned sídhe, and Vicky took out her sPad. It took her a good thirty seconds to snap it locked again and shrug. 'Do you remember that book I lent you, Conrad? *The Leys of Old Albion?*'

'I do. I've still got it somewhere.'

During the Victorian era, once the Invisible College had been opened to women, there was a boom in books for the newly Entangled world, and one of them was a fully illustrated book covering the truth of magick in pre-Reformation Britain as it was then understood – the Fae, Gnomes, Dwarves, Trolls, Dragons, Druids, Witches … you get the picture. And pictures was the point of Vicky's reference.

'Imagine tearing it up and découpaging all the pictures onto that door. I have no idea how *anyone* could get in there unless they were born to it. There's Fae magick, a hint of the Morrigan and the gods only know what else. Human, too. Way beyond me. And what the hell is that smell?'

I went a little closer, and she was right: curry. Had someone brought one of the dishes up here during the wedding? I peered at the ground. 'Look out for moles.'

'Eh?'

I reached into the long grass. It's not usual to find litter in the Fae Realm. I held up a plastic packet. 'Curried mealworms. Want to have a look, Boss?'

'And spoil my digestion? No, thanks. Shall we go?'

'I just need a moment to check that hive,' I said.

The Morrigan had gifted Elvenham Grange with not one but two swarms of bees at Beltane – the regular ones down below and what I now know to be Fae bees up here. Exactly what makes them 'Fae bees' is something I'm not allowed to discuss, but I wanted a closer look, and blow me, didn't they actually *glow* with Lux? When not busy giving birth, Myfanwy has said that only the Fae themselves can harvest the honey, and that we'll get lots of brownie points from them if we invite them to do so.

We descended to Mittelgard, and by unspoken agreement, we took a leisurely walk around the garden before heading back inside.

'What are your plans?' asked Vicky. 'It feels like I haven't seen you properly for *ages*. I got to see rather more of Mina than I'd bargained for on the hen weekend, but you not so much.'

'I'm looking forward to the selection weekend.'

'That's because you're a sadist.'

'Before then, we've got to be in Derwent to release the Red Queen on Thursday, and I believe that I may be having afternoon tea with the Allfather.'

'You what?'

'Yes. I have to fly the Wasp to Cartmel Racecourse and then take tea with the Allfather and another of Homer's victims. On the whole, I think I'd rather fight a dragon.'

Vicky raised her eyebrows. 'I dunno about *that*.'

'Perhaps. And after the Red Queen, I've been summoned to a Pack Council in Birk Fell.' I shrugged. 'After the selection board, we're shuttling between here and Middlebarrow Haven for a couple of weeks, then we're going on our proper honeymoon. If nothing else gets in the way.'

'Oh, aye? Where are you going?'

'Mina got the cruising bug when we did that jaunt with my parents. And then I'm afraid there's business in London. You know, I've been thinking: I reckon that Judge Bracewell only recruited Tom so that she could discuss her final rulings on the Flint Hoard with him.'

Hannah laughed. 'Very cynical, Conrad. Not even Marcia would do that.' She paused. 'Okay, maybe she acted sooner than she would have done. And here's a weird thing. After you two disappeared in a puff of rainbow smoke, I heard one of the Shear Magic girls saying that *Mélisande* needed a drink, as if she were a special guest.'

'I've given up trying to figure out what was going on in Faith's household,' I told them. 'I'll wait for the book Alice is allegedly writing to discover that. If I live long enough.'

I needed to be in London for several reasons, and I wasn't going to mention any of them here. The launch of Mowbray College is going to be massive and, yes, I'll be consulting the boss about it in time, but not today.

There was lots more to discuss, though: thanking Hannah again for the Wasp, reliving some of the highlights of the wedding, dropping a couple of hints about our involuntary trip to Asgard, asking how Vicky's romance with Jay Hawkins is getting on. You know the sort of thing.

There was one item that overrode all of those, and that was when I got a call from Lady Celeste Hawkins while we were admiring the marijuana plant: Saffron had been discharged from Jimmy's Hospital and was now convalescing at Cherwell Roost in Oxford.

'There's only one problem,' said Celeste. 'She nearly died, but she doesn't believe it. She's going to heal too well for my liking, because she's already talking about returning to work. Or "returning to duty" as she puts it.'

Only someone's mother can get away with saying things like that.

'Let's go in,' I said. 'And focus on the most pressing question of all: who I'm going to select for the team tomorrow.'

'Eh?'

'Extra fixture for the Clerkswell Wizards because of the cancellations, and I'm still the acting captain. Priorities, Vicky. Priorities.'

Postscript

Afterword
By Dr Francesca Somerton

If you're wondering how Conrad's account of his 'Honeymoon in Valhalla' came to be included here, along with his notes on the first Akademia Working Party meeting, then you'll have to ask him, because when I pushed him on what the Allfather had said he became rather vague and insisted that a full account should be sealed away. Having read it, and read what he told Mina, you can probably see why it should form the last chapter of the fairy story.

Conrad's adventures continue in **Second Nature***, and Alice will be back, too.*
Watch out for the **Thirteenth Book of the King's Watch** *coming from Paw Press.*

Author's Note

How was it for you?

Other voices have butted in to Conrad's adventures many times: Saffron, Mina, Cordelia, Tom Morton… and of course Vicky got not one but *two* novellas all of her own. I know. But this is the first time that a completely new voice has had (almost) a whole book to themselves. So why?

If you've seen why it took so long to write *Third Eye*, you'll know that I simply couldn't shoehorn Douglas Geldart's story *and* Conrad's view of the wedding *and* what happened to Mina into one book. I decided to focus on Conrad for *Third Eye*, and I decided that it was about time we saw what a sídhe looks like from the inside and what it's truly like to be one of the Fae. Given that a very young Squire was part of Shear Magic, the obvious answer was to tell Alicia's story from the beginning. I hope you enjoyed it for its own sake and also for what she reveals about the behind-the-scenes goings on, both within the People and at the hen party / wedding.

So where next?

It took just over two years to produce the *Three* novels from the King's Watch. I hope it will take less time to produce the next one: *Second Nature*. Before then, however, I'm going to be working with my little sister on her cosy mystery series featuring the Caffè Milano girls. I hope you'll forgive the interruption.

Being an Independent Author means that you need a great team around you, and I'm thrilled to welcome a new editor to #TeamPawPress: Philippa of Lexical Peaks.

Arriving in a series at Book 12 is no easy task for an editor, and she really went the extra mile to understand the universe of the King's Watch, what readers have got used to and how I've rendered the stories. The fact that she started with Alicia's story didn't help, either. I'm very grateful to Philippa for all the hard work, care and attention she's lavished on my manuscript. It goes without saying that any remaining typos and violations of the English language are down to me, not her.

Thanks also to the other members of the team: Rachel for the cover and Katie for her work on the website. An additional note of thanks is due to those who read the first draft – Asen, Lore, Lucy, Nina, Paula and Sheila.

Finally, this book could not have been written without love, support, encouragement and sacrifices from my wife, Anne. She's been very patient with Conrad over the years, and for that I am very grateful.

Until the next time,

Thanks,

Mark Hayden.

www.ingramcontent.com/pod-product-compliance
Lightning Source LLC
Chambersburg PA
CBHW031304210726
48287CB00005B/1408